COMING
TO TERMS

A novel by Jonathan Bower

The Carraig Press

A Paperback Original from
The Carraig Press,
P.O. Box 32, Bantry, County Cork, Ireland
First published by Trafford Publishing. for the Carraig Press, Ireland 2007

Note for Librarians: A cataloguing record for this book is available from Library and Archives
Canada at www.collectionscanada.ca/amicus/index-e.html
ISBN 1-4120-7265-4

*Printed in Victoria, BC, Canada. Printed on paper with minimum 30% recycled fibre. Trafford's print shop runs
on "green energy" from solar, wind and other environmentally-friendly power sources.*

TRAFFORD
PUBLISHING™

Offices in Canada, USA, Ireland and UK

Book sales for North America and international:
Trafford Publishing, 6E–2333 Government St.,
Victoria, BC V8T 4P4 CANADA
phone 250 383 6864 (toll-free 1 888 232 4444)
fax 250 383 6804; email to orders@trafford.com
Book sales in Europe:
Trafford Publishing (UK) Limited, 9 Park End Street, 2nd Floor
Oxford, UK OX1 1HH UNITED KINGDOM
phone 44 (0)1865 722 113 (local rate 0845 230 9601)
facsimile 44 (0)1865 722 868; info.uk@trafford.com
Order online at:
trafford.com/05-2160

10 9 8 7 6 5 4

For H.

Also by Jonathan Bower:
AFRICA AND AFTERMATH
GAEL AND GALL

One

There is a kind of man who has always had to rely on himself, because he has found that others in his life cannot be trusted, particularly those close to him in childhood: parents, brothers, school fellows. So he gets into the habit of working things out for himself, of being very rational. His beliefs are reduced to a minimum and replaced by a pragmatic and somewhat jaundiced empiricism. Dominic was this kind of man. The emotional crises and betrayals of childhood had left him with a deep distrust of everything that was not clear, that was not verifiable, that was not scientifically sure.

Something of all this could be seen in his appearance. Though a tall man over six feet in height, with heavy-boned limbs and a strong round head, his eyes betrayed a lack of confidence, and his way of holding himself a kind of dogged refusal. Yet his eyes were warm, and his slightly self-deprecating smile ready.

He was a man of paradoxical idealism. If his trust in others was betrayed, he still believed in trusting. There would be others or another more worthy of it. His emotional life was like an experiment where he kept getting the wrong answer. But he would not give up his search for the right one.

It was contrary to all his empirical expectations that now in middle life he began to have vivid premonitory dreams. In the first of them, he dreamed that he was talking to his wife, and that she was trying to make him understand something. The words were spoken, and accompanied by gestures of effort and irritation, but for some reason, he couldn't grasp their meaning. This paralysis of communication left a lasting impression in his sleeping mind. The next morning it was still with him, and it haunted him with a sense of regret.

Later, at the embassy, he found the first of her farewell letters. He sat down straight away in his office with its tall oriental windows and began to read it.

'Paris, 3 mars.

Cher Dominic,

I know I should have written to you sooner. I kept on saying so, but I couldn't. Please forgive me. Don't think that you are the only one who is suffering. I have been suffering so much all these years, struggling to adapt myself to you, to be as you wanted me to be. But I couldn't . Now I know that I must get free. I must escape. But it hurts me almost as much as staying on and living the impossible struggle with you.'

He read on without much shock. He had realised some months before that she had decided to leave him. He had gone through the crisis then. Now he was just living the ashen confirmation. The letter and the dream he had had seemed part of the same experience.

That first time, the premonition of the dream did not strike him. But some days later he had another dream of Nicole. They were staying at her parents' summer house in Var, in the south of France. It was a warm morning of early summer. The cicadas were beginning their frenzied buzzing. Inside the house it was cool and dark. One unshuttered window showed a brilliantly coloured scene of pine wood, mountain, and sky. He called through the open bedroom door to Nicole.

'Are you getting up?'

She didn't answer. That was strange, it was past ten o'clock. He felt a small chill of fear and stood up.

'Darling, are you all right?'

He walked quickly into their bedroom. It was even darker there. At first he thought that all was normal. She was lying in bed still, perhaps asleep. As he approached her he noticed a strange redness on her face, which glistened slightly. Soon he was leaning over her to see what it was. Gradually he realised that there was no longer any skin on her face, that the flesh was bare and alive. A skein of blood filmed it and moved with a slow, fluid momentum. Horror and panic caught at him. He wanted to kill her, to put her out of this macabre anarchy of the living carcass, to end her obscene lingering in life, but he could not. The flesh moved of its own, and he could not kill it.

He woke up with a sense of dread, and it soon gave way to emptiness. There was no light yet. He thought it must be about four a.m. Now he had a long morning without sleep to get through, as on so many days since the crisis. His sleep had been destroyed. He wondered if it would ever be restored.

Later in the day, as he approached his letter box in the embassy, he thought that there might be a letter from her. Yet he immediately discounted it. Things like that could happen once, but not twice. He pulled open the small door of the box and saw the envelope with the familiar handwriting and French stamp. The aura of the dream surged into his mind as he took the letter out and put it in his pocket. He was certain that it contained only confirmation of the previous one - more explanations, more recriminations, more pain and regret.

He heard footsteps behind him.

'Hello, Dominic.'

He turned, it was Sylvia. Her sharp face with its strange,

feminine fragility gave him pleasure.

'Hi, Sylvia. How are you? I thought you were sick. Someone said you had flu.'

'I had, but I'm better. In fact I was quite delirious, and wrote a couple of delirious poems. '

'Interesting. Were they good?'

Dominic thought of his own delirium that refused him peace morning after morning. That didn't come from any virus, it came from the poison of life.

'Well, they are intriguing. And you know, the funny thing is that my son is doing 'Kubla Khan' in English at school. Anyway, what's your news?'

'Bad, Nicole's going to stay in Paris. It's over for good.'

He realised how strange the expression must sound to a foreign ear - 'for good'. He and Nicole were breaking up, but for him it was anything but good.

'She'll come back. Don't worry. She's doing just what I did. She feels she has to live in Paris and experience what it has to offer. I had to live in London. Then I came back, and look, now I'm as settled as anyone.'

'No, Sylvia, this isn't a phase she's got to pass through. It's a new beginning. There's no coming back.'

'I don't agree. You'll see.'

He smiled at her, picked up his briefcase, and went out.

He read the letter at home later and it was as he had thought. Some of the phrases stood out and lodged themselves in his memory: '...good luck that we can separate and not sink in despair' and 'I must embrace the future, so must you.' As he read, it seemed that the emptiness he felt, the sense of loss, became gradually more solid. Each stroke made the crystal of his new state more clear cut, more irreversible.

Two

After a week or so, he had his third dream of premonition, but it was not about Nicole, it was about Emma. Though he had not seen or heard of her for five years, the five years of Nicole, now here she was, suddenly, in a dream. They were wandering in the bedrooms of his grandfather's old house, Blaistow. The bedrooms were on various levels, filled with old, heavy furniture, and they were connected by irregular passageways. He felt the sense of eager mystery that always made his visits to the house as a child so exciting. Now Emma was with him, close to him. He touched her lightly from time to time. They didn't talk, but there was a complicity between them. They went from one room to another and he realised that they were looking for a bed, for somewhere to be alone together, this was the agreement. He led her into one of the passages connecting a bedroom at the front of the house with one at the back that had only one small window and was always dark. There was a large, high double bed in it, he remembered. They passed a lavatory with its old apparatus and its faded blue carpet that smelled faintly of stale urine. He opened the door of the back bedroom and was aware of memories which floated just beyond the reach of his consciousness. He went in first and almost at once pulled back and shut the door. He had seen in the obscure light his parents on the high bed. They were both naked, and his father's body was sprawled across his mother's, the white flesh crossed

over in arms and legs, like trees that had been cut and fallen
together, completely without order.

'What's wrong?'

'My God, it's Mother and Father. They are in there naked.'

'Oh it doesn't matter. There must be another empty room
somewhere. Why don't we go back to that front room?'

'Emma, it's always being walked through, that room, to get
to the lavatory in the passage. Anyone might come in.'

They hesitated together in the darkness. Then he put one arm
round her small back and the other hand on one of her breasts.
Almost at once he felt the nipple rise under the material of her
pullover. Her hunger was like an old memory, extraordinarily
sweet, that flowed into him. It unlocked a happiness deep, deep
in his mind. He was afraid almost to release it, but it was released.
With it came the insistent impulse to tell her how much he wanted
to submit, to surrender to this happiness, but it was so strong that
it could find no expression. He just repeated her name two or three
times as he looked at her face, hidden in the close darkness.

The extraordinary, flowing release of the dream was cut
short as he woke. He looked at the shuttered window. Thank
God, he thought, it was light. It was after dawn. He would only
have to lie there for an hour or so.

Later, as he approached his letter box, he wondered whether
there would be another letter from Nicole. He opened it without any emotion. There was a letter, but it was not from France.
The stamp was large and strange, and the envelope had faded
blue piping, not the familiar French blue and red. As soon as he
picked it up he recognised Emma's handwriting. The premonition of his dream filled him now with a sense of being a victim,
of being borne along by some stream of fate. Yes - it would happen to him, he was helpless, and now he had these warnings in

advance. There was her handwriting, strangely irregular, as if every letter had its own character. There was hardly any overall slant. Yet it was absolutely fixed in its irregularity. The crooked cross of the 't' was always exactly the same, the slopes of the various tails consistent in their variety. It was almost an amateur handwriting, a self-taught one, where each letter had gradually assumed its form, but now never varied. It gave finally a somewhat scratchy impression, but it was emphatic and rigid.

He looked at the stamp and the post mark. Spanish, King Carlos. That made a change from those unending series of portraits of Franco. Posted in Cordoba. How extraordinary - what was Emma doing in Cordoba? And writing, after five years of complete silence. No contact whatsoever. For a moment he wondered if some bizarre encounter had thrown Emma and Nicole together. Had Nicole told her that their marriage was over? No, no, it was impossible. He tore off a strip down the side of the envelope and pulled out the letter. It was a thick piece of paper, a page torn from an exercise book, with lines. The message was short.

Dear Dominic,

I'm sitting in the spring sunshine. The trees are covered with their fine, pale green leaves. Suddenly I had the urge to write to you, to find out where you were and what you were doing. It's very strange, and somehow I feel wrong to lose contact completely with someone one has loved, as has happened between us. Maybe you'll find this impertinent and completely out of place, but I would so like to hear from you. You may not have realised it when we were together, but you were terribly important to me, and you still are.

Love,
Emma.

The letter had a very powerful effect on him. He sat in his office, reading its short, single paragraph again and again. He stared out through the dusty windows at the city, which stretched away in white and beige to the ragged outline of Jebel Kabir, the mountain to the south. As his eyes took in the view, his beating heart and the excitement that Emma's letter had stirred in him transposed him back to another world. The past where she had been with him was recreated. From the emptiness of his present loss, it had redeeming comfort. As in his dream, her presence and that intricate confidence that their being together gave him was palpably real.

He knew that he had no right to her. He had rejected her coldly five years ago and had made no effort to contact her since. Yet now she had written, and he could not contain the feeling that she was still his, that they were still as they had been. The memories had been unlocked and they had repossessed him. Yet they were vague, he could not picture her face or hear her voice. But he could feel the contentment of being with her flooding him. He was shocked and overjoyed that the emotions that surrounded her deep inside him were still so powerful. His marriage with Nicole suddenly became an object, floating free in his mind. The reality now was Emma, those five years ago, in Alexandria.

Three

'We've been invited to lunch tomorrow, at Dick and Maree's.'

Dominic lowered the Egyptian Gazette newspaper and asked Lynda:

'Oh, who are they?'

'The P.D.G. of Pyramid Oil and his American wife. They're darlings. It's at a friend's house actually, not theirs. In Agami.'

'I'm not sure if I can make it. We've got work all morning at the institute. When is it going to start?'

'Of course you can make it, Dominic. It won't start until one thirty at the earliest. Bring Rory with you - it's more or less open house when Dick and Maree are entertaining.'

'But you said it was at someone else's house?'

'Same thing. This is Alexandria, not Britain. Thank God.'

True, he thought, it was Alexandria. Not, possibly, the Alexandria of Durrell's famous quartet - had that ever really exited, or was it only a magical invention of the writer's Baroque pen? - but still Alexandria. A place where everybody seemed to know everybody else, a place of teeming contrasts and intimate, friendly decadence. And a marvellously liberating place for someone like Lynda, who had grown up among Brighton's stiff, white, rather lifeless facades.

He looked at her across the large sitting room of the apartment, and wondered whether it was Egypt or marriage or time that had changed her so much. When he had first met her, maybe four years before, she had been sharp, caustic. But now she was almost a social dilletante - nothing was worth taking seriously. Her life was now simply too enjoyable for her to harbour the Marxist bitterness that she had once poured out with such venom. And being her guest was a pleasure, not because she and her husband Charles lived in probably the finest apartment he had ever seen, but because she filled it with such an informal, generous open-handedness. She had become the antithesis of the calculating, envious, intolerant woman he had thought her before.

The apartment *was* fine. They had heard of it at some party. Old Ali, or was it Hassan, or his aunt, who owned it, and had let it for years and years to distant relatives from Cairo? Now it was empty, and the whole point was that it just couldn't be let on the open market. It would be torn to shreds in less that a month. No, it could only go to relatives, or friends. A young English couple? With no children? That would be perfect. Lynda and Charles were soon installed. They couldn't believe their luck. The place was a palace, a museum of antiques, vast. The dinner table seated twenty-four. The salon had three separate sitting areas. Turkish and Persian rugs covered the parquet floors. Hand-painted Chinese screens adorned the walls. And yet the rent Lynda and Charles paid was risible - two hundred and fifty Egyptian pounds a month. This was Egypt before the 'Opening'– before innumerable American, Japanese, and European firms descended on the country with Sadat's blessing, took up every apartment and villa, and sent rents shooting over the thousand mark. This was only 1975, when the 'Opening' was just a word, just an idea.

So his friends were living in this luxury, and he was enjoying it as their guest. Not without twinges of uncertainty - it really was disproportionately opulent. It was almost as if they were squatting in the living quarters of a ruling class that had simply packed up and fled. Which of course was fairly near the truth. Egypt had had its revolution, but it had been rather benign. A lot of wealth had survived, though many of its owners had gone, to Lebanon, to Geneva, to Paris, to wherever. So the houses and the apartments were still there, preserved status symbols of the elite of King Farouk's era. Maybe now they were a little faded. The cover of the huge sofa Dominic was sitting in was a little frayed in places, he noticed. But, but, the place was still splendid. He poured out a whisky from the bottle with its familiar Saccone and Speed label, and asked Lynda:

'Will you have a nightcap, Lynda? A Scotch? Or something else?'

'Yes, a small brandy."

She reached over and took the glass.

'Thanks. You'll enjoy it tomorrow. Dick is such a sweetie. Of course he's always half drunk after office hours. Maree's still very American, even after years with fusty old Dick. They're an odd combination. Oh, and Emma will be there. You'll meet her.'

'Well, I'll really try to make it, Lynda,' Dominic said, but he tried not to sound too enthusiastic. He had heard about Emma, and Lynda had her pairing-off tendencies. He didn't want to encourage her.

Four

At twelve-thirty next day, Dominic managed to avoid talking to anyone after the conference, and slipped out of the institute. It was a hot August day. The air was close and humid around him. He opened the door of his old, white sports car and bending double, eased himself into it. This required some agility. First he had to sit in sideways onto the seat, taking care not to crack his head on the hard-top window frame. Once the body was in, the legs had to follow. Dominic's were long, and he had to pull them up almost to his chest to get them clear of the door sill. Yet once inside, he could stretch them out into the long tunnel, where his feet were exactly placed to operate the pedals.

He started the engine and pulled out into the quiet side street, full, like almost every side street in the quarter, with piles of building materials. There were apartment blocks going up all round the area. Soon it would be just like the Corniche. The urban explosion in Egypt was limitless - a nightmare, a monster, that sucked enormous numbers of people into its maw every year. Surely it couldn't go on. Cairo had now - what did they say - eight million people? Or was it ten million? In any case, it was appalling. It must end in catastrophe. It probably would; he had been interested to read in a history of the country that the population of Cairo had suffered wild oscillations, shooting up periodically, then crashing down, usually as a result of famine or plague. What sort of debacle would end this present surge, whose signs were now all around him - piles of sand and gravel, bags of cement stacked in doorways and huts and closely guarded by watchmen, iron networks for reinforced concrete, shouts and bangs of building workers?

'It's got to stop,' he muttered to himself as he drove his car carefully over a heap of reinforcing rods that had recently been dumped in the street, but as he turned into the busy main road, the sounds of hammering and concrete mixing continued behind him.

He took the lake road, the long way round to Agami, which was on the other side of the city, to avoid the torment of the rush hour. Soon he was speeding past the miserable houses on the fringe of the city. The lake came up on his left, a dull, dirty expanse of violet blood. The breeze roughened its surface and the choppy waves had a pink-brown froth at their crests. It was an infernal sight, with its puce colour, a sea on another planet. Dominic had heard that it was caused by an alga. Or perhaps it was just massive chemical pollution from the industrial plant at the head of the lake, which looked like a refinery of some sort. Maybe the purple alga had invaded the lake to consume the refinery's sulphurous wastes - a symbiosis of the twentieth century. As he pulled onto the coast road, he was struck by the lake's unearthly beauty.

His car rose through the ochre hills that ran along the coast just behind the dunes. Soon it was winding down through scattered palm groves to the Agami turn-off with its police post. There was only one policeman there, sitting in the shade, and Dominic was not stopped. He swung round into the resort road and waved at the policeman in his drab uniform.

What an extraordinary place Agami had become. Once it had been a stretch of deserted coastal dunes and sandy scrub belonging to some bedouin. Now it was a summer resort like no other in Egypt - far enough away from town to keep something of its country character, yet near enough for everyone who was anyone to have villa or beach house there. Like Cairo and Alexandria, it was growing, growing.

Soon the tarmac ran out and Dominic's car shook and creaked on the stony track. Lynda had described to him where the house was, but he found the tracks confusing. Was this one the second or third after the Moroccan-styled villa that he had identified a few moments before? He thought it was the second and was about to drive on when he noticed a group of cars parked under the shade of some causurina trees. That would be it. Most of the cars had white customs plates - they belonged to foreigners. As he pulled up and parked, he saw Rory's red Fiat among them. Good old Rory, he thought, never late for a free meal.

The first moments of meeting someone who is to become a lover are often intensely vivid in the memory - the words spoken, the sharp edge of feeling. But perhaps because he had been warned of Emma's presence at the party, Dominic had put a check on himself and on how he would react to her. Later, when he tried to think back to what had passed between them that first day, he could only remember the visual scene clearly, but almost nothing of the conversation.

He first noticed her as he was talking to Lynda and Rory. She was sitting out in the garden, in a deck chair. He was struck by the girlish delicacy of her oval face. Her child-like body lay straight in the chair, her arms by her sides, and her hands with their long fingers turned over the front bar of the chair. Her legs were thin and beautiful, he saw at once. She was wearing shorts and a white pullover with a university crest printed American-style across the front. Her breasts made two points under it.

Eventually Lynda took him over and introduced him to her. He learned that she was at Oxford, studying English, and was on holiday, staying with her parents. He looked down into her acute, greyish eyes, blinking in the sun as she talked and looked up at him. He couldn't remember later what she said, but he did remember that in those first few minutes, he knew that he was going to pursue her, that he had chosen her.

But for the moment, he decided to play a waiting game. He drifted back to Lynda and the others.

'Somebody should do something about it,' Lynda was saying, as her red lips and small white teeth closed on the back of a large prawn. 'Lester is a queer as a coot. Someone must tell Mike and Jane about it. Imagine him inviting Stephen to go round to his house to play table tennis. Honestly, the last time Lester played table tennis on that rickety old table of his was before I arrived in Egypt, I can tell you.'

'Oh, it doesn't matter, Lynda. Live and let live, as you English say. Lester is harmless. Stephen enjoys his company, and he wants to go and play table tennis with him, that's all.'

It was Ronald, a Dutchman with a rather Latin face, who had spoken. Lynda was not convinced.

'Would you allow your son to visit the house of a well-known queer, especially if he looked a bit like Mick Jagger and was fifteen years old? Or is it fourteen? '

She turned for support to her husband.

'Fourteen, I think,' Charles replied, 'but he's got a moustache sprouting on his upper lip. That I have noticed.'

'There you are - the critical time. It shouldn't be allowed. If no-one else is going to tell Mike and Jane, I shall.'

Dominic wondered how the parents would react. So Lester was a well-known homosexual. He had heard his name mentioned but had not met him. He imagined a man in his forties, with a fattish face and slightly bulging eyes - a caricature. This Lester was in fact the first homosexual known to all that he had ever come across.

'The whole thing sounds very Egyptian, doesn't it?' he put in.

'What do you mean?' Lynda asked. It was clear that she disapproved of homosexuality and felt sufficiently at home in Egypt as to want the practice to have nothing particular to do with the place.

'I mean English and other foreign homosexuals coming to Egypt to escape repression at home. You know, like E. M. Forster. The first real love of his life was an Alexandrian police-man, or was it a bus driver?'

'But that's the whole point,' Lynda said, 'Stephen isn't a homosexual. He's just an ordinary kid who could be corrupted by Lester."

'Then there's no problem,' Ronald said in flat Dutch tones. 'If he's an ordinary kid, he won't be interested at all. He will just say to Lester: "Go to hell".'

'I wish one could be sure. Anyway, I'm going to talk to Mike and Jane about it. They're new here, they don't know about Lester.'

Lynda consumed another prawn.

'Bah, you English, you're always worrying about being homosexual. Either you are or you are not,' Ronald said. The subject did not seem to interest him.

'Hey, ' he almost shouted at Dominic, 'will you play a game of racquets with me after lunch?'

'Yes, sure,' Dominic replied. 'But give me some time for digestion. What about three or four o'clock?'

'Four would be fine,' Ronald said. 'I have to pick the kids up from a friend's house after lunch and bring them to the beach.'

'Good. Four o'clock then.'

He liked Ronald, with his open and frank character. They drifted together over to the food table to help themselves to fruit salad.

Later in the afternoon, they were on the beach playing as arranged. Dominic found Egyptian racquets an excellent game. He wondered as he played why it had never spread anywhere else, at least in Europe. With bats larger and heavier than ping-pong bats and with an old tennis ball, two players take up positions maybe ten, twenty feet apart - the distance depends on the standard of play - and just hit the ball back and forth. No points, no rules, no winner, no loser. You simply try to keep the ball in the air as long as possible. If one player hits a strong straight shot, the other can only parry defensively, sending the ball back high and slow. This gives the first player another chance to hit hard, and so on for several exchanges until he either hits wide or the other fails to return.

Ronald and Dominic played for about half an hour. Even in the strong breeze, that always blew in from the sea over Agami beach in August, they were soon hot and covered with sweat.

'OK, now we swim,' Ronald suddenly shouted, hitting the ball off into the breakers. They threw down their bats and plunged in after it.

Five

During the first days of the following week, Dominic often thought of Emma and wondered how he was going to approach her. The more he delayed, the more difficult the approach seemed to become. He felt an impediment building up.

'Maybe I'll just let it drop', he thought. 'She didn't seem to show much interest in me. She seemed rather flat. Do I really want to start with her?'

Yet as he reasoned thus, he knew he was just temporising, just playing with his intention. It was displacement activity in his head, he was going to approach her, he had decided. Yet it took courage, and the longer he left it, the more courage it was going to take. He seemed unable to control his inhibiting speculations.

'Maybe she'll refuse straight away. Or she'll be terribly deadpan, completely unenthusiastic. I'll seem a fool. And she's only nineteen...nineteen.'

His brain went on and on day after day with this slow torture of prevarication.

'Hello.'

'Hello, Emma? Look, this is Dominic here'.

'Oh, hello.'

Her voice sounded interested, but it had the sing-song intonation of a smooth, professional receptionist at a London hotel.

Too late. He had to say it now.

'I was wondering whether you'd like to come over to Lynda and Charles's tomorrow night for dinner?'

His voice went curt and hard in his nervousness.

'Oh, that'd be very nice.'

The intonation was exactly the same. Maybe it was real - why did he think it artificial?

'Good, Fine. About eight then?'

'Eight? All right. There's only one problem though. Can you come and pick me up? Daddy hates going out at night and I hate Alex taxis.'

'No, that'll be fine. Charles can tell me how to get to your place. See you tomorrow at about eight then.'

'Yes, thanks. O.K. Till tomorrow then.'

'Bye, Emma.'

'Bye.'

He put the phone down. His body relaxed. The first, crucial step taken. In the whole panoply of the universe, in the vast un-knowable maelstrom of its actions and reactions, he had put out his hand towards her. Of the million, million changes occurring every second, he had effected this one, his first step towards Emma. Everything would now be different for him and for her, because they would come together and know each other.

Yet it had hung on a thread, the thread of his vacillating will. He might not have acted. He had thought of reasons for not acting. He had delayed it. He had skirted it. In similar situations in the past, he had not acted. But finally, he did not know how, the balance was tipped. He had acted. What was the mecha-nism? How did the will finally break through the fear and the inhibition? What impenetrably intricate process decided it?

But it was decided.

Six

The next day Dominic met Rory for lunch at the Sporting Club in Alexandria. Before eating, they sat on the terrace in the shade of a flamboyant tree, whose fine, pennate leaves filtered the vertical sun and whose blossom blazed scarlet. They drank fresh lemon juice in large glasses.

'You know, sitting in a place like this, one wonders whether Egypt has had a revolution at all,' Dominic said.

'It wasn't so much a revolution, more of a palace coup.'

'What about Nasser and his Arab socialism?'

'I mean there really wasn't so much social change. Nasser was more a national deliverer than a social revolutionary.'

'Yet he kicked out the monarchy, and a whole ruling class with it.'

'Did he? That ruling class had simply been a military caste. Of course they were also capitalists when they were granted huge estates. But I'm sure a lot of them survived, even in the armed forces and in the administration.'

'He did confiscate some private fortunes, but this club, it's carried on as if nothing has happened.'

'Yes, it has. You know what the Egyptians say about their revolution? It's one of those Egyptian jokes. There's that revolving restaurant at the top of the Kennedy Tower in Cairo. Have you been up to see it? Well, it turned just once and then something broke in the mechanism and it hasn't budged an inch since. The Egyptians say that Nasser's revolution was like that restaurant. It made one turn and then stopped dead.'

Dominic laughed. The Egyptian joke, usually political, often obscene, was one of the characteristics of Egyptian life that he found most engaging.

'Perhaps it was like most things Arab, a lot of show, a lot of emotion, but not much follow-through.'

'Yes, exactly. There was no real revolution here. Some hugely rich people had their property "sequestered", I think the word is, but the principle of private property remained absolutely valid. Mahommed, after all, was a merchant. None of this Christian nonsense about money being *per se* evil. And that's why an Islamic country will never go really communist. Some communist officers might take it over, like in Yemen, but they won't get anywhere.'

'Now that's an interesting idea. Russia was one of the pillars of Christendom, with the Christian revulsion against wealth. Now it's communist. You're saying there's a connection.'

'There could be. Money evokes such moral fervour in the west, that is, in Christendom, or what's left of it, but I really don't know Russia.'

'I wonder where China fits it?'

'Oh, I wouldn't stretch the analogy. Let's just say that Islam never had a moral hang-up about money, as long as the differences aren't too glaring.'

'Well, in Farouk's Egypt, they certainly were glaring.'

'Yes, so there was an adjustment, to even thing up a bit, but not to overthrow the property owning system altogether.'

'And the sporting Club remains. And I suppose we can be thankful for it. My God. It's huge, just like the Guizera Club in Cairo. It must cover a square mile at least.'

'I suppose these clubs were started by the British. But the Egyptians have certainly taken them to heart. Just look around. Most of the people here are locals.'

'More British than the British. I have friends in Cairo - you know, Cherif, Khalil - who spend every afternoon at the club playing tennis or squash.'

'It's a surprise, isn't it? I suppose you came out here like me, fed on post-Suez anti-Arab propaganda. You expected the place to be virulently anti-British and anti everything British.'

'Maybe I did. Anyway the fact is that they're more assiduous sportsmen than we are.'

'Speak for yourself. Last time I played sport was when I was forced to at school.'

Rory's spindly frame and unhealthy complexion seemed to confirm it.

'I mean the sporting club - it's a very British institution,' Dominic went on.

'Oh, I agree. And the Egyptians obviously love it as much as you do. Nasser may have thrown out the Suez Canal Company, but the clubs, he held on to those.'

They finished their glasses of juice, and then went inside to have their meal.

Dominic returned to Lynda and Charles's apartment after lunch and had a long siesta in his bedroom. Normally he allowed himself only to doze on a sofa in the drawing room, with music playing on the stereo to prevent himself from falling deeply asleep. Today he abandoned this restraint and gave himself as excuse the fatigue he felt after his morning's lecturing on 'Future horizons in scientific and technical co-operation' to a plenary session of the conference.

As soon as he closed his eyes he began to think of Emma.

He felt a small contraction of fear at the idea of making the first physical approach to her. There had been something too observant about her manner when he had met her, she was all sharp monitoring, vigilant. This was too conscious for him, it directed too clear a gaze at him. It unnerved him. It seemed she didn't have any insouciant warmth, that he could flow into and that might arouse him.

'But it's probably not her at all. It's probably me,' he reasoned.

For he had not had any contact with a woman, physical, sexual contact, since he had arrived in Egypt, and that was nearly six months ago. During the first couple of weeks in the country, he had felt an intense and promiscuous sexual excitement with almost every woman he met. But as soon as he was forced to realise that for one reason or another, she would not really do, the excitement died. And the erections which had caught him in the most inopportune moments, faded.

Now, he noticed, there was almost no spontaneous sexual excitement in him. He presumed it was partly because he was getting old - he was, after all, past thirty. Perhaps he had already used up his stock of spontaneous sexual hunger, that stream of imaginings and responses that had for so long seemed endless. Like everything else, one just took it for granted, and now, he was shocked to realise, it was going. Anyway, he reasoned, most of the time it had only been because he had no active sexual life, no partner, that this stream flowed. The only satisfactions it ever met with were the solitary ones of masturbation. Now it was fitful, faltering. He felt a sting of panic. He wondered whether he could in fact respond to Emma. Had the mechanism broken down completely? If he approached her, would he be excited by her, would he get that hot, sweet flow in his genitals, or would he be impotent? The possibility had never occurred to him before, because his endless fantasies and imaginings had always made his body an automatically aroused thing. Now he circled the fear of impotence in his mind. Before, all he had to do was to dwell on some sexual vision or association and his body would respond, his cock rise up hard and the skin pull tight over his balls. He tried now to break through this new apprehension to such a vision, but it was no good, it was too forced. His imagination did not catch onto it, it had no power, and left him feeling empty. Yet in this emptiness, he must approach Emma and win her.

What sort of girl was she, besides being very much younger than he was? What sort of sexual experience did she have? He knew she had no-one at the moment, but not much about her past. A friend of his, an old colleague, who also knew Lynda and Charles and who had come out to stay with them for a holiday, had tried to get her. From what he had heard, he had not been very successful. This friend had talked rapturously of her for a few days during his attempt, that he knew. But he had got nowhere and never spoken of her again to anyone.

I wonder why she didn't like him, he thought, in the drifting associations before sleep. Was it that absurd romanticism of his, that I for one never took seriously? Her sharp eye saw only tactical pretence in it. Well, I certainly won't swoon over her like he must have done. I'll have to be cool with her. She's one of the few available British women here - I mustn't let her believe I'm just a hungry dog after her. They often become vain and egotistical, foreign women in Arab countries, where the Arabs run hungry, denied their own women. Like Lynda. Well, I'll give Emma no reason to indulge her vanity, if she has any.

Towards eight o'clock that night, he was driving with

Charles along the wide avenue that led past the university to the suburb where Emma's parents lived. A faded elegance was cast about by flamboyant trees and lawns and the imposing brown-stone buildings. On some of the islands in the middle of the road there were huge, hand-painted portraits of Nasser and Sadat. The quality of the portraits was not very high, and the faces had naïve, caricatured expressions. It made one feel that Egyptians were lagging very far behind in the technology of the symbol and the audio-visual brilliance of the west. It was as if they were still watching silent films, unwilling or unable to launch themselves into the era of the more exacting talkies. These enormous faces of Nasser and Sadat, how could they inspire or impress? To Dominic they seemed clumsy and dead.

'It's the first on the right up there after the fruit stall - you see, the one with the bright light,' Charles said, pointing.

Dominic saw the huge bulb, it must have been two or three hundred watts, hanging above piles of oranges, bananas, and mangoes.

'Right.'

He pulled the car round. A few minutes later they drew up outside a white house with a large garden hidden by a high wall. He got out of the car and rang the bell at the gate. It was an answer-phone with a dim light. Almost immediately he heard a sharp voice.

'Hello?'

'Hello. It's Dominic. Is that you, Emma?'

'Yes, hello. I'll be right down.'

He heard the front door of the house close and her steps as she came to the gate. The thought that already there was a connection between them struck him. She was walking towards him, unseen, she had accepted the proposal of his will, she was doing what he wanted. Complicity and acceptance even now, right at the beginning.

The gate opened. He was shocked almost by her physical presence, so suddenly real, in front of him. She was wearing a sort of trouser suit in light cotton, with coloured embroidery on the collar and cuffs of the blouse. Her small face seemed thinner and more grown-up than at the lunch party. Yet there was no make-up on it, he noticed. Her hair was pulled up on each side, and fell down over her ears in braided strands.

'I hope you found your way all right,' she said with a vehemence which he could not interpret. Was it nerves or self-confidence?

'No trouble. Charles came with me. He's in the car. I'm afraid there won't be much room. Still, you're very thin'.

He put his hand out and touched her waist. The soft body did not pull away. Yet he felt that he had made a crude gesture, for she stood there, silent. He regretted that he had touched her without invitation, but the soft feel of her side lingered in his mind with its own justification.

'I think it would be better if you sat in the middle. Do you mind? I've got a little cushion, it shouldn't be too uncomfortable.'

He opened the car door on Charles's side.

'Get out Charles and let Emma in.'

Charles got out and greeted Emma with a kiss on each cheek.

'Hello Emma,' he said. 'You're looking very nice.'

'Am I? Thanks. Hello, Charles,' she replied.

'All right. Now let's see if we can all actually fit in,' Dominic said.

He held open the car door for her. She bent her thin body

and got in. He went round to his side, leaned in and got the cushion on the drive shaft tunnel for her to sit on.

'Is that all right?'

'Fine,' she said in a voice a lot less intimate that the one she had used with Charles. He felt that he was much further from her than Charles. He would have to struggle over a great distance to get close to her. The quality of her voice seemed to cut him away from her. Yet as he got into the car, body first, then legs, in his usual way, he had to press up against her quite closely. He felt the soft, yielding pressure of her breast. Then he slammed the door and straightened up his body to give her more room. Charles got in on the other side.

He started the engine and drove off. They only touched now when he turned corners, and this he purposely did more abruptly than usual. The physical contact with this woman, this young girl he didn't know at all, who didn't know him, but who, he was sure, knew that he had decided to pursue her and who was ready for him, filled him with an uneasy excitement. He drove with exaggeration, making the car's exhaust give out a raucous clatter.

Charles asked Emma how her parents were, and she began telling him about a function they had been to that day. Again Dominic felt distant, left out. There was more between Emma and Charles than between Emma and him. Yet there was the crucial sexual connection between them, tentative and hidden as it might be. That would be enough for him. Let her talk to Charles. It didn't matter. After all, he had no intention of trying to impress her, of being terribly likable.

'How long have you been in Alexandria, Dominic?' she asked him later in a slightly strained voice.

'We got here the week before last, for the summer conference, you know. I can tell you, Rory and I have already become quite accustomed to the style of Lynda and Charles's place. You've been here before, of course,' he said, as he pulled up outside the rather ugly block that housed their splendid apartment.

'Oh yes, many times. I was at all those planchette evenings last year. Wasn't I Charles?'

'Yes, you were, and I suspect you were the one who asked those rather obscene questions,' Charles said laughing.

'That's not true,' Emma protested, as they got out of the car.

They went into the building, across the large, empty hall, devoid of windows, and into the small lift.

'Who else is coming?' Emma asked as the lift began to ascend. Dominic felt a flicker of embarrassment that her question was directed at him as if to draw him into the intimacy that already existed between her and Charles. Even as they stood in the lift, her body was closer to Charles than to him.

'I'm not sure. Some friends of Lynda's, isn't that so, Charles?'

He repaid the gesture of her question with a deliberate, flat vagueness. Charles answered her entirely naturally.

'Well, first there's Ali and Sybil. And Miriam, and Mohsen. And some new chap called Khaled, who's in the navy. That's the lot, I think'.

The lift came to a stop and the door slid back. Dominic was next to it.

'After you,' he said to Emma.

Her thin body moved briskly before him. It was frail almost, yet it had an extraordinary momentum, a cogency which he found daunting. How could he impose his physicality on hers?

Yet he was going to attempt it. The worry of this vision and the silence as they waited in front of the door ended quickly when it was opened. Rory stood there.

'Well, hello... Emma, how are you?'

He seemed very pleased to see her. For a moment, Dominic wondered if Rory might move towards her as well, and get there first, supplant him.

'How nice to see you again so soon,' he was saying.

'Hello, Rory. Charles didn't say you'd be here,' she replied.

'Oh, I'm one of the family - almost. I'm staying here too. Dominic and I share the guest suite.'

Dominic wondered whether Emma had been thinking of Rory when she'd asked who else was coming to the dinner. Had she accepted his invitation simply as a means of seeing Rory again? He felt repelled from her.

After meeting the other guests and shaking hands with them all in the Egyptian manner, he sat with Emma on a sofa and drank his whisky. She had a glass of wine.

'What kind of whisky is that?' she asked.

'It's a Scotch. Why?'

'It looks so pale, and your glass is nearly full.'

'Oh, that's all water. I've got into the habit of drinking whisky like this out here, just a small one and then filling up the tumbler with water.'

'I wish Daddy would drink it like that.'

'Why, does he overdo it?'

'I'm afraid so. It doesn't seem to affect him very much. Everyone says he holds it very well. But still, he drinks over half a bottle a day.'

'Mmm, well, funnily I find I'm drinking less and less as I get older...'

He hesitated, having touched on his age, looked into her clear, nineteen-year-old face, and then pushed himself into the posture of a bent old man with a shaking hand holding his glass. She laughed, and he smiled back.

'I just don't seem to like getting drunk any more. Maybe I've been drunk too often.'

'Well, Daddy's never drunk, that's one thing.'

'Just pickling his liver slowly and surely?'

'I suppose so. I hate drunk people, don't you?'

'It depends.'

'Well, I do, especially men. I hate it when they begin to slobber over one... over me, as if being drunk is some excuse for pushing themselves on me. Ugh!'

She gave a little shake to her body, like a dog coming out of dirty water.

'Well, with this kind of diluted whisky, I call it Egyptian whisky, you can be sure I won't get slobbery or drunk.'

'Jolly good.'

A sympathy seemed to be struggling into life between them. Emma looked at him for some moments in silence. He returned her gaze. Then his fell to her mouth. How extraordinarily delicate it was - a thin, pointed mouth, very, very young, and behind the thin lips, small white regular teeth, designed, it seemed, only for nibbling. As he watched, it stretched into a smile, with sharp points on each side.

'*A table, s'il vous plait,*' Lynda called out, and people began going into the dining room. The huge table was set at one end. As Dominic and Emma went in, Emma started talking to Lynda, and without trying to prevent it, Dominic found himself sitting down on the other side from her. He had let himself be separated from her and felt a sense of weak passivity. He would now lose what he had just gained.

Sitting beside him at the table on one side was Miriam, an Egyptian woman of indeterminate age, late thirties or forties, very elegant, an *habitué* of European circles. She was very fluent in English and once or twice switched to equally efficient French. Then she began talking of her time in Italy, and it was clear she spoke Italian as well. Cosmopolitanism *a l'outrance*, Dominic thought. He wondered if she had a foreign parent, or even two, and was just living in Egypt.

'But you are Egyptian, aren't you?' he put in as she made a remark about how dreary life was in Alex now, compared to Rome.

'No, I'm Turkish,' she replied, as if it was a question frequently asked, and one to which she had a satisfactory answer.

'Turkish, really? From what part?' he asked.

'Oh, I was born in Cairo. But we are a Turkish family, pure Turkish.'

'You mean both your parents came from Turkey?'

'No, but all my ancestors. You see, we have never married into Egyptian blood.'

He was struck by the idea that for her, nationality was a question of blood. Where you were born and brought up she seemed to consider only a circumstance. What counted was blood. That was where the self-image, the sense of identity came from.

Rory had been listening to the exchange.

'Turkish, nonsense, Miriam,' he said. 'You're as Egyptian as can be. Raised here for generations. Why don't you want to admit it? Bamboozled by the British?'

'Bamboozled?' Miriam repeated uncertainly.

Dominic felt Rory was stepping over the edge of discretion. He looked at Miriam. She seemed hurt. Her face may have had a blush in it, but with her dark, smooth skin, it was hard to tell. Her skin certainly did look Egyptian.

'But I don't even know Arabic,' she said, stammering slightly on the a of Arabic.'

'That's disgraceful,' Rory said in mock horror. 'But it doesn't prove you're not Egyptian. You're Egyptian - you're part of this extraordinary, pluralistic, polyglot, chaotic, enchanting people. Don't say you're not.'

Miriam took the rebuke with good grace, she seemed a little surprised at it only. Dominic wondered if she came out with her Turkish origins because she thought British people were more respectful of the Turks.

'Well, maybe I've spent too much of my life away from Egypt,' she said reasonably.

'And lived through an era in which the British poured contempt on Egyptian nationalism,' Rory said with bitter force.

Dominic felt he must change the subject.

'You know I heard an amusing story the other day, about someone I suppose you'd consider Turkish - King Farouk.'

He smiled at Miriam, trying to win her confidence. She smiled back.

'When he had to sign his abdication document, he couldn't write his name correctly in Arabic. He made some sort of spelling mistake in it.'

She laughed openly. So did Rory, but his laugh was full of contempt.

Dominic's anecdote had served its purpose, the subject was dropped.

Lynda and Charles had acquired, probably with the flat, an old house servant from Upper Egypt called Ahmed, who was now carrying round from guest to guest a large dish full of keftah meatballs. He was, though half blind, an extremely good cook. Those who had already started eating were complimenting him on his efforts. His black face smiled with satisfaction. Obviously the Egyptian guests knew what they were talking about, but he had his doubts about the British. Did they really appreciate the savour of his keftah? Under his care his two employers, Lynda and Charles had, he felt, begun, but only just begun, to appreciate good food. When he had first started to work for them, they had had the distressing and quite uncivilised habit of rushing through their meals, not seeming to notice them. Or even worse, and this would put him into a sullen mood of protest, they sometimes read, both of them, books propped on glasses, while consuming what he had prepared with such care for them.

But now, he reflected with satisfaction, perhaps because of the frequent presence of more civilised Egyptians, they were beginning to take their meals seriously, to emit noises of approval while eating, to linger at the table, and often to fall into contented sleep afterwards. In a word, to eat well.

'Your national service doesn't seem to have lasted long, Khaled,' Lynda said across the table to the naval man.

'I'm only out on sick leave.'

'But you're not sick, are you?'

'Of course not. Why are you English so logical?'

His square face broke into a wide smile, curling back his upper lip.

'No, I had to come home for Freddie's engagement,' he went on. 'Our family doctor arranged it.'

'So you're going back soon?'

'After a week. Anyway there is not going to be a war while I am away.'

'Thank God,' Miriam said. 'Poor Egypt, we have had too many wars. Now we need peace.'

'What do you think, Khaled?' Charles asked. 'Will there be peace, or are all these withdrawal agreements just going to be a breathing space?'

'We need more than a breathing space,' Ali put in, 'to repair our army and get ready for the next war. We need a lifetime.'

'No,' Khaled said, 'I think we have turned a corner. Egypt has proved to herself and to everybody that she can fight. Now we are ready to make peace.'

'Is Sadat strong enough to do that?' Charles asked.

'But Charles, who was it that told us recently that Sadat is in fact a CIA agent?' Lynda asked.

Ali and Khaled roared with laughter.

'It's not impossible,' Ali said when he had recovered. 'The CIA were very involved with the Free Officers' Movement during and after the revolution. And look at what Sadat has done since he took over - everything to push back the Russians.'

'Launching the '73 war, that was hardly pro-American,' Charles said.

'No, it was just a little anti-American. But as soon as we had taken the famous Bar-Lev line, we stopped advancing and just dug in. We didn't want to anger the Americans really. After all, we are so looking forward to having a Coca Cola factory here in Egypt.'

Again the Egyptians at the table laughed without restraint. Dominic watched them, amused. This was something that he had been completely unprepared for - their all-encompassing sense of humour.

'Well, whether you get peace and Coca Cola here in Egypt,' Rory said, 'you certainly won't get peace in Palestine.'

'We have suffered so much for the Palestinians,' Khaled said. 'What have they done for us?'

'So now you're prepared to abandon them and live comfortably?'

'Well, they are their own worst enemies, don't you think?'

It was Emma, with her clear, precise voice.

'How exactly?' Rory asked back with a complete absence of the warmth he had shown her at the door.

'All their terrorist attacks, Munich, that school - now they're making trouble in Lebanon. Daddy says...'

But Rory cut her off.

'You've been reading too many western papers, Emma. Anyone fighting for their rights against western interests are, by definition, terrorists. What else can the Palestinians do, for God's sake?'

'It doesn't do them much good, shooting up a plane at an airport, does it?' Charles said.

'No, it doesn't. It gives western propaganda the perfect and perfectly spurious excuse to damn them. You all...'

His arm make a quick sweep in front of his body, just missing his glass of wine.

'Yes, even you Egyptians, you've got this propaganda cancer in you.'

'Cancer? What an exaggeration,' Emma said coldly.

'What else is it? A people is uprooted, kicked out, killed, and abused, first with the help of Britain and then of America, and what do I hear from you... criticism of those who committed the crimes? Oh no. Instead I hear condemnation of the feeble responses of the victims. It's grotesque.'

Rory was white in the face.

'I still say you're exaggerating. In Britain, we hear both sides of the issue. We do have a free press, after all,' Emma replied.

'Oh, don't be so naive,' Rory said. 'Have you actually looked through the British press to see who reports from Israel? The Guardian - Eric Silver. What religion do you think he is? The Times - the same thing. The BBC - Jenkins. He's a self-confessed Zionist. It's like sending a member of the communist party to report on the situation in the Soviet Union. You're getting a hopelessly one-sided picture.'

'You are right, Rory,' Ali put in. 'We have known this for a long time. No-one listened to our side of the story.'

'Maybe the Palestinians should become like the Jews then,' Donimic suggested. 'You know, spread slowly and surreptitiously into the countries of the west - Europe and America - and when they're in, start making their voices heard.'

'They won't be allowed to,' Rory said. 'I don't know how the Jews got about, but now, we've got immigration controls. It's too late. The Palestinians are just going to be crushed, without respite, without mercy. What I can't stand is that people, decent people, instead of placing blame where it belongs, on the Zionists and their helpers, castigate the Palestinians as terrorists for trying to get some of their own back'.

'It does seem so unjust,' Lynda said. 'But we mustn't let politics spoil the evening. Rory, have another glass of wine, Ali?'

Both accepted, and the conversation turned to Freddie's engagement. Khaled began to describe the intricacies of the ceremony to Emma, and Dominic listened in. The whole business sounded more like the actual marriage - it was a very formal procedure, conducted before the assembled families and friends.

The dinner, like most meals in Egypt, was long and unhurried. Because he was working early next morning, Dominic suggested to Emma soon after midnight that he take her home.

Once out of the apartment and on their way down to the car, a silence of strangeness re-established itself between them. What they had said to each other during the dinner party had been pleasant enough, but it had not broken down the reserve he felt with her. There had been no careless flow of conversation, releasing his spirit into hers and hers into his. The effort of will was still necessary to cross the distance between them.

They drove through the quiet streets in the particularly dark quality of the Alexandrian night. The street lights were incapable, it seemed, of holding it back. Perhaps many of them were not working. Those that were cast a purple-white glare around them, making the leaves of the trees silvery against a black ground. In between these illuminated palls was obscure darkness. Unlike Cairo, few people were about.

Finally, it was Emma who broke the silence.

'How long are you going to stay in Alex, Dominic?'

'Well, the conference will last about four weeks, in its various forms. We've got to be back in Cairo at the beginning of September. And you?'

'I suppose I'll go back some time in the middle of September. I've got so much work to do. At the beginning of the vacation, I thought I'd have plenty of time, but for some reason I can't seem to get down to the reading.'

'It's the sea air.'

'Possibly.'

'What stuff are you doing this year?'

'The Romantics, mostly - Coleridge, Wordsworth, Keats. And for the novel, George Eliot.'

'Yes, all that is certainly a lot of reading.'

'If I could only get really started, I'd be able to apply myself.

But getting started, that's the problem.'

They were swinging into the small side street where she lived. For a moment, Dominic thought he might lean over and kiss her lightly on the mouth before she got out of the car. He pulled up and looked directly at her in the metallic glare of the street lamp. Though her face was so close to his, he felt in the sudden stillness that she was a long, long way off. The air between them became like a transparent, plastic solid. As he stared at her she was being telescoped slowly away from him in this paralysing medium. He must say something to her to break this reverie.

'Well, Emma…I hope you enjoyed yourself.'

It was hopelessly impersonal, cliched, but it was all that came.

'Yes, it was nice. Lynda and Charles are such a nice pair, aren't they?'

'Oh,' she went straight on, as if to forestall any advance he might have in mind, 'Now where are my keys?'

She rummaged in her Greek woollen bag.

'Ah, there they are. Well…' she looked up with a punctuating smile, 'thank you very much for a nice evening.'

'A pleasure.'

His reply was equally mechanical. Absolutely impossible to reach out now, to touch her, he thought.

'Well, bye then. See you soon.'

'Yes, goodnight, Emma. See you.'

She got out of the car and briskly opened the high garden gate. With a small wave, which he returned, she disappeared.

Seven

Because he had failed to make another date with her, and because no intimacy had sprung up between them, Dominic let one day after another go by without contacting Emma again. Afternoons of tennis at the Sporting Club with Ali, meals in town with colleagues at the conference, visits, visits, interminable visits in the Egyptian style to friends' houses for drinks and easy-going talk - in this way, days and nights were filled.

When he thought of Emma, he wondered if he should give up his pursuit of her. They didn't seem to suit each other in some visceral way. Maybe it was easier to recognise this. It was easier not to struggle.

The following Saturday night, after dinner at Ronald's beach house in Agami, Lynda suggested that they all go to the Agami Palace.

'What on earth is that?' Dominic asked.

'Our local nightclub - yes, O.K.' Ronald said.

'But I'm not going to stay all night Ronald,' his wife Elizabeth added as they all got up to go.

When they got there, the Agami Palace was as full as the Maidan al Tahrir in Cairo during rush hour. Bodies jostled against bodies in the dark, it was almost impossible to make progress. Somewhere in the middle of the space, dancers, under a hail of stroboscopic lights, writhed and sweated to crushingly loud music. Lynda knew many of the people there and greeted them as she led the way successfully to a table where waiters were assembling chairs for them to sit on. They crowded round and Lynda gave the orders. One was sent to get a bottle of whisky and a bucket of ice, others for dishes of olives, humus, stuffed vine leaves, and another to fetch the manager. He soon appeared in dinner jacket and velvet bow tie.

'*Mais, Leenda, comment ca va? Comme tu es belle ce soir!*'

As she stood up he held both her hands and drew her towards him to land a kiss on each of her cheeks.

She must be a very regular customer, Dominic thought, as he observed this unrestrained greeting and familiarity. It jarred on him, but Lynda and Charles obviously found it completely normal - they were chatting away to the manager like old friends. Perhaps they were old friends. Yet he felt sure there must be in the exchange between Lynda and the manager some of that special stimulus that foreign, and therefore 'free' women have for any Arab man. She could not but be, for him, a woman with a special heat. Dominic could feel this heat from Lynda, and from Sybil and Elizabeth as well, as it bounced back from the faces of the Egyptian men who surrounded them. It was a heat that never came off an Egyptian woman, like Miriam, who sat opposite Dominic, sipping her fizzy drink. Her heat was hidden, by control, by repression. A quick surge of sympathy for her, and annoyance that she was drinking such a worthless product of the west, made him stand up.

'That's enough of that poison water, Miriam. Come and dance.'

She jumped up.

'Yes, I would love to.'

They fought their way to the dancing area. Dominic noticed

that everyone had the latest chic in dance styles. Even Miriam, who he had thought might be a bit old for rock, moved expertly. It seemed that the whole of Egypt was now dedicating itself to the disco revolution as eagerly as it had previously followed Nasser's. In the intense noise, conversation was impossible. He and Miriam could only exchange occasional smiles.

With a sudden chilling in his stomach, Dominic noticed, on the other side of the dancing area, Emma in the arms of a middle-height, dark-haired man. He was holding her close and seemed to be talking into her ear. Dominic thought she had seen him, and was on the point of waving to her, but no, the thick body of the man turned, and she turned with him, without any sign of recognition on her face. Numerous moving bodies quickly hid them again from his view. He realised his heart was beating much faster. To what purpose? He looked at Miriam, smiled at her, and waited for it to quieten.

Later, at the table, he heard Charles say to Lynda: 'Look, there's Emma.'

Dominic was talking at the other end of the table to Ronald. He continued speaking, pretending not to have heard Charles, with his head turned away, but he listened intently.

'Where?'

'Over there.'

'Who with?'

'Can't see. Some bloke.'

Lynda's next remark was barely audible in the noise, but he felt sure he heard it right.

'The first of this summer's crop.'

Eight

After the night at the Agami Palace, Dominic allowed the days to pass without contacting Emma. Learning that she went through men, that many had been where he hoped to go, first of all filled him with a repellent irritation. That heat which the European woman gave off in an Arab country, she too had exploited it. Even though she was nineteen, the age at which an Egyptian girl could only meet a man surreptitiously in the afternoon in some café, she had already had a 'crop'. All, no doubt, like that tight-shirted, hairy individual he had seen her with at the nightclub. He imagined the mixture of hunger and flattery, vanity and brashness, with which they had pursued her. And she had acquiesced, time and time again. Why had he allowed himself to be unnerved by her sharp, monitoring look? These Egyptian men had probably brushed it aside with hackneyed compliments: 'You arre my angel,' or ' You arre the most beauutiful girl in the worrld.'

But at the same time as being repelled by the knowledge that she had been with many men, he also felt a coarsening impulse to approach her and get her much more brusquely. He came from that generation that had grown up just before the pill, from the pre-permissive generation. He had never had a one-night stand, never met a promiscuous woman. It was outside his realm of experience. Now here was a nineteen-year-old, a student at Oxford, who was that new breed, for whom sex was no longer the profound tension that it had been for his generation. She could just take this man or that, and she had had a string of them to prove it. Knowing this about her provoked him. All the probing, the difficulties, the slow yielding, were irrelevant with her. If she fancied a man, that was all that was required. Bed and sex followed forthwith - it was as easy, as basic, as that.

'Well, I'll adopt exactly the same approach,' he decided. 'I'll just let myself go with her, and if I like it, fine. If I don't, then out.'

The fact that the second week of the conference was nearly through seemed to make no difference. If it was going to happen between them, it was going to be quick, and anyway, if she was used to going through men, it probably wouldn't be an affair of any importance.

The next Saturday, another visit to the Agami Palace was planned over lunch. Dominic, Rory, and Hugh, a visiting lecturer at the conference, had rented an apartment in a small building not far from the nightclub and planned to spend the weekend at the resort. Without any of the hesitation which had preceded his first phone call, Dominic now rang Emma again.

'Hello, is that you Emma?'

'Oh, hello, Dominic. Nice to hear from you. How are you?'

She seemed friendly, enthusiastic even.

'Fine. Look, we're all going to the Agami Palace tonight. Would you like to come?'

He tried to sound as off-hand, as unconcerned as he could, and the flat tone of his voice verged on rudeness even to his own ear. Yet her reply was immediate.

'Yes, that'd be lovely. Just what I need.'

'Good. We'll probably eat there as well. O.K?'

'Super.'

'I'll pick you up about eight then.'

'Well, actually, I'm going to be in Agami myself this afternoon, with Mum and Dad.'

And with that Egyptian boyfriend, Dominic thought.

'Do you remember the house where we had lunch that day? Where we met?'

'Yes, sure.'

'Well, I'll be there. Pick me up from there, if you like.'

'No problem. Well, about, oh, about eight-thirty.'

'That'd be lovely.'

Well, she certainly sounded keen enough, he thought as he put the phone down. Maybe the Egyptian lover-boy has been discarded and she's ready for something new. Maybe she's tired of inane compliments.

Driving out to Agami that evening, Dominic took the more direct route through the city. It continued on through miles and miles of residential and industrial suburbs, where the streets were full of people, donkey-carts, buses, bicycles, cars, children, cats, lorries, and heaps of rubbish. It needed only a momentary loss of concentration, and one would kill or be killed. Yet remarkably, there were no accidents. Everyone skirted death in this haphazard chaos, but miraculously escaped. All trusted to Allah's will, and his will was sparing. Its benign power made a bumper pass just a few critical inches away from a child's leg, stopped a donkey-cart just before it crossed the path of a hurtling bus, and allowed Dominic's small white MG the fraction of a second in which to pass between a vegetable lorry and a taxi reversing out into the main road.

In this bedlam, there was only one rule of the road - don't hit anyone. Everything else was permitted.

Some hours later, Dominic, Emma, Rory, Charles, Lynda, Ali, and Gamal, a huge Egyptian who seemed to be suffering from that disease which produces excessive growth of the lower jaw, hands, and feet, were seated round a table in the Agami Palace. Lynda and Charles had been greeted in exactly the same, effusive way as on the previous Saturday. A meal had been ordered - hummus, kebabs, salad. Plates of half-eaten food and pieces of bread lay strewn over the table. A bottle of Scotch was in the centre. It was nearly empty.

Emma sat beside Dominic in a light cotton dress which left her lithe, brown arms bare. Looking at her, he noticed the taut skin curving over the muscles of her shoulder and then flattening on her upper arm. The moulding, the smooth bulge of her flesh, was perfect.

They said almost nothing to each other, some pleasantries in the car before arriving, and now in the deafening music of the nightclub, some shouted remarks over food. He glanced at the others seated round the table. They too seemed smothered in noise, staring blankly towards the dancers, their heads propped on their hands, some smoking. Occasionally one would wake from immobility and reach out for the whisky bottle. Dominic was sure that they were all sliding into boredom. After all, if one didn't dance, one certainly couldn't talk, one could only sit and stare. And yet probably everyone considered that they were living it up, that this, the nightclub, was the acme of leisure. For Egyptians in particular, Dominic thought, this was the good life that they must have too, since they had seen it all in the movies. He looked from one face to another - Egyptian or European, they were expressionless, empty.

Was Emma bored as well? He wondered. There was a kind of willful commitment about the way she sat and looked at the dancers, as if she was really trying to find them entertaining. She pushed her glasses back on her nose from time to time, to get the scene more clearly in view. One of her fine, thin legs, folded over the other, wagged in time to the music.

'Are you ready for a dance?' he said loudly into her ear.

With a quick movement, she turned her head to him, gave him her sharp-pointed smile, and nodded.

He followed her into the crowd of bodies, and as he did so, he felt a surreal force pulling him after her - the concurrence of their intentions. Now there was no question between them, they had accepted each other. They had approached, circled, hinted, drawn back, and now come forward again. In spite of the meagerness of what had passed between them, of the pleasure they had so far given each other, the matter was settled. Her thin body moved in front of him towards the dance, and he followed, passively drawn along by her motion, his will playing no part.

When she turned to face him on the floor, there was an instant in the flash of a white spot light when the brightness of her eyes and the glitter of her glasses broke into this drifting ease. But he ignored it and moved close to hold her. It was a slow, as the Egyptians called it, but he held her with her right arm out from her body in the formal ballroom stance, and put his right hand lightly round the small of her back. Without any pressure from him, she came slowly, delicately closer to him as they danced. Her body, with light, floating movements, began to touch his and establish an intimate contact between them. He felt in its lightness a kind of innocent submission and it delighted him. He let go with his left hand and brought it to her back to join the other. Very gently he held her as he brought his body full up against hers. She met his advance and he felt the soft pressure of her breasts against his chest, of her belly against his sex. She dropped her head onto his shoulder and he bent his own so that his nose and lips were on her thick, straight hair. He breathed in the warm smell of it. They moved together with a slow, easy movement. This was the first love between them, where the language of their touching brought more joy than their dry, abstract contact of words. He felt sure that he had moved through the cold shield of her gaze, vigilant behind her glasses, to a new, warmer acceptance. The way she held herself against him had a purity that loosed from him a wave of relief. He pressed her with gentle force against him, feeling to enclose her small body in his. He searched the soft warmth of her flesh. A sweet, flowing pleasure ran into his sex, and he felt it swelling and pressing against her. She felt it too and brought her belly more closely against him. He was filled with happiness so intense that the crowd around them became carelessly merged in it. The whole nightclub was now intimate, floating in this new world of Emma's body and his and their warm complicity. His erection became stronger, strident, and they moved together with small, close movements.

Eventually the music ended, and they pulled apart slowly, easily. He looked down at her, smiled, and said:

'I'd like to repeat that.'

She smiled back, and as she did so, another record began, with a strong, booming bass. It was not a slow. They moved off the dancing floor and back towards the table where the others were still seated in poses of mute emptiness, as when they had left them. He realised as they approached the table that his erection must still be obvious, but he did not try to hide it. He was filled with a sweet calm that he and Emma were now sure to be lovers, and he was happy that others should see it.

They sat down again and he pulled his chair towards hers

and held one of her hands in both of his. She leaned her head easily against him.

'The others don't look very happy,' he said to her, and hoped that they did not hear. She shook her head slightly in agreement, but without saying anything, as if it was no concern of theirs.

'Not like us,' he said.

Again the smallest movement of her head against him.

Ali emptied the last of the Scotch into his glass and shouted to the others:

'Shall we get another bottle?'

'Not for me,' Charles said. 'Lynda?'

He turned to her.

'Oh, let's. It's only eleven.'

Ali stood up and gestured to a waiter.

Rory stirred and asked Lynda to dance. As they went off, Dominic noticed Ali's face falling into a dead mask. He stared at the empty bottle in front of him. Was it whisky or Lynda he wanted most?

An argument was developing at a nearby table. Suddenly Dominic wanted to get away from this atmosphere of ritualised emptiness, this nightclubbery, in which only crude emotions could flourish. What did it all have to do with the delicate sympathy that was growing between him and Emma?

He said to her: 'Shall we leave?'

As the words came out, he realised that this was the final invitation to sexual union, spoken without forethought, but now irrevocable.

Her reply held no shock.

'Yes, let's, it's so loud in here.'

They got up, shook hands with everyone at the table and made their way to the dance floor. They pushed through to Rory and Lynda.

'We're off, Rory,' Dominic shouted over the music.

'Can I have the key?'

He made a turning motion with his hand. Rory nodded and got the key from his trouser pocket. Lynda looked on. Dominic took it quickly. The two of them knew now that he and Emma were going to sleep together. There was a sour blankness on Lynda's face, and for a moment Dominic thought that it was disapproval, but perhaps it was the effect of the heat, the dancing. Emma kissed her goodbye. They walked away.

The apartment was not far from the nightclub, in an area where three and four storied buildings were going up in disorganised profusion. They climbed the stairway to the front door. Emma went first and again Dominic noticed the extreme youthfulness of her small body. He, over thirty years of age, she, nineteen.

Inside, he looked at her face. Was she nervous? Was it all really so easy for her, for young girls these days? She seemed quite relaxed, though now there was a silence between them. He felt she had fallen into a numb state of waiting. But she was calm.

'I'll go to the bathroom first. I want to have a quick shower. The bedroom's that one.'

He pointed. She went into it straight away, her arms hanging at her sides, one hand holding her woollen bag.

He went into the bathroom, took off his clothes and showered quickly. As he dried his body, he looked at it and it seemed a strange object that didn't belong to him. Aware that Emma was undressing in the bedroom, he felt a gripping of excitement in his stomach, and imagining the movement of her thin thighs, his cock began to swell and rise on him. It had a strange objectivity, it was a force outside himself. He wrapped the towel round his body to hide it and went in to her. She was sitting on the bed quite naked, with her back against the wall. Her knees were drawn up and her arms were around them.

He went and lay on the bed beside her and put out his hand to touch the white side of her body where the ribs formed ridges. Her breasts were pressed against her thighs. They were white, and large for the thin torso. She had taken her glasses off, and as she looked at him, he felt that she couldn't see him clearly, that she had fallen further into her passive silence. She had decided to make love with him, she had given up control, and she was slipping further and further into abstraction. She was naked beside him, but he felt she was drifting away into an abandonment that was impersonal.

Suddenly she said: 'Won't be a moment.'

She got up quickly from the bed.

Her body was more womanly without clothes. He watched her disappear into the bathroom.

Some minutes later she came back, walking naked, with her breasts hanging heavy. He saw her bush of hair, large and thick, above her beautiful legs. She went over to the chest of drawers, and searched in her handbag. Eventually she found what she was looking for, and he heard the small snapping sound of a pill being pushed through foil. He saw her swallow it with a gulp of water from a glass she had brought in.

This was the free generation, he thought. No more fumbling, shame, embarrassment. No more clumsy struggling with contraceptives as the heart beat painfully. Just one pill each day, regularly, and then, if one liked someone, there was no impediment.

She came to the bed, and got in quickly under the sheet. He moved over her and began kissing her thin, girlish mouth. He put his free hand on her breast and squeezed its roundness. She broke away from the kiss and reached over for the light switch. She caught the wire and let it run through her fingers until she found the switch.

The darkness blocked her off from him completely for a moment. She brought her face back to his and he found her mouth again. He pushed his tongue into her and even this entry filled him with a sense of wonder that she was really a woman, not a girl. Yet she remained distant from him in the darkness. With his hands he caressed her body but it was as if he did not know who it belonged to. Who was she? He wanted to find her, to love her, but suddenly she seemed unknown. His cock, that had hardened when his tongue had gone into her mouth, now began to weaken. Yet she was really there, her body given up to him. He felt her thighs, their smooth taut skin over her lithe muscles. He rubbed her thick bush, and she responded with squirming motions, pressing her sex against his touch. He felt the nipples rise on her breasts and her mouth remained open wide, a wet space for him to fill. He grew hard again and clutched at this excitement. He pulled his body up over her and she opened her legs for him. His cock pushed against her thick hair, and balancing himself, he put down one hand to try to direct it into her. But she seemed closed and dry, unyielding. He pushed harder, vainly. He could not find her. Why did she not help him? His excitement would die if he didn't get into her quickly. But he could not. He pushed against dry, thick hair, and he felt his cock weaken. She lay, her arms round his back, waiting. He couldn't find her opening. He was lost.

He moved off her. A sweat broke out on his face from his failure and the exertion. He continued kissing her, but now she was only further away than before, drifting inexorably away.

'We seem to be a bit hesitant,' he whispered, trying to reach her again.

She answered with a small movement of her head, no words. He wondered what she was thinking, this woman he hardly knew. Why had he rushed at her? She was with him now in the darkness but he had failed to take up her offer. Why had he not let his love for her grow as it would? Was it because of what he had heard Lynda say of her? Or because they would have only a few weeks together before she returned to England? Now it was too late. It hadn't worked. His instincts couldn't adjust to the faster pace of her kind. He stopped kissing her, and lay beside her in the darkness. Neither of them spoke again. Eventually, with a strange sense of aloneness, he drifted into a fitful sleep.

He awoke with the sharp, early morning light breaking into the room through the laths of the shutters. Emma was lying on her side with her back to him. He didn't know if she had woken or not. They had thrown off the sheet during the night, and he lay facing her, looking up and down her back, at the deep curve of her waist, and the long crack between the cheeks of her buttocks, the rounded, full flesh. She was perfectly still, just her quiet regular breathing. He was free to stare at her nakedness. And her young body was beautiful. As he looked at her, the womanly swelling of her hips, the curved fullness of her behind pushed slightly back towards him excited his will to possess her, to get into her. He remembered how he had made love to another woman, thin like her, on a holiday in Greece, often from behind. Her buttocks had twisted and turned as he was in her, in a brutal, completely unrestrained way. She had given him her body at its most basic and she had relished its pleasure without any reserve. He had looked, looked, enthralled by her rearward, writhing abandon.

Here were Emma's curving white buttocks, just like hers, and his sex hardened and rose as he imagined how they might move. He shifted closer and pushed up under them. She moved slightly. So, she was awake. She raised her upper leg a little in silent, furtive complicity with him. Otherwise she lay perfectly still. It was enough. He found the wetness of her, and pushed up into it. Guiding himself with his hand, he got into her. She was small, but not very. He came quickly to orgasm. She remained passive, still. Afterwards, he stayed in her, filled with relief. But it was tinged with shame. They were lovers, but only through the detachment caused by his previous failure. It had been a forced, not a loving start.

He lay holding her in tandem. She put a hand behind her onto his thigh. After a time he reached back to take his watch from the bedside table.

'It's half nine. Shall we get up?'

'All right.'

'What would you like for breakfast?'

'Nothing much. Tea, yogurt if you've got some. And figs, I really do love figs.'

'O.K. I'll go down to the fruit man and get some.'

He put on jeans and a shirt and went out to the car. At the fruit stall, he pointed at the figs, luscious, purple, with their skins split and their carmine hearts oozing juice. He asked for a kilo, and when the fruitseller confirmed the order, he gave Dominic the name in Arabic: tyn. A word almost without a vowel. What a strange name for figs, Dominic thought. So meager a word for so generous a fruit. He would have expected something longer, something more descriptive of its character. He took the fruit in a funnel of newspaper and carried it to the car.

When he got back to the apartment, Emma was already sitting at the table in the living room with Rory and Hugh. Rory was wearing an Egyptian galabiya of a creamy, ochre colour, decorated with brown silk piping. It hung loosely on his sparsely fleshed frame. Hugh, about fifty, out for the conference from Britain, was the typical Englishman abroad - shapeless khaki shorts and a shirt designed to be worn with a tie, but instead with the sleeves rolled up and the collar unbuttoned and sticking out awkwardly.

Dominic greeted them.

'Look at these, ' he said, spilling the figs onto a plate.

'Oh, yummy,' Emma enthused.

'They do look good,' Hugh said. 'But I say, shouldn't they be washed rather carefully first?'

'I'll do it. You sit down and have some tea, Dominic,' Emma said and took the fruit out to the kitchen.

'Well, how was it at the Agami Palace after we left?' Dominic asked Rory.

'You didn't miss anything,' he replied, 'except for a fight at the next table.'

'Oh?'

'Well, an Egyptian fight. You know what I mean.'

'An Egyptian fight? Do they have local martial arts here then?' Hugh enquired.

'Anti-martial arts. Theatrical arts. Very civilised arts - to avoid the possibility of anyone getting seriously hurt.'

'But I thought Egyptians were terribly excitable, terribly violent,' Hugh said.

'Oh, certainly they're excitable. They just explode, no restraint at all. But the whole thing is rendered harmless by the anti-martial arts. It goes like this. The combatants exchange harsh words. Soon they move on to insults. Their companions are alerted. Then they jump to their feet and start shouting. Companions, passers-by, gather round. Things hot up. Personal honour is abused. Curses. Then the first physical contact. Arms, which have up to now been flailing in gesticulation, begin to shoot out. They push each other violently. Now the seconds intervene. They try to restrain the combatants with remarks of support and "that's enough" and "no more". Then they start to push the combatants apart. This brings the conflict to sudden climax. Sure of the restraint of their friends, the combatants give themselves over completely to their rage. Held back firmly, they struggle to hurl knock-out blows at each other. The blows never land. A paroxysm of curses ensues. It's clear that but for the intervention of the others, there would be killing. Then it's all over. The combatants are pushed back from the conflict zone. They are led away. Now they're explaining to their seconds what they would have done, what lessons could have been taught. The seconds say "yes, yes" and pour out sympathy.

Really quite civilised, don't you think?' Rory concluded.

'Well, it certainly sounds better than the typical brawl in England where people slash each other with broken bottles,' Hugh said.

'And yet it gives everyone the necessary satisfaction. With us, everything has to be controlled by self-restraint, the Protestant way,' Dominic said.

'But it's so silly,' Emma put in. 'They all look to me like children, blustering and blowing. All exaggeration.'

'Yes, of course, Emma,' Rory agreed, 'but don't you see, they enjoy it!'

He laughed.

'I suppose they do. Like a childish game.'

She handed round the bowl of glistening fruit.

As they ate, sinking their teeth again and again into the soft, juicy, sweet flesh of the figs, Dominic looked over at Emma and felt a calm joy that in spite of the night before, they had become a couple. Rory and Hugh deferred to her now with the subtlest gestures, in recognition that she was joined to Dominic and therefore part of the household, its new member. It gave Dominic a profound release, a resonance in his soul that he had not enjoyed for many years.

The group spent the day reading, eating, and listening to music. The hot, humid air of the Alexandrian coast made any exertion unwelcome. Only on the beach, where the strong breeze came in slightly cooler from the sea and the crashing breakers, could one do anything more vigorous. Dominic and Rory played racquets, but the lack of co-ordination of his friend's unathletic body made the game uninteresting. They soon broke off, and Dominic and Emma went in swimming. Emma swam well, her agile strokes sending her through the water swiftly and easily. Dominic admired her vigour, her mastery. They exchanged smiles and talked across the warm, green water that held their bodies close in hidden, fluid conjunction.

Later they lay together on the beach. Emma was stretched out with her eyes closed, her long hair clinging to her head, flecks of salt drying out on her skin. He tried to read a book on nineteenth century philosophy. It was rather tedious - the interminable counter attack waged by the religiously minded against the advance of science. What hindered his sympathy was the fact that in his own life, in his own rejection of religion, he had suffered no angst. The process had been painless. It had not left him in any way bereft. He couldn't really feel for the distress of these nineteenth century thinkers, hankering after the thrill of metaphysics. One might as well hanker after the illusory thrills of childhood.

He let the book fall and his gaze wander. The beach was full of people, almost all Egyptians, with an occasional party of foreigners. One such was a family group not far away. They were French perhaps, and they had young children. The smallest was a little girl of about three years of age. She was completely naked, and ran about freely. Her skin was brown except where her miniature bikini bottom normally covered it, where it was white and striking. She ran close to Dominic and of her small, healthy body, her sexual part, white, swollen, strange, seemed the central and most conspicuous feature. He stared at it with shock and wonder. The crack was so long and so large in that tiny body, the mark of her gender, her destiny, the harbinger of her role. It filled him with a quiet awe. This was what made woman, this deep cleft, these two round ridges of flesh on either side. This was the fundamental physical imprint that rendered this child, and all women, utterly other from him, from man. It formed the gulf, the unbridgeable distance between them, and constituted the reason for the whole struggle to become one. He looked at Emma. Her cleft, covered, hidden, was the mysterious and unknowable goal that he sought. Other men would in turn seek the white cleft of that child when she had grown. She did not know it now. She carried it in innocence, this mark, this destiny. Looking at her, Dominic was thrilled by the alien, unalterable nature of her female form.

Later that evening, Dominic and Emma went round to Ronald's bungalow not far away for a barbecue supper. Ronald had invited Dominic earlier in the week and when he had rung him at midday to ask him if he could bring Emma, Ronald said at once:

'We would love to see her. Ya, ya, bring her.'

He was relieved that Ronald seemed to like Emma unreservedly. He must have known her for a couple of years at least - probably as long as Lynda and Charles - yet he had made no remarks when he had told him that Emma was spending the weekend with him, no innuendoes about her past, her previous boyfriends. He seemed to be very pleased to hear that they were together. Perhaps Lynda's remark had been exaggerated. Was she jealous? After all, Emma was a lot younger, and being unmarried, freer.

It was in fact Lynda who opened the door to them when they arrived at the bungalow. She greeted Emma with a kiss on each cheek.

'Hello, lovie. Hello Dominic. Come on in. Ronald is still on the beach, playing with the kids. Elizabeth is cooking. I've got Charles working on the barbecue grill.'

'Can we help?'

'No, no. come and have a drink with me.'

They sat down.

'Here's some red wine. Is that all right?'

'Fine,' Dominic said and smiled. Lynda was cheerful.

'Heavens, what a scene you missed last night. There was almost a fight.'

'Yes, Rory told us about a dust-up of some sort.'

'It happened right next to our table. Everybody got terribly worked up.'

'So Rory said.'

'It all started with a remark someone made about me.'

'About you?' Emma asked. 'Did you know them then?'

'Only vaguely. But one of them had met me once at one of Khaled's parties. Anyway, when this other bloke made the remark about me, Khaled's friend told him to shut his trap, that he knew me.'

Lynda's eyes opened wide as she described how remark had led to riposte, riposte to insult, insult to blows.

'Honestly, they would have killed each other if they hadn't been pulled apart. Imagine...'

Her mouth opened in mock horror. Dominic wondered if it was the phlegmatic English style of Charles that gave her a taste for such excitement.

'Oh, I'm glad I missed it,' Emma said. 'I hate scenes like that - Arab men getting into stupid rages, like schoolboys. Why can't they grow up?'

Lynda was taken aback by this censure.

'But the Egyptians are so excitable, so passionate about everything, aren't they?' she countered.

'But what's the point? It's all blow for nothing.'

It seemed to Dominic that Emma was talking from personal experience.

Elizabeth appeared carrying plates of olives and white cheese. As she greeted them, Dominic was struck by her statuesque beauty. She was very Nordic, large-boned, quite heavy, with thick rich blond hair.

'How are you enjoying your work down here?' she asked Dominic. She spoke English even better than Ronald did, with a slightly American accent. Of all the nationalities that Dominic had come across abroad, the Dutch had impressed him most. They were cosmopolitan, open-minded, vigorous. He told her something about the conference, but with the English reflex against talking shop, answered her question briefly.

'Where's Ronald?' she asked Lynda.

'He's still on the beach.'

'Go and tell him to bring the children in, will you please?'

She pulled a golden lock out of her eyes.

'Can we help?' Dominic asked.

'No, thanks. Everything is ready. Including a new marinade for the fish. An Egyptian friend who owns a little restaurant showed it to me.'

'What's in it?

'It's mostly oil, garlic, parsley, and spices - I'm afraid I don't know the names in English. Has Charles got the fire going?'

She went out onto the patio, leaving Emma and Dominic alone.

'Dominic,' Emma said, turning to face him. 'I'm afraid I can't stay with you tonight.'

He felt a sudden jolt, he sprang awake in all his senses. He could feel himself breathing, hear his heart beating.

'Oh, why?'

He tried to sound neutral, but all the resolution of the day they had passed together had drained away in an instant.

'Well, last night I had an excuse for staying out. I told Mum and Dad I was going to the Agami Palace and would sleep at Lynda's. But tonight that won't do - twice in a row.'

A wave of relief passed through him. So she wasn't so modern - she had to deceive her parents, it was for their benefit that she was retreating.

'That's OK.'

He leaned over and kissed her on the mouth.

'When am I going to see you next?'

'Tomorrow night might be a bit difficult. I'll come on Monday evening. You'll be in town, at Lynda's?'

'Yes, I finish work at one. I'll be there all afternoon, waiting for you.'

'Oh, it seems a long way away. Sorry I can't stay tonight.'

He felt that she was trying to express an understanding of the fragility of their sexual connection, and of the need to strengthen it. Her smile was a reluctant recognition that this would have to wait.

'It's all right, Emma. Till Monday then,' he said gratefully and kissed her again.

There was a sudden cackle of laughter on the patio. The children had returned. Elizabeth came in with Ronald.

'Hey, hey,' Ronald said when he saw them. 'Dominic, Emma, lovely to see you.'

He kissed them both, as an Egyptian would.

'Sorry I wasn't here to welcome you. Look, I must go and change. We're eating on the patio. Go and join the others.'

Over dinner the conversation, as so often in expatriate circles, was about other people. As soon as Lester was mentioned, Lynda described the part she had played in putting a stop to his goings-on with Stephen.

'Jane was really angry with me. Said I should have warned them long ago. Well, why didn't anybody else? Why was it left to me?'

'Everybody thought they should mind their own business,' Ronald said flatly.

'But that was just it. Jane was furious. She said there was a conspiracy of silence. And she blamed me more than anyone because she said I was her friend and knew all about Lester.'

'What actually happened?' Elizabeth asked.

'Nobody knows. And that's not what matters.' Lynda answered in a categorical tone. 'It's not what actually happens, it's what people think, or rather assume, will or has happened.'

'Yes, people always assume the worst,' Charles agreed.

'Guilty until proven innocent,' Emma put in.

'Guilty anyway. That's what everyone would think. That's the trouble - you can't let a young boy like Stephen keep company with Lester.'

'But what about all those schools in England then?' Ronald asked. 'Those private schools that for reasons we foreigners can't understand you call "public schools". Does everybody in England assume that the teachers and boys in them are all homosexual?'

He looked round at them with a quizzical smile. Charles broke the moment's silence.

'Well, some are, but it's very much frowned on.'

'Frowned on? What does that mean?'

'Disapproved of. It's absolutely taboo.'

'Extraordinary. You know in our country, it's only the stupid children of the rich who go to private schools. But you English, you go on torturing your children by locking them up in these schools. Boys without girls. No contact. And when the boys get interested in each other - it's absolutely taboo. You're really crazy, you English.'

'I agree, it is rather repressive,' Dominic admitted.

'Bah, it's completely perverted,' Ronald said. 'You do everything you can to make your boys homosexual, and then repress them with taboos.'

'Does Stephen go to one of these schools?" Elizabeth asked.

'Yes, he's at Harrow, isn't he, Charles?' Lynda replied.

'Well,' Elizabeth concluded, 'he probably won't need much encouragement from Lester in that case.'

'Why do you do it?' Ronald asked. 'Why do you English carry on and on with this boarding school business?'

'It's a long story, I'm afraid,' Dominic said, 'but I suppose this perversion, as you call it, is the result of that other well-known English vice, snobbism.'

'But public schools are simply the best schools there are,' Charles said.

'Impossible,' exploded Ronald. 'No matter how good the teaching is, there are some things I would never do to my son - or my daughter.'

'Well, we seem to have survived.' Charles said.

'Survived, yes, but in what way?'

Ronald looked at Charles and Dominic, and as if to cover his insinuation, added:

'Was it all necessary?'

'Possibly not,' Dominic said. 'In my old school, they're admitting girls into the sixth form these days.'

They would be only a year younger than Emma, he realised with a shock.

'Ah ah, you left too soon,' Ronald said and laughed.

'Oh, that's not much of an improvement,' Elizabeth said. 'Even with the sexes together in a boarding school, it would still be like a zoo. It would just be sex in a zoo.'

'I went to a completely co-educational boarding school.' Emma said.

'And was it like a zoo?' Dominic asked her.

'No, I don't think it was.'

Nine

Another week of work began at the conference. Dominic's contribution was in the field of technical co-operation. Now in the third week, he was familiar with most of the participants. They were receptive and lively. He enjoyed his work.

From time to time he wondered why such energetic and intelligent people as the Egyptians had lagged behind in the age of technology. What was at the root of their lack of progress?

At regular intervals throughout the day, the hypnotic call to prayer of the muezzin drifted into the conference, and Dominic thought that perhaps Egypt, and the world of Islam as a whole, was still dominated by the word - the machine had not replaced it as it had in Europe and Asia. Invariable formulae of words, chanted and read from generation to generation, still held this civilisation in thrall.

Yet once Islam had been vigorous in science, leading the world in fact, and there seemed to be no prejudice in the religion against science on a priori grounds. What had gone wrong? Perhaps in its heyday, Islam had simply been the most enlightened of the realms of the word of those times. Now the less enlightened realms, in Europe, in Japan, had been swept away, and replaced by the new technological realm of the machine. Islam lived on anachronistically, and had been overtaken.

And this very fact, this resultant inferiority, made Muslims more loyal to their word rather than less. They lived, Dominic believed, an almost incurable dilemma. Clinging to the word, they sought help with the machine - information, training, aid. But were their hearts in it? And probably more important, did prestige in their society accrue to the machine and to those who understood it? If not, if moving up in their society meant distancing oneself from the machine, becoming technically ignorant and incompetent, then surely their progress was hamstrung. He recalled that at the beginning of the conference, the chairman had welcomed them and then given them an elaborate apology because the stencil cutter was out of order. He spoke of the machine as if it were a magical black box, impossibly complicated, something quite outside his powers of comprehension. He was ultimately responsible for it, yes, but when it malfunctioned, he admitted to being utterly helpless. He could not take any decision, any action in its regard. He must wait for the advice of the expert. The expert, alas, had not yet been found. His apology wound on and on in labyrinths of excuses.

What struck Dominic was the chairman's hopeless incapacity to enter into the reality of this machine, to hazard guesses about it, to make intelligent suggestions as to what might be done with it, to have any opinion at all about it. No, it was impossible - for this man at the top of the ladder, confident of his prestige, the machine remained totally other, outside him, nothing to do with him. It was left entirely in the hands of a lower order, those who lacked power and prestige, and also, no doubt, any great competence or conscientiousness as well.

Late on Monday afternoon, Dominic was reading a chapter of Willey's "Nineteenth Century Background", this one on Carlyle, another metaphysician fighting against the scientific revolution. He wondered how it was that this man of bombastic, domineering incoherence had been so influential. Probably not because of the quality of his metaphysics, rather because he had written a work of political propaganda on the French revolution which had resonated perfectly with the post-Napoleonic chauvinism of Britain. Yet in spite of his influence, the scientific revolution of Britain's culture had proceeded.

Dominic's thoughts were interrupted by the doorbell. Ahmed was off duty, so he went to answer it. Emma stood there, in shorts and a man's shirt with dark brown stripes. Her hair was gathered up on each side and tied with short lengths of ribbon. She was wearing dark clip-ons on her glasses.

'Hi, Dominic,' she smiled with a nervous, quick movement of her lips.

'Hello, Emma. You look so summery and... *a l'aise*. Come in. How are you?'

'Fine. I've been helping Mummy all day with jam making. Very domestic. I must have eaten half a pound, tasting it all the time.'

'Your mother is the traditional wife then, jam making and all that.'

'No, she just likes it. Well, I suppose she is. She's a marvellous housekeeper. Daddy has so may business friends to entertain. They're always charmed.'

'You say that with a hint of disapproval?'

'Well, Mummy's such a talented person. She could have done anything.'

'Maybe she preferred to marry and have children.'

'Shouldn't think she had much choice.'

They had gone into the small corner sitting room. They sat down on the sofa, and Emma sat lengthwise, facing him, with her legs on the cushions. He looked at their smooth skin. She shaved her legs, they were shiny, like wax.

'What are you reading?"

She picked up his book and was examining it.

'Mm, this is on my reading list. What on earth are you reading it for?'

'Why shouldn't I? You literature people think we should obtain dispensation to approach your field?'

'No, I suppose not. Still, it's strange... what do you think of it?'

'Oh, most of the metaphysics in it is so much nonsense.'

'Why do you read it then?'

'Masochism.'

He grinned at her.

'What did you get up to yesterday?'

'Daddy wanted to look at one of his wells, and we went with him. It was terrible - we spent the whole day in the car.'

'Any oil?'

'No, just sore behinds and stiff necks. I'm still creaking.'

She flexed her shoulders.

'You need a massage.'

'Yes, I do.'

'Shall I give you one?'

'Yes, please. I'd like that.'

'Come into my bedroom then.'

His heart beat faster. His mouth suddenly went dry. Almost without knowing it, without even a kiss, he was going to see her nakedness again, they were going to be on a bed together. What would happen this time, in the bright light of day? As they went into the room, he couldn't avoid the apprehension, the fear, that he wouldn't be aroused by her. Before he realised that he was repeating the same pattern as on their first night, he said:

'Look, I'm rather sticky, I'll go and have a quick shower while you're getting ready.'

In the bathroom, he wondered whether she would take off all her clothes. He had never massaged anyone before, or been massaged. Why had he suddenly suggested it? Would she detect his lack of expertise, and think it was simply a ruse? And would she expect him to make love to her? Would he be able to?

He went back into the bedroom with only a gaffiya, an Arab head scarf, wrapped round his waist. She was lying face down on the bed, with a small towel covering her behind. She was lying quite still. He knelt down beside her.

'I hope I don't prod you in the wrong places. Here goes.'

She gave a little laugh, and he began. First he worked her shoulder muscles, and then pressed her neck on each side with his thumbs. He felt her go limp.

'Oh, that's good,' she said.

'Is it?' He was relieved. 'I used to get very stiff there - from driving. Just at the base of the neck.'

'Oh,' she let out a breath. 'And between my shoulder blades. I'm sure there's a knot of tension there.'

'What exactly is a knot of tension?'

'Where all the nerves are knotted up and tense. You know - they talk about them in yoga.'

'I can only feel muscles and bones. There aren't any knots.'

He drummed her back with the sides of his hands.

'What about your legs?' he asked.

'They're all right. Just the small of my back.'

He was getting near the sexual zone. Would she turn over?

'Yes, harder. I'm so stiff there.'

He went back and forth from the spine to the flanks. She was quite thin there, the spine stood out clearly.

The exertion bathed him in a film of sweat. It ran and dripped from his forehead onto her body. He felt uncomfortable and uncouth.

'This is hot work. I hope that's enough.'

He gave her a little pat on her behind and got off the bed.

'I'm sweating like a pig. I must dry off.'

He went back to the bathroom and wiped himself with a damp face-cloth. It gave him relief. He dried his face and chest and returned to the bedroom.

Emma had turned slightly on her side. The towel was still draped loosely across her body. A dark shadow went in under her raised hip. He lay down beside her, and put an arm round her body. She brought her face to his and they began kissing. Something in the light passivity of her kisses, the oblique angle of her body to his, her quickening breath, excited him and he felt the flow of his erection. He pushed his tongue into her mouth and her body against his, feeling the small round cheeks of her buttocks. He wanted to go into her at once but he feared that she was not ready and that it would be difficult again. He caressed her belly and stroked her thick bush. She pushed against his hand. Apprehension stopped him from putting his fingers into her to see if she was aroused. He brought his hand back to her breast and squeezed it. He made an abrupt movement to get over her, and she at once turned on her back and opened her legs to receive him. With his mouth fastened on hers, he put down his hand and strained to enter her. She moved her pelvis and put her arms round his neck. The crisis was over, he felt her wetness and was in her. She started to move vigorously, independently of him, apart. Her mouth remained open, but her tongue was passive, it did not meet his. He felt the strangeness of her as they struggled towards orgasm. His came with a dim release, a hollow resolution. She stopped moving soon after him, and they lay still for a long time. He stroked her hair, now undone, with his fingers. Their wet bodies gave off heat.

Eventually he rolled off her and they lay side by side. With one hand he held her fingers between his, and in this first relaxed peace between them, he allowed his thoughts to wander and to explore what had happened with her. It seemed to him that against many odds, mostly of his own apprehension, and across the many years which separated them, they had come through to union, to a certainty which could grow.

Emma broke the calm silence.

'Must stop this you know.'

'Oh?'

What could she mean?

'Making love without precautions.'

'Without precautions? Are you serious, Emma?'

He propped himself up on his elbow and looked at her face. Free now of the distorting shield of her glasses, it had a complete openness.

'Afraid so.'

'But Emma, that's incredible. Where are you in your cycle?'

'Somewhere in the middle, I think.'

'In the middle? My God! But that pill you took in Agami before getting into bed, what was it?'

'An aspirin.'

'An aspirin? But I assumed it was the pill.'

'No it wasn't. I thought I had a headache coming on. I often get headaches from too much reading. I didn't want one to spoil our first night together.'

Dominic flinched slightly. It had been spoiled anyway. A shadow of fear passed through him.

'But good God, Emma, you take a pill, so obviously, before getting into bed, what did you expect me to think?'

'I don't know. I didn't think about it.'

'Didn't think about it? And what if you got pregnant?'

She gave him a small smile of resignation.

Suddenly he felt a surge of love for her and he hugged her and kissed her neck again and again.

'You little devil, and I thought you were the super modern girl, completely organised.'

He laughed and bit her shoulder. This new revelation broke down any reticence left in him, and brought him close, close to her. He forced her to tell him about her cycle. When had she had her last period? Was she regular? With a tremulous excitement they calculated that their first night together had probably been bang on her ovulation time. Now, three days later, they had compounded the risk.

'Emma, you're crazy. What we've done is terribly irresponsible. You could easily, easily get pregnant. Then what would we do?'

The idea of this young girl of nineteen, her body thin and smooth in its youthfulness, with a child, his child, growing in her, thrilled him. After so long he would know this unique adventure.

'I don't know,' she replied. 'I haven't really thought about it.'

'But all your other boyfriends that I've been hearing about. What did you do with them?'

'What other boyfriends? Do you mean Alexei? We didn't do it very often. He used to wear a contraceptive.'

'And the others? I got the impression that you are pretty active.'

'That's not true!' She seemed genuinely affronted. 'Who told you that? I haven't had much experience at all. And I gave up Alexei ages ago.'

Was this just for his benefit? Had Alexei been the dancing partner he had seen her with in the night club?

'But Emma, Emma, we've made love right at the critical time - twice. What happens if you get pregnant?'

'Do you think I will? Well, I'm sure of one thing. I'd never have an abortion. Couldn't stand the idea.'

'You mean you'd go ahead and have a baby?'

She answered him with a very faint smile. The thrill in his voice seemed to have affected her. Her eyes were open to him with a brave fearlessness. He kissed them with many light kisses, then her face, over and over, in a kind of reverie.

Ten

Dominic saw Emma whenever he could over the remaining weeks of his stay in Alexandria. His early hesitations gave way to a strong and surer knowledge of her, and a confidence that their union has passed the early tests.

They made love many times, and it was best when it happened abruptly in some unplanned place or time. Once he went to her house to take her out for a meal. She was not ready and invited him up to her room while she changed. He sat in a chair, looking out through the oriental arch of her bedroom window into the palm trees of the garden as she searched in her wardrobe. The flocculent August sky was turning a pale rose. Warm, jasmin-scented air came in through the window along with the distant sounds of the traffic from the main road.

'Shall I wear this or this?' he heard her ask. He turned and saw her standing in her bra and panties holding two galabiya-style dresses alongside her body. He went over to her.

'Let's see.'

He put his hand out to one of the dresses to feel it, to hold it up for inspection, but his eyes slid quickly from it to her face, and there he saw such a clear expression of trust, of acceptance of him in her room, in her world, that he felt a strong rush of feeling for her. He started kissing her with a quick, generous passion, and she, for now they knew each other well, opened her mouth at once to him. He gripped her body hard in his arms, venting force on her. She yielded to it. They heard her parents in a nearby room talking and moving about. Yet they both started to draw each other towards her bed. A wild delight filled him as he pulled off her underwear and she quickly, impatiently tried to undress him. At any moment her mother or father might come in, but they would not stop. They were adamant in their claim on each other. He rushed into her but she was ready, pressing up against him. She too was excited by the danger of discovery, by the thrilling contiguity of her two states - daughter, controlled, obeying, and woman, triumphing in sex, living her force.

As they lay in the sweating heat of their spent passion, the twilight about them reddened and quickly gave way to an enveloping darkness.

On another afternoon, they had made love in the beach apartment in Agami, and afterwards started to read, lying together on the bed. Their bodies were close, his legs twining amongst hers. A naked unity held them, though they read different books, their minds exploring separately. This paradox filled him with happiness. They were free to think apart, to become engrossed independently, while all the time, their limbs rested on each other, and they lay as one.

The door opened suddenly and Hugh came into the room unannounced.

'Oh, sorry,' he said, seeing them in such naked intimacy and retreating.

Dominic looked up at him and smiled, but was sure he saw a shadow of resentment pass across Hugh's face. Was it the resentment of the older man forced to witness the easy, lost pleasure of youth? Or was it, Dominic wondered, jealousy of him for taking this young, much younger girl? When Hugh had closed the door, Dominic's and Emma's eyes met for a moment. She raised her brows in a small flicker of sympathy for Hugh's embarrassment, but he felt a triumph of domination over the older man. Hugh was alone, dying slowly in his heart, yet Dominic could only feel jubilant in his own fulfilment. He shook off the shadow of Hugh's resentment without remorse.

Only occasionally did the sense of weakness that he had felt with Emma at the beginning visit him again. Once they had been alone together in Charles and Lynda's apartment in the afternoon. They were reading, she, stretched out on a couch, a book of poetry, and he, something scientific in connection with his work. Suddenly he threw his book down and got onto the couch, climbing over her body, kneeling over her.

'I can't do any more work. What are you reading?'

He took the book out of her hand and laid it down open beside her head. It was Yeats, and the poem on the page was: 'Her Vision in a Wood.'

'Read it to me,' she said.

He began, crouched over her, his hands pressing the cushion on either side of her head, his arms straight, holding himself above her. He tried to read the lines well, to give them force, but they were obscure. Emma listened, seeming to give herself over to them. Suddenly he felt her hands going quickly to his fly. She opened it in a trice and slipped a hand inside and caught hold of his balls. He was completely disconcerted. Her movement had been so peremptory. She held him brusquely, as if she had a right to take him whenever she wanted, there, at the most central part of his manhood. She owned him. Young as she was, now she possessed him.

He tried to read on but he caught less and less of the meaning of the words. His voice sounded hollow, yet she continued to look up through glittering glasses at him, feeling him, gripping him, possessing him, as he read. He felt that he was performing for her, but he could not. A cold perspiration broke out on his forehead. He wanted to stop, but forced himself to continue. She stared at him, she must have seen him sweating.

'Oh, I can't read it when you're doing that,' he said suddenly, and rose up away from her. She let go of her hold on him, and looked at him with a silent surprise as he left her and retreated. Her arms fell down to her sides.

In the evenings he would often take her to Asteria's Pizza restaurant. It was usually full of young couples and young families. The enormous social energy of the Egyptians gave the place an air of fete. Beautiful girls, some with faces that might have been taken unchanged from the early Coptic portraits of Fayyum, others that seemed to have stepped down from a frieze in the Valley of the Kings, these he loved to watch. They were all made up elaborately, their eyes flashing in dark lines of kohl.

And there in front of him sat his English girl, transposed from a quiet green quadrangle of Oxford, not, perhaps, as beautiful as they were, but one of his own tribe, sharing his culture, who would still interest and intrigue him when these Egyptian girls had lost their looks and sunk into obesity.

Often they talked of literature, of poetry.

'I envy you so much, you know,' he said to her once, 'being able to spend all your time reading literature. For me it was a joy that I had to squeeze in between endless practicals in the laboratory and slogging away in the library. Yet this is what you're doing, full time.'

'Oh I do enjoy it,' she said, 'though it's hard work too, you know. Weekly tutorials, essays, papers...one can't read for joy alone. It's much more serious than that.'

'Nothing is more important than the joy of literature, the

unique encounter between the reader and the word, and the enrichment he gets from it.'

'He or she you mean, don't you? But studying literature is not experience alone, it's analysing it.'

'Analysis - that's the affair of science. Why try to erect a pseudo-science of art? You'll kill the joy.'

'Nonsense, you don't understand.'

She didn't seem to want to continue the discussion, yet he thought the issue of great importance. Why didn't she? Was it because of a kind of arrogance, that literature was her area, her life? What did he know about it, an amateur? Then again, he wondered if it was his overbearing way of arguing that put her off. After all, he had had discussions like this many times before. He knew exactly what he wanted to say, whereas she, she was young, she was just gathering her force. Did she find him bullying? Did she think he was attacking her, undermining her?

They pulled apart in the silence that followed. He into his search for the reason for her withdrawal, she, he knew not where. When he next spoke, it was to draw her attention to a fat boy at a nearby table who sat in front of ice-creams, cakes, and bottles of fizzy drinks, like some modern day pasha. His parents looked on with beaming pleasure as he poured the calories into his overfed body.

The next day, Ronald joined Dominic for drinks in the club bar.

'How is Emma?' he asked, in his direct, slightly over-loud manner.

Dominic took the glass offered and sat back in his chair.

'Why do you ask?'

'Well, we like her very much. We are very glad that you and she are together. She had that terrible boyfriend before.'

'The Greek?'

'Yes, the Greek. He was completely unsuitable. We didn't like him. She was just making a fool of herself. Wasting herself on him.'

'*Chaqu'un à son gout*,' Dominic said, gratified but curiously embarrassed.

'Yes, well, you and her, that's much better.'

Ronald's dark features broke into a broad smile. Dominic couldn't reply. There was something so morally upright and clean about Ronald and Elizabeth and their marriage - to be approved of by them was somehow taxing. Was he really good for Emma? A small stab of guilt cut into his mind as he remembered his willful, cold approach to her. If Ronald knew all that, would he still praise him?

'When are you going back to Cairo? Soon, eh?'

'Yes. We've got just one more week of the conference. Then it's all over. Including, who knows, me and Emma. She'll be going back to Oxford at the beginning of September.'

'Both of you, you must come round and see us before you go. Come to dinner. Ring Elizabeth any time.'

'Thanks, we'll do that. And what about our proposed expedition to the wadi east of Agami? Can we fit that in next weekend?'

'I hope so. I really want Willem to see the avocets. He's starting to love birds now. If we went on Friday evening, we could birdwatch right through the dawn on Saturday morning.'

'That's a splendid idea. I don't know if Emma likes birdwatching' - he knew so little about her, he realised - 'but I'm sure she'd like to come with us.'

'Good, good. We'll sleep in our tent, and you two can sleep in the Landrover.'

'That sounds fine. We certainly wouldn't be very comfortable in my car. Oh, by the way, I meant to ask you, have you ever heard the karawan?'

'The what?'

'The karawan - that's what the Egyptians call it. They don't seem to know anything else about it, except its name. It's a night bird, with a strange, beautiful call. Have you heard it?'

'Yes, I think I know the bird you mean. In Cairo we were staying once and in the middle of the night we heard this call, a strong crying sound.'

'That's it!' Dominic said excitedly. 'Nobody can tell me what it is. I've asked everyone. It comes out particularly on moonlit nights. I've heard it often, often, but I've never seen one. What do you think it is?'

'I don't know. I wondered what it was too, that night in Cairo. Is it an owl?'

'It could be. I thought that at first. A night flyer - that fits. And the cry is something like our screech owl - barn owl, you know, the one with the heart-shaped face.'

'Yes, I know the one you mean. It might be that. Or a North African variety of it. I'll ask other people at work if they know. What do you say the Egyptians call it?'

'The karawan. We really must find out what it is.'

'We must, yes.'

'That bird's call is one of the most beautiful, most haunting things I have experienced in Egypt. I love it.'

'The karawan,' Ronald repeated.

On the following Friday night, Emma and Dominic were in Ronald's Landrover, he on the front seat, she on the back. Though it was August, the sea breeze buffeting over the dunes came in through the windows and was cool. They lay huddled under blankets.

'This is our last weekend. I really don't want to go back to Cairo, but unfortunately I've got to. We have another conference beginning at Ain Shams University in early September,' Dominic said.

He stretched his arm over the back of the seat and sought her hand.

'Emma, this has been so short. We're really only just getting to know each other.'

'That's the trouble with university holidays. They're so deceptive. When they start, you think, goodee, two whole months. Then in no time, they're over.'

The off-handedness of her reply cut short his urge to talk about their just-growing love and what might become of it.

'Well, anyway, when are you going back to Oxford?'

'I'm flying on the thirteenth. And I've really got to do heaps of work before then. I've been so lazy.'

She seemed more preoccupied with this than with the fact that they were passing their last nights together for months - maybe, he wondered, for ever?

'You'll stay with me in Cairo on the way through?' he asked - now that she had crushed his sentiment - in as casual a voice as he could.

'That'd be nice. You live out near the airport, don't you?'

'Yes,' he answered shortly, struck by her command of practical detail. Was that all it meant to her - a convenient place to sleep before her flight?

She brought his hand to her breast, and he started to caress it. He was almost indifferent now, the impending separation and the way she talked of it made him feel that what they were doing was of little importance to her.

He felt her nipple go hard and she started to pull on his arm.

'Come over,' she whispered.

He got up and climbed over the seat. He struggled awkwardly in a half-kneeling position to get his underpants off. She was naked, waiting for him. He abandoned himself to her heat. She wanted him in her, that was enough. What did it matter how or for how long? Her mouth became completely open, passive, and he pushed his tongue deep into it. It seemed she just fell back, taking, empty. He must fill her.

Her body began to move and twist, and he felt a desire to exhaust it, to master it. He was thrilled by an abstract sexual struggle between them. He pulled out of her suddenly and catching he shoulder made her turn over. He gripped her by the waist as she knelt and went into her again. He held her fast from moving, so that each movement was his, so that each intention of his yielded exactly the pleasure he sought. He thrust remorselessly into her, pushing her body violently with each stroke. Her head was near the window, and it banged against it. She was unconcerned, centred completely in the struggle for release. Eventually it came to him in shuddering waves, in which he seemed to fall further and further into a space outside himself and her. He could only dimly hold on to his body and his spirit. He was object, abstracted. He collapsed onto her. She still moved, still struggled, now that his grip was loosened, but eventually she too gave way. Across a distance, he felt her yield, but he could not tell if she had really had the same release as him.

'All right, you two, up you get.' Ronald opened the front door of the Landrover and shook Dominic by the shoulder.

He woke out of a dream in which he had been driving among mountains, taking a road into an area he did not know, into dangerous, mysterious country. It was hidden, blocked off by the mountain range. He had never ventured into it before, but now that he was there, now that he had broken through into it, there was a marvelous fresh unfolding in everything he saw - blue mountains rising up as in a procession before him, great trees spreading in the clear light, villages crouching on slopes far away.

He opened his eyes. It was still dark.

'We've got about fifteen minutes before the light comes.' he heard Ronald say. He pulled himself up on the seat and looked out. He could just make out the shape of the date palms waving against the starry sky, the profile of a sand dune. Emma stirred on the other seat.

'We're getting up. Do you want to come with us?' he asked her.

She gave a short moan and then said. 'No, I'll stay, too sleepy.'

'All right,' he replied, but he felt a disappointment in her. She would not share with him this small exploration.

He got out of the Landrover and pulled on his clothes. Ronald, Elizabeth, and Willem were already dressed. He went over to them.

'All set? I've got my glasses…bird-book. Anything else?'

'Have you got your camera? Willem, where is our tripod?'

The boy answered in rapid Dutch and went into the tent.

'I'm going to try out my new telephoto lens on the avocets - if there are any,' Ronald said to Dominic.

Elizabeth stood wrapping an anorak round her body tightly. Her blond hair, blown by the wind, almost covered her face. Willem reappeared with the tripod, and after a final check of the rest of the photographic equipment, they set off. Ronald led the way.

'There's a small cluster of mimosas near the mouth of the wadi. That's where we will hide,' he said in low voice.

'But the sea wind will take our smell to the birds,' Willem protested loudly.

'God verdomme!' Ronald hissed, 'If you talk loud like that, Willem, there won't be any birds left to see.'

What an acute child, Dominic thought, but did birds actually smell? Such a basic consideration had never crossed his mind. Surely they did not - sight and sound were what they relied on. Yet he wondered if anyone had done any research on it.

'I don't think birds can smell, Willem.' he whispered to the boy, hoping to restore his confidence. He thought Ronald had been too brusque - the habits of parenthood.

'But we have to be quiet, though, 'he added.

'OK,' the boy replied.

'That's the water,' Ronald whispered, pointing out to the left. 'Now be careful.'

They followed him over the flat sand. Soon they could make out the clump of mimosas on the edge of the last dune before the sea. They worked their way behind it and then dropped down into a small depression in the sand. Creeping along, they got in amongst the bushes. The heavy, hanging leaves brushed their faces. From the breakers on the shore nearby, a low roar came in over them.

'This is fine,' Ronald decided. 'We will have a very good view here. Willem, give me the tripod.'

While he was setting it up, Elizabeth laid a rug on the slight incline of the sand for them to lie on. Stretched out, their heads just showed above the crest. They could make out the little lake of the wadi behind the sand bar. A faint light gave its surface the appearance of scratched steel. Dominic turned on his side and looked up. Now he could see the clouds - frothy, piled masses. Dawn was breaking. Within minutes an amber-pink light filled the sky and the towering cumulus became coloured down, suspended and milky soft. Stratus behind and above it shone brighter. The glowing, turbulent heavens, full of warmth, seemed to be enfolding the earth as if this day were one of the days of creation. Dominic felt his stomach go light, his breath catch.

'Look at the sky,' he said to them.

Already it was changing, the masses of salmon pink turning into amber greys and blues.

The birds had been calling in the dawn light around them. Sparrows in the palm trees chattering, and waders piping their reedy notes at the water's edge. As the minutes passed, the scene filled out. They were very near the water, five metres or so. Some stilts walked up and down, close enough for them to see their fragile legs clearly, with their knee joints like knots in stiff red twine. Half way round the pool of water, a large heron stood motionless, save for an occasional raising or lowering of the head, with its huge, spearing bill.

Another large bird flew past them on silent rounded, grey wings. Its flight had an owl-like quality, with an almost metro-nomic wing-beat, a perfectly constant momentum, and no de-viations from its path.

'What's that?' Dominic asked.

'It must be a reiger - a heron,' Ronald replied. 'Look at the beak -so big.'

The bird circled the water and was coming back past them. It tilted over suddenly and they saw its large red eye and the long white crest feathers, like two bald quills, stretching along its grey back.

'Look up herons,' Ronald said to Willem, but the boy had already found the page.

'Interdaad. Een kwak - look, look,' he showed the illustration to Dominic.

'He's right. Yes, that's it, Ronald - night heron, we call it. Definitely. What a strange bird. That eye - as big as an owl's.'

The heron floated past them again, its broad wings moving up and down in perfect, regular rhythm. Then it made its way over to a grassy patch near the water and settled, its neck and shoulders hunched as if under a dark grey cloak.

'There are some egrets right over there. Look, Willem,' Ronald pointed.

Dominic was surprised that father and son spoke in English. Was it out of courtesy - they didn't want him to feel left out? He appreciated it keenly. What English family could do the same by going into Dutch or any other language?

'Oh, look,' the boy suddenly said with suppressed excitement.

In an instant there before them, circling in a flock of about fifty, were the avocets. Black and white bars on their wings beat and flickered like a huge semaphore signal announcing their arrival.

'Superb. They're larger than I expected,' Dominic said.

They were as big as curlews, round and plump, but their delicate up-curving bills gave them a gracefulness as they wheeled and turned together over the wadi. Almost like the passing of a heavy shower, they suddenly fell from the air and settled in the shallow water. Soon their bills were swishing from side to side, searching for food.

'What are they called in Dutch?' Dominic asked.

'Kluut,' Elizabeth replied.

'I suppose we get our name from French. Kluut - funny. You know, we should revert to the Latin names when we're bird-watching together. Let's see, avocet…Ricurirostra avosetta. Ah, so our name comes from Latin. I wonder what it means?'

Ronald and Elizabeth mounted the long lens on their camera and began taking photographs of the black and white birds in the now brilliant morning light.

'This one was great Elizabeth,' Ronald said enthusiastically. 'I got him full in the frame.'

'Keep shooting,' Dominic advised him. 'They seem to be moving off.'

Sure enough, the avocets were making their way along the water's edge to the far side of the pool.

Dominic looked up over the clustering palms. The dark shape of a familiar Egyptian kite was gliding in the distance - its long forked tail twisting this way and that. Another Egyptian summer's day had begun, with its heat, its struggle, its timeless acceptance.

When they got back to the Landrover, they found Emma stretched out in a deck chair, reading. She lowered her book as they drew up and said:

'Well, did you have a nice time? See plenty of birds?'

Dominic was irritated by the question - as if one counted up the number of birds seen, like some sort of contest. She really wasn't interested, didn't understand what it was all about. Nature was a world, a reality, that she could not penetrate. It was hardly surprising - traipsing round from one oil-field to another after her father, how could she find her feet in any one place, how could she connect? Her spirit, rendered brittle by too much movement, was held together not by a deep connection with nature, with landscape, but by man-made culture, the books she was reading. He felt sorry for her, denied this richness, and contempt that she had this limit.

'OK. What about some breakfast?' Ronald asked as he unpacked his gas stove.

Emma sprang up from her chair.

'Yes, please. I'm really hungry. Must be this fresh air.'

Elizabeth spread a rug on the hot white sand, and they gathered together on it. Willem was first at the food. He broke a piece from an Egyptian oil cake, dipped it in honey and then cream and began to eat. The others followed suit.

Twelve

'When are you going back to Oxford, Emma?' Rory asked.

'Middle of September. Not long now.'

Dominic, standing beside her, remarked to himself how often people initiated topics of conversation which might bear uncomfortably on their friends' feelings. Here now was Rory, rubbing in the fact that Emma had another life to go to. Well, he himself had another life to go to, in Cairo, so why should he take Rory's enquiry personally? Because, he realised, there was the unknown in Oxford that threatened. He could wait patiently in Cairo for Emma's return, but would she wait for him there?

'I envy you and on the other hand I don't,' Rory went on.

'What do you mean?' Emma said, with one of her quick movements of her head.

'Oxford, you know. On the one hand all that beauty - old squares, Gothic towers, the river, gardens, and on the other hand, that awful, monastic smugness the place breeds - that Oxford complacency.'

'I don't think Oxford is either of those things for me. My college is far from beautiful and I'm certainly not complacent. I have to work too hard.'

'It'll come, it'll come. You're just starting your Oxford career. The initiation period. After a year or two, the magic will begin to work. You'll be completely Oxfordised. Then it'll be too late.'

'Well, Oxford certainly isn't a monastery any more,' Dominic put in. 'More and more of the colleges are taking women students.'

'You don't change a centuries-old institution in a couple of years, Dominic,' Rory replied with what sounded like impatience. 'Look at the House of Lords, for God' sake. Plenty of peers from the working class, but still the same infantile lordship nonsense, the same tugging of forelocks.'

'There's something in what you say,' Emma conceded. 'My girlfriends seem to spend most of their time complaining that Oxford men, well, lots of Oxford men are so... so useless.'

'What do you expect?' Rory said. 'Turfed out of their boarding schools and then straight into these old, monastic cloisters.'

'You're forgetting all the nurses and the language school students,' Emma said. 'Hundreds and hundreds of women.'

'I hope to God some of them get their hands on them, that's all,' Rory said and drained the beer from his glass.

Dominic felt little inclination to explore with them this topic of the sexual life of Oxford undergraduates. He wondered how he could break off, even if it meant leaving Emma with Rory. But his friend had already removed another glass from a tray Ahmed was carrying round and had started again.

'But all that is not the problem. The problem is the intellectual cotton wool, the cozy provincialism, the firm conviction that everything in the garden is rosy.'

'Have you ever been to Oxford?' Emma asked flatly.

'As much as I want to. I've read what has come out of it and that's more important - in history, in philosophy. I'm not sure about Eng. Lit. They may be all right there.'

'What's wrong with Oxford philosophy? I would have thought Ayer's "Language, Truth, and Logic" was about the most sensible thing written this century,' Dominic put in.

'Oh, it's sensible all right - so damned sensible that it's convinced English philosophy not to bother itself with any of the great questions facing us."

'Like what?'

'Like politics, like history, like the destiny of mankind.'

'But Ayer's whole point is that it's very difficult to talk scientific sense about such matters.'

'So we all sit back and refuse to talk about them at all? Is that it? Well, that is it as far as English philosophy is concerned. Meanwhile the world goes to hell.'

'The only thing I know about Oxford philosophy was that film about the Oxford don who fell in love with an Austrian princess,' Emma said with a smile.

'That was perfect, that film, the cloying love affair of the English intellectual with the upper class, and running through it all, a blithe ignorance of what's happening in the world outside.'

'I thought it was super - Michael York was gorgeous.'

Dominic registered this remark with a slight jolt - how many Michael Yorks were there at Oxford right now?

Lynda, with a large brandy in one hand and a cigarette in the other, joined them.

'What's all this intense discussion about, you three?' she said with a forced smile. 'Not politics, I hope.'

'No, Rory's just trying to persuade me not to go back to Oxford,' Emma said, 'but he's not succeeding.'

'What, are you working for Dominic?' Lynda asked with an arch look.

Dominic saw it and felt a sting of embarrassment first freeze his face, then begin to colour it. What an absurd suggestion, but was that how she saw it - that he didn't want Emma to go back, he didn't want to lose her? It was obscurely humiliating. He must deny it.

'Not at all. Rory just thinks that Oxford's intellectual calibre is not all it's cracked up to be.'

Now the three of them were looking at him. Could they detect his discomfort? His cheeks began to burn. He sought refuge in his glass, which he raised in front of his face. He lowered it empty and said: 'I must get another drink,' and left them. He saw a puzzled concern in Emma's eyes as he moved past her.

He went over to the other side of the room, where he found Khaled and Elizabeth talking to another Egyptian couple. In his agitation he broke peremptorily into their conversation.

'Khaled, are you still shirking national service?'

Even as he did so, he knew that he was being rude, over-bearing, but it was too late. Elizabeth stopped talking, and looked at him with surprise. He hoped she would excuse him.

'I'm just out for a weekend, Dominic. Just two or three days. And how are you?'

'My service for the nation here in Alex is over. We go back to Cairo on Monday.'

'Did you like Alexandria?'

'Yes, very much. It wasn't what I expected, but I've enjoyed it very much. It's much bigger, busier than I thought.'

'You are right. Alexandria is so popular these days. It's far too crowded.'

It was the Egyptian woman he didn't know speaking. She was about fifty, with a great mass of blond hair piled up in an old-fashioned coiffure. Her fat face matched her corpulent body.

Her eyes had a heavy, fatigued look.

'It was so much better in the old days,' she concluded.

'Samira, you're always saying how much better it was in the old days,' Elizabeth protested.

'Oh, but it was, Elizabeth. Where we live, there were only villas around us, such elegant villas. You know what it's like today.'

'Where do you live?' Dominic asked.

'Baulkli. It's on the Corniche. Do you know it?'

'Yes, I've been working out near there.'

'Well, it used to be a very elegant suburb - before the revolution. Now all the good houses have been knocked down, and apartment buildings have been put up instead. It's so vulgar now.'

Dominic found her snobbery not quite real, for how could Egyptians, the warmest people he had ever met, really be snobs and coldly dismissive of others? No, no, they could not. They didn't really mean it. This hankering after the good old days before the revolution, it wasn't snobbery, it was merely nostalgia.

'We never knew the old Alexandria,' Dominic said. 'We only know the new, but it's still a fascinating place. That old restaurant we went to last week for example. What was it called, Elizabeth?'

'The Union.'

'Yes, that was it. Incredible - they say it's been exactly the same since before the revolution.' He smiled at Samira. 'Nothing has changed, not even the staff, it's got the air of a kind of pensioners' refuge.'

'The Union used to be so gay in the old days,' Samira said. 'Didn't it, Adel?'

She sought support from her husband. He merely nodded

apathetically, and swaying gently, lowered more of his whisky.

'I love those old waiters,' Elizabeth said. 'They're so sweet.'

'I suppose the owner just won't replace them. They'll work until they drop dead - and that might be any day now.'

'Do you remember the one who served us last time, Dominic?'

'Yes, the chap with the stoop?'

'And the funny stomach.' She made a curve with her hand to indicate its profile, one that any Egyptian might be proud of. 'He's the slowest of them all. He put things down on the table incredibly slowly, like a ... a tortoise.'

'You mean poor old Ragab,' Samira said with sympathy. 'He used to be in the service of King Farouk, you know. That is where he learned to serve with so much dignity. He must be more than seventy now.'

As she was speaking, Dominic looked past her into the hall and noticed that Ahmed was opening the front door. Two or three Egyptians were coming in, and behind them, Lester. They were talking loudly. They strode into the salon as if with fixed purpose, but for the moment that purpose seemed merely to get drinks. They made straight for the drinks table at the far end of the room. Dominic looked back to Elizabeth. She was talking about Farouk.

'Is it true that he had an enormous collection of porno-graphic pictures, Samira?'

'In Mansoura Palace? Oh yes, it is true. But, you see, that was only when he was old and fat. When he was young, he was so good-looking.'

'Really, was he handsome then?'

'Very handsome. And he was always chasing other men's wives. Of course, no-one could refuse.'

Would Samira be old enough to have been commandeered by Farouk, Dominic wondered? Hardly; unless the king commandeered minors as well as wives.

From the end of the room there came the sudden crash of broken glass. A hush followed, and in it, the voice of Lester could be heard hurling abuse.

'Fucking bitches, I hate them.'

One of his companions was trying to calm him. All heads turned to look.

Lynda was approaching.

'Puritan bitches, fascists...'

The words came out uncontrolled, slurred.

Dominic said 'excuse me' quickly to his group and moved towards Lester. There might be trouble if Lynda closed in, and knowing her, she probably would. Where was Charles? Dominic looked round but couldn't see him. Nor anyone else who might take charge of the situation. As he got near, Lynda was already in front of Lester, speaking with a voice contracted with hate.

'Will you stop making an exhibition of yourself and spoiling my party. Nobody invited you.'

'And nobody invited you,' Lester bawled, 'to poke your puritan bourgeois nose into my private life.'

'I didn't poke it in. I was merely asked about your habits, and I said what I knew.'

'And you gave your nasty, bitchy advice, didn't you? You want everyone to do just what you want, don't you? You're all the same. You bitches have got to have it all your own way.'

'How dare you,' Lynda spat at him.

'How dare you...how dare you,' Lester sneered. 'Just because you've got a cunt, you think you rule the world. Why didn't you leave me alone? Oh no, you had to poke your fascist nose in. You hate anything you can't have yourself.'

'That's grotesque! If you think you can corrupt a young boy, well you can't.'

Lynda's voice was like a saw cutting through splintered wood.

'I loved him, why shouldn't I? Why? Why?'

Lester lurched forward, but Dominic could see that his spirit, far from reaching a climax of aggression, was teetering on the edge of breakdown. He stepped between him and Lynda, took him by the shoulders, and looked him fixedly in the eye. Lester returned his gaze. Dominic saw revolt move like a shadow across his face, but the reaction of submission was more powerful.

'I loved him. Why not?'

Now the rage was breaking up into self-pity. Lester's eyelids were suddenly suffused with red.

'It's all right. You'd better go now, Lester,' Dominic said with complete finality.

'I've lost him. They won't let him see me.'

Lester's face crumpled and tears rolled down his florid cheeks. Dominic steered him out of the room to the door. One of his friends followed.

'Will you take him home?' Dominic asked him.

Lester could hardly walk. He was sobbing in a drunken haze of loss and shame.

'Yes, I'll take him,' the friend answered.

'They don't understand. They hate me.' Lester was saying. 'They hate me.'

Dominic closed the door behind them.

When he returned to the salon, the party was running back on its normal rails. A multiple chatter had been re-established.

Where was Emma? He looked from one group to another. Presently he saw her seated alone on a sofa, turning the stem of her glass between her delicate fingers. She had a disconnected look. He went over to her and sat down.

'You look rather distant,' he said, and wondered whether her pre-occupations had already shifted back to Oxford, even while she was still with him.

'Do I?'

She turned and smiled with a clear innocence.

'I was just thinking.'

'What about?'

'The stars.'

'The stars!'

He laughed.

'What stars?'

'The ones we're born under. I mean I'm Cancer, and I seem to be a perfect one.'

'Oh, those stars. Anyone less crab-like I couldn't imagine.'

'Don't be so superficial - the Crab is just the name, I mean the type.'

Dominic had not the slightest enthusiasm for the new, fashionable metaphysics - astrology, gurus, drugs.

'What type am I then?'

'You're a Pisces. Anyone can see that.'

'Well, as a matter of fact, I'm a ...'

He tried to think of another sign, and then finished with 'Gemini' as convincingly as he could.

'Nonsense, you're a Pisces - mobile, slippery, at home in your element.'

'Sorry, I'm Gemini,' he repeated.

'Don't lie. I saw your passport the other day.'

'You cheat!' he remonstrated, but it reassured him that she had found out his birthday that way and then foisted on him the cliched attributes.

'And another thing, Pisces never believe in astrology,' she said with a hint of contempt.

'I certainly don't.'

A silence followed. He wondered what Lester's star was. Was there one for homosexuals, were they helpless against their disposition, all ordained? That also he could not believe. He looked at Emma. Her face was impassive, with her glasses sitting on her nose. How could she be hoodwinked by all that nonsense? She was young, that was it. It was just a silly enthusiasm. He wished she would see through it, and yet at the same time he had a contrary desire to enter into it with her, to erase the years and experience that separated them, and to believe with her. Bitterly he knew he could not.

'Are we going to stay together tonight,' he asked her, 'even if I am fishy?'

She smiled and turned to him.

'I'm afraid I can't. I'm expected home. But I'll come round tomorrow. We can spend the morning together before you leave for Cairo.'

He took her hand, and looking straight ahead, said 'Pity.'

As he woke up next morning, he was aware of a diffuse sense of distress. He felt as if he were being borne along by a river with the branches of trees that might arrest his fate out of reach. Should he struggle to reach up and grasp them, or should he let himself be carried along by the great momentum of the river? He was being borne away from Emma. Was it in his power to exert himself, to move against the flow, somehow to bind her more tightly to himself? Then again, did it matter?

Was what they shared worth struggling for? He felt there was little commitment in it from her side. Why search for more? Let it go at that.

He was reading the French language daily in the long, sun-filled salon when the doorbell rang. That was her. Ahmed shuffled into the hall and opened the door before he stirred himself. Emma came in carrying her Greek bag weighed down and full of books. He stood up to greet her.

'Hello.'

'Hi, Dominic. What are you doing? What a horrible smell. Here, let me open some windows.'

He looked at her in complete passivity as she threw open the French windows leading onto the balcony, and others at the far end of the room. The noise of the traffic, horns honking incessantly, filled the room.

'God, what a din,' he said.

'Better than that horrible smell of stale tobacco smoke,' she replied. 'There, now I can breathe.'

She was right, the warm morning air was fresh and clean as it poured in. Yet he was repelled by this absorption of hers in domestic, physical details. The river was bearing him on. They sat down on the sofa in front of the open French windows.

'Where are the others?' she asked.

'They've all gone out. We're alone.'

'I wanted to see Lynda.'

'What about?'

'Oh nothing, it doesn't matter.'

'Well, she's gone off to recruit support. To lobby for her side in the Lester Stephen business. People seem to be falling into two camps, one pro her, and the other anti.'

'Which camp are you in?'

'I really don't want to get involved. I don't know whether to condemn Lester or not. Of course Lynda assumes I'm on her side, and I feel I owe it to her. I'm her guest, it's a debt of friendship.'

'I hate it when everybody gets so worked up about things like this. Such a waste of time. They've nothing better to think about.'

'I dare say you're right.'

She seemed to be lumping the whole circle, him included, into the category of useless, expatriate triflers. Probably because of that, he pursued the topic.

'But there's something very powerful, something completely unexplained about people's reaction to paedophilia - in Britain at any rate.'

'To what?'

'Paedophilia, you know, men having sex with minors, young boys particularly.'

'Well, it's just weird, isn't it?'

'Obviously, but why are people so intolerant of this weirdness? Is it good old Christian puritanism? Is it fear? What?'

'I heard Lester last night. He accused Lynda, and women in general, of being jealous of him.'

'Do you think that's it? Why should women care?'

'I don't care. But when I think about it, it gives me the creeps.'

'Why exactly?'

'Well, it's so uneven - a grown man and a boy. I mean it must be very painful when they do... you know what I mean.'

'Sodomy.'

'Yes, it must be terribly painful for the boy.'

'That may be so. But Lester - can you imagine him harming

a fly? He is as weak as butter. Would he hurt anyone? I'm sure he wouldn't.'

'It does seem hard to believe, I agree.'

'No, the basis of the whole thing is much, much deeper than that. The tyranny of the normal. It's as if everyone feels deep down that sex is a repressed force, an area of great pressure, of competition, certainly. They know instinctively how easy it is to divert it, to let it flow into homosexual channels. And if that happens, it renders the struggle so much more frustrating. It undermines their whole competitive heterosexual quest. They can't abide it. They can't allow others to escape. It's as if every-one is struggling to, let's say, build houses with bricks. There's competition for bricks. You've got to really fight for them. Then someone comes along and grabs the nearest bits of wood, and makes a house of that. No trouble. Why go to all that effort to get bricks? But the brick builders know that you have to get bricks. That's what building is all about. So the wooden house must be crushed. It's because they're so stressed getting bricks that they're so intolerant.'

Emma was listening to him, but was she following his argument?

'Do you see what I mean?'

'Yes, but that's far too mechanical an explanation.'

'Maybe you're right.'

He decided to change the subject.

'What books have you brought with you?'

She pulled them out.

'Romantic criticism - Wordsworth.'

A small chill of alienation came on him as he looked at them.

'Oh, give work a rest. Let's talk instead.'

'What about? Not Lester.'

'No, no, about us. We're far more important, aren't we?'

She turned her face to him and smiled. Her glasses caught the sunlight. He noticed that some grime was lodged between one lens and the rim. He put up his hand and took them off, and then began stroking her long hair.

'I'm really going to miss you, you know.'

The cliché constricted his mind, but what else was there to say?

'Are you?' she replied.

'Emma...'

He drew her up from the sofa and into his bedroom. Lying beside her on his bed he felt a wavering in his spirit between his will to possess her, and so stave off their separation, and an acceptance of defeat. He started to kiss her, but even as he did so, he began a slow, inexorable process of withdrawal. But their mouths knew each other and their bodies moved together as they had learned to. He clutched her breasts with a force coming from nostalgia and regret, and she began to undo his belt. Were they going to make love, couple on this last morning? No, he became aware that the retreat of his spirit was slowly gaining power over the contrary surging of his body. Emma's hand was caressing him, but its crude movements further pushed him to retreat. His erection faded. His kisses became colder.

'Funny, on our last morning, I just don't feel like it,' he muttered to her. He was grateful and relieved that she did not ask him why he had begun in the first place. She brought her hand out of his pants. He lay with his head on her breasts. There was a calm between them.

Later they had lunch in a nearby restaurant and they talked about Oxford, its buildings, its activities, its joys and frustrations. It was like going back to school. Dominic held himself from any more cliches, any sentimentality. He tried to be cool, as she was. He said goodbye to her outside her house, kissed her on both cheeks, and clambered quickly into his car.

In the late afternoon he was on his way back to Cairo. He took the delta road. The lowering sun beat down on the land that had yielded more crops than any other on earth. The delta of the Nile, the land that had received the healing flood since the dawn of time, but which now, since the Aswan High Dam, had begun a new era where the fertility was steadily draining away. No more laying down of the new silt every year. Would there be a crisis in fifty years' time, the soil exhausted?

The straight road ran along through the flat landscape. Villages and towns came and went, with their brown mud buildings joined to the brown earth. They were both of the same element. They seethed with the fellahin - men and boys in striped galabiyas, women in black.

Then on past the wide, open fields, with workers' backs bent over in a line, and areas of vivid green fodder shining with the evening light among darker areas of foul medames, the Egyptian staple.

Suddenly Dominic's eye caught sight of great, grey structures off in the distance. They rose above the plain - pure forms, sharp-topped, and curved. For a moment he thought that they were buildings of some sort, and he struggled to understand their dimensions. He sped on towards them. In an instant, their bulk was transformed into surface. They were giant sails. The feluccas which bore them were hidden from view, moving imperceptibly on the sluggish water of a canal or distributary. The arching canvases seemed fixed like in a painting; they belonged to a different epoch, removed, calm, pure.

As he approached the next town, Mahalla Kubra, the Place of the Bridge, he noticed a large sign warning travellers that they were in a military area and that photography was forbidden. It struck him that the sign was a completely ineffective gesture. No doubt the Israelis had perfect photographs of the bridge, the town, everything. In fact, it was not so much a gesture, more of a symptom - of Egypt's uneven struggle to confront an enemy who had proved much more powerful, the enemy that had destroyed their entire air force in a day in June 1967. The sign had been put up in the aftermath of that defeat, a witness to fear. There were no signs like that going up after the War of Ramadan. Now the signs were proclaiming a different message, of force and dignity regained.

He slowed the car as he approached the bridge. Before he reached it, a man in army uniform stepped into the road and raised his arm. A spurt of adrenalin spread in Dominic's stomach. A check-point - and he was sure that his car papers were not in order. But there was no escape. He pulled up. The soldier remained on the kerb side. Dominic could see now that he was an officer. He leaned across the passenger seat and looked up at him through the open car window.

'Salam alekum,' he greeted him in what he hoped was a suitably respectful manner.

The officer leaned down and almost pushed his head completely into the car.

'And to you peace. Are you going to Cairo?'

'Yes, I am.'

'Can you help me? I am going to Cairo too.'

'Of course, yes. I am at your service. Welcome.'

He opened the door, and the man squeezed himself into the car with difficulty. He was in his forties, and was as fat an any self-important man of his age in Egypt should be. His uniform bulged with well-being and self-indulgence. Dominic wondered what he would be like in war, in the heat of battle. It was impossible to guess. One thing though, he realised, he would now have no trouble getting through any roadblocks ahead.

The officer asked Dominic where he came from. When he learned that he was British, far from reacting with hostility, he switched from Arabic to halting English and became even more talkative. His brother had worked for the British in Cairo. What was Dominic doing in Egypt. Technical aid? Very good. Science and technology, ah, that was what Egypt needed very badly. Egypt must develop. Dominic agreed. Egypt had so many problems, the man continued. How to feed everybody. Great problems.

'Tell me, do the British love segess?'

'Sorry?'

'Segess. Do the British love segess?'

Dominic struggled to understand. Segess? What on earth was that?

'We Egyptians love segess too much. It cause grreat prroblem. Too many people. Population grow too fast.'

'Oh,' Dominic exclaimed. The penny had dropped. What an extraordinary question.

'Well, I suppose the British don't love sex as much as the Egyptians.'

'We Egyptians sink about segess all ze time. It take all energy, make us very tired.'

Dominic laughed to himself. The poor chap must have one or maybe more of those fiery bedouin women at home, giving him no peace. Egypt's problem had led him inexorably back to his own. The two were obviously linked.

A car horn sounded behind them. Dominic looked in his mirror and saw Rory's red Fiat waiting for an opening to overtake. Traffic was pouring past them in the other lane. He hoped Rory would have patience. Eventually there was a gap and the Fiat sped past. Rory waved, and Dominic saw that Khaled was in the front seat, his hand poised in a precise gesticulation. Three other young Egyptians were in the back, some friends of Khaled's from the navy probably, going up to Cairo for a wild night before reporting back for duty on Monday. The red car soon disappeared among overloaded taxis and lorries all rushing breakneck towards the capital.

Dominic and his passenger followed, and before long the teeming suburbs of the city engulfed them. The sky was carmine, and the thinning palm trees held aloft against it black, radial spikes.

Thirteen

Dominic resumed his normal life in Cairo, his work each day in the Ministry building downtown, lunch at the Guizera or Heliopolis Club, followed by a short siesta before returning to the club for tennis or squash. Perhaps a reception in the evening at the British residence in honour of some visiting dignitary, or a visit to the house of an Egyptian friend. The heat, the regular twelve hours day and twelve hours night, the irrepressible social instinct of the Egyptians, the sheer teeming life of the city - all seemed to speed time on its way in a daze. He succumbed, he was happy.

Only occasionally did he think of Emma. She belonged to another world - the world of Agami, of the sea. Here was dust, city, and the river. But when ordering an anis at the club, he would suddenly miss her presence, for they had always had anises together at lunch in Alexandria. Or when he lay drying in the sun on the grass beside the pool at the club, he would open his eyes suddenly, hoping to see her lying beside him. At night in bed when he thought of her, the ambivalence of his emotions troubled him, waves of recoil made him question the memory of their coupling together. He felt it was useless to try to hang onto the fading vision of her face.

He noticed that Rory never mentioned her in their conversations. Was that jealousy, or was it that he considered their relationship incongruous - he, Dominic, an adult, wasting his time with an immature girl? But who was Rory to talk? He seemed to have no sexual interest in his life other than a sordid evening with a prostitute about once a week. He regaled Dominic with the details of these encounters. The cruder, the more squalid they were, the better he seemed to like them. Dominic wondered at his utter detachment from these women, at the ice-cold libido that spent itself with them. The whole man remained completely distinct, untouched. There was something unhealthy, maimed, about it, hiding behind the indifference.

'But don't you want anything more from women than this half hour's crude fucking?' he asked him once.

'What do you mean? Continuity, love, all that kind of thing? No, I don't have any wish to get involved. I don't want any long term entanglement.'

'I don't seem to be able to avoid it,' Dominic said, for when he looked back on his weeks with Emma, he felt that he had been struggling all along to achieve just that - to get involved, to be entangled with her.

'Anyway, enough about women,' Rory cut into his thoughts. 'I've been meeting some friends of Khaled's in the air force, and they're rather interesting. There's a lot of ferment going on, I can tell you. Come over this evening and meet them.'

'What kind of ferment?'

'Basically opposition to the Americanisation of Egypt. You'll see.'

'All right. I'll come round after the club. About seven or so.'

When he arrived at Rory's flat, the group were already well into heated discussion. Khaled introduced him to two men he had not seen before: one with a thin, sad face, and the other, Ali, fatter and rounder. There were also two women with them, an Egyptian who worked at the British Council and an English girl who was teaching in a Heliopolis language school. Lotfi, the man with the sad look, was obviously drunk. He dominated the gathering with a voluble stream of talk.

'You see it was all arranged in advance. Sadat said to the Americans "Look, I must fight, but I don't want to fight seriously. I just need a little victory for public opinion. Then I'll do anything you want".'

'You really think the Americans knew in advance that there was going to be a war?' Rory asked.

'Of course, of course. And they warned the Israelis. They told them it was coming. But the Israelis were so proud, so overconfident, that they didn't believe them. Then bang, we got over the canal. We completely over-ran them. The famous Bar-Lev line that they had been boasting about for years. We took it all in twenty-four hours. They were completely unprepared. The roads to the passes were open. So what did Sadat do? Take them and get the whole of western Sinai? Oh no, that would have really upset the Americans, that could have really threatened Israel. It would have turned America against Egypt. So he stopped - right on the canal. Said to the army "Very good boys, but that's enough. No more". And I'm sure he told the Americans. And they told the Israelis. So the Israelis took all their tanks, all their planes, and hit the Syrians.'

'It was a war on one front, only one front. First Sinai, then Golan,' Ali said, reaching over for another bottle of beer.

'Exactly,' Lotfi continued, 'and then, when they had pushed back the Syrians, they were ready for the Sinai again. And that was where Sadat got a shock. He had played the game with the Americans, but now the Israelis were not going to play it with him. Their pride was hurt, the pride of their army. So Sharon just disobeyed orders and attacked and broke through. Sadat said to the Americans "Look, this is not fair. Stop them at once". And they did - not at once, but they did stop them Then the withdrawal agreement. Then buddy buddy with America. Yes, Nixon, no, Nixon. It's disgusting.'

Lotfi stubbed out his cigarette and immediately lit another.

'But how could Sadat have had his secret agreement with the Syrians to attack and then expect the Americans to help him?' Rory asked.

'Because he had already shown the Americans that he was their man. He had kicked out all the Russians. So help was what he wanted in payment for that.'

'Then the whole war was a clever plot at the expense of the Syrians.'

'Exactly, Syria gained nothing. She lost men, and land. She was betrayed.'

'But you have to admit,' Dominic put in, 'that Sadat the betrayer was successful. He pulled it off, the first Egyptian leader to do so.'

'Successful? What have we won? A strip of desert on the other side of the canal. Worth nothing - nothing!' Lotfi almost shouted with vehemence.

'But that strip has allowed you to open the canal, and that is already bringing in millions.'

'It has brought us some money, but it has turned us into America's little dog. We are Nixon's pet dog now. We have betrayed the Arab cause. We have let down our Syrian allies. We have sold out to the Americans. Why? Because Sadat married an English woman and wants to be loved by the Europeans and the Americans.'

'Sadat must be killed.'

Ali's round face was expressionless as he uttered the verdict.

'The whole policy of Egypt now is horrible.'

His vocabulary in English was more limited than Lotfi's.

'In the air force now, many say that we must have second revolution.'

'Exactly,' Lotfi came in again to resume his flow. 'Sadat must go. All this new economic policy must go. The "opening" - who is benefiting? The rich, the speculators, the importers. And all the time, Egyptian industry is being strangled. The cost of living is going up very fast. There are no flats for young couples. The people cannot survive. The government is completely corrupt. We must get rid of them. Shoot them all.'

Rory's servant came into the room with a large dish of spaghetti and laid it down on the table before them. The English girl began serving and at last the talk lost its unswerving drive and broke into remarks and silences. Dominic had found Lotfi's conspiracy theory at the expense of the Syrians convincing. It certainly seemed to fit the facts of the war.

'Are you in the air force too, Lotfi?' he asked him.

'No, I have left the air force. I had enough.'

'Oh yes? What are you doing now then?'

'I am a pilot in Lufthansa.'

'Lufthansa? Really? You mean you're working in Germany?'

'Lotfi has just married a German woman,' Rory put in.

'That's right. Now I am German. German job, German wife, German house.'

'Well, well,' Dominic said, eating his spaghetti. After all that talk, the burning diatribe against Sadat and his betrayal of the Arab cause, here was Lotfi washing the sand off his feet and opting for Europe. Was the diatribe just hot air then? Was there any real passion, real commitment in the air force, or anywhere else in Egypt? Would Sadat live to a ripe old age? Dominic thought that if Lotfi was anything to go by, he would.

Some days later, Dominic was sitting in his flat drinking tea as the muezzin called out the evening prayer. All the windows were open and the air had begun to cool. Now it was the walls that seemed to be giving off heat. Though he was wearing only a loose galabiya, the tea made him perspire.

His caffeine induced reverie was interrupted by the ringing of the telephone. He leaned over and picked it up, thinking it was probably Rory.

'Hello.'

'Hello. Is that Dominic?'

'Yes. Emma. Goodness, what a surprise.'

'Is it?'

'Of course. How are you?'

'All right.'

'Good. Hold on a minute.'

He pulled the phone onto his lap and relaxed.

'Emma, lovely to hear you. Did you get my poem?'

He had written her some verses the week before, telling her he missed her.

'Yes, it was sweet. Thanks.'

'So what have you been doing?'

'Nothing much.'

'What - you mean you haven't been working as planned?'

She seemed flat, completely without interest. What was wrong with her, he wondered?

'No, I haven't.'

'That's not like you - the brilliant student.'

'No. Actually...I'm pregnant.'

His mind blurred suddenly. The words seemed to resonate

in his head. The second in which he perceived them disconnected itself from the normal flowing of time.

'Emma, are you sure?'

'Yes, I'm sure.'

'How many days late are you?'

'Oh it's not that. I'm getting morning sickness every morning. There's no doubt about it.'

Now that the shock was passing, he felt a dumb surge of joy. But he was afraid to express it to her.

'Good God, Emma, so it's happened.'

'Yes. I just thought I should tell you.'

'But of course. How do you feel about it?'

'I don't know really.'

'What's that supposed to mean?'

She cut him off.

'Mummy's coming. I'll have to go. Bye.'

'Emma, write to me.'

'Yes, bye.'

The phone clicked. He was alone with this new knowledge that she had his child growing in her. His joy gave way to sympathy for her - she seemed so bewildered, like a young girl who had done something wrong without knowing quite what it was. She was young, nineteen, yet she was entering into her full adulthood. And through her, he was too. His sense of distance from her, his feeling that their union required too much effort on his part, gave way to a new gratitude. He longed for her letter. What did she want to do?

It came four days later, not to his flat, but to his office at the Ministry. Rory told him as he came in that it was there. He found it on his desk. There was her writing - the idiosyncratic letters leaning this way and that. On the left side of the envelope were written in big capitals the words: 'Private' and 'Urgent'. He felt a grip in his stomach and his heart began beating as he sat down and tore open the envelope. The letter was short, just one page. She was completely sure, she said, that she was pregnant, and had decided to go back to Oxford early and have an abortion. She would not be staying overnight with him as planned. She realised it was all her fault. That's life, she concluded abruptly, with her love, and a little net of kisses round her name.

Just as he had been taken by surprise by his earlier joy, now too he was shocked by the coldness that seeped into him. He was unsure whether it was because she had decided to abort or because she was just going to go straight back to Oxford without seeing him. What did that mean? It was intolerable.

When he got back home at lunch-time he rang her. Her mother answered.

'Is Emma there, please?' he asked in forced social cheerfulness.

'Yes. Is that you, Dominic? Hold on a moment. She's just coming.'

Nothing strained or portentous about her voice, he noticed. Obviously she didn't know.

'Hello, Dominic.'

'Hello, Emma. I just got your letter.'

'Oh.'

'Emma, please don't go straight back to Oxford. Come and see me as we had planned.'

'Do you want me to?'

'Yes, I do. Please. It would be awful if you just disappeared. When are you flying?'

'Next Saturday.'

'Can't you come on Friday then?'

'All right. I've got a friend staying. Can I bring him?'

A friend? Who was he? She had never mentioned any friend coming to stay while he was in Alex.

'Yes, of course. But you'll come?'

'Yes. We'll come on the three o'clock train.'

'Shall I pick you up at the station?'

'No, no. We'll get a taxi.'

'All right, Emma. Till Friday then.'

'Bye then.'

'Bye darling.'

He put the phone down with a sense of great relief. It seemed very important to him that she was coming, that they would spend some hours together, no matter what she had decided to do. He longed to see her and hold her in his arms. The hurt that she would ignore him, avoid him and return to her other life, had been erased. He would have her with him soon.

Fourteen

'Peace to you. How are you?'

'Very well, thank you, Bey.'

'And how is the family?'

'Well, alhamdulillah.'

Dominic gave the man the small red twenty-five piastre note. That was the normal fee for cleaning a car.

'Thank you,' the man said, and his long, deeply-lined face broke into a grin.

'That's a good job. She's very clean.'

'I am at your service, Bey.'

It was typical of Egyptian life, this human, man to man exchange between the privileged and the labourer or odd-job man - the rubbing together of lives, rich and poor. The conversation he had just had with the car park attendant at the club may have been short, but it was marked by courtesy and warmth on both sides. Some of Dominic's British friends thought such sentiments were a sham - there could be no real common feeling or interest between this man, struggling on the edge of poverty and destitution, and someone like Dominic, the rich foreigner, or any other wealthy Egyptian member of the club. The sham served merely to obscure the struggle of the classes, and the poor's implacable desire for justice. But Dominic had never believed that a man's worth lay only, or even primarily, in what he earned or what he had. How therefore could a man's relationship to another depend simply on possessions? Did it really mean that he and the attendant who had just washed his car were class enemies, just because he possessed a car and the other didn't? He would not believe it. Almost every day he saw the attendant. They exchanged greetings. They didn't need to. Over the months they had got to know each other. He knew what clothes the man had, or rather how few he had. He learned of the man's family and where they lived. He noticed the swollen knuckles of the man's hands, and the way the fingers flexed sideways when they gripped the handle of the bucket in which he carried water. He saw how the man's legs shuffled in a knock-kneed way as he walked. Was the arthritis in his hip joints as well? It probably was.

All these things Dominic had got to know, and no doubt the attendant had been just as observant of him. A relationship had grown up between them, and a friendship, of that he felt sure. He knew if the man asked him for help, he would give it, and if he asked the man, unlikely though that was, it would be the same. The gross inequality between them in money, in class, was not everything. Of course the only reason they came into contact was because the poor man could find no other work than this, standing in the club car park day after day, collecting five or ten piastres from car owners who chose to give them, and less frequently earning twenty-five for cleaning a car. But in that contact there was not just the dumb exchange of service for money. How could that yield the warmth or the certainty of friendship? For Dominic was convinced that between him and this poor man, there was a friendship. It was something he felt just as surely as he felt anything.

He drove out into the broad tree-lined avenue leading to the Roxy roundabout, past the huge, cream coloured palace that had been commandeered to serve as the headquarters of the still-born union between, Egypt, Libya, and the Sudan. Every day, the enormous building received its squad of bureaucrats in their official cars. What they did was anyone's guess. The so-called union had been an empty dream of Gaddafi's in the early days. Now it was derided as evidence of his rampant megalomania. Yet the Palace of the Union remained in operation. People still worked there. The whole affair was irrefutable proof that once civil servants have been given jobs and offices, it is almost impossible to take them back.

Dominic pulled right after the Palace into one of the main axes of Heliopolis, called in Arabic, Masr el Gedida, New Cairo. This huge suburb had been built as an architectural set-piece, rather like Nash's Regency development in London, but on an even grander scale. Its style resembled nineteenth century British imperial building in India. The company that had built it had been Belgian, but Dominic did not know the name of the architect. Nor had he seen any books on the subject. Yet it was a magnificent architectural achievement. Certainly the buildings were now often shabby in their detail. Cinemas had developed the tasteless habit of sticking their garish posters on the pillars of most of the main facades. But if one stood in the middle of a street, one could see that the buildings achieved an impressive unity, and a mosque or church described in the distance domes, spires, or minarets in striking, exotic harmony.

Dominic parked the car opposite Groppi's and went over to the café. He ordered coffee, fried eggs, and toast. The crowds of the evening shopping period filled the streets and he watched them with interest. The cake shop attached to the café was doing a brisk business. He decided to call there before going home and buy some Turkish delight. Groppi's Turkish delight was the best in Cairo.

Fifteen

On the following Friday evening at a little after five, Dominic heard footsteps coming up the stairs to his apartment. They stopped outside the door and the bell rang. That would be Emma and her friend, he thought. He went quickly to open the door, wondering how she would seem to him, now that there was this astonishing new connection between them. She was standing, her case on the floor on one side, a duffle bag on the other, in a denim boiler suit, with braces over her shoulders. The extraordinary vividness of her face he had forgotten. She smiled at him with a quick, nervous movement of her lips.

'Hello, Dominic.'

She stood still, as if her not moving symbolised a confused acceptance of her condition and her responsibility for it.

'Hello, Emma,' he said in excited recognition, but he felt constrained from kissing her in front of the other man, who waited a little behind her.

'My God, that's heavy. You carried it all the way up?' he said, taking her case, and ushering the two of them into the hall.

'It's full of books, that's why,' she replied. 'I brought them all out, full of good resolutions, but I'm bringing most of them back unread.'

They were inside. Dominic shut the door.

'Dominic, this is Robert. Robert, Dominic.'

He shook his hand. Robert was young, about the same age as Emma, but his youthfulness made him seem both familiar and insignificant, whereas Emma's had at first made her curiously formidable.

'Robert is the school friend I told you about, remember?'

She didn't seem in the least embarrassed. What was Robert doing, staying with her? Dominic couldn't remember her telling him anything about him.

'So you went to what Ronald calls the zoo?'

'Zoo?'

'Oh nothing. A Dutch friend of ours thinks public schools are zoos. Come in and sit down. What would you like to drink? Beer, tea, wine?'

'Tea, please,' Robert replied.

Dominic looked at Emma.

'Yes, tea for me too, please.'

'Won't be a moment.'

He left them and went into the kitchen to prepare it. He could hear them talking together. Before he had finished, Emma came into the kitchen.

'Can I help?'

There was a banal matter-of-factness about her which disappointed him and at the same time was a relief.

'No, it's all right. Hey, Emma, this Robert character, are you with him? You know what I mean.'

'No, of course not. He's just a very old school friend - absolutely Platonic. You are funny.'

'Well, how am I to know? He might be your old true love, come to rescue you in your crisis.'

'Robert? Not likely, he couldn't rescue a kitten.'

'So he's just a friend. Thank God for that.'

He kissed her quickly on the mouth. He put the things on the tray and picked it up.

'Shall we go in?'

She nodded and followed him. Robert was looking through his records in the sitting room, a standard time-filling exercise, and at the same time an important cultural ritual.

'I see you've got "Blood on the Tracks",' he said, looking up.

'Yes. Do you want to hear it?'

'Please. I haven't heard it. It's a good one, isn't it?'

'The best for ages. The best since, oh, since "John Wesley Harding".'

He put the record on. Robert became more significant - he liked Bob Dylan. "Tangled Up in Blue" filled the room. Dominic raised his voice.

'This is really a come-back album. "Nashville Skyline" and all that stuff afterwards -terrible. But this is the old Dylan.'

Robert nodded his head enthusiastically.

They sat, drinking tea, listening to the music, and talking in snatches about Alexandria, the end of the holidays, what was on in London.

Eventually Emma said: 'I'm going to have a bath. Show me where things are.'

Dominic got up and took her case into his bedroom. She sat on the bed and pulled off her shoes.

'I'm afraid there are only two bedrooms. You'll have to sleep either with me or with him.'

She looked up with a pursed mouth.

'Look, I told you. Don't be silly.'

'Terrific. You're sleeping with me.'

He pushed her over flat on the bed, and lay on top of her.

'Emma, I can't believe this. I'm so glad you came. When can

we talk?'

'Not now. Get off. I want to have a bath.'

He rolled off her. His sudden openness to her was checked. She was behaving as if everything were perfectly ordinary.

'All right.' He got up. 'Here's a towel.'

He pulled one out of a drawer and handed it to her.

'Now you go out and keep Robert company. He's shy and a bit uncomfortable.'

Dominic left her.

After supper Emma and Dominic sat outside on the balcony in the warm night air. The traffic on the airport road, Sharia Aguza, was a distant, muffled roar. He stretched out his hand in the dark and took hers. For some moments there was silence between them. The baby, the seed that was growing in her had not been mentioned. Now, at last, he knew they would speak of it.

'So, it happened,' he said.

'Yes, it did. Of course it was my fault.'

'I suppose so, but I had something to do with it.'

'It was probably that first night. I was so stupid.'

'Far from blaming you, I feel...well, I don't know, I'm terribly pleased.'

'Are you really?'

'And a little amazed. You know, that out of our very...'

He just caught himself from saying 'forced affair' and changed it instead to ...

'...short affair, should come such fruit.'

'Yes, it is rather amazing, isn't it,' she said, and squeezed his hand.

'Do you really want to have an abortion?'

'Why, what alternative is there?'

'We could get married. You could have the baby.'

As he said it, a sudden transformation of viewpoint had taken place in his mind. Now he and she were solidly united together, and everyone else was ranged outside them. Marriage was perfectly easy in this framework, a detail almost. He was suddenly convinced of their union.

'Do you think we could? When? At Christmas?'

'Yes, at Christmas. Would you be swelling by then? Probably not. God, it would surprise people.'

'It'd really drive Daddy to drink.'

'I can see the look on Lynda's face when I tell her. Cynical old Rory can be best man.'

'Mum would love it. She's really taken with you, you know.'

'That's a good start - getting on well with my mother-in-law.'

'When shall we announce it?'

'Tomorrow.'

'Oh, it sounds so lovely. But there's Oxford. It would be so difficult.'

'Would it?'

'Yes. As soon as I really knew, there seemed only one solution, abortion.'

He wanted to remind her that she'd said that she would never have one, but refrained.

What was the point of rubbing it in? It would only make her more determined. And was he trying to dissuade her? He didn't know. But he did know that the thought of marrying her in Alexandria at Christmas, and caring for her as her thin young body swelled with their child thrilled him and offered him a vision of wonder, of beauty, in which he would be transformed.

'Shall we go to bed then?'

They stood up, and as he looked at her, he struggled to break down the ineffable separateness that made her and him unique and individual. He fought in a moment of hallucination against the awful distinction between his will and hers. No matter what he said to her, even if he begged and pleaded, she alone, in the inviolable separateness of her own will, would decide. And if he begged and pleaded, he felt with dread that she would definitely go on, she would have the abortion. So he must not struggle. He must let her go free in her will. He must trust her. There could be no compulsion.

The moment passed. They went into the flat. Robert had disappeared. While Emma was in the bathroom, Dominic un-dressed and wrapped a blue sarong round his waist. He had stopped wearing pyjamas because he had caught a common Egyptian skin infection, dhobie's itch, in his groin, and was treating it with a sticky ointment which stained clothing. Emma came back from the bathroom with a towel round her, took it off, dropped in on a chair, and slipped into bed.

He got in beside her.

'I like your cloth -lovely colours,' she said.

'Do you? I'm wearing it because I've got the cursed dhobie's itch. Here.'

He pointed.

'The doctor has given me some horrible ointment for it.'

Now she would know why he wasn't going to make love to her. Maybe she wouldn't want to anyway?

'If I had the baby, would we be able to look after it, Dominic?'

'Yes, of course. No problem - I'd get an ayah.'

'Oh, it would be so exciting.'

'This is the country for having babies in, that's pretty clear.'

'Mummy would be thrilled.'

He put his hand on her firm, small belly.

'It's in there. It's in there.'

'Yes. A girl or a boy, do you think?'

'Look, I've waited thirty-three years for this, I don't care.'

'Let's see... what sign would it be born under?'

'What sign? Emma, you're the end.'

He caught her hair and pulled her face to his, giving her small kisses, one after another. Then her lips parted and she held his mouth on hers. The kiss became a new exchange, in which he discovered again the strange, delicate hollowness of her mouth. The heat of their excitement burst up and their bodies twisted against each other. He felt her touching him with very light stroking fingers. She pulled up his sarong. She wanted him, she didn't care. He got over her and she opened for him. He entered her surely and easily, hoping that he was not dirtying her or the sheets with ointment. She gripped him round the back and her mouth sucked him deeper into her. He felt a sudden uncontrollable sweetness for her, a love that had never existed between them until this moment. He moved with an ecstasy of freedom in her and she enclosed him. His climax came in pure waves. Unheeding afterwards, staying in her, he moved down her body so that his face was on her breasts. They drifted into sleep.

The next morning she was already in the kitchen when he woke. He looked at his watch. Eight fifteen. The flight was at ten and they had to be at the airport a good hour before. He got up and went into the kitchen. Emma was dressed. She was wearing a dark blue velvet jacket over her jeans suit, and her hair fell on it in a harmony of deep colours. She turned when she heard him. For a moment they looked at each other in a short recognition of the love they had taken and given in the night, and then she said:

'You needn't bother to get dressed and come to the airport, Dominic. Robert and I will be quite OK. We'll get a taxi.'

He felt it as a cut, but replied: 'Whatever you like.'

Later, as they had a hurried breakfast, the mood of closeness between them gave way to more casual remarks which drew Robert into the conversation. Had he enjoyed his holiday? Yes. It had been his first in Egypt. So, Dominic thought, he had come all the way out to Alexandria just to spend a week with Emma. Was he in love with her? Probably.

Putting a last piece of bread into her mouth, Emma got up from the table.

'Time to go. Robert, go downstairs and hail a taxi. We'll follow with the luggage.'

When he had left the room, Emma came to Dominic and kissed him quickly on the mouth. He tried to hold her but she slipped away and picked up her case and duffle bag.

'You take Robert's things,' she said.

He allowed himself to be ordered. He picked up the bags and followed her out of the flat. She went down the stairs in front of him, her heeled shoes making a sharp clacking sound on the tiled steps. The dynamic of parting already controlled them, and cut away his impulse to fill these last seconds with any grasping communication - that he was so glad she had come, if only for a night, that he loved her, that he hoped she would decide to have the child and they would marry.

But their steps took them on down. It was almost automatic, dazed. As they pushed open the front door of the building, the bright morning sun blinded them. Robert was standing on the pavement with a taxi already waiting. Dominic put the bags and case into the boot. Emma and Robert got in and their doors slammed shut.

'Lil matarr,' Dominic instructed the driver.

'Haadher,' the man replied.

Emma wound down her window. Her narrow face, framed in her hair, her glasses sitting on her nose, the colour of her velvet jacket, her smile, the black surround of the taxi window - this image Dominic would always remember, for it was an image locked with tense emotions which could not find words, which feared futility, which yearned for consent.

As the car pulled away, they drained from him. He had not even waved. Had he said goodbye?

During the days that followed, he went over again and again in his mind what the future might hold if Emma decided not to have the abortion. Buoyed up with the new love he felt for her, he imagined their happiness and the excitement of their marriage at Christmas. Of course everyone would assume that Emma was pregnant, but what did that matter? They loved each other, they had made a child, what better basis was there for marriage?

It would mean her leaving Oxford. Would that be so important? She was studying English literature. What career did that fit her for? Teaching in some dreary English school? She would hate that, he felt sure. She could have her children, and then go back to university later if she wanted to . She's only be, what, twenty-five or so? Then she'd know what she wanted to do. It might not be English. In any case, what exactly was she doing in her present course? Only reading. She could do that anyway. He felt sure he loved, valued, and got as much from English literature as she did, though he was a scientist. As he had once argued with her, he believed that there was no science of literature, no body of knowledge that the university could impart that was denied the ordinary reader like himself. He thought that the whole idea of a university teaching the literature of one's own living language was spurious. It was, in fact, a subtle perversion. The artist, the creator, no longer confronted the public directly, he reached them through the intermediary of the academic. So he would be saddled with received opinion, doctrine, established values. He would, in the long run, be smothered. And the reader would be smothered also.

Emma would be better away from Oxford, reading what she wanted when she wanted. She could do that married to him and bringing up their children. That would take six, seven years of effort. Then she would be free to study again, to launch herself into the world of work if she wanted to.

About a week after her departure, he got a letter from her. It was just one hurriedly written page. She had had a new idea, to have the baby and take one year off from Oxford, then return and finish her degree. What did he think of it? She must know at once.

In the first instant, though the plan was so different from the future he had been imagining, he thought: -Yes, we could do it. But then he began to question its basis. Emma could not raise a child in a year. What would happen when she returned to Oxford? Whether the baby went with her or stayed with him, it would mean the splitting of the family. No, it was completely unrealistic. It sounded more like a proposal to avoid having an abortion that a proposal to marry and found a family. She wanted to have the child and continue to be an undergraduate. With him in Egypt? It was impossible. And yet, the child would be born, their child. They would surely be transformed by it. Maybe Emma would, having had it, renounce Oxford and be, instead, a mother. But did she want to marry him? She said nothing of it in the letter. Suddenly he was beset by doubts as to what she really felt, what she wanted of him. Might she just discard him, even if she had the baby?

He sat down to write a reply to her letter. He began by saying that the one year off plan was unrealistic. The question was, did she want to stay with him and have a family? He could not answer that question for her. Yet if she wanted to have the child none-the-less, then of course he agreed to it. Even if... He tried to imagine the life the child would have if they did not stay together. Being shunted from her to her family, to him, and back again. Awful for the child, for everyone. So really it was a question of marriage or an abortion. Yet that was not what she was proposing, and she wanted his answer. He struggled to finish the letter but could not. He tore it up.

That day went by, and another. He fretted but could not write. He kept thinking, if she loves me, she will have the child and marry me. If she does not, then she will not.

In any letter he would plead, he could not help it. Yet it was something she must know and decide herself.

On the third day after her letter, he drove to the post office on Ramses Street and sent her a telegram. In it he said: -Cannot say yes or no. Your decision I accept. Love and understanding. Dominic.

Sixteen

'How goes Lotfi and the second revolution?' Dominic asked Rory as they sat beside the club swimming pool having lunch.

'Oh, Lotfi's gone back to Munich, to his German wife. Haven't seen much of Ali either since that evening at my place.'

'Lotfi was certainly on his high horse then. Did you really believe his conspiracy theory about the war?'

'Wouldn't put it past them. In any case, we'll probably never know. Most of the crucial things in history never get told. Take the last world war for instance Churchill's brilliant feint - history books still haven't heard of it.'

'I haven't. What feint?'

'The Battle of Britain, the diversion of the German bombers onto civilian targets instead of RAF airfields.'

'Are you trying to say that Churchill was responsible for the Blitz?'

'That is exactly what I am saying. And furthermore, I have immense admiration for what he did. It took terrific nerve.'

'What exactly did he do?' Dominic asked with open hostility. He found the idea repellent.

'Look, Dominic, you're just an innocent. Reared on the Dam Busters' March, comics, Kenneth More with his goggles, that kind of nonsense.'

'There's no call to be patronising. I may not be particularly well-informed about the Second World War, but this idea that Churchill caused the bombing of English cities is preposterous.'

'Is it? Is it? Have you ever read anything about the Battle of Britain? Look at the facts, man. Germany is in the process of knocking out Britain's air defences in order to invade. She's winning, that's to say, the fighter airfields are getting knocked out. End of August 1940. Then two German bombers get separated and dump their bombs on London before turning back. What does Churchill do? He grasps the opportunity. Bombs Berlin.'

'Well, there you are. The Germans started it. Churchill just retaliated.'

'For God's sake, Dominic, don't just trot out the stock response before you've found out some of the facts. That's what I detest, peopled having opinions, smug, self-satisfying opinions before they've bothered to inform themselves as to what actually happened.'

Dominic flinched under Rory's attack but said:

'Well, the facts you've given me do not exclude my interpretation.'

'But that's just it, I haven't given you half the facts. I said Churchill hit back. But how do you reply to two stray bombers dropping their bomb loads? More or less in kind. You send maybe one squadron. But Churchill sent a whole fleet. Again and again. Hitler ranted and raged against the brutality of the English and warned that he would strike back at their cities. So Churchill hit him again. Hitler took the bait. He swallowed it. The Luftwaffe wasted its bombs on useless civilians and the airfields were saved. It was a desperately close-run thing. But Churchill, the old war dog, the absolutely brilliant tactician, had saved the day.'

'Maybe I don't know all the facts, but it sounds preposterous.'

Dominic felt sharp discomfort. One thing he and his family had never questioned was the valour, the uprightness, the morality of Britain's war against Hitler.

'Of course it sounds preposterous - to you, because you're just averagely informed. Which means that all you've ever heard is the official version, the propaganda. You think the Blitz was something the Germans started. I suppose you think Dresden was a military target? Look, if the Germans had won the war, all this, the whole area bombing policy, the Churchill bombing in 1940, all this would have been our war crimes. They would have had their war trials, and they'd have wrapped it up with the usual propaganda of the winning side. The prerogatives of the victors. But in fact we were the victors, so it was all pushed aside. It was just ignored. Some of it couldn't be suppressed - Dresden, the atomic bombs. I suppose you think they weren't war crimes?'

'But who started it all? The Germans deserved everything they got. So did the Japanese.'

'Splendid. Innocent civilians are innocent only if they're on our side.'

'Are you suggesting the Germans we bombed didn't support Hitler?'

'Do you know that they did? They didn't have much chance to express their opinions, did they? That's the irony of it. In a democracy, the civilians actually assent to a government and its policies, and in that sense, they are no longer innocent. In a dictatorship, they have no choice, they're helpless.'

'They shouldn't have allowed themselves to be dictated to, then.'

'There I agree entirely. But what I can't stand is your smugness, Dominic. We only do what we have to do, the others commit war crimes. It's moral humbug, and worse than that, it's stupid - just ill-informed, complacent, received opinion.'

'All right, you say Churchill deliberately provoked the Blitz on British cities. How the hell do you know? What gives you such special insight?"

Dominic's voice had a cutting edge that shifted the dispute onto a more personal level.

'Nothing at all - just a bit of common sense, and the willingness to look at the facts. To go beyond the convenient, comfortable view.'

'It's all mere speculation. You've got no proof.'

'Oh for Christ's sake, Dominic. I've got no proof that Santa Claus doesn't exist. Look, accept for one moment that Churchill did come to the bombing feint decision, do you think he's going to leave it in the cabinet records, put it in his memoirs, tell all the world about it? Grow up. If you want to discuss politics, show some nous as to how politicians work.'

'But something like that is bound to get out.'

'Yes, but proof of it isn't. Most cabinet papers aren't released for thirty years, and some are never released. Never. And of course Churchill's decision wasn't recorded as such, only the bombing orders were signed. Of the policy, there is absolutely no record, no proof that it ever existed. That's obvious, isn't it?'

'Perhaps,' Dominic admitted. He did know about the Official Secrets Act and the stifling hold it was said to have over British public life.

'Perhaps? Well, anyway, let's talk about something else. How is Emma?'

Dominic was taken aback. His immediate reflex was to retreat. He did not want to talk about Emma. Why should Rory know all about her too? He reddened.

'Fine, I suppose. I haven't heard.'

His voice was completely flat.

'Ah-hah. Well, I'm going to have some interesting sex tonight.'

He relaxed. Rory was not going to question him further about Emma.

'Another whore? The usual?' he asked.

'Not this time. Khaled is up in town, and he's promised to bring round two girls - old college friends, so he says. These will be the first clean Egyptian women I've got my hands on. I'm looking forward to it.'

'Well, it'll be a change, no doubt.'

'Yes, but will it be a change for the better?'

Rory laughed dryly. Dominic looked at him, and for the first time found his taut face, and his strident opinionated manner distasteful.

When Rory returned to his flat after the argument with Dominic, he did not feel that he had triumphed over his friend. He knew that he had been condescending, and regretted it, for he liked Dominic, and really wanted to convince him rather than alienate him. Yet once into an argument on politics, he couldn't help but see Dominic as the apotheosis of the half-baked liberal. True liberalism he considered one of the fundamental supports of his political philosophy; it was the limited, unprincipled liberalism of Dominic and his British political culture that he had begun to regard critically and to rail against. The trouble with this liberalism was its insouciance, its lack of any depth. When faced with Dominic's unquestioning acceptance that whereas murdering Jews in concentration camps was a war crime, murdering civilian Germans in burning cities was not, he was filled with rage and revolt. The revolt came from his disagreement, the rage from the fact that Dominic, a British academic, a man of some learning, an intellectual even, was quite unaware of the problem, or at least had not confronted it in his own mind. And of course as a result, knew almost nothing about it, save what everyone knew. And what everyone knew, Rory more and more concluded, was what everyone was allowed to know. There was a filter, there was control. It was immensely subtle, but it was there. As regards the way the British media presented the Arab-Israeli problem, there were obvious clues - the over-whelming preponderance of Jewish correspondents reporting from Israel, the strong links between the British Labour Party and Zionism. But that was just one issue. He detected similar bias and control in many other areas. Ireland, of course, which caused him so much personal anguish and distress, since he was from Northern Ireland. That had been the beginning of his bitter enlightenment, of his realisation that woolly liberalism, liberalism that accepted whatever comfortable formulae were handed down, liberalism that never thought things through, was not enough.

He had come to detest that liberalism, and when Dominic, his friend, showed himself to be thoroughly formed by it, he felt a sense of utter hopelessness. It was so pervasive, it would take years and years of effort to erode it in an individual, and many more in a people, in a whole political culture. Yet he felt he must fight for this goal, impossibly distant though it appeared. He did not know exactly how. But certainly he was not going to spare Dominic's feelings, leave him in his comfortable ignorance. Or anyone else he cared for, or who cared for him. It was a price that he expected both he and they had to pay for friendship. If the friendship was broken by the struggle, then it was hollow, illusory. As for the wider world, there was perhaps no hope that truth should gain on falsehood, that morality should dislodge hypocrisy. The world, he felt sometimes in a panic of despair, was immutable. The growth of human culture a mere incident in the timeless evolutionary fight of the human species amongst so many. That blind fight didn't change, it possessed an infinitely great and complex momentum. Human progress was a self-deception, the struggle for the good hopeless.

Yet he knew he was caught in it, he must fight, even if it was all useless. And progress was real, even if it was infinitesimal. Democracy was better than autarchy. Slavery had been abolished. That was the whole point - one had to struggle constantly against a feeling of hopelessness, that oneself didn't count, that others were immovable. They weren't. Dominic, for example, he felt he could lead out of his blinkered opinions, but he would have to be less harsh. Next time he argued with him, he would try to be so.

As Dominic made his way home from the club, his mind was also still absorbing the questions and impressions of the argument. He was troubled, not so much by the historical issue in dispute, but more by the inadequacy he had felt when confronting Rory's battering enumeration of facts that he did not know. He had sunk into a sullen reaction. Now his resentment was slowly yielding to rivalry. All right, he would read up on the matter, he would not allow Rory once more to assume the role of know-all. This resolve brought him some relief.

He put the key into his front door and opened it. On the floor inside, a postcard lay, picture side up. He recognised at once a view of the Corniche in Alexandria. His heart immediately began a heavy, dull beat. Had Emma come home? Decided against the abortion? He picked up the card quickly and turned it over. Only two words were written on it, followed by a question mark. For a moment his brain couldn't take them in. They were completely meaningless. Suddenly he realised that they were Latin, a name. He pronounced them slowly: Caprimulgus aegyptius. Then he noticed a small R at the bottom of the card. Ah - it was Ronald with a suggestion as to the identity of the karawan.

Caprimulgus - he smiled to himself, and went straight to his bookcase and took out Collins' 'Birds of Britain and Europe'. Ronald and he had the same book, Ronald's version in Dutch. Elizabeth had once pointed out to him with indulgent mockery that the publisher obviously considered that Britain was not part of Europe. The title of the book proclaimed it. Did all British bird-watchers agree, she asked humorously? He had admitted that they probably did.

The book covered not only Europe, but North Africa and the Middle East as well, and was therefore their standard reference. He looked Caprimulgus up in the Latin index, and aegyptius was the first one listed. Page 185. He turned to it. Opposite was an illustration showing a typical nightjar, but it was much paler than the British species - a light sandy beige. He read the entry. Certainly the general description fitted - nocturnal habits, desert or semi-desert habitat. But the critical piece of evidence for the karawan, its extraordinary call, was not convincingly described. This bird, according to the entry, made a variety of noises: 'tukl, tukl', 'kre-kre-kre', a clear 'u' or an 'o' with metallic timbre, and the nightjar's 'churr'. Whereas the karawan always called with that unmistakable reedy, piercing cry. Metallic, yes, but not a 'u' or an 'o', and Dominic had never heard any churring. That sound he would have recognised at once.

No, he decided against Caprimulgus aegptius. He would send a note and tell Ronald. They must think again.

Seventeen

The weeks of October and November slipped by. The great heat of Cairo's summer was giving way - autumn brought cool, freshening air at night, and now in the mornings it was clear and sunny, without the pulsing heat that made men dread the coming of torrid afternoons. The fasting month of Ramadan had come and gone, and at night the streets of the city, which were crowded then with the faithful released from their fast, were now relatively quiet.

The change in the weather had been gradual. There had been no drama of the coming of the rains, or the abrupt turning of the colour of leaves. Egypt was easing herself into winter with a slow, but almost sensual relief.

Dominic waited throughout these weeks for word from Emma. A letter came towards the end of November. He opened it eagerly, but as he read, his spirit became numb. It was almost banal, with an introductory sentence in which she apologised for not writing - she had 'kept putting it off', just as he had, she explained, but not through any 'ill feeling'.

But surely, he thought, it was her turn to write to him? She had the news to tell, he could only sit and wait for it. He had waited, with faint dread, all those weeks, and yet she had not bothered to send it, because he had not written to her? How absurd. Was the pregnancy, his and her child, and what she had decided to do about it, not infinitely more important than whose turn it was to write? Evidently not. He read on. There was nothing, nothing at all on the subject in the letter. Emma merely announced that she had changed her mind about staying in England during the Christmas holidays - another surprise for him, he did not know she had made it up - and was going to come 'home' to Egypt instead. She was flying on Sunday, the 9th. December. Could she stay with him on that Sunday night, before proceeding to Alexandria the next day? That was all. Just the warning that she might be bringing an American girlfriend with her, then the almost brusque 'Love, Emma', surrounded by its net of kisses, the last of them scrawled quickly.

Dominic allowed some part of his hope to find refuge in the brief equivocality of the letter, but more consciously he told himself that their adventure in the creation of life had been cut off. Emma must have had the abortion. The embryo they had begun together was no more, was finished. Now he could only wait, to hear it from her mouth.

Some days later, as he drove from his office at the Ministry to the club, he realised how much he had come to love Cairo and its irrepressible and chaotic atmosphere. Black and white taxis wove in and out around him like minnows jockeying for position in a turbulent stream. Bul-buls, the current craze, twittered from cars that specialised in the latest gadgets. This one was a chirping device which sounded whenever the brakes were applied. They competed with the incessant blaring of horns.

Then, as they all waited, becalmed in disarray at a traffic light, a boy suddenly appeared on a bicycle, threading his way with astonishing speed and dexterity through the mass of vehicles. He was holding the handle-bars with only one hand, and there were obviously no brakes for him to apply. In any case, braking would have been almost impossible, for on his head he was carrying a huge wooden tray piled high with aesh baladi, the brown, flat pitta bread of Egypt. They were fresh from the oven, blown up hollow, yet they all remained exactly in place as the boy glided left and right, with his free hand balancing the heavy, precarious load. One mistake, one hesitation, and the whole lot would come crashing down among the impatient wheels of the stalled traffic.

The lights changed and the teeming metal horde started to lumber forward amid a chorus of horns. The boy on the bicycle was ignored. Vehicles poured round him. Surely he could not stay upright in all this? But no, as Dominic changed gear and slipped between the pavement and a shuddering lorry, he just caught a glimpse of the boy suddenly swinging out left and across the oncoming traffic lane, tilting alarmingly, and then, with a flourish like a champion skier doing a spin stop, sweeping up to a bread stall and depositing the great wooden tray of bread into the waiting arms of the stall owner without mishap. The whole manoeuvre was consummate, inimitable, perfect. Not a single loaf had fallen.

Meanwhile Dominic and the rest surged on up the pitch black street and swept round the Roxy roundabout. With a stab of alarm, Dominic noticed some police standing in the roadway stopping cars ahead of him. His car papers were definitely out of date, he knew, but he had put off going to Alexandria to have them renewed. The heat, the incomprehensible bureaucracy were too daunting. Now he might cop it.

He slowed. A policeman standing in the middle of the road stared at his number plate. That was the trouble with a sports car, it always attracted attention. When he was almost level, the policeman's hand came up, but after a moment's hesitation, it gave him a quick wave through. As Dominic passed, he mumbled a 'thank you' in Arabic, and accelerated away. Escaped this time. They weren't checking cars with the special customs plate today - it was somebody else's turn. Relieved, he headed up to the club gates.

Eighteen

'What do you think, Mark, is she here to try to settle a major arms contract on the side, or is it simply routine?' Dominic asked.

The British consul, a tall man about Dominic's age, with a shiny, boyish face, smiled.

'Routine - just feeling her way before the next election.'

'Which you hope she'll win?'

They were talking at a reception in the British ambassador's residence for Margaret Thatcher, the new leader of the Conservative opposition.

'Strange, isn't it?' Dominic continued. 'Every political figure of any note has to come to Egypt sooner or later. Living here, one has the feeling that the place is creaking on the edge of collapse. But no - American congressmen, French ministers, Germans, and now Thatcher, come trooping out to Cairo. Egypt still counts.'

'Well of course it does. Mostly because it's so unpredictable. For years everybody thought Sadat was quite ineffectual, and then bang, the October War. All the visits since have no doubt been partly to prevent a recurrence. '

'What are Thatcher's views on the Middle East then?'

'I don't think we've had anything clear from her on it yet,' Mark answered with the non-committal reflex of the diplomat.

A man wearing a buttoned-down collar and a dotted silk tie

joined them.

'Hi, Mark. How's tricks?'

'Hello, Jim. Fine, and you?'

'Not bad. Just had a good look at your leading lady. She's cool.'

'Jim, this is Dominic Erbury, here on technical development. Dominic, Jim Cram, American first secretary.'

'How do you do?'

Dominic shook his hand and thought his face lacked definition.

'Hi. Yeah, I really like her. I had a few words with her, I mean, I figure she's got the east-west thing sorted out.'

'I suppose you're right there.'

'It would really be great if she became your next prime minister, but would the British accept a dame like that?'

'If the Conservative party can accept her, I think the rest of us can. What do you think, Dominic?'

'You know the joke about Wilson being the best conservative prime minister we've ever had? Well, you could say that Thatcher is the best male party leader we've had. She's not exactly...'

'Feminine? Into cookies and high heels?' Jim concluded for him.

'No, but it's not her being a woman that interests me, it's something else.'

'What, that a grocer's daughter has stormed the establishment?' Mark asked with a trace of malice in his drawling, home county accent.

'Not that. It's that she's a scientist. If she becomes prime minister, she'll be the first real scientist to have done so.'

'She was a scientist,' Mark said. 'Have there been any scienlist presidents of the US, Jim?'

'Scientists? Hang on. Maybe there've been some Christian scientists.'

He laughed.

'I suppose it's a bit of a hobby horse with me,' Dominic continued. 'I'm a scientist, and in a sense I feel confident of Thatcher. She's been trained in the disciplines of thought which should be just as applicable to the business of government as to the business of understanding the physical universe.'

'Do you think it would really make a difference?' Mark asked. 'Politics is anything but scientific.'

'I'm afraid that's true. But at least a scientific training should filter out some of the more credulous illusions of political life.'

'That God is on our side, you mean?' Jim said.

'Yes, but more the subtle and pervasive tendency to absolutism, or should I say, the unwillingness to confront other viewpoints.'

'Are scientists really any better at that than the rest of us?' Mark asked.

'They're not angels, certainly,' Dominic said. 'But if someone comes along with evidence contrary to yours, you, as a scientist, can't dismiss it simply because you don't like it. You're forced to weigh it on its merits. It's not so much a virtue of will, of disposition, more one of method or habit. But it's the only reliable way to arrive at the truth, that's clear. I just hope that if Thatcher came to power, that method would help her.'

'You're being a little too sanguine about the nature of politics, Dominic. Do you think that if it were shown clearly that nationalised steel was better than private enterprise steel, Thatcher would drop privatisation?'

'I hope she would,' Dominic replied with a small shrug.

'We shall see,' Mark said dryly. He looked over the heads of the crowd. 'It seems she's getting ready to go. I'll have to leave you.'

The group broke up. Dominic caught sight of Rory near a window, talking to a woman with thick, wavy, straw-blond hair. He edged his way towards them. As he approached, he noticed that Rory wasn't wearing a tie - the only man in the reception not to be doing so. Dress habits in Cairo were still fairly formal. The ambassador, for example, was in a creased grey suit, bought in England probably a decade ago, now mildly shabby. Why couldn't the British dress better, Dominic wondered. And here was Rory, with an open neck, and a blue and white striped jacket that made him look as if he was about to go out sailing.

As Dominic reached them, Rory was talking stridently to the woman, his gaze going out over her head. She was listening with rapt attention.

'It's hopeless, it'll take years and years. Centuries. You haven't a chance. Here, Malthus is king. Mindless fornication in the sweaty cleavage of the Nile. You can't stop it. Screw, and worry about the results bukra.'

'We've got to try anyway,' the woman put in.

Dominic was pleased to find that her face fitted perfectly the Pre-Raphaelite luxuriance of her hair. She looked like his imaginary vision of Tess of the d'Urbervilles.

'Ah, Dominic, this girl here is trying to control Egypt's birth rate. Annabel, this is Dominic. We work together.'

'Hello, What do you do then?' she asked brightly.

'Our work is humdrum, insignificant,' Rory replied for him, 'whereas yours is apocalyptic.'

'That's rather melodramatic. In fact I spend all day talking to women's groups.'

'Must be up-hill,' Dominic said and smiled.

'Well, indirectly so. The women are receptive enough, it's getting the men to heed the message that's the problem.'

'Typical, typical,' Rory said. 'Good God, in Ireland it's that man the Pope who tells everyone what to do in bed, or rather what not to do, while the women themselves are clamouring for the pill.'

'I hope Irish women are more ready to disobey the Pope than the Egyptian country woman is to disobey her husband. Female emancipation has so far to go here.'

Annabel's voice had a surprising and delightful gruffness.

'Talking of emancipation of women, did you talk to Mrs Thatcher?' Dominic asked her.

'I certainly did. I told her exactly what I felt about her miserly cutting of school milk when she was minister of education.'

'Really? How did she take it?' he asked, impressed at the forthrightness of her manner. He could just see her speaking her mind.

'Oh, she just smiled and said that much though she regretted it, it had been necessary.'

'Terrific,' exploded Rory, 'a real Cromwellian answer, that one! Anyway, the bird has flown - this thing's all over. Annabel, join us for dinner at the Brochette. I'm meeting a Palestinian friend there. You coming, Dominic?'

'I'd love to,' Annabel said. 'Wait a moment, I'll just tell Peter and Mary.'

She left them.

'Have you met Ezzedine, Dominic? He works at the Palestinian Radio.'

'No, I don't think I have.'

How did Rory get to know all these people, Dominic wondered?

Half a hour later, they were sitting in the obscure recesses of the Brochette Restaurant, waiting for their order, and eating humus, olives, ricotta, and strips of hot Egyptian bread. Ezzedine was a man in his late thirties, chubby in his face and body, with a small tuft of hair left isolated on his forehead by a hairline retreating on each side. He had a heavy, melancholy expression, which was relieved by the languorous appeal of his fine eyes. He was describing the difficulties that they had at the Palestinian radio station. One minute they were encouraged and championed, the next they were shut down.

'It must be rather perplexing,' Annabel said with emphatic sympathy. Dominic thought that she sounded like a lady commiserating with her servant over the death of a dog. But he felt she was quite sincere; accents often gave the wrong impression.

'We are used to it,' Ezzedine said, closing his eyes in punctuation, and showing them his long, curving lashes. 'We are only pawns. Egyptian interests are more important than us and they always were.'

'But don't you think that now that Egypt and Israel are on a more equal footing, and signing agreements, something will be done for the Palestinians?' Dominic suggested.

'Yes, surely something will happen now,' Annabel added reassuringly.

'Nothing will happen. Nothing will happen. Nothing will happen!'

Ezzedine for a moment seemed to have lost control. His eyes stared into space and bulged alarmingly.

'He's right,' Rory put in. 'Arab regimes anywhere only support Palestine for their own ends. The rest is hypocrisy. They're all dictatorships, devoid of any ethic of government. They have no democratic legitimacy. So they trot out their Palestinian sympathies and slogans to give themselves some kind of credit in the eyes of their masses.'

'That's unfair. Egypt has gone to war three times with Israel. Thousands of Egyptians have died. Palestine was the whole reason for those wars.'

'It may have been the original reason, Dominic,' Rory replied, 'but it certainly wasn't the whole reason. Anyway, I'm talking about all those thirty odd years since Israel was set up, not just the two or three months of war. The Palestinians have had to live through all that, dispossessed, kicked out, pushed from pillar to post.'

'That is right,' Ezzedine said. 'It is a terrible life, rotting in refugee camps in Jordan and in Lebanon. And when we try to fight for our rights and attack Israel, then we are driven out by our Arab brothers.'

'But why don't they support you?' Annabel asked.

'Quite simple,' Rory put in. 'Human nature, in all its vileness. The victim doesn't attract sympathy, he attracts more abuse. That went for the Jews in Europe just as much as it goes for the Palestinians today.'

'Is there no Christian charity then?' Annabel asked.

'Don't make me sick,' Rory replied heatedly. 'What did Christian charity do for the Jews in Germany? The Nazi party hunted them down and killed them and what did Christian Germans do? They joined in, they loved it! What is Christendom doing for the Palestinians today? Keeping their oppressors in business. No, no, Christian charity has nothing to do with it. Human vileness, that's what it's all about.'

'A Christian country is responsible for it all, Annabel,'

Ezzedine joined in. 'Balfour was a Christian. Was that charity, to give our land away to foreigners?'

'No, I suppose not,' Annabel replied. 'But where were the poor Jews to go?'

'That's it,' Rory said flatly. 'Europe - your Christians - persecuted the Jews, and instead of doing something to purge its evil, it shoved them off into Palestine. Anything to get rid of them. My God, I've just realised something - Israel is the largest, greatest, most efficient Jewish concentration camp ever.'

'What a horrible idea,' Annabel shuddered.

'That's absurd,' Dominic said. ' The purpose of the Balfour Declaration was to help the Jews, not to get rid of them. It was 1917, not 1945.'

'To help the Jews? Is that so? Well, I've been reading up a lot on the Balfour Declaration, and the standard interpretations are distinctly hollow. Britain never gives anything away unless it's in her own interests - if she helped the Jews, it was only in return for something.'

'What?' Dominic asked.

'That's what I'm trying to find out. And I think I'm getting close.'

'Whatever the reason was, it destroyed my people and my country,' Ezzedine said.

'Oh, it was terribly unfair,' Annabel concluded.

'It was evil,' insisted Rory. 'Corrupt motives working on vile human nature. First persecute the Jew, then aid and abet him to persecute the Arab. There's no such thing as Christianity in it, nor justice, nor morality.'

'Maybe the United Nations will, in the end, be able to bring about some kind of solution,' Dominic said, more to try to give Ezzedine a grain of comfort and bring the discussion to an end than because he believed it. He was tired of Rory and his harangue. The man was becoming a frenzied prophet in this cauldron where Egypt and the rest of the Middle East were boiling.

'The United nations,' Rory laughed with scorn. 'What a joke. If you think the United Nations as it's presently constituted can impose a just solution in the Middle East, you're in a fool's paradise. The United Nations is just a club run by the major powers. If their interests are threatened, out comes the veto, and the whole thing stops. That's the Security Council. As for the General Assembly, it can pass resolutions until it's blue in the face, no-one will take the slightest notice.'

'We have lost all hope in the United Nations,' Ezzedine agreed lugubriously.

Because of the presence of Annabel and Ezzedine at the dinner, Dominic had to wait to ask Rory how he had fared with the 'clean' Egyptian girls. The next day, lying beside the swimming pool at the club, he broached the subject casually to Rory, who was reading a biography of Arafat in a deck chair. Rory put the book down.

'Oh, it was fun!' he said with laughter. 'But it was a farce. I suspected as much when Khaled whispered to me as we went into action -Remember, only brush.'

'Brush - what's that?'

'That, old cock, is as far as you can go. Brush, it means rubbing up and down outside, it means no penetration.'

'The clean girl must remain a virgin?'

'Mine did, certainly. I was going to ignore Khaled's instruction, but when we got down to it, she made me promise, brush only. Well, I'm a gentleman, after all. What could I do?'

'How amusing. The brush, I must remember that.'

'Otherwise, it was amazing. Those girls were keen, I can tell you. As soon as we got them into the flat, one of them went off to the kitchen to make coffee. Go in and get her, Khaled gestured. So I did. Just walked straight in and grabbed her up against the fridge. She was gorgeous. Had her squirming like an eel in seconds. Hot as hell. She started taking her clothes off right there in the kitchen. What breasts! Aureoles like bursting fruits. Huge. I couldn't believe it. But then, as I say, I had to promise not to do it.'

'Full marks for your self-control,' Dominic said, genuinely surprised. A sweaty and relentless struggle would have been more in keeping with what he knew of Rory's character.

'And are you going to see more of her, or was it just the usual one-night-stand?'

'No. Next week, same thing. Or better, I hope. But I'm definitely going to have to brush up -sorry - on my Arabic. I want to take Aisha through every non-penetration routine I know.'

'*L'amour a l'egyptienne.* How long will you be able to put up with mere foreplay?'

'No idea. In any case, whenever I need the real thing, I can get it for a consideration. From each, according to my need.'

He gave a dry laugh.

Thinking about the conversation later, it bewildered Dominic how Rory could so compartmentalise his dealings with the opposite sex. It was willful, powerful, even if it was ultimately immature and sterile. Dominic always felt the need to move towards an integrity in sex, to find the whole woman and to be the whole man to her. It was the only healthy way. In his deep, puritan soul, he despised Rory, but some part of him envied the other's careless, unprincipled sexual greed.

Nineteen

Emma's flight was due at 21h.30 and Dominic drove his white car along the straight, tree-lined road out of Heliopolis towards the airport a good hour before. He could never quite get used to the twenty-four hour clock, and no matter how many times he checked that 21h.30 was 9.30 p.m., he never had full confidence in his calculation. The mind, it seemed, was perversely, incorrigibly attached to old norms. It was the same with Farenheit and Celsius. A temperature was not really a temperature unless it was translated back to the old Farenheit scale which had measured the heat and cold of his childhood. Was this bone-headed inflexibility of the brain a synecdoche for a much wider enslavement to past habits, emotions, and reactions? Was one always struggling, more or less unsuccessfully, to confront the new with the ineffective tools designed for the old? How many blunders of an individual or a nation were the result of such incongruity?

A jumbo jet came floating in towards the runway on Dominic's left as he drove along the open stretch of road approaching the airport. It was extraordinary how the great aircraft held itself aloft. It seemed, because of its huge size, to be moving impossibly slowly through the air. Was it Emma's flight? He tried to make out the insignia on the tail-plane but couldn't.

It took him quite some time to find a place to park the car. At the entrance to the airport building, people seethed as in a great ant-heap where the lines of input and output were disturbed and confused. Streams heading towards and into the building writhed through streams coming out. There was no system, no in-door, no out-door. Human emotion was the only controlling factor, the arbiter of progress in one direction or another.

Just outside the doors, Dominic came up against a family reunion which was blocking the way. Mother, father, brothers, and sisters caught at the returning son as if he might at any moment be dragged back away from them and they must physically hold him fast. His head was jolted as they planted kisses on his cheeks, left and right, again and again.

Those who could not get through had to wait, overwhelmed by the strength of the emotions they saw expressed before them. But as they waited, their nervousness mounted. Before long, one or two felt the surge of panic, and Dominic watched as their emotions grew even stronger than those of the re-uniting family. They forced their way through the group and broke up the exchange. He and the others followed in their wake. The stream in was re-established.

Once through the doors and into the airport building, he made his way to the balcony which overlooked the customs hall. Beams, piles of building materials, and rubble lay everywhere. The airport was undergoing major re-development, and it looked as if it had been doing so for a generation. Meanwhile millions of passengers passed through it, in and out of the great heart of Egypt. For almost an hour, Dominic looked down on the scene below with unflagging interest.

He knew at once when the London flight started to come through. There was something unmistakable about the combination of blotchy white skins, irregular features, and shabby or crudely coloured clothing, which set the British apart in the crowd of Egyptians and foreigners. He felt a strange mixture of sympathy and revulsion at their unbecoming appearance. They looked almost as dowdy as people from the Eastern block - marginally smarter than the Jugoslavs, but no match for the Italians who came in behind them.

Soon he picked out Emma. She at least looked charming, her hair auburn, falling in light waves, her pale denim-suit. She carried one reasonably sized case. The perennial traveller, he thought. He appreciated with a sudden, sharp emotion the unique connection between her, down there in the crowd of travellers, and himself, standing up on the balcony among so many strangers. It seemed almost miraculous. Only she mattered to him, and he to her. All the others had no significance. He watched her with delight. Of all those waiting, she would seek out only him. His breath came quickly.

Some moments later, she was through the customs check and walking with long, purposeful strides towards the exit. Her eyes moved from side to side in front of her and eventually rose to take in the balcony where he stood. He waved his hand at the same moment and she spotted him instantly. She waved back and her thin mouth stretched into a wide, brilliant smile.

Dominic felt lifted with a quiet joy. They would not clutch at each other like the Egyptians, but still, they loved each other in their own way. He turned to go back down to meet her.

Emma was cheerful and full of questions as they made their way to the car. Was the weather still warm? What was happening in Cairo? How was Rory? Did he have any holidays over the Christmas period?

He gave her the news as they drove back to his flat. At first he was disappointed by the triviality of her questions and comments. The issue of the abortion hung in the air between them, yet she seemed interested only in commonplaces, in gossip. But soon he responded to her and began to enjoy himself, describing Rory's new experiences with Egyptian girls, and speculating whether this would lead to a reformation of his character.

Then it was Alexandria. Was Lynda still at war with Lester? Had he been there since the summer? Had he seen her parents?

In his flat the conversation continued. They had wine to drink, and its effects and her cheerfulness gave him a resigned pleasure. If she was unconcerned with the past and what it meant to them, then he would not try to make her talk of it. She would do so when she chose.

They decided to go out to Groppi's in Heliopolis for some supper before going to bed. Emma took her case into the bedroom and then went into the bathroom. Dominic waited for her. She returned to the bedroom saying that she must change into something, but that she wouldn't be long.

He finished the wine, and felt the sting of his full bladder. He got up and went into the bathroom. He had already got his fly open and his penis out before he reached the lavatory bowl, and as soon as he could, he let his urine flow. Immediately he saw, floating in the water, staining it with strands of bright red, a bloody tampon. A quick revulsion passed through him. The rough, chalky texture of the object, rolling over in the stream of his piss, the spreading cloud of blood, the sweet, acrid smell that he breathed in, filled him with a cold nausea.

She had thrown it there. She had taken it out of her body, and just thrown it into the water. She had not even bothered to make sure she had flushed it down. The indifference of her act burned him. She couldn't have cared whether he saw it or not.

The wave of nausea gave way to a slow, hateful anger. He felt dismissed, crushed.

He came out of the bathroom and walked quickly in to confront her. She was sitting on the side of the bed, completely absorbed in putting on eye make-up. He stood rigid before her.

'So you had it.'

'What?' she asked casually, looking up at him at last.

He felt his anger flare at her. Didn't she have any inkling what he was talking about, of what he had been waiting for months to hear from her?

'The abortion,' he said in a rasping voice.

Now she recognised the restrained anger in him and for a moment her eyes widened in fear.

'Yes, I did have it.'

'Why didn't you tell me, instead of leaving that bloody tampon floating in the lavatory bowl?'

He wanted to bear his indignation down hard on her.

She fended it off.

'Oh, did I? Sorry. You didn't ask me. I thought you weren't interested. Yes, I had it. It was beastly.'

So it was answered, the question that had been in his mind so long. Now there could be no doubt.

'I was so frightened, as you can imagine,' she went on. 'I cried the whole day afterwards. And all the examinations, they were dreadful. I felt like a used object. And so cut off from everything. Outside, there was the real world, Oxford, lectures, my friends, all going about their normal lives, whereas there I was inside, going through a sort of self-sacrifice. Still, my gynaecologist was terribly sweet.'

Dominic sat down beside her on the bed as he listened. His anger was draining away. With a deadened detachment he noted that she did not say anything at all about her feelings for him or his feelings for the aborted child.

'If it hadn't been for him, I might have had a nervous break-down. I hadn't told anyone what I was doing, not even Heather, so he was the only person who could give me any sympathy, any warmth.'

'You didn't tell me,' Dominic said with bitter resignation.

'No, well you were so far away, and I didn't want to worry you. It was all my fault anyway.'

She gave him a small smile.

They got up and left for Groppi's. Over supper, Emma talked on. It seemed it was a great relief to her to be able to spill out all her experiences to him. He listened as sympathetically as his sense of his own rejection permitted him. He wished he had been there to help her through it, to be with her, but perhaps she would only have felt more uncomfortable, his emotions to contend with as well as her own.

Her gynaecologist had brought her a white rose the morning after the abortion, she said. He had held her hand and told her that everything was all right. When he had left her, she laid the rose beside her head on the pillow and started to cry. She cried a long, long time. She couldn't stop. She didn't want to stop. Afterwards, she felt much better, healed in her spirit, though she still hurt so much.

When they got into bed, Dominic saw her nakedness again with wonder. He had forgotten how her breasts hung from her body. He had forgotten how the smooth, thin flesh of her thighs ran away from the sandy bush of hair between them. He had forgotten the slope of her shoulders.

He began to kiss her lightly, as if re-claiming her, here and there on her body. She moved towards him. Eventually he brought his mouth up to hers as if to forge a new beginning and she kissed him with a force that brushed aside his tentativeness. It shocked him, it was so abstracted from all she had told him, all she had been through. Yet it roused a distant heat in him. His tongue once again felt the hollowness of her small mouth. Her arms tightened round his neck and her body pushed against him. He got up over her and hugged her with a force that made her gasp, and without touching her sex with his hands, he pushed in at her. He felt her legs yield open. She accepted him brusquely, pushing against him so that his entry was quick and deep. She moved vigorously, and his mounting to climax became a struggle of wills, of his rhythm against hers. He felt that he was drawing back into himself, into a blackness where the sexual conjunction with her was distant, peripheral. With a sudden breaking, his release came in sharp spasms, and the blackness consumed him, spreading through his body. Emma pushed and twisted under him, but he was hardly aware of her.

The next day after work, he drove back to his flat to pick her up and take her to the club, where they joined Rory for lunch. Emma and Rory greeted each other enthusiastically, and as Dominic looked on, he thought ruefully how uncomplicated simple friendly acquaintance was. It expected nothing, it required nothing. Whereas he always suffered his burdened expectation of Emma. He could not be just carefree with her as Rory was now.

They sat down, and drank beer in the warm, clear sunshine. The usual club characters were scattered round the pool - the squash coach sunning himself in an aura of perfect fitness, the old man who did yoga immobile on the grass in a lotus position, one of the young stars of the swimming team with superb shoulders.

'It's so nice to be back,' Emma was saying to Rory. 'I feel completely Egyptian again. Isn't that funny? Yesterday I was in the Bodleian. Today, I'm here.'

'The wonder, or rather the dislocation of the jet age,' Rory said. He took a cigarette and offered one to Emma. She took it. Dominic wanted to put in a critical remark but let it pass. He hated her half-hearted social smoking.

'One day Oxford,' Emma continued, drawing the smoke into her lungs - Dominic winced inwardly - 'the next day, Cairo. There just seems to be no connection.'

'I remember telling you that Oxford was a provincial backwater - one of the most beautiful in the world, of course - but a backwater.'

'Oh don't start on about Oxford again,' Emma pleaded. 'Tell me about Egypt instead. What have you been doing since I last saw you?'

'Meeting a lot of people. Reading. Writing.'

'Really? What are you writing?'

'It's a play I hope to put on next spring. The central character is a Palestinian girl who's raised in a refugee camp in Jordan or Lebanon and who is raped by an Arab businessman.'

'Heavens, that sounds rather ... I mean where are you going to put it on?'

'Not sure yet. Yes, it's outspoken, it hits hard. I see it as an allegory of the Palestinian people on many levels. That's what gives it its power, its significance.'

'Be careful,' Emma said, 'politics and art don't mix.'

'Nonsense,' Rory shot back. 'That's a standard cliché of Eng. Lit. Yeats's finest poetry came when he engaged with Ireland's war of independence. Tolstoy, the Russians, do you think they kept out of politics?'

'No, it's strange that,' Dominic said. 'Politics in a Russian novel seems perfectly acceptable. But in a modern one?'

'That's simply fashion, degenerate fashion.' Rory said. 'The worth of any culture depends on how far it treats the really important issues, individual or collective. Any culture that proscribes any issue is just corrupt.'

'But modern politics, in Britain anyway, is so boring,' Emma said flatly.

'That's because there aren't any modern politics in Britain - just two parties aping each other trying to keep the same show on the road: the mixed economy, the House of Lords, the monarchy, the rump of empire in Northern Ireland and elsewhere, the BBC-ITV duopoly, the whole works.'

'What do you want,' Dominic asked, 'the Tories to go fascist, Labour communist?'

'No, I don't want that. But there are certain things I do want that aren't just echoes of the old, outworn order. A solution in the Middle East for instance.'

'Is art the right medium to work in then?' Emma asked.

'It's the only medium I can work in right now. It may not be very effective. Who can say what effect Tolstoy's novels had on the disintegration of Czarist Russia? They had some effect, I'm sure of that.'

'That was Tolstoy,' Emma said, 'but in any case, politics in art bores me, whether it's all that stuff in "Anna Karenina" about reforming and educating the serfs, or these modern leftist playwrights.'

'But don't you see, Emma,' Rory said in tones that betrayed no self doubt or mockery, 'that's because you belong to a degenerate culture.'

'And what do you belong to,' Emma retorted, 'the new purifying commisariat of regenerated culture? Ugh!'

Dominic intervened quickly to end the exchange.

'It's funny, but I have to admit that since I've come to Egypt and become concerned with the situation here, I don't seem to be reading much fiction. Much more history. I don't quite know what that means. Probably that one has phases when one is primarily interested in oneself, and so in the modern psychological novel, and others when one is interested in the world around one, and how it came into being.'

'That's just it. Literature for the first, and history, non-fiction, non-literature, for the second,' Emma said.

'I disagree. I will not be proscribed. Anyway, enough of it.'

Rory leaned back in his chair in sudden irritation.

'Ah, the food,' Dominic announced.

They were served and began eating. The unfocusing effects of the beer turned their conversation to the weather in Britain before Emma's departure and other trivialities.

Over the following days, Dominic and Emma kept mostly to their own company. Emma did not wish to see more of Rory, because he was always 'going on about politics'.

For their lunch, Dominic usually make salads or omelettes; for dinner they went out to eat in one of the restaurants on the banks of the Nile. In the afternoons they had siestas listening to music.

They made love once or twice each day. Though the fears of not responding to her that had haunted him at the beginning of their relationship had vanished, Dominic now felt a nagging detachment from her, a sense of anti-climax which had become ingrained. She responded as much and as intently as ever, as if with real passion, but he observed it from a distance. It did not excite him, it did not move him.

The second afternoon as they lay together, their bodies sticking skin to skin with the drying sweat of sexual exertion, Emma bean talking about her last few weeks at Oxford.

'I got terribly depressed. Everything seemed so empty. It was the after-effects of the abortion of course. I just couldn't concentrate on anything. Work got me down. I thought maybe I should go and see a psychiatrist.'

'Really? Was it that bad?'

He felt for the first time a real sympathy for her.

'It was like being in some kind of vacuum. I wanted to break out, to do something - anything. But I didn't know what. I was awfully tense.'

'Couldn't you talk to anyone?'

'No, anyone I could have talked to know my parents. So, well, Heather, Clare, any of my really close friends, every time I wanted to tell them, I couldn't. I had this block - Mum and Dad must never find out.'

'But don't you think they realised you were pregnant before you went back in September?'

'They might have. Mum might have. One morning when I was looking green, she asked me straight out.'

'And what did you say?'

'I said "of course not, Mummy". I think she believed me.'

Dominic wondered at what must have been the hard, bare-faced strength of her lying. Hadn't she given herself away with a flicker of the eyes, an infinitesimal hesitation? Probably not.

'You were afraid your girlfriends wouldn't be as good at lying as you are?'

'I couldn't be absolutely certain of them, so I didn't tell them. They wouldn't have been able to help me anyway. They wouldn't have understood. That was the worst part, feeling that no-one had had a similar experience, that I was so utterly alone. And then wondering if I could be desirable, if men could still want me after it.'

'Oh?'

He felt the skin contract on his cheeks.

'Anyway I slept with two men on the play to prove that to myself.'

'What play?'

'Didn't I tell you? I helped with the props on the college play. Robin and John were on it as well.'

'Convenient,' Dominic said. The rancour was coming out.

'Well, they seemed happy enough to sleep with me. Of course, it wasn't much good - either time - but still it was reassuring.'

'You mean you just had one fuck with each?'

'There's no need to be crude. I suppose they realised I was in a pretty disturbed state. So they shied away. Still, it reassured me. I recovered my confidence a bit.'

'I'm so glad.'

'Oh, don't be stupid. You're not jealous are you? For heaven's sake, it was nothing.'

Dominic didn't reply. He sat up and stared ahead.

'I suppose you've had no-one since I left?'

'As a matter of fact, I haven't,' he replied, feeling that his truthfulness added to his humiliation.

He got up and left her.

Emma returned to Alexandria soon after. Dominic put her on the train in Ramses Station. They agreed that he would visit her the weekend following the next. He would stay as before with Lynda and Charles.

He drove back from the station to the club and had a game

of tennis with one of the young coaches. Later in the evening, as he drank coffee after supper in his apartment, he felt the echoing strangeness of being alone after the three days with Emma. He was aware that in that time something had become desiccated in his feelings for her. She had changed, a poignancy had gone from her. The fact that she was so much younger than he was had lost its significance. His wonder at her youthfulness was dead. Of course they were no longer joined in the adventure of her womb. That was now ash, ash of her will and her decision.

He still thought of himself and her as being a couple, but their relationship was now ordinary, a matter more of usage than of inspiration. He gained a satisfaction in thinking of her in this new way, in questioning whether she could ever really move him deeply again. She had lost her fragile mystery and its power over him.

Twenty

Some days later, Dominic went to lunch at the house of Mark Darlington-Smith, the British consul. His cheerful, slightly ungainly wife opened the door and welcomed him.

'Hello, Agnes,' he greeted her. 'I hope I'm not late. One forgets how long it takes to get from Heliopolis into town in the rush hour.'

'No, not at all. Do come in. Go and join Mark and the others in the sitting room. I've got to pop into the kitchen and check on things.'

He did. It was a small party. He noticed at once Annabel, sitting next to Mark, in a frock which reminded him of London summers and which went perfectly with her flaxen hair. He shook hands with Mark and smiled and said hello to Annabel.

'You've met Ed Small?' Mark asked. He pointed him toward a dyspeptic-looking sixty-year-old in a beige safari suit.

'Briefly, yes. How are you?'

He shook hands with the man and noticed that when he said something, the movements of his mouth seemed to resonate in small vibrations of the sagging cheeks and the pouches under his eyes.

'And his wife Cynthia?'

'How do you do.'

'And Jim and Martha of course.'

Dominic greeted Mark's opposite number at the American Embassy and his wife with a 'hi' and sat down.

'So, all on your own again, Dominic? Agnes tells me that Emma has flown.'

'Yes, she has, I'm afraid. Obviously she had to go on to Alex before too long.'

'Who's Emma?' Annabel asked with the forthright manner that Dominic had noticed in her before.

'Ah,' replied Mark, 'she is the cause of Dominic's new reputation as a cradle snatcher.'

Dominic smiled first at Mark, then at Annabel.

'Oh?' Annabel said. 'How old is she then?'

'Nineteen, I believe,' Dominic replied.

'That's it,' Ed put in, 'get 'em young.'

It looked as if he had followed his own advice - Cynthia was a good ten years younger than he was.

They all laughed, including Dominic.

'I'm doing my best,' he said.

'Wow, that reminds me of the time we crashed the state boundary, Martha. Remember?' Jim began. 'I was just out of high school, and Martha was underage. I was trying to get her out of earshot of her folks. We were heading for a ski resort up in Maine. Then I just flashed on it as we drew up to a road check. Wow - this is a federal offence, abducting a minor.'

'Yes, and do you know what he told the cops?' Martha exclaimed. 'That I was his sister. His sister, for God's sake.'

She gave a guttural laugh. Jim looked discomfited.

'Hell, I had to play it safe. Your folks thought we were twenty miles down the road at the Freemans.'

'Yes, well it was OK. The guy let us through. Otherwise he might have busted us for incest!'

'That would have been tricky,' Mark said, tongue literally in cheek.

Ed broke in.

'Ach, America is still a puritan country. People are so damned religious there. I read recently, I can't remember where, that thirty-seven per cent of Americans still believe in hell.'

'And the devil presumably,' Dominic added.

'Yes. And of course, far more of them believe in heaven. That's American optimism for you,' Ed chortled, and his face shook with an afterwave.

'What you guys forget,' Jim said, 'is that religion is what a lot of America was originally about. The Pilgrim Fathers and all that.'

'Yes, but at least you Americans managed to get the principle of the separation of church and state into the constitution,' Annabel said. 'Whereas in Islam, there's no distinction.'

'Right,' Jim agreed, 'and it's going to block their progress all along the line.'

'Surely that's more in theory than in practice,' Mark said.

'No way,' Martha came in emphatically. 'It's down in the book. God's word, that's it.'

'Yes, yes, I know that,' Mark replied, 'but when it comes to running an actual Islamic country, like Egypt for example, quite obviously the laws now in force are nowhere near the same as those in the book.'

'Maybe,' Jim said, 'but more and more Egyptians think that they should be.'

'Then the problem lies,' Dominic said, 'not so much in the nature of the religion, but in how religious, I mean how obedient, the adherents are. All religions are pretty much as bad, or as good, as each other.'

A small change in the lines of expression on the faces of Jim and Martha showed that this remark produced first shock, then hostility.

'I disagree,' Martha said. 'There's a fundamental difference between a religion which says this is the actual word of God, like Islam, and ours which describes Christ's life and teachings.'

'Aren't you forgetting that Christ is meant to be God?' Dominic asked. 'Therefore Christ's words are the words of God.'

He was warming to the argument and the issue. His opponents seemed to be victims of an unconscious assumption that Christianity was indubitably better than Islam.

'But our word of God never gave inferior status to women,' Martha said, as if her point was a trump - unanswerable.

'Wait a minute,' Dominic said. 'What about the refusal of the Catholic and Anglican churches to allow women to be priests? That's allotting them a pretty obviously inferior status.'

A short silence followed this remark.

'You have a point there,' Jim said. 'We certainly disagree with the Holy Father on that issue.'

'There you are then.' Dominic replied with as much good grace as he could. 'All religions have their absurdities. What about the Christian business of loving your enemy? Nobody takes that seriously. What about the Christian idea that woman is the source of sexual iniquity? So you burn witches - about four million of them by current estimates.'

'Christ never advocated burning anyone,' Martha objected.

'No, he didn't, but Christians did,' Mark said.

'Exactly,' Dominic continued, 'it's not what the religion actually says that counts, it's what is done in its name.'

'I think you're right,' Mark agreed, as Agnes came in and

joined him on the sofa. 'What I find interesting - we were talking about it the other day - is the degree of theological abstraction, sophistication really, in Islam, compared to Christianity.'

'What do you mean?' Jim asked guardedly.

'Well, whether it is more advanced to say -Here is the word of God given to me in a vision, or to say - Here is the son of God walking amongst us. I think the former more sophisticated myself.'

'Why is that?' Jim asked.

'Well, you can see the development of theology as a movement towards abstraction. First man worships things, you know, the sun, statues, then the man-God of Christianity, then the message of God.'

'Yes, it struck us the other day, driving past Khan Khalili,' Agnes said, 'where all the donkey traffic is, that two thousand years ago a poor man on just such a donkey appeared, and people started believing he was God. It's absolutely astonishing to think about, when you look at any man on a donkey in Khan Khalili today.'

As they went to the table to eat, Annabel said:

'According to your theory Mark, Buddhism should be the most advanced religion. I don't know much about it, but isn't it a sort of very abstract, very spiritual belief? Nothing idolatrous, or 'our God is better than your God' about it. In fact, no God at all.'

'I believe you're right. I'll have to confirm that when I'm posted to New Delhi.'

They sat down and began the meal with a discussion on where Mark and Jim had already served, and where they would like to go next. The food was tolerably bad. Dominic wondered how it was that Agnes, after exposure to the richness of Middle

Eastern cooking, could impose her bland and completely uninspiring English tastes in her own kitchen. Yet it was so. The
meal was without any excitement, and ended with a kind of
half-hearted chocolate eclair. Dominic left the table bored and
with his hunger hardly satisfied.

Back in the sitting room for coffee, he sat next to Annabel.
The pleasure that the beauty of her blue eyes, fresh complexion,
and strongly bowed mouth give him eased his disappointment
with the table.

'What news of Rory?' she asked him.

'I haven't seen him for a few days. Emma found him a little
hard to take. His political sermonising put her off.'

'He is very politically minded, isn't he? I wonder why he
didn't go in for journalism, instead of technical development or
whatever it is you're in.'

'I shouldn't imagine many papers would be prepared to
print his views.'

'Too much bias on the Middle East, you think?'

'Heavens, he seems biassed about almost everything. He
rails against the hallowed balance of the British media - says
it's a device to eliminate uncomfortable dissension from the de-
bate.'

'Odd, isn't it? We take it for granted, moderation, balance.
And then we come across someone like him who finds it objec-
tionable and calls it all into question.'

'He is a very rebellious character. And he has extraordinary
ideas on history, on the Battle of Britain, for example.'

'What does he say about the Battle of Britain?'

'More or less that Churchill decided to use civilians as fodder for German bombs.'

'That's a horrible idea. But how?'

'As a decoy - he provoked the Germans into bombing civilians instead of airfields.'

'How did he do that?'

'By bombing their civilians.'

'Daddy was in bomber command. He never told me anything like that. I'll write and ask him about it.'

'Do. That would be interesting. Anyway, that's one of Rory's theories.'

'He is unusual. Does he live in Heliopolis too?'

'You haven't seen his place?'

She gave a little shake to her head.

'It's almost a museum piece. Really extraordinary. You know this mock Louis Quatorze style that's so popular here in Egypt? Well, he's got an apartment almost at the top of a huge block, built, I should think, in the last ten years, and it's absolutely full of the stuff. It's wildly incongruous.'

'With chandeliers?'

'Enormous ones. And all around, Rory's domestic chaos - books, papers, unemptied ashtrays, bottles, general squalor.'

They were interrupted.

'We're thinking of going to the Guizera for a swim,' Mark said. 'Would you like to come Annabel, Dominic?'

'I'd love to,' Annabel replied, and Dominic said that he would go too. He realised that he wanted to see Annabel's plump Saxon body in a swim suit.

Mark asked Ed and Cynthia if they were interested.

'Good God, no!' Ed exploded and his sagging cheeks shook with the words. 'I'm off for my siesta. Exercise at this hour, baking in the sun? Not on you life.'

They all prepared to leave.

Dominic was not disappointed with Annabel's body. She

wore a bikini. Her bottom was round and jolly, her breasts high, ample. She had delicate wisps of blond hair under her arms, unshaven in the French manner. He speculated that she was free, and thought that, but for being with Emma, he would have pursued her. He watched her swimming up and down with a small sense of regret. She moved with strong, confident strokes, and her blond hair streamed behind her. Sodden, it had lost its curling waves, and was now languorous, a golden echo of the ripples that flowed over her body.

When Dominic next saw Annabel, their roles were reversed. He was the doer, she the spectator.

'I thought it must be you,' she said.

He straightened up from under the bonnet of his car.

'Hello, Annabel, Eh, a spot of bother - my motor's misbehaving.'

The forced style of his words made him feel more uncomfortable, though he used it to try to make light of his predicament. He was dishevelled and perspiring. But she was all sympathy.

'Oh dear, I hope it's not serious. What's wrong?'

Disarmed, he felt easier and explained.

'The engine has overheated. I should have stopped earlier, but I was hoping to get home. The water pump seals have gone. Water's been pouring out. And stupidly, I haven't got a spare can in the boot. One should always carry water in hot climates.'

Perspiration ran down his nose and fell off in drops.

'I'm afraid I'll have to abandon ship,' he said, as he wiped his forefinger across his brow and flicked the sweat away.

'Will you really?'

Dominic looked at her through the painful glare. In her cotton dress with its bow front and flowery pattern, he felt she could be on the way to a university regatta in England.

'Oh, it's all right. I'll get Rory to come down with me later this afternoon when it's cooler and tow me back to Heliopolis.'

'Have you got a tow rope then?'

'Yep, that is something I do carry.'

'Well, I'll tow you. I've got the agency car for the day. It's that Fiat over there, do you see?'

'No, no, don't bother Annabel. Really, we can do it later.'

For some reason that he didn't have time to analyse, he was reluctant to receive assistance from this sympathetic and forthright girl.

'Nonsense. Get out the rope and fix it on. I'll reverse back to you. Won't be a moment.'

She walked off to her car. Dominic noticed the strong curves of her calf muscles as she did so. They were covered with fine, golden hairs which gleamed in the sunlight. He blinked the stinging sweat from his eyes, and then leaned into the car and got the keys out of the ignition. He opened the boot and extracted the tow rope from the spare wheel well.

A few minutes later, after he had asked, for the second time -Are you sure you want to take all this trouble? - and Annabel had shot back -Of course, do let's get on with it, the two cars were firmly attached. With a wave of her hand, she got into the Fiat and started the engine. She let the clutch out rather smartly and both cars lurched forward. Dominic feared for the rope, but no, it held. They were under way. Again she waved at him, and he waved back, though there was something about her vigour that he found slightly unnerving. Still, she was getting him home, out of the dusty inferno of the midday Cairo rush hour. They crawled past the City of the Dead on the ring route out to Heliopolis.

When they were in Dominic's flat after the successful completion of the towing operation, he smiled at her broadly, with a quick realisation that his sense of embarrassment at receiving her help had been absurd.

'Well, Annabel, what will you have? The reward for the pilot - a large rum on the rocks?'

'No thanks, I've never liked rum. We're not a naval family. Give me,' she smiled back as broadly, 'a long, long gin and tonic, and at least three slices of lemon.'

'Right you are. Beer for me - rehydration essential.'

He went to the kitchen and returned with the drinks. He drank off his beer almost at one draught, the sharp stinging in his throat giving him keen pleasure. Annabel drank more slowly.

'What bliss,' she said. 'I finished my bottle of duty-free gin ages ago. I never knew I had such a craving for the stuff. Now I only get it when I visit diplomats and people like you who can use the tax-free shop.'

'Can't you?'

'No, for some reason, the agency feels that tax-free booze and family planning should not go together, even where personnel are concerned. Ridiculous idea, don't you think?'

'Oh, it's probably the Egyptian government who haven't given them permission. They didn't pay the necessary bakhshish to the official concerned. That's where the problem is.'

'You could be right. I do wish they would pay up.'

She giggled and drank.

'I'll just go in and wash up a bit,' Dominic said, ' and then I'll take you to lunch at the club. OK?'

'That would be lovely.'

As he scrubbed the oil and dirt from his nails in the bathroom, he was excited at the thought of Annabel sitting there in her flowery summer dress on his sofa in the next room, waiting for him to rejoin her. With the light, floating feeling in his head from the cold beer, he now thought that an approach to her would be so simple, so straightforward. That bluntness of hers that he had first found too direct, now seemed only to make their growing intimacy freer of obstacles.

'I see you're fond of Braque,' she called in to him.

'Yes, that's a copy of one in the Tate that an American friend did for me. Do you like it?'

'Yes, I do quite. But why didn't he copy a Picasso? I'd have much preferred a Picasso.'

'No, Picasso's just a dabbler. Braque is the real painter's painter."

'Phoey!' he heard her retort.

They had lunch on the club terrace. Dominic talked about his car.

'God knows if I'll be able to fix it. There's no MG garage here, of course.'

'Isn't there?' Annabel asked between mouthfuls. She ate heartily.

'No usual British incompetence,' Dominic answered, throwing his hands up. 'Here we are in an ex-British protectorate, and who has cornered the car market? Fiat, with the Germans taking what's left. It really makes me sad. But it's typical of the British - our old aristocratic values still dominate. Even in the empire, it was infra-dig to be in trade, and now most of the imperial markets seem to have slipped away. When did you last see a British car in Cairo?'

'There are hardly any, it's true.'

'Right. So I'll have to send all the way back to England to

get a new water pump. Imagine - for an MG. When we were running things out here, the place should have been crawling with them.'

'Sell it and buy a Fiat.'

'I suppose I should. But I have this curious sense of loyalty. I'll keep her, even though she's years out of date in terms of engineering.'

'Nonsense,' interrupted Annabel, 'you'll keep *her* for one reason only, to keep up your dashing image.'

He could not deny the truth of this and coloured. He was discomfited that she should point out this more venal motive for owning a sports car.

'You may be right,' he offered with a forced smile.

'Of course,' she insisted. 'You'd be lost without it. How could you pick up young girls like...what's her name?'

'Emma.'

'Emma, yes. It's extraordinary the weakness young girls have for noisy, low-slung cars like yours.'

'I hope that's not all she sees in me.'

'Perhaps not. But you've only got yourself to blame if you can't get your car repaired, if you're the victim of British commercial incompetence, as you put it.'

He was silenced by her clear-sighted taunt.

'MG know your weakness, and now they've got you hooked.'

'I must admit, it is a bit like a drug. Just the name MG still has an extraordinary hold over the imagination. What do you think it is - good advertising?'

'Not really - just snobbery, elitism. Like that appalling habit of spending hundreds of pounds on getting a special number plate. It makes me seethe. If people paid that money to Oxfam for example, think of the good they could do. But no, they spend it on a silly number. And the Queen herself is to blame, sitting on top of the pile with her ER II Rolls Royce. It's so senseless, and so vulgar.'

'Good Lord, Annabel, you don't spare any of us. You're very severe, you know,' Dominic said with admiration as well as discomfort.

'Certainly,' she replied.

He realised that this exposition of his vanity meant that he stood lower in her esteem than he had hoped. His fantasy of making an easy pass at her receded. As if reading these thoughts and pursuing her own in a parallel fashion, she suddenly said:

'Why don't you take me round to visit that friend of yours, Rory? You told me he lives nearby.'

He forced himself to reply:

'Why, of course. Yes, just down by the Roxy roundabout,' in a voice that he hoped did not betray his reflex of jealousy. He waved for the bill.

When they stood later outside the front door of Rory's apartment, Dominic distinctly heard a woman speaking in Arabic somewhere inside. He glanced down at Annabel, but she was impassive. Whether she had heard the voice or not, she gave no sign. After a long delay, the door opened. Rory stood in a creased galabiya and looked at them with an expression of unconcealed lassitude.

'Hello, Rory,' Dominic said as he ushered Annabel in. 'Hope we're not disturbing you. Here's Annabel. We wondered if you'd be good enough to give us coffee.'

Rory looked from him to Annabel and a flicker of animation passed over his features.

'Sure, come in. Annabel, yes, how are you? Sit down.'

He cleared a pile of old newspapers and numerous books off a sofa.

'What a God awful day,' he exhaled, his eyes staring out in front of him. 'I spent four hours at the Faculty of Science in Ain Shams this morning, trying to get this Assiut project off the ground. Hopeless. I wish now I hadn't suggested it in the first place. The Egyptians are quite clearly going to apply the donkey principle with a vengeance.'

'I believe I did warn you,' Dominic said.

'Yes, well, it's my own damn fault.'

'What's the donkey principle?' Annabel asked.

'You pile the work on the donkey, the one who's fool enough to do it. The corollary is, never volunteer.'

'Well, I've had a bad day too,' Dominic said. 'The car's out of action. And I hoped to go to Alex this weekend.'

'That's all right. I'm going down with Ali on Saturday. I can give you a lift. But we're heading off into the delta somewhere next day, so you'll have to make your own way back.'

'That will be OK. Thanks.'

A girl came into the room, a plump Egyptian with dark Nubian skin and a shy manner.

'Nemat, this is Dominic and Annabel.'

Rory pronounced each name slowly and pointed. Nemat smiled broadly and sat down. She was beautiful.

'She doesn't speak any English,' Rory said quickly. 'So, coffee? Or a drink?'

'Coffee will do fine,' Annabel replied.

'Yes, coffee. We've just had lunch,' Dominic added.

Rory spoke to Nemat in rapid Arabic and she got up and went out to the kitchen.

'That was pretty fluent,' Dominic remarked.

'Can I help her?' Annabel asked.

'No, stay where you are. Nemat's a good girl - she thrives on serving me. Can't keep her out of the kitchen. Or out of my bed, for that matter. But that's another story.'

He stubbed out a cigarette.

'What have you been doing since I last saw you?' he asked Annabel.

'More of the same - visits to family planning centres.'

'You've got your work cut out there.'

They talked about the demographic growth in Egypt. Nemat brought in four cups of Turkish coffee, piping hot. They sipped them slowly.

'I wish you could have a chat with Nemat about family planing,' Rory said. 'Then all those bed sessions I mentioned might go a bit further.'

Annabel was quite unembarrassed. She laughed.

'We only talk to married women.'

'Too bad.'

Later, Annabel said she must leave and got up abruptly. Dominic got up too. She drove him back to his flat. They exchanged a few remarks. Annabel did not mention Rory or Nemat. As he got out of her car, he thanked her again for towing his.

'Not at all. Thank you for lunch. Bye, bye. See you soon,' she said as she drove off. Dominic wondered if in fact she would.

Twenty-One

At a little after nine o'clock on the following Saturday morning, Rory pulled up outside Dominic's apartment building. In Egyptian style he blared the horn to announce his arrival. Dominic leaned out over his front balcony to check who it was, and went down quickly to the car.

'Sorry if we're a bit early,' Rory said as Dominic got into the car. 'I wanted to clear town before the traffic builds up.'

'No, I was ready. Hello. Ali.'

'Hello, how are you?'

Ali's English phrase-book greeting was accompanied by a warm smile that made it more eloquent than any more sophisticated formula. That was one of the lessons Egypt had taught Dominic - human communication, if it had enough heart, could easily jump the conventional barriers of language, class, or background.

They pulled out into Sharia Aguza and headed in a wide arc up the Nile valley and round the enormous spread of old Cairo towards the Pyramids. They would then swing north-west onto the desert road to Alexandria.

As they passed the City of the Dead, the brilliant morning light etched the domes and minarets of the Mamlouk mausoleums, showing up in sharp relief intricate Islamic patterns of carved stone. A great dome, beige brown, its surface an endless interweaving of lines which jumped from one Gestalt form to another, caught Dominic's eye.

'That's particularly fine, that one,' he said pointing, and touched Ali's shoulder.

'That is the tomb of Sultan Quait Bey,' the Egyptian replied, pronouncing the 'b' of tomb so that the word had a more morbid ring. 'It is very big tomb. Many people are living in it.'

'Living in it? Really?'

'Yes, all this you see, the City of the Dead, is full of poor people. They have nowhere else to live, so they come here.'

'Evidently it's not a city of the dead anymore,' Rory said. 'Some of these tombs are huge buildings. The living have reclaimed them.'

Now they wound up the ascent to the Citadel, where Saladin's walls still stood. The Moquattam Hills came up on their left, a sharp escarpment which marked the eastern edge of the Nile valley. As they turned west, the slender minarets of the Mohammed Ali Mosque cleared the profile of the fort and soared upwards, an exotic tribute to the glory of Ottoman architecture.

Soon the bustling life of Khan Khalili, the old medina, was all around them. Blowing his horn incessantly, Rory rushed through the traffic with the verve of a long-time Cairo resident. Dominic was in the back, and felt his right foot pressing again and again on the floor. Rory had the unnerving habit of leaving his braking to the very last split second. Why couldn't he do it sooner?

Ali in front seemed completely resigned to his style of driving and turned on the car radio. The soft, lilting voice of Abdulhalim Hafez filled the car and blotted out the cacophony from the street. Ali began to wave his head slightly from side to side, and joined in with a high falsetto, following the elaborate curves of the melody almost exactly. Each verse ended with one word, repeated again and again: abadan.

'What's that word, Ali, abadan?' Dominic asked.

'It means never. He is singing for his son. The mother left them. It is very sad song.'

Soon they crossed the river and headed out on the Guiza Road. The nightclubs massed on each side, an endless ribbon development witnessing the self-indulgence of the rich. How did they all find customers, Dominic wondered? Weren't there far too many? Certainly they completely destroyed the approaching view of the Sphinx and the Pyramids, that seemed to huddle behind neon signs and concrete buildings at the end of the road like an abandoned film set. To appreciate these monuments now, one had to approach them from the desert, where their magnificent, pure forms rose uncluttered from the sand as in the time of their creators.

The red Fiat forked right onto the desert road, and they were soon among a cluster of stony hills. The pyramids were now hidden from view behind them. Ahead lay miles and miles of desert.

Some time later, Ali pointed out over to the right, where a large entrance arch straddled a road that had left the main road a few minutes before. The Egyptian flag with its bands of red, white and black, and its central eagle, flew nearby.

'That is an air force base,' Ali told them. 'You see? It is now important. They are repairing it. Before, the bases on the side of Israel were important, on the east side. Now it is the west side, facing Libya.'

'So much for Arab brotherhood, Arab solidarity,' Rory said.

'We will never have Arab unity. When one Arab is supported by America, the other is supported by Russia. The superpowers play with us like, you know, pieces in a chess game.'

'And now it's Egypt's turn to be played with by the Americans.'

'Yes, so the Russians are playing with the Libyans. Now they are getting the MIGs and the tanks that we need so much after the war.'

'Aren't you getting what you need from the Americans?'

'We are getting only promises. Sadat said "go" to the Russians, and then fought the war with the Russian weapons. Now they send no more spare parts. We must ask for spare parts from the Chinese.'

'When you think of it,' Dominic said, 'Sadat took an enormous risk, waging a war just after severing relations with his main arms supplier.'

'He didn't exactly sever relations,' Rory said, 'he kicked out the personnel, the advisers, so that he could wage the war. If they had stayed, they'd never have allowed it.'

'Possibly, but it confirms the theory of a strictly limited war, doesn't it?'

'Yes, it does. So where does the problem of new arms supplies leave you now, Ali?'

'We are very weak. We are afraid that Sadat will do more and more to please the Americans, so that we can get new American planes.'

'Shit!' Rory said abruptly. 'Look, a police check.'

Ahead of them on the road a solitary policeman stood with his hand up.

'You talk to him, Ali. I haven't got a proper registration book for the car, just a bit of paper from the Alex customs. It's months out of date. Here.'

He reached into the glove compartment and handed Ali

some pieces of paper and his license and passport. They drew up alongside the policeman. He was a fat figure in an ill-fitting uniform, sweating in the glaring desert heat, his neck unbuttoned. Ali greeted him and they conversed amicably. The pieces of paper were handed over one by one. Gradually the policeman's remarks became more hesitant and subdued. Ali's, in contrast, became longer and more emphatic, and his hands came into action as if their gestures were indispensable in conveying the necessary information. As the exchange went on, Rory began to bite his finger-nails nervously.

'I know the feeling,' Dominic sympathised. 'Why is it so damned difficult to keep one's car papers in order?'

'Uh, uh, this looks bad,' Rory said quietly.

Ali got out of the car as the policeman went to the front and back to check the number plates. He came round to Rory's window and delivered a remark in Arabic with an impassive, fatigued air. Rory replied haltingly:

'I'm sorry, I don't understand.'

The policeman shrugged and started walking towards a blockhouse, the only building in sight, a short distance from the road. Ali followed him, and after some paces, they stopped and a new exchange began.

'We've had it. He said something about the irregularities in the papers - must see his superior about it.'

But a few minutes later, Ali had left the policeman and was walking back to the car. He was smiling broadly.

'OK, we can go,' he said as he got in.

'Great,' Rory shouted, putting the car in gear and moving off. 'How did you do it?'

'The usual way -bakhshish. I gave him two pounds.'

'Good man! What was the trouble?'

'He wanted to report you to the commander. So I thought it would be better to offer him a bribe before he did that.'

'Did he drop any hints?'

'What?'

'Did he suggest it?'

'No, I just said to him -But officer, we are willing to make a contribution.'

Rory exploded in laughter.

'Make a contribution - that's good.'

'You must be diplomatic,' Ali explained. 'As I gave him the money, I said -For the children.'

Rory chortled.

'You must teach me those phrases, Ali.'

They broke their journey for lunch at the Halfway Hotel, and in the middle of the afternoon they arrived outside Charles and Lynda's apartment building in Sharia Patrice Lumumba. Rory was staying the night with some cousins of Ali in downtown Alexandria, so Dominic went up in the lift alone.

Charles let him in. His melancholy face brightened for a moment as he greeted Dominic, but quickly lapsed back.

'Hello, Charles, I expected to see Ahmed. Your car wasn't outside.'

They walked into the long salon where shafts of yellowing sunlight slanted in.

'Lynda took it. She's gone to Mamoura for the day. Well, how is Cairo?'

'Good, good. It's cooler now - really splendid for tennis.'

They sat down. Dominic noticed a detective novel open on the sofa. He picked it up and looked at it absentmindedly. Surely Charles wasn't reading this rubbish?

'Cairo's fine,' he went on, ' but of course there's a snag.

Emma's down here.'

'I saw her yesterday, at the Consulate Christmas party. She said you'd be coming later this evening.'

'We left earlier than planned.'

'She looked rather drawn, I thought. She seems to have lost weight.'

'Oh?' Dominic said, feeling a prickling of discomfort. Was she showing physical signs of the ordeal of her abortion that he had not detected?

'Probably the college food,' he went on, and to change the subject, asked Charles if there was any Alex news.

'Nothing worth talking about,' the other replied in a flat voice that sounded bitter. He said nothing further and they fell into silence. After a pause, Dominic said: 'Well, I'll ring Emma,' though, as he stood up, he felt a curious reluctance to do so. Being in this flat, as he had been last summer, with Emma living at her parents, suddenly seemed tiresomely repetitive. It was as if they were having to start over again.

The feeling was reinforced when her mother answered the phone and told him that Emma had gone to the beach for the afternoon.

'She thought I'd be coming later,' he said. 'The service is at what, six o'clock?'

'Yes, that's right, but you'd better be there earlier, to get a good view. It'll probably be quite full. Emma would be so disappointed if you were miles away at the back. She's been practising like mad all week.'

'All right, I'll be early,' he said with a small laugh. 'Are you in the choir too?'

'Good heavens, no. Emma is the only musical talent in the family.'

'I'll see you in church then, Maree. Some time before six.'

'Fine. I'll tell Emma.'

Between the telephone call and the carol service, Dominic's feelings wavered between two impulses: the first to locate the warmth that seeing Emma again should bring him, the second a recoil that came from a sense of purposelessness when he thought of their affair. The enormous dimension that their future together had held during those weeks before her abortion was now empty. The few days she had spent with him in Cairo had added nothing, save for the sense that his need for her and his search for some new growth between them were incongruous. For he could find no similar need or search in her. At the beginning, because she had been so young, he had felt that she was unreachable, delicate, profound. Now he knew more of her - the decisiveness of her will, and the concentration on herself that took no cognizance of his feelings. The prospect of contending with these drained his emotions.

That evening he went into the Anglican church in Alexandria in a mood of uncertainty. Finding a place among the congregation, which could have been that of any church in England save for the odd, distinctly American family, he sat down and then looked towards the choir. He saw Emma at once in the front row on the left, and was not prepared for the sharp effect the sight of her had on him. She looked so small and tender, sitting there in her blue velvet dress, her hair pulled back by combs from her cheeks. She was almost like a schoolgirl. And he was coming to hear her sing. The school concerts of his own youth echoed in his mind. Now he was the visitor, the intruder, from outside.

The impression grew stronger when the service began. The vicar walked in with an arch solemnity, and his voice carried such a strong colouring of ecclesiastical pomposity that Dominic had to restrain a laugh of ridicule which tugged at his stomach. He feared that the man's pretentiousness would spoil whatever nostalgic pleasure the Christmas carols would give him.

Two small girls with shining blond hair and with lighted candles in their hands had been called up to the altar. The vicar instructed them to light two larger candles on either side of the rails, and then two that stood in front of the rows of pews, and finally two on each side of the door at the back of the church.

The little figures walked past Dominic with their eyes firmly fixed on the flames flickering close to their faces. It was touching - if a bit surprising in an Anglican service.

Candles? As if sensing that this high church style might provoke a reaction in the congregation, the vicar intoned:

'These candles symbolise our joy at this Christmas time. I hope their light will fall on you all as did the light of the angels who came to announce the birth of the little babe Jesus.'

Now his chin fell towards his chest.

'But these are real flames, so we must take care with all these young ones in our midst. You will see, we have placed a bucket of sand just here,' - he pointed to near the pulpit, - 'and another back there, near the church door, should any emergency arise.'

His face came up abruptly, and he surveyed them with a fixed smile.

Dominic strained to look over the heads and sure enough, there were the buckets of sand. His stomach again began to quake. That was the trouble with high church frolics, Anglicans had so little experience of them. With this absurd fire drill, the vicar had rendered the whole thing ludicrous. But looking at the children's faces, Dominic saw that for them at least, it worked.

The carol singing began, and in the beauty and associations of the familiar melodies, he was slowly drawn into the communal celebration.

Emma's solo was the second verse of "Once in royal David's city". Her small voice with its irregular vibrato came down the church to him and he listened with strained attention. She sounded at once distant and intimate. The choir joined her and then the whole congregation. Dominic sang strongly, feeling for her a mixture of tenderness and admiration.

They all sat down for the next lesson and he stared at her. Though her face was turned in his direction, she gave him no sign of recognition.

Outside the church he saw Dick and Maree and went over to join them.

'She *was* good, wasn't she, Dominic?' Maree said at once, laying a hand on his arm, unashamedly the proud mother.

'Yes, she was,' he said, but he thought her over-indulgent and added:

"A most accomplished young lady, I must say,' with an exaggerated accent and mock gravity. Maree seemed not to notice this unpleasantness, and he immediately regretted it.

'Of course, "Once in royal David's city" is one of my real favourites,' she continued. 'It brought me right back to our little church in Bluewater, North Dakota.'

This reminder that Maree was American made him reflect that Emma seemed so completely English - there was nothing of the enthusiasm and openness of the mother in her.

For some moments they stood among the crowd in a silence he found irritating. He could think of nothing to say to break it. Maree and Dick exchanged short greetings with people who passed near. The vicar hovered about the church door shaking hands. An air of respectable and cohesive boredom enfolded them. Beyond the small garden surrounding the church,

Dominic could see the streaming cars and metro trains of the oblivious Alexandrian night - this city that had known so many religions.

Suddenly he felt an arm slip round his and he looked down. Emma was at his side and greeted him. He bent to kiss her. She didn't have her glasses on, and he saw that her eyes were glistening.

'Well, how did I sound?' she asked excitedly.

'You were perfect, darling,' said her mother.

Dick stood there mute, as if long ago he had resigned the role of praising Emma to his wife.

'Are you going to go straight to the party dear, or are you coming home for a drink first?'

'No, we'll go straight on, Mum. Don't wait up for me. Bye.'

With that she pulled Dominic by the arm, and led him out of the churchyard. He found this small resignation to her will both novel and pleasing. Now that he no longer had a vision of where their relationship should go, he was happy to follow her.

'Where's the car?' she asked.

'I'm afraid it's in Cairo. We'll have to get a taxi.'

'If we can find one. I hope it doesn't rain, that's all.'

At her curtness, his pleasure left him.

'Look, you stay here, and I'll come back with one.'

A gust of wind from the harbour brought spots of rain with it.

'Oh come on. It doesn't matter,' she said.

Out in the street, the quiet, circumspect world of the Anglican church was pushed aside by the teeming traffic. They walked over to the square where the Cecil Hotel stood, imposing, dark green-brown, along one side.

'There's a cab,' Dominic said, 'by the hotel.'

They went to it and got in. Emma gave instructions to the driver.

A moment later Dominic took her hand.

'It was in a mirror in that hotel that Darley first caught sight of Justine.'

'Yes. I've often wondered which one. Maybe the one in the foyer. It's so shabby now, stains and blotches everywhere.'

'Perhaps it was all a dream, Durrell's Alexandria.'

'He wrote it as if it was - recollected in tranquillity on his Greek island.'

'Where are we going?'

'To Helen's. She the vice-consul. *Le tout Alex* will be there.'

'Good Lord, I hope there won't be all those French-speaking Greeks. My French isn't up to it. I'll be exhausted after half an hour.'

'You'll just have to listen a bit more, instead of talking all the time.'

'All right, I'll try.'

Her rebuke did not affect him. He felt it was conversational banter, nothing more.

At the party Dominic drank beer and did find someone to talk to in English, an Egyptian he had met during the summer conference. He was a lecturer at a technical college outside the city, and though he was built more like a businessman who had enjoyed many business lunches, Dominic discovered that he was a keen squash player. So they talked about the sport, in which Egypt was one of the strongest nations. Were the Pakistanis going to stay on top for ever? Who were the young Egyptian players who might challenge them? Dominic suggested Gamal Awad, the seventeen-year-old prodigy of his own club in Heliopolis.

They exchanged phone numbers and agreed to meet for a

game on Boxing Day.

Emma passed near him, and Dominic called her and asked her to dance. They moved in amongst the others. He watched her body as she danced in front of him with ease but without sensuality. She had probably learned it at school, not in London discotheques. When a slow began, he put his arms round her and she slipped against him and rested her head against his chest. Her hair warmed his cheek and he smelled its now familiar odour.

She leaned back and said:

'Do you think I'm very spiritual?'

'Spiritual? As opposed to sensual? I don't know. Why do you ask?"

'I've just been talking to a really interesting man. He's German, I think. He says I have a strongly spiritual aura. That he could feel it.'

'I prefer to feel your body.'

'Yes,' - she gave a small laugh - 'but this man, Hans, I think his name is, says I should take up meditation and , as he put it, come into my spirituality.'

'I shouldn't think there's much harm in that.'

'Don't be so condescending. He runs meditating groups at his house. He wants me to come to them.'

'Ah ah. Soon it'll be extra tuition - just you and him.'

'Don't be absurd. He's as old as Mum and Dad. That's him, over there.'

She nodded in his direction, and he located a thin man of about fifty, wearing a turtle-neck sweater of shiny, synthetic material. A device of some kind hung from a thong around his neck. His face was yellow and lined, and his blond hair was combed forward so as to cover the balding area in front.

'I wouldn't trust him with any of your orgone if I were you.'

'Orgone? What's that?'

'Some other crackpot's name for sexual energy.'

'Why do you think he's a crackpot just because he's interested in the spirit?'

'Because the spirit is a crackpot idea. Give me the body, give me the real.'

He gripped her more tightly.

'No, seriously, Emma, when you're my age, you realise that human warmth is what's important, not mantras and self-deception.'

'Yes, Grandad.'

That silenced him for some minutes. They moved together a little mechanically. Dominic noticed Charles sitting alone in a chair.

'Look, there's Charles. I didn't know he was coming. Good, he can give us a lift back. He doesn't look very cheerful, does he?'

'Haven't you heard?'

'Heard what?'

'About Lynda. She's having an affair with an Egyptian woman.'

'Really? With a woman! After all that business last summer with Lester.'

'You should see her. She's called Nefretiti. Titi for short. It's not her real name of course - she's called that because she really is like her namesake. She's got the same long neck and narrow face. Really quite beautiful.'

'Extraordinary that - how you see a face today that you're sure you've seen before on an ancient sculpture. So this woman is a Queen Nefretiti in our midst.'

'To look at, yes. Charles has been taking it fairly stoically. Though of course he's obviously depressed. Poor chap. One can't very well talk to him about it. It's rather difficult.'

'And where's the logic? Good God, one minute Lynda is hounding a homosexual, the next she's having a Lesbian affair. It's really too much. What makes her think it's OK for her?'

'Oh, I've kept well out of it, but I can tell you, it's the event of the season.'

'Luckily I didn't put my foot in it with Charles earlier this afternoon. I thought he was at a bit of a loss.'

'Everyone's sorry for him, and for Nefretiti's husband. They've got two small children.'

'We only need a sickening prostitute now and Durrell's cast is complete.'

'Some of those Greek blokes over there probably know one, if you care to ask.'

'I don't think I will. Without Durrell's magic, she would be as uninspiring as this idea of Lynda and her Nefretiti.'

'It's not an idea, it's a fact.'

'We're the only normal people around.'

As they left the party with Charles, Hans came up to Emma and fondled her hand in farewell. Dominic looked on as he insisted that Emma should visit him any afternoon. Sunset, he revealed with a portentous look, was the most fruitful time for meditation. Emma responded with an enthusiasm that grated on Dominic, but they parted without a *rendez-vous* being fixed. Maybe, Dominic hoped, she would let this charlatan, this self-deluding riddler, whatever he was, drop.

On the way back to the flat, the three were silent. Charles drove, and Emma and Dominic sat in the back. He had his arm round her shoulders and looked out into the glistening streets as the night rain poured down. It was so different from Cairo. He remembered their first date, when the same three of them had come back in his car to Charles's flat. He had felt peripheral then, but now it was Charles who was cut out. He and Emma were a couple, enduring. But, he thought, a couple with so many incongruities of feeling and intellect. Her enthusiasm for this spiritualism, for example. How could he take that seriously? It was just immature dilletantism - the sort of thing silly young undergraduates had done when he was at university. That was it of course, she was a student, going through all those poses that he had found absurd in his day. Now, ten years later, he was witnessing them again. How could he be any more sympathetic now?

Besides, he had begun to measure an emotional shallow-ness, emotional limits in her, which, though he was content to be with her and to make love to her, cut off his impulses to try to understand her more deeply.

She had said that she would spend the night with him. She could tell her parents that she had stayed with a friend. So they followed Charles into the flat. Lynda was not there. Charles wandered listlessly about, tidying up books and glasses. They said goodnight to him and went straight to Dominic's bedroom.

He undressed her quickly and caressed her almost disinterestedly. She stood before him shivering slightly as he cupped her breasts in his hands, and she put up her face to be kissed. She made small moans as he ran his hands down each side of her thin, curved body and then gripped her tense buttocks. She pressed herself against him and began to pull him towards the bed. As he kissed her neck, her head fell back with a gesture that he felt betrayed exaggeration or some obscure dishonesty. But his body knew her and desired her, and lying beside her on the bed, he pulled off his clothes. He felt a possessive relief when he pushed into her.

But as they moved together, strongly, vigorously, he realised with sudden clarity that they were now taking from each other what they wanted, that they must be satisfied with its limits, and that now it was, and might always remain, an exchange of habit.

Next morning they woke and the dull grey light of the winter day kept them lying in.

'After Cairo, this weather reminds me of home,' Dominic said, 'like the service last night, the Christmas carols.'

'This is home for me, if anywhere is.'

'Still, the service, you must have had ones like it in school. We did.'

A vision of rows of chairs, the grand piano, the ballroom with its Adam stucco, and the crowd of parents ranged like obedient visitors from another world, passed through his mind.

'You've never told me about your school romances, Emma - how you lost your virginity.'

She propped herself up on one elbow.

'Haven't I? There's not much to tell. I just decided one day to do it.'

'Just like that, no long love affair?'

'No. There was a boy I was involved with. We were so very, very close. We met each other every day, we talked to each other about everything. He wrote me beautiful poems. He had almost exactly the same tastes in literature as I had. We understood each other like...that.'

She crossed one finger over another.

'But he wasn't the one you did it with.'

'No. We talked about it over and over, but we decided that

our relationship was too precious - it might spoil it if we had sex. We wanted to keep it spiritual, perfect.'

'Perverse, perhaps. How sad. So who did you decide on then?'

'It wasn't sad. It was beautiful, tender, with Tom. You don't understand. But we just didn't want to do it together. Eventually I did it with another boy, a rugby type, nobody special. I got it over with.'

'Did you enjoy it?'

'Not particularly. But I wasn't expecting much. Anyway, it wasn't very painful. It was funny, he was quite gentle and bashful when I told him I wanted him to do it with me. I told Tom afterwards of course, and said what an anti-climax it was and how we'd done the right thing to keep our relationship Platonic. He seemed relieved, but I don't know why, it changed something between us. We lost that absolute closeness we had before.'

'But Emma, why, why couldn't you have done it with him? Why someone else? Didn't you love him?'

'Of course we loved each other. I remember so well sitting on a window ledge in the library one summer evening, and Tom telling me that he loved me and that he thought I was the most perfect companion that he could ever have.'

'But there was something missing.'

'No, we felt it was perfect as it was.'

'And so you had this loveless deflowering.'

'I soon got over it.'

'And continued on your merry way.'

'What do you mean by that?'

'You know, the impression I got when I met you, that you had been pretty active, making up for all that lost time with Tom, delayed promiscuity.'

'Look, I thought I made it clear, I was not in the least promiscuous before I met you.'

'You were a fast mover though. We didn't wait all that long, did we?'

'You seemed to want it, didn't you?'

'Yes, I admit I did.'

Her retort had stung him, reminding him of his first failure with her.

'Well then?'

They got up and dressed. They were to have Christmas lunch at Emma's home. He got her present out of his bag and slipped it into his jacket pocket.

'What about Charles?' he asked her. 'Where's he spending the day? It'll be bloody for him if he's on his own. Lynda isn't back, is she?'

'Isn't she? Well, I'm afraid he can't come with us. Mum and Dad have already invited the Randals and the Taylors. With us, that makes eight. Besides, if Charles comes on his own, everyone will feel sorry for him. It'll be embarrassing and ... he's probably going out to a restaurant with Lynda and crowds of Egyptian friends. That's her style these days.'

'Well, all right.'

Dominic too felt the reflex to shun the victim, to keep his pain at arm's length.

They had a well-cooked meal and over-ate hugely. After it, they exchanged presents. Emma gave Dominic an old brass coffee pot, and seemed pleased with the silver Bedouin anklet that he had got for her. In the evening they sat about drowsily, as Dick played a record of Latin American guitar music, a present from another guest. The rhythmic harmonies rolled into Dominic's mind along with the comforting mood of this strange room, with Emma curled up on the sofa beside him, and her parents now a familiar presence. Even so, he held himself away from them, on the periphery of his contentment. He was reluctant to feel that he was in any sense settled with Emma.

On Boxing Day, he went to the club for his game of squash. Cherif, his Egyptian partner, beat him soundly. After the game, they sat drinking lime juices in tall glasses. Dominic pleaded Christmas over-eating and drinking as an excuse for his poor play and said he wanted a return match next time he was in Alexandria. Cherif laughed and accepted.

After the game, Dominic went home and took a long bath. The exhaustion of his body seeped into his spirit. As he lay motionless, his mind seemed to drift away into a careless satiety and isolation. The conversation that he had had with Emma on Christmas morning, what she had told him of her early sexual experience, floated in and out of his consciousness, giving a new context to his feelings for her. There was a continuity between the puritan conflict of her first lover affair at school and her abortion, that had, he felt, stunted his unfolding commitment to her.

In the early evening, he called at her house. Dick let him in, and led him to the sitting room. The central heating was oppressive and he noticed that Dick had a tumblerful of whisky on the table beside him.

'Just whiling away the day with Paul Scott,' Dick said, holding up a book as he sat down.

'What is it like? Everyone is talking about this new, Indian, quartet.'

'Oh, I like it very much. Of course my family were in India. I was born there, you know.'

'Really? I didn't. So you have a colonial tradition in the family? Now you're in that quintessential post-colonial enterprise, the oil industry.'

'Yes, there's something in that. Anyway, I feel at home in Scott's India.'

'It's rather strange, isn't it, this wave of nostalgia for India and all that in Britain.'

'I don't think so. When you consider how predictable, how boring life tends to be in England today, a book like this offers not so much nostalgia, but escape.'

'Maybe it is escapism. I've always thought it was more longing for the old assurance of the imperial past.'

'I shouldn't think so. Just interest in an infinitely exotic and varied country.'

He pushed his thick glasses up his nose and reached for the glass of whisky.

Dominic liked him. For a moment he could find no connection between this father and the daughter who yesterday had joined her body to his. There was a crucial difference of character that he could not identify.

Dick asked him if he wanted a drink, then raised his book and took up reading again. Dominic looked round the room, at the bookshelves, the pictures, the karamc hangings, and saw them as the culture from which Emma had grown.

She came in a few minutes later. Her hair fell from a long parting down over the sides of her face. She wore a dark blue woollen sweater and jeans.

'Hello, Dominic,' she said as she sank on the sofa beside him. ' Did you have a good game?'

'Yes, thanks. Cherif was much fitter than I expected.'

'Who won then?'

'Oh, he did.'

She gave him a sympathetic smile, but the movement of her eyebrows expressed a certain satisfaction.

'Well, where would you like to eat?' he asked.

'Where were you thinking of - Asteria's?'

Her question lacked any enthusiasm, as if this choice was both predictable and unattractive.

'Well, yes, I was thinking of Asteria's actually,' he said defensively. 'But if you like, we could go somewhere else.'

'No, it doesn't matter.'

She got up.

'Bye, Dad.'

Dick looked over the top of his book and replied with a grunt.

As they sat among the potted rubber-tree plants and the climbing creepers in the restaurant, Dominic remembered their meals there in the summer. That was probably why he had wanted to take her there again this evening - those memories were still touched by the newness and adventure of their first weeks together. Now he looked across at her as she cut into the thick pizza on her plate, and could feel no echo of them.

'Bored with our old haunts?' he asked suddenly.

She registered his gibe with a slight flicker of her eyelids, but replied:

'Well, their pizzas are still the best in town, I suppose.'

'That's something at least.'

In the silence that followed, a girl at another table caught his eye. She was waving at them. He touched Emma's arm and pointed.

'That's Sandra, one of your admirers.'

'Really?'

'She was at the party. You didn't notice her?'

He shook his head.

'Must have admired you from afar then. She told me she thought you were dishy, tall and gentlemanly or something.'

'Did she now. Well, that's gratifying.'

'She's very keen on you. Said I was lucky to have you, and that I should hold on tight.'

'But you won't, will you?' he said, before he had time to think whether it was wise or not.

'Won't I?'

'No, something'll stop you. Just like something stopped you from making love to that boy at school. The mechanism doesn't quite work in you - love doesn't work, that is.'

'How do you know?'

'I can feel it. You go through the motions, but it doesn't really work. You can't get outside yourself, into the other person. You didn't really love that boy at school at all, did you?'

'I did.'

'No, you didn't . But you were perfectly happy to have him write all those poems to you. He thought you were the perfect companion, that flattered you, but when it came to the final jump, the real thing, you couldn't do it. You couldn't genuinely give, so you just threw your sex at someone else.'

'But we decided together.'

'That's what you say. But he was probably only agreeing to what he knew, he sensed, you had all along decided. Do you think men aren't aware? That they aren't sensitive to how a woman feels towards them? That they're not easily put off? Poor fellow, I can just see him, going along with your absurd Platonic proposal merely to save himself from hearing from you more bluntly that, after all, you really didn't love him.'

Her face had gone pale. She stared past him, suddenly at a

loss.

'Be honest, Emma, you've never loved anyone, have you?'
She did not reply.

'You're always acting the part. You don't really believe in it.
At school - your defloration - and after that, your Greek boyfriend here, what did he mean to you? I got the impression not
much.'

'But it's not my fault. What did I do wrong?'

'If you can't see, there is no point in telling you. There's a
block. You go along with it, you tinker with it like a child with
a toy, and then inadvertently you pull something out and break
it. Then it's too late.'

'I don't want to break anything.'

She seemed genuinely distressed, and he relented. He felt
now a concern for her and the isolation he had exposed in her,
for the absence of any passion in her young life. She looked at
him steadily. He took her hand across the table and held it for
some moments.

They finished the meal in silences broken only by short remarks. Strangely, he sensed a relief in her after his attack. She
was more relaxed, paradoxically warmer.

It was dark when they left the restaurant. He hailed a taxi. In
their last few minutes together, they talked of when they would
next see each other. Emma had to be back in Oxford on the 9th.
of January. She would stay one or two days with him on route.

Dominic had the taxi driver pull off the main road to a café
where the long distance taxis for Cairo waited and filled up.
He saw that there was one waiting, half full. He patted Emma's
knee and said:

'I'll phone.'

They kissed shortly.

'Masr?' Dominic asked the taxi usher. Nobody used the Arabic name for Cairo, from which the English name is derived. The old, pre-Islamic name was the only one current.

'Masr,' the man answered, and opened the front door of the Peugeot for Dominic. The two back seats were already full.

A few minutes later, the last place, beside Dominic in front, was taken by a woman. He couldn't see her face well in the darkness, and though she was being seen off by a man, who she talked to out of the side window, she was travelling alone.

A shout summoned the driver who had been drinking coffee at a nearby table. He got in and collected their fares. Before setting off, he paid a small commission to the usher. Dominic wondered why drivers observed this practice. The usher seemed to him completely superfluous. Perhaps it was just another way of spreading the available income down the social scale. Maybe the ushers did serve a real purpose, if only on occasion - arbitrating between contending passengers as to who should get the last seat.

Soon they were in darkness heading along the flat roads of the delta. Dominic was uneasy as the speedometer crept past 100 kilometers per hour and the station-wagon vibrated and rattled. The other passengers seemed unconcerned. From what he could make out, the men in the back were discussing a forthcoming football match between Al Ahly and Arab Contractors, two of the biggest Cairo clubs. The driver did not join in. He drove nonchalantly, save when another vehicle came against him, when he flashed his lights continuously at the on-comer, and received the same blinding flashes in return.

Don't they understand what dimmed lights are for, Dominic wondered. The flashes left the road ahead in pulses of black invisibility. But then perhaps this incessant flashing served merely to reassure the two drivers that each of them was, at least, awake.

The woman next to Dominic did not talk to the other passengers. Her body pressed lightly against his from time to time. He thought of saying something to her, but didn't. The darkness seemed to relieve him of the necessity, and the swaying motion of the taxi made him drowsy.

Later, the woman opened her handbag and took out a packet of cigarettes. She offered one to Dominic.

'No thanks. I don't smoke,' he said to her in Arabic. It was one of the phrases he had learnt early and often had occasion to use.

She stretched her arm across in front of him and offered the cigarettes to the driver. He took one. They lit up and smoked, though he did not start talking to her. Yet he seemed to have accepted the cigarette with bonhomie.

Towards midnight they passed through the last delta town before Cairo. They would get to Ramses Station at about one-thirty. Dominic hoped he'd be able to find a taxi for Heliopolis. The metro would have closed down by then.

Though they were not going round any corner, he thought he felt the pressure of the woman's thigh against his increase. He shifted his body away from her a little. A second later, the pressure increased again. In an instant his drowsiness evaporated and he was wide awake. He moved his thigh away a second time. Almost straight away the pressure was re-asserted. The woman *was* doing it. He peered out of the corner of his eye at her, but she was looking straight ahead. Now the pressure was unmistakable. He accepted it, he didn't, he couldn't pull back any more. He let his thigh press back against hers. She started giving him little pushes. A promiscuous exchange had begun. His heart beat violently. These pushes, a slight rubbing up and down, were passing into him in this dark enclosed space with strangers all around him. How could she, an unknown, Egyptian woman, be doing this to him? He could hardly believe it. His breathing became difficult.

Now she had brought her right arm across and was lightly scratching him. The blind sensations ran up his leg and caught hold of his sex. His cock began to swell with an inexorable, uncontrollable force. Her scratching fingers caught and squeezed his leg, then slid upwards, exploring, teasing. His excitement almost made him gasp. His trousers constricted him uncomfortably as his erection strained with hot, sweet force. He looked down. The bulge in his crotch was large and unmistakable. Might the driver see it? Still her fingers stroked, squeezed, now pulled at the flesh of his leg. He surrendered to the flowing, violent pleasure it gave him, that seemed to blot out everything in a dark delirium. He existed only in this contact between her hand and his thigh, and in his straining erection.

They came into Cairo city, and sped down the empty streets towards the station.

'You'll come with me?' he whispered into her ear. He saw her head give the slightest of nods.

The taxi stopped in the station forecourt and they all got out. Dominic could hardly straighten his body, his cock was so rigid. He put his hand into his trouser pocket and rearranged himself. He took the woman by the arm and steered her away. Now he looked at her face and saw that she was about his age. She was not good looking, but she had pleasant, open features.

'Where do you live?' she asked him.

'Masr el Gedida,' he said. 'We'll take a taxi.'

They stood waiting, and he began to shiver from the cold night air and the weakness in his legs.

A taxi pulled up. They got in and he gave the address. When they were sitting together in the back, she immediately began again the same, dark, anonymous provocation. Her hand now made very quick movements to his fly, where she felt his tense erection. He put his arm round her back and caressed the side of her breast.

They arrived outside his flat. The building was in darkness. He paid the driver and hurried in with her and up the dark staircase. He opened the door of his flat and turned on the light. He led her to the couch. As they sat down, he put his arm round her and asked her her name.

'Olfa,' she said.

Now he examined her. He noticed how her eyebrows were plucked. They were just pencilled lines, with sparse hairs along the middle of the lines. His gaze fell to her mouth. It had a thin coarseness that made him at once sympathetic and condescending to her. After the dark excitement of the taxi, now he was seeing the reality of her body, her class, her culture.

'This is a very good apartment,' she said, looking around. 'How much do you pay?'

'A lot. What do you want to drink? Whisky? Tea?'

'Whisky.'

He left her, and the sexual heat ebbed out of him. Gone was the burning sweetness that insisted on gratification. His sex was emptying of it all. He got two glasses, half filled them with whisky and went back to her on the couch. Now he wished the whole episode hadn't happened. He desired her not at all.

They drank together, and she slipped her hand inside his shirt, but in the bright light that had revealed her, and in their inability to find anything to say, there was no return to the blind physical response of before.

Eventually he stood up and said:

'Let's go to bed'

She followed him to the bedroom. He took off his clothes quickly and didn't mind that she saw him hanging, flaccid. He got into the bed. She went to the bathroom and when she came back, she was dressed only in her panties and bra. They were black with lace edges. Her body was fat and she had large breasts. She switched off the light and got into bed.

Dominic let her nestle against him and he held a breast with one hand. It was soft and yielding. He lay still, unwilling to kiss her or to try to manufacture new heat between them.

After some moments she started to stir. She drew the covers off. Then she got up and turned round to kneel beside his body. He felt her take his soft cock in her fingers and then into her mouth. Slowly her tongue moved over it from side to side in a gentle, patient motion.

He was astonished. This had never happened to him before, a woman setting about bringing him to erection in this calm, measured way. He felt the blood flow back, his swelling in the wet softness of her mouth. The physical response reasserted itself and made his recoil from her a fading irrelevance. Soon he was stiff, and the strokes of her mouth long and steady.

He pulled at her body and she came up. He caught her shoulders and turned her away from him. She rolled over and he moved into her from behind. She was wide and loose, and he wondered whether she had been circumcised, whether her lips had been cut away. He liked the easy, loose friction as he moved in her. She made small sibilant noises and moved a little with his rhythm. He came to climax slowly, and without pulling out of her, he lapsed into sleep.

Next morning, they woke late, and Dominic realised with

annoyance that he would be late for work. He bundled Olfa out of the apartment and apologised for the haste. He asked her where she wanted to go, and she said the Hilton Hotel. He laughed inwardly. He hailed a taxi on Sharia Aguza and they set off. He would get out at the Ministry, and she could go on from there alone.

'Here's some money for the taxi,' he said.

'I need more money. Give me more money.'

There was a crude insistence in her voice which did not surprise him, but confirmed his realisation that she must be a prostitute. He took two five pound notes from his wallet and gave them to her.

'I must pay the taxi back to Alexandria. Give me more.'

'No, that's enough,' he said firmly, with a slight smile.

She didn't argue, but instead wanted to know when she could see him again.

'Next Saturday, in Alexandria.'

He didn't want her to show herself again at his apartment. He hoped she hadn't taken note of the name of his street.

'Same time, for the taxi, like last night.'

He lied, hoping that this was the best tactic for escape.

'At the café?'

'Yes, at the café. At ten o'clock.'

She repeated the details twice. She seemed pleased at the prospect and he felt a small scruple at his subterfuge. He stopped the cab a block before the Ministry and jumped out, leaving her with a 'masalama'.

The taxi drove off and was soon lost in the morning traffic. He laughed to himself and began walking towards the Ministry. Would he tell Rory that now he too had sampled the fabled Egyptian whore? No, he decided he wouldn't.

Twenty-two

Dominic's siesta was interrupted by the ringing of the telephone. He awoke in a brief panic of disorientation, and with a lingering feeling from his dream that something important remained to be done. Now it was too late, he couldn't remember what it was. He picked up the phone and said hello. At once he recognised the flat vowels of Ronald's Dutch voice.

'Hey, Dominic, we heard you were in Alex. You should have come to see us. What happened?'

'Sorry I didn't drop by, Ronald, I had very little time down there.'

'And all of it was for Emma, eh? You young lovers...'

'Young? Look, I'm older than you are Ronald.'

'Are you? She's not.'

Ronald laughed.

'Anyway,' Dominic said, 'Emma and I aren't so loving either.'

He was no longer gratified that friends thought of him and her as a couple. He felt that they might not remain one for long.

'Well, I didn't ring you to talk about that. I wanted to talk about the karawan. I think I've identified it.'

'Really? Well, what is it, Ronald?'

'Athena noctua.'

'Noctua I understand, but Athena?'

'Little owl in English. Listen to this: "call a loud ringing kiew, kiew, habitually uttered by day, song remarkably like opening sequence of curlew's song". And also this: "Often flies at night and hovers for insects in dusk". That sounds like the karawan, doesn't it? The only problem is that the karawan calls at night and not during the day.'

'Well, we're getting warm. Certainly the size is about right. I saw one flighting over the Nile recently in Cairo, and it was about the size of a little owl. Maybe there's a north African variety.'

'Well, there's the spotted little owl, but it is found only in southern Iraq.'

'Southern Iraq? That must be very like the Nile delta - all those swamplands of the Tigris and Euphrates that Thesinger wrote about.'

'Yes? Well, I think it could be some sort of small owl, like the little owl.'

'Could be. We're certainly a lot closer than any of the Egyptians I've asked.'

'Exact. I asked an Alex friend about it recently and he said -Yes, I know it. He gave me a very vague description, and I asked him where he had seen one. Do you know what he answered?'

'Where?'

'In a zoo in Switzerland.'

'Oh, they're hopeless. I've got a story that's almost as good. An Egyptian woman swore to me that she knew it - she works in the British library and I was looking through their bird books. I asked her to describe it. -About this big, she said, and completely yellow. It sings beautifully. My friend has one in a cage in her house. Of course what she was talking about was a damned canary.'

Ronald's laugh down the telephone was almost painfully loud.

'These Egyptians, they care too much about eating to know anything about birds. But we're coming to Cairo soon, with Willem. We'll go on an expedition together and solve the mystery once and for all.'

'Good, Ronald. I look forward to that.'

They said goodbye and wished each other a happy New Year.

A few nights after his conversation with Ronald, Dominic dreamt that he actually found a karawan. He was driving out to Agami past the purple lake when he suddenly saw an Egyptian in his headlights, standing by the side of the road. The man waved frantically for him to stop. He was wearing a galabiya with blue stripes, and he had a long white cloth coiled round his head in the Nubian style. Dominic pulled up and the man said in an agitated voice that he had chickens to sell. He pointed to a cage on the ground nearby made of wooden laths and began telling Dominic that he must sell a chicken today, otherwise his children would go hungry. Dominic said that he didn't want to buy one, and wondered why the children couldn't eat a chicken themselves. The man pulled him by the arm and led him over to the cage. He held it up so that Dominic could see inside. There were five or six chickens in it, and he noticed at once that one of them was dead, and the others were so cramped that some of them were forced to stand on its body, their footing precarious. They swayed uncertainly, holding their heads out low, and blinking their round eyes.

'Why is one dead?' he asked the man.

'That one is a karawan,' the man replied. 'My son found it and put it in the cage, but the chickens killed it.'

'I want to buy it. How much?'

They quickly agreed a price and the man opened a flap on the cage and took out the carcass. He handed it to Dominic. The flesh was cold and the feathers had been almost entirely stripped off. Only some on the wing remained, and they were freckled, like those of a pheasant.

Dominic brought the bird back to the car and examined it in the headlights. The beak was blue and looked like a hawk's, and when he held it between his fingers, he was surprised to find that it was soft and pliable. He wondered whether this was because it was a young bird, a nestling. Yet it was quite large, bigger than a pigeon.

He got into the car and threw the bird on the passenger seat. He started the engine and drove off. He was excited and wanted to show the bird to Emma, who was waiting for him in the apartment. But as he drove along, he noticed that it was rotting on the seat beside him. Its skin was suppurating and the innards were spreading out from a hole in the abdomen. Gradually its head became a flattened, sticky mass. It would all have decomposed before he could show it to her. He pressed down on the accelerator but the car would not go faster.

In any case, it made no difference. All that was left of the carcass now was a dark stain. He still hoped that a microscopic analysis could be carried out on the liquid, that the bird could be identified from what was left. But who would be able to do it? A sample of the cells would have to be sent to Britain. It would all take so long. By then, they would probably have broken down completely. He felt a very deep distress that the karawan had slipped from his grasp. As he stirred into the first waves of wakefulness, the dream faded. He opened his eyes. Dull, pre-dawn light bathed his room in greyness. It looked alien, as if he had woken in a tomb.

Some nights later, Annabel, Rory, and Dominic sat in the open-air theatre near the Sphinx, waiting for the beginning of "Madame Butterfly". The production was French, but the singer in the title role had an Arabic name.

'She must be Lebanese,' Annabel said.

'Or Egyptian, working in France,' Rory replied. 'Why do you assume that she's foreign?'

'Just a guess.'

'She could just as well be Egyptian. They have a long operatic tradition here. Probably got going in the nineteenth century when the premiere of "Aida" was staged here for the opening of the Suez Canal. There used to be an opera house in Cairo, but it burned down some years ago.'

'Maybe it was as well,' Dominic said, 'I very much like this open-air opera, with the Sphinx staring over our heads, and the Pyramids ranged behind.'

'It is romantic,' Annabel agreed, 'but I'm sure the acoustics will be awful.'

As she spoke, they could hear the braying of a donkey some distance off.

'But it all adds colour,' Rory laughed. 'Anyhow, this religious silence with which we listen to classical music in the west is a bit suffocating, and it's completely out of place in Arabic music. If you particularly like a phrase or line in a piece of Arabic music, you cry out just as you please.'

'Doesn't that make for cacophony?' Annabel asked.

'No. The cries are expected, they don't go on the whole time. It's just a different convention.'

The lights dimmed and the sad story of Madame Butterfly began.

After the opera, they drove to the Pyramids. The moon was nearly full and their pure, massive forms towered up and away from them in the pale light. They took the narrow road that wound up through the rocky desert above the plateau on which they stood. Turning a corner, they were confronted by the three great monuments in an oblique line down below them. Rory stopped the car and turned off the lights. The unearthly beauty of the tombs thrilled them. For many minutes they sat and looked in silence, awed by these stone mountains raised in human defiance of time and death.

Driving back, they came close under Cheops' side. Annabel said suddenly:

'Why don't we climb up?'

'In those clothes?' Rory said. 'Anyway, isn't it forbidden?'

'But there's no-one about. Let's.'

He stopped the car.

'You're on,' Dominic said and got out. Annabel and Rory followed. A car passed them on its way to a nightclub in the desert nearby. Otherwise the place was empty. Annabel tucked her skirt into her panties and led the way.

'An Egyptian friend told me you have to go up one of the corners.'

They followed her and started to climb. Looking carefully for their footing and avoiding the piles of dust and rubble on the blocks, they hardly noticed the land spreading out dimly below them.

About half way up Rory began to complain that he couldn't go on. He was no athlete, his twenty cigarettes a day were telling. Annabel and Dominic continued and about ten minutes later they reached the small platform at the top. They sat down panting. Their hearts beat dully as they looked across to the great spreading mass of the city to the north, fringed on either side by dark areas of irrigated farmland, and cut through by the curving black veins of the river. The Moquattam Hills rose up on the far side. All around behind them stretched the desert, grey in the moonlight, as if coated with volcanic dust.

A chill wind blew and Annabel began to shiver.

'We'd better go down. Oh, it's been wonderful. I'm so glad we came up.'

She threw her arms round Dominic's neck, and kissed him quickly on the mouth.

'You and I climbed Cheops together,' she said.

Dominic was embarrassed by her sudden approach.

'Yes, well,' he smiled at her, 'we've got to get down again.'

She kept her hold round his neck and looked up at him. He wondered if it was a declaration, but then she said:

'Yes, poor Rory, we must get back to him - only half way up to magnificence.'

She let go her hold and they began their descent.

Rory was waiting for them in the car, smoking. They got in and Annabel described the scene from the top to him.

'It was marvellous. You should have persevered. We felt so exalted, spiritually as well as in fact. The four lines of the tetrahedron running down below us in perfect symmetry. And Kefren in front, with its white crown and rough sides. I feel terribly privileged, don't you, Dominic?'

She turned in the front seat and appealed to him.

'Yes, it was beautiful,' he said.

'While you've been up there,' Rory said, 'I've been contemplating the passage of time, the fragile link of memory and stones with the past. You know, I became aware for the first time of my own temporality, my own mortality. I mean really aware.

We all know we've got one life, that death must come, but it's something, the end of our lives, that we really can't imagine. We can only reason about it, not feel it. But looking up there at the Pyramids, I suddenly felt it - the passage of my life as a minute event, as just a small stretch of time, one passage in an endless series. And I felt how pathetic it was. We all have this limited, fixed passage. For most of it we're diverted by the potential of our wills . We're too busy thinking of what we should choose, what we should do. But seen from outside, a human life is no more the deluding internal series of choices, it's just one passage in a host. It's not so much bleak, it's utterly humbling.'

The other two were silent, their thoughts running into their different associations.

'I suppose it was thinking about the thousands who built all this that got me going,' Rory said, starting the engine. 'What choices had they, for God's sake? Not much more have we.'

Twenty-three

On her way back to Oxford for the spring term, Emma came to stay with Dominic for three days.

On their first evening, he took her to dine at a restaurant in Zamalek, in the heart of Cairo. It was a pleasant open-air place beside the river, which flowed past black and rippling. They ordered food and drank red wine, while Emma described how everyone in Alexandria was still up in arms about Lynda's affair with Titi. Charles appeared more and more dazed. Emma thought he was heading for a nervous breakdown. Titi's husband was talking of divorce.

They were served hors d'oeuvres and began eating. When he had satisfied the sharpest pangs of his hunger, Dominic said:

'And us?'

He felt a curious resentment that Emma should talk with such interest of others' relationships while never referring to their own.

She looked at him with a stiff expression on her face.

'Us? How do you mean?'

'I wonder what's going to happen to our affair.'

'You should know that.'

'Should I?'

Her easy tactic of passing the responsibility to him irritated him. He found it too pat, just a way of avoiding saying what was in her mind.

'I mean, you're off to England for another term - back to those two fill-in lovers of yours.'

'Shouldn't think they'll be very much interested in me.'

'And if they were?'

'Oh, for heaven's sake.'

He knew he was picking a sore to no purpose. She would reveal nothing. All he would achieve would be a cold withdrawal in himself and guilt in her.

'All right, let's drop it.'

But the impulse wouldn't let him.

'It's just that it's a bit different from the last time you went back, isn't it?'

'Thank God it is - if you knew what it was like then.'

'I thought we were getting married. I was happy.'

'You didn't have the problem.'

'That's all it was then, a problem.'

'Well, of course it was a problem. Be reasonable.'

'So hack it out. Get rid of it.'

She let her knife and fork drop onto her plate and looked at him with baleful eyes.

'Well, this time, you've no problem. You're free as a bird, aren't you?'

An unmasked bitterness went out towards her with the words. He saw her eyes glisten and then blur as tears started to gather in them.

'You're just trying to hurt me.'

'You imagine you're incapable of hurting me?'

She began to dab her eyes with her napkin. Then with a brusque movement she took off her glasses and stared past him, over his shoulder, at the river. She mastered herself and her face became a bloodless mask. For a time they were silent. He went on eating mechanically, but the pieces of meat that he chewed seemed unwieldy in his mouth. He could hardly initiate the swallowing to take them down. His hunger was numbed.

'It's just that...'

He wanted to say that he needed some declaration from her of how she felt about him before this second long separation, something that he could hold on to, but in a slither of cowardice or pride, he finished:

'I wonder where we are going, that's all. I didn't mean to hurt you.'

He put his hand across and held one of hers. She accepted his gesture, put her glasses back on and said:

'Let's not spoil the last couple of days.'

His resolve to get a clearer truth from her had failed. Now he acquiesced, though he knew it was evasive, corrupting, sentimental.

'All right.'

They drove home up 26th. July Street, which was unusually empty because of the cold wind that had sprung up, and then turned north into Ramses Square. As they passed the station, the statue of the Pharaoh stood huge and implacable, gazing out through the blinding glare of the floodlights.

They went to bed as soon as they got back. Dominic lay motionless on his back, unable to find the small remarks that usually came to him, the cues for their unimportant exchanges. Emma sat at the dressing table, combing her hair. When she had finished, she walked to the bed and sat down on his side. She bent over him, but he did not look at her. To his surprise she brought her face down to his and kissed him on the mouth. He realised that this was the first time in their relationship that she had begun, that she was the initiator. He responded slowly, as if it was unnatural to follow this new exercise of her will, but even so, it gratified him.

The next day, he told Emma that Rory had invited them for dinner.

'We don't have to go if you don't want to,' he said.

'No, it's all right. I'm surprised he can cook.'

'I shouldn't think he'll be doing the cooking. He's probably roped in Annabel for that.'

'Annabel?'

'You don't know her? As far as I can make out, she had displaced Nemat in his affections, though his affections are never very marked.'

'A girlfriend? That should make the evening more interesting.'

'I like her a lot. She's got such a direct, vigorous way about her. She's completely unselfconscious.'

His enthusiasm was quite clear. Did she notice? Did she even care?

'Well, I must go and get ready.'

She went into the bedroom and took longer over it than usual.

Rory was already half drunk when they arrived. As he poured wine for them, he spilled some on the table. Annabel reached over with a paper napkin to mop it up but he flicked her hand away.

'For God's sake, stop fussing. Just let it be. It isn't the first wine stain on this table.'

He handed Emma and Dominic their glasses.

'Your health,' he said.

He tilted his head towards Annabel.

'Always trying to clear up and clean up. No sooner in the

place than she wants to organise it all. Get it spic and span.'

Annabel sat watching him with a face free of rancour.

'She can't understand that I like squalor. I like to have my things around me.'

'Yes, well the food is ready,' she said. 'Shall we eat here or in the dining room?'

'Oh let's eat here,' Rory said. 'I'll tidy up a bit.'

This last, mocking remark was followed by a sweep of his arm across one end of the table. Newspapers and books piled up against each other into a heap and then fell off the table onto the floor. Rory looked down at the heap.

'Ah, here's the book I got out for you to read, Dominic,' he said, picking up a paperback. 'To give you some more informed ideas about the British blitz on Germany. Of course we called it "area bombing" - nice euphemism that, don't you think? It meant wholesale slaughter of civilians.'

Dominic took the book. It was "The Destruction of Dresden". He felt irritation at being reminded that his determination to read up on the subject of the Battle of Britain and to discover how the tide of the battle had turned had come to nothing. He had no new information with which to confront Rory. He let the pages of the book run open under his thumb. In the middle were six or so pages of photographs. He stopped at them, and came to one, a full-page photograph of a city, devastated, with one dark building standing intact in the centre ground. No doubt it was Dresden after the raid.

'Read it,' Rory said. 'It may not be accurate on the actual number of people killed in Dresden, but then that's not surprising. The place was full of refugees and afterwards it was so blasted that a proper body count was impossible. Anyway, Irving's figure is probably wildly out. But establishment British historians have put the total at sixty thousand dead. That's about the total of our civilian dead for the whole of the war. Got it? A good two days' work.'

'Is that so?' was all Dominic could offer as a reply.

'It is.'

'Then you would think everyone would know about it.'

'My dear fellow, everyone doesn't know about it because the government doesn't want everyone to know about it. You're still labouring under the illusion that once the truth is established, once it gets out, everyone will hear it. It's not like that at all. In politics, truth isn't qualitative, it's quantitative.'

'What on earth does that mean?'

'It means that truth doesn't drive out falsehood because it's qualitatively better. It does so only if it's pushed out more than falsehood is pushed out. Some people know about Dresden and they've come out with it, but the government and those who follow their lead have been pushing back in the opposite direction much harder. The result? The truth hasn't gained any purchase in the public mind. The average man or woman just doesn't credit it. You, for example.'

His finger pointed at Dominic and then at Emma.

'The truth isn't qualitative, Emma, because you have to be told it again and again before you take it in. Most of the time, you see, people are trying to push it back with lies.'

Annabel was kneeling beside the table serving them.

'Tell them what your father wrote you.'

Rory put his hand on her shoulder, and though she was intent on what she was doing and facing away from him, there was a small reaction to his touch which made Dominic conclude that they were already lovers.

'Yes, it was interesting,' she said. 'I wrote to my father

about Rory's theory and the whole question of civilian bombing, and he told me a very disturbing thing. He was in Bomber Command and a friend of his was in one of the bombers that attacked Dresden. He told Daddy that he and all the crews were informed in the briefing that the city centre was crowded with refugees and that the bombing target was the central market place. He felt very uncomfortable but of course they all went off and did it. But when they got back, something really sinister took place. A film team came down to make a propaganda film and they held the briefing again. This time though, there was no mention of the masses of refugees, and the bombing target was the railway yards. Daddy's friend said he never felt so sick in his life. It's a horrible story, isn't it?' she concluded, looking from one face to another.

Dominic sensed in her that categorical insistence on the truth which he had always held to be one of the most valuable traits in the English character. Why then was he loath to accept the story? He was loath, he felt an immediate impulse to provide excuses, to put things into perspective. Hadn't the Germans slaughtered five million Russians and six million Jews? He put the book back on the table.

'Well, I'll read it, Rory, though I can't say I'll be particularly sympathetic.'

'Read it, that's all I ask. Sympathy can only come from knowledge. It'll probably come slowly. We can't expect you to have a conversion overnight.'

There was a mocking tone in the words that stung Dominic. He must not let it pass.

'In any case,' he said with a flatness that he hoped would sound like a rebuff, 'my sympathy or lack of it seems rather academic, doesn't it? A useless anachronism. After all, modern warfare, the whole nuclear business, is Dresden and nothing but, only thousands of times more lethal. Everybody is committed now to the same kind of war - genocide.'

Far from being put off, Rory's face responded with enthusiasm. His eyebrows went up and his mouth spread in a wide smile.

'Now you're getting the picture,' he said loudly. 'The war crime has become the common currency. But let's call things by their right names. Dresden, Hiroshima, Nagasaki, all were war crimes. And any nuclear war would inevitably be the greatest war crime in the history of humanity. That's why we haven't had one - yet.'

'So what should we do, join CND?' Dominic said with clear sarcasm.

'Christ, no. Unilateralism would produce a situation exactly like the end of the last war. America had the bomb. Japan didn't. So naturally America used it. That's the thing about evil, about cruelty. It's used against the weak, the helpless, not against the strong. Do you think they would have dropped it if the Japs had had one. Of course not.'

'You're right about cruelty and weakness,' Annabel said. 'Look at rape, wife-beating, baby battering. And in nature too, when you come to think of it. The predator picks the weakest, the most defenseless prey. That's the law of life.'

'I'm afraid so. For all that, we try to struggle against it in the human world,' Rory went on. 'But what I insist on is that we face up to it. See crimes, our crimes particularly, for what they are. Not cover them up with lies and ignorance.'

'But that's just it,' Dominic said, 'these crimes you're talking about aren't our crimes. We had nothing to do with them. It's pretty easy for us to admit to them because we weren't responsible. We've never killed anyone. It's when you have, when guilt burns you, that you start covering up. That's obvious, isn't it, and only natural.'

'Point taken, but a political culture can only make progress if its opinion formers expose the crimes committed by others in the society that those others naturally want to cover up. It's bound to be a constant, up-hill struggle, but it's what democracy, the freedom of the press, is all about.'

'You consider yourself an opinion former, then?' Emma taunted.

'An opinion former of my own opinion, that's one sure thing. Otherwise I'd just have somebody else's opinion foisted onto me, like all the rest. Like you.'

'Politics isn't my overriding interest. Why does it have to be?'

'It doesn't have to be, but it should be. If you've got the least glimmer of intelligence. I assume you have.'

Dominic wanted to stop this. Some part of him was gratified to see Emma being worsted and her egoism exposed, but he had been made uncomfortable by Rory too often not to feel for her a contrary sympathy.

'Oh, let's spare our women the heavy burden of war and its responsibilities. I'll certainly read the book and tell you what I think.'

Emma looked at him with clenched hostility instead of with relief.

'Do that,' Rory said. 'It's the only good thing Irving wrote. Now he's gone completely awry. His last book proposed that Hitler wasn't responsible for the holocaust of the Jews. Still, anyone's work can be good and bad.'

When they got back to the flat, Emma went straight to bed.

She seemed antagonistic towards Dominic when he made small remarks. He left her and went into the bathroom, wondering how she could go to bed without cleaning her teeth. This was the self-indulgent, slovenly side of her that he had noticed before - her clothes lay scattered round the bedroom in confusion, she ordered food in restaurants and then left it half-eaten. As he brushed his teeth and stared at his sallow face in the mirror, he wondered whether she had been the spoiled child at home, or whether she had developed such habits at her school.

He dropped the toothbrush into the mug on the basin and went to the lavatory. As he pissed he thought, yes, her mother can't see any fault in her, it must have started at home.

His train of thought was interrupted as he felt a hotness in his urethra with the flow of urine. Was his bladder over-full? Had he put off going? He didn't think so.

When he went back into the bedroom, Emma had already put out the light. He got into bed beside her, and curved his body against hers. He brought his hand up over her thinly covered ribs and held one of her breasts. He squeezed it gently. She moved her body slightly and he felt his hand removed by her hand and placed lower down round her belly. The intimacy was unwelcome. He wondered why, but soon his thoughts drifted back to the dinner conversation and then to Rory and Annabel. What was the nature of their relationship, what did they like in each other? It was a strange pairing.

Gradually his thinking lost cohesion, disconnected, and he fell asleep.

The next day was their last together. Emma was to take the plane to London in the early afternoon. Dominic woke first and listened to her even breathing. Her hair was spread around her head, dull reddish brown. Gently he stroked it up away from the back of her neck, exposing the fine wisps behind her ears and the white skin underneath. She stirred and turned over. Opening her eyes for a moment, she made a small sound. In spite of her rebuff the night before, he moved against her. He desired her in her unfocused waking with slow, insistent force. He pulled her against him. She started to breathe with a different rhythm and he knew that she was yielding. Yet when he rolled her body back and went into her, she seemed for a time numb and inert, as if her will still refused him. But gradually, as he moved in her, he broke through to her heat and she began to twist and press at him with increasing energy. He wanted to stop her, to slow her, but he could not bring his will to bear. He let go, and his orgasm came with hot, gripping waves. Their sweetness, their force, seemed to overpower him. Gasping, he spent himself in her still restless body.

After breakfast, he felt a tension in her which their lovemaking had not resolved. Though he believed now that the sexual impulse in her was troubled, a reflex of guilt and his wish to please her forced a reaction from him. He could not leave her be, to suffer her own contrariness or to forget it.

'These are our last few hours. What's wrong, Emma?'

She sat on the sofa opposite him, and in answer to his question, stared fixedly at the arm of the sofa where her hand rested. She began to run her finger along a seam of the cover.

'I can't see I've done anything. What's up, for God's sake?' he insisted.

'Oh, you don't even notice,' she at last replied.

'Notice what?'

'How condescending you are. It's almost instinctive. You're just not aware.'

He looked at her without speaking. Now she had begun. He

would hear it all.

'That insufferable remark you made last night - Let's spare our women the problem of war - I suppose you think that wasn't offensive?'

'Look, Emma, I only meant...'

He tried to remember what he had meant.

'I only meant that, you know, fighting a war is a man's business. Women are spared it. Thank God, most of them sit it out at home.'

'Nursing soldiers in battles, working in munitions factories, working in offices in London when the bombs are falling - that's sitting it out at home, I suppose.'

'No, of course not. I only meant that, well, women don't do the actual fighting.'

As he said it, he wondered whether in fact that made much difference.

'That's only because they aren't told to. A woman could be just as good a ...pilot as a man.'

'Maybe she could,' he said, but immediately the question of whether a woman's nerve would hold under the stress of combat rose in his mind. He decided not to express it.

'Maybe she could,' he repeated, 'but do we want her to?'

'Do we want her to? Who is we? That's what I can't stand in you. You just assume that men can decide. It doesn't seem to occur to you that it should be the women who decide.'

'I never thought they'd want to.'

'Just as you never thought they'd want to be educated, to work, to vote, to have the same rights and opportunities as you men.'

'There is a difference, Emma, for heaven's sake.'

'No, there isn't. Underneath, there's the same principle at

work - that men decide what is good for women and what is not.'

'You're just lumping everything together. Of course I'm in favour of votes for women, equal rights, all that. It's just that there are still some differences that limit what a woman can do. That's obvious.'

'Is it? What's more obvious is that men use such differences, and have always used such differences, as a justification for the suppression and exploitation of women.'

'Well, don't include me in that. I'm not in favour of suppressing or exploiting women. I don't think that they're by nature suited to fighting in wars, that's all.'

'What are they suited for then?'

'Having arguments with men. Oh, I don't know...'

As he looked at her resentful face, uncontrollable associations linked his desire to win over her in argument with what he knew of her and what he despised.

'Things like astrology.'

'What exactly do you mean by that?'

Her hostility was out like a sharp knife.

'Take yourself, this nonsensical enthusiasm you have for the stars, meditation, you know.'

He didn't need to finish. She jumped to her feet.

'You're so...boring,' she at last delivered, and strode past him out of the room and into the bedroom. He heard her throwing herself on the bed.

She didn't stay there long. About five minutes later she reappeared. He looked up from the book he was reading as she sat down in the same position on the sofa. They stared at each other for a moment and he felt a sharp regret at the growing split between them. He wanted to know now how he could please her

- if only he could find out what she felt for him, what she really thought about their future, then he would overcome this new bitterness and find her again. He would get rid of all this nagging division.

'Look, Emma,' he said, 'I'm sorry for being so boring.'

She looked back at him without any relenting.

'No, you're just pathetic,' she replied.

He thought she would go on. She didn't. There was no remorse in her.

'I don't seem to be much good for you, do I? And while I'm about it, I'd better give you some other bad news. I'm afraid I may have picked up something - down here.'

He pointed to his crotch. She brought her hand up in an automatic movement and pushed her glasses back up her nose. Her brows became ridged and her mouth opened as she breathed in fear with this new information.

'It may be nothing,' Dominic went on, 'just a tingling so far. It may be a mild urethritis. Nothing to worry about. Anyway, you should have a check-up when you get to Oxford.'

As he spoke, he saw her face contract away from him, go out of focus. There was no way back to her now.

'I'll let you know if it develops. As soon as I can. In any case, have the check-up.'

She made no reply. She sat quite rigid. He went and sat beside her and tried to take her hand. She pulled it away.

'Emma,' he began, but he had nothing to say to get through the barrier that she had clamped down.

For the last hours together, her silence was never broken. Dominic felt his instincts revolt against her. He watched her pack her things, he took her to the airport, he stood with her as she checked in, but she addressed not one word to him. His few remarks or questions hung in the space between them, useless, grotesque.

How could she maintain this inhuman silence? He could hardly stand to remain with her. But it was not for long. She opened her bag, took out her passport, put her boarding card and ticket in it, and then walked away from him to the exit gate.

It was a strange torture for him not to rush after her with his goodbye and a plea for forgiveness. But a sure sense of hopelessness prevented him. He watched her proceed past the police into the crowded departure area. She did not turn her head.

Twenty-four

The weeks that followed Emma's departure were for Dominic weeks of his disease. The morning after she left, he went to the lavatory and noticed at once that the end of his urethra was stuck together rather like eyelids after sleep. His piss forced its way through the blockage and came out at an odd angle. There was a hot, itching gratification all the way along its passage from his bladder. Later that day he noticed that his underpants showed a tell-tale stain of discharge. Now he knew he was infected. In the evening, he took out the list of doctors supplied to British expatriates by the embassy and chose one that was on the Heliopolis side of town.

He walked down to the Roxy roundabout and took a service taxi into town. There was no woman sitting next to him this time, and he cursed the chance that had set him next to the one from Alexandria, with her insidious disease, whatever it was.

The doctor's surgery was in a shabby apartment building in Sharia Adly. The stairway up to it was anything but clean, but once inside, Dominic was relieved to find it was as hygienic as any he had visited in Harley Street for his check-ups before going abroad.

Soon he was called in. The doctor was about sixty years old, with silver hair cut short so that it formed a thin bristle on each side of his head. He looked out over old-fashioned, half-focal spectacles. Dominic gave him his personal details.

Eventually the question came:

'And what is the trouble?'

'I think I've picked up a venereal infection,' Dominic said, struggling to hold his embarrassment in check.

'Oh?' the doctor responded phlegmatically. 'Let me see.'

He waggled his bony finger at him, and Dominic stood up and undid his fly. His cock had shrunk inordinately small through nervousness and apprehension, a reaction he had been subject to since childhood. As he looked down at it, he wondered how an ailment in such a small limb could so demoralise him.

'Do you have a discharge?' the doctor asked, and leaning forward over his desk, he caught hold of Dominic's penis between thumb and forefinger and pulled it in a brisk milking motion. A small drop of clear liquid with a globule of yellow pus appeared on the end. He let the penis fall.

'Go for an analysis. And take a course of these injections.'

He scribbled out the prescription and gave it to Dominic.

'Here is the address for the analysis,' he added, putting another note into an envelope and handing it to him. 'Come and see me as soon as you get the result.'

It had all been so short, so matter of fact. Dominic's spirits picked up as he paid the receptionist and left. He felt he'd be fixed up in no time.

The next afternoon he went to the laboratory for his analysis. First the assistant squeezed a discharge sample from his penis as the doctor had done, and then removed it with a platinum wire. Taking a culture dish, he spread the sample carefully over the surface of the jelly nutrient.

Dominic assumed that this would be all, but the assistant then asked him to turn round, lower his trousers, and lean with both hands over a low table. He placed another culture dish on the table so that it was directly under Dominic's hanging penis. As Dominic waited immobile, the assistant went to a nearby table, put on a polythene glove, and lubricated the index finger with vaseline. He returned and stood behind Dominic. He placed his other hand firmly on Dominic's lower back, and the lubricated finger he thrust into Dominic's anus, pushing far up into the rectum.

The sharp, stinging sensation of the entry took Dominic by surprise, and as the assistant's finger began to press hard against the prostate area, this was supplanted by another, more powerful, hot ache. Its hotness crept gradually down his urethra and Dominic realised that the pressing finger was forcing on him a slow, painful ejaculation. He felt wretchedness at this crude commandeering of his intimate sexual functions and a self-loathing at his humiliation.

The assistant stopped his massage for a moment, and looked round Dominic's stooping body to see if any drops had fallen onto the dish. They hadn't. Dominic felt they still had some more inches to travel.

The assistant resumed his massage more violently, and Dominic felt that he was being almost lifted off his feet. Eventually two or three drops of fluid fell onto the dish.

'I think that's it,' he said with a gasp.

The assistant looked round again to inspect the dish.

'OK,' he said, and withdrew his finger from inside Dominic's body. He picked up the dish and held it to the light.

'OK,' he repeated. He counted on his fingers. 'Come back on Friday.'

Dominic left the laboratory and walked down the stairs in a state of numbness. His legs trembled, and he barely took in the details of the large foyer that led to the street. Once outside, he hailed a taxi.

In contrast to the demoralising effect of his visit to the laboratory, getting the injections was almost a cheerful exercise. One of the young assistants in a chemist's near the club led him to a small cubicle on the right of the counter, where Dominic presented a bare buttock. The needle going in and the antibiotic following it were hardly painful at all. Dominic was able to talk to the assistant good-humouredly, and he left the chemist's without any unpleasant after-effects.

On the Friday, he returned to the laboratory and picked up the result of his test. The envelope was not sealed and as soon as he got into the street, he opened it and inspected the contents. There were two sheets, the first stating that the prostate fluid and discharge both contained Diplococci neisseria, and the second listing which antibiotics the bacteria culture had been sensitive to and which ones it had resisted. He noticed at a glance that it had resisted most, but was sensitive to penicillins.

He went straight to the doctor and was soon admitted. He passed over the test result and the doctor read it through.

'Gonorrhoea, you've got gonorrhoea,' he said.

Hearing the disease named was like a weight pressing on Dominic's chest. He found it difficult to breathe.

'I told you last time not to have any sex relations. Now you must inform all your partners that they must see a doctor.'

'I've done that already.'

'Good. And how are you now?'

'The discharge seems a little less, but the irritation is just as bad.'

'You have been having injections for what, four days? We shall change the medicine. Take these.'

He scribbled on a pad, tore off the sheet and handed it to him.

'Two tablets, four times a day. Come back in five days.'

The new prescription was for ampicillin, and when Dominic got home, he took out the information leaflet with the bottle of pills and read it. The drug was recommended for gonorrhoea. There were no side effects.

Each day, Dominic hoped for a dramatic improvement in his condition, but it never came. In the morning he noticed with depressing familiarity the evidence of the discharge during the night. Every urination gave him the same hot, stinging sensation. He wrote a short letter to Emma in which he told her that what he had feared had in fact happened, but that it was even worse - he had gonorrhoea. He told her that he had caught it off an Egyptian woman that he had slept with only once, and that he was sorry and felt wretched. He advised her to have her check-up without delay. That was all.

On his next visit to the doctor, he complained that the drug did not seem to be curing him. The symptoms had eased only slightly.

'You have probably picked up a new infection. I told you to stop sexual relations.'

For a moment he was silenced by the rush of his indignation.

'I assure you, I have not had any relations since my first visit.'

The doctor looked at him over the flat tops of his glasses.

'No? Perhaps it is resistant. Maybe we will use ultra-violet radiation.'

To Dominic, this sounded sinister, bizarre. He couldn't remember ever having read or heard of such treatment for bacterial infections.

'In any case, you must go for another analysis.'

The doctor wrote out the sheet.

'And continue with the present antibiotic. We shall see.'

Dominic was sure there was a tired scepticism in the last remark. There might also have been a hint of prurient gloating. He took the note and left quickly.

The disease now became a constant, nagging presence, and the fact that it was not cured filled him with a sense of hopelessness and desperation. Every day he put his mid-morning pills in a small paper packet to take to work. At the office he swallowed them surreptitiously, hoping that Rory would not come in and catch him in the act.

He could no longer drink, and when asked why, said that he was on antibiotics for tonsillitis. He dreaded having to give his excuse to Rory, who would surely see through it, and quiz the truth out of him.

He submitted to the humiliation of a second analysis, and picked up the results three days later. They were exactly the same as the first.

Again he sat before the doctor's desk, demoralised, helpless.

'You have a new infection,' the doctor told him tersely.

'But that's impossible. As I said, I have had no relations since I first got the symptoms.'

'The analysis report says that they found both intra and extra cellular bacteria. Extra cellular, that means a new infection.'

Dominic felt that he was being brow-beaten. The fact that he had suffered such guilt over picking up gonorrhoea in the first place meant that this persistent new accusation was intolerable. But he did not answer back. Instead the link of confidence between him and the doctor was broken. He didn't care now what the doctor thought.

'Well, you must continue with the ampicillin treatment. If there is no cure in a week, we shall use the radiation treatment.'

He pointed over to an apparatus standing near a bed in the corner of the surgery. Dominic looked at it and vowed that it would never be used on him, whatever it was.

The following day, he rang through to the Ministry and said that he would not be in for work because of his tonsillitis. He went to town and crossed the Nile to the west bank and walked down to the British Council building. He knew that the library was particularly well stocked with medical books, and he intended to read up everything it had on his disease.

Early in his researches he learned that there had been alarming developments in gonorrhoea in recent years, particularly since the Vietnam War. Resistant strains had developed which did not respond to normal doses of penicillin. It was found that whereas injections of one hundred thousand units had previously controlled an infection, now doses of half a million were required. Some army doctors were treating the disease with doses of one million units injected into each buttock. Some other antibiotics were also recommended in case of resistance to penicillins. One was kanamycin, though this drug had potentially dangerous side effects.

After a whole day in the library, Dominic felt he was reasonably well informed, and decided to treat himself. He was sure that he now knew more about gonorrhoea than the doctor, and he had certainly read nothing about radiation treatment. He returned to his flat in Heliopolis and straight away checked the dose of penicillin in his first course of treatment - only seventy-five thousand units, with streptomycin. He checked the sensitivity chart from the laboratory. All the mycin drugs had had no effect on the culture. He decided to go on a five day course of half a million units of penicillin per day.

That night he went to the chemist's and said that he wanted two injections of a quarter of a million units of penicillin each. The assistant who had given him his previous course served him, and placed the two packets of the drug on the counter while he prepared the syringe. Dominic checked the expiry date and saw that there were still two years to run. The drug would be in good condition.

A few moments later he was in the cubicle and the needle went into his right buttock. But this time, the stronger dose of antibiotic brought with it a searing pain. He had to use all his will not to move, not to pull away. The needle was extracted. There was a delay, and then it went in again on the other side. A second time the scalding fluid entered his tissues. He clenched his jaws tight.

As he left the cubicle the assistant said goodbye in his jovial manner. In reply, Dominic could only force himself to smile. 'Must put on a good front,' he muttered to himself as he walked out of the door, still in pain.

Thrown back on himself by his disease, he avoided social contact, and spent more and more time alone in his flat. He listened to music a lot, mostly Handel, Scarlatti, Corelli, and other composers of the Baroque period. There was in their music such a celebration of order and harmony, such an unbridled desire to please, which was balm to his depression.

When he thought of Emma now, it was as if she belonged to another era, the era when he was healthy. All that seemed irretrievably lost. There was no life left in his sexual fantasies or memory, just decay. He began to believe that the mechanisms of his libido had received a crushing blow from which they would never recover.

One morning he woke and discovered with some surprise that he had an erection. He decided to masturbate, wondering whether it would give him any physical pleasure. The orgasm came normally, but the pulsing contractions, the flow of the semen, were hot and stinging. The pleasure was now tainted with subtle pain.

Afterwards, he lay looking at the liquid sinking slowly into the towel where he had spilled it. At least it looked normal. Yet in his mind, the emptiness that his disease had brought him spread further.

In the evenings he read the book on the bombing of Dresden that Rory had given him. The horrors of the attack lifted him out of himself and diverted his pity to its countless civilian victims. He discovered how the area bombing raids on Dresden and other German cities had been mounted. First came the low level attacks by Mosquitoes with their marker flares, then the large explosive bombs to damage buildings, and finally the incendiary bombs, rained down in a great circle to create the fire storm. In it, the inhabitants were literally burned alive.

He learned also that Britain had been the only power at the start of the war to possess large, four-engined bombing aircraft suitable for heavy bombing, and that throughout the war, Bomber Command had pressed to pursue its strategy of area bombing of civilians. The terrible attacks on Dresden, Hamburg, and other cities were only the final culmination of this strategy, though by then the efficiency of the operations had improved dramatically. Even Churchill, who had ordered them, seemed horrified by the results, and, it appeared, had dishonestly tried to shift the responsibility for them onto the RAF.

Dominic read of the protests against area bombing that had been expressed at the time by some politicians in parliament and by a few church leaders. They had been dismissed. This was in the end the most appalling message of the book - how easily, even in a society as humane as Great Britain's, the mechanisms of war could squeeze pity out of the hearts of ordinary decent men. Bomber Harris was, as likely as not, a good chap, yet he had been the main instigator.

And since the war, the huge rush of moral indignation, the force of humanity's revulsion had been directed almost completely against the evil of Hitler and Nazism. And there had been so much of it that those responsible for the slaughter of Dresden had escaped notice and any retribution. They were passed over, excused, almost forgotten about.

The realisation that so many civilians in German cities had been killed and that their deaths had contributed so little to the winning of the war eventually effected a change of perception in Dominic's mind. Hitherto, when he had thought of the war, he had held the series of events that made it up in the matrix of a moral structure that had justified his nation's and the allies' fight, irrespective of how cruel that fight had been. Now a subtle but profound reversal had taken place: he saw the war as a series of events in which great societies clashed and inflicted unjustifiable cruelties on each other, but where these cruelties were in fact incidental to the real nature of the struggle. They would serve for the erecting of the moral framework in which both sides viewed the conflict, and because the victors were left with the field of propaganda as with the field of battle, so it would be their framework which would survive and persist. The real course of the war came first, the moral framework was then imposed. It appealed for sacrifice, and when the war was over, justified it. Dominic felt as if, quite suddenly, he understood war as a reasonable person must. Britain and the Allies had fought Germany not because Hitler was a fascist and because he persecuted the Jews, but because he sent his armies over the national borders of eastern Europe. That was his principal crime, it wouldn't have mattered if he had remained democratically respectable and had not been a racist, the war would have been fought just the same. Only the a postiori moral framework would have been different.

Of course, of course, Dominic concluded, and when Britain or rather the West was in a war for which they themselves were to blame, the episodic, spluttering war of the Middle East, the process was exactly the same. Again the justifying moral framework was constructed and most people believed in it. The Jews were fighting for their lives, the Arabs were bullies. The Palestinians? Why didn't the Arabs absorb them? And in any case, they were terrorists. This was the West's moral framework of the Middle East, and Dominic had long thought it grossly one-sided and unfair. Now he realised that such frameworks were always, by their very nature, unfair. Every war unleashed the mechanisms of cruelty in men, and also unleashed the insidious process of self-justification. There was no firm moral ground, save only in the individual, secret heart.

Dominic returned one day from work, and found a letter under his front door. He saw at once that it was from Emma - her spidery hand, the British stamp. There was no surge of affection in him as he picked it up.

'Dear Dominic,' it began.

'As you saw, the revelation that you had caught a venereal disease upset me very much when you told me that day I left

Cairo. But I held in my indignation and didn't blame you, because somehow I felt that it would be of no use. Now that I have your letter telling me that it is gonorrhoea, which you caught from an Egyptian woman, I must express the shock and disgust I feel. I shall ask you nothing about who this woman was, where or when you met her, but that you have introduced this pollution from her into us, into me, is revolting. I thought such things could happen only to other people, never to myself. Now you have exposed me to such a horror. I feel utterly degraded by you and cannot forgive you.

I had hoped that you, older and more experienced than me, might have enriched my life, but in fact you have dragged it down and made it sordid. It is hard to believe that you, to whom I gave everything, have repaid me with a horrible disease.

Emma.

p.s. I have now had a check-up, and the doctor says I seem all right, but I have to go back in a week's time.'

Dominic's reaction to the letter was intense and confused. He felt the sting of her words and part of him was filled with shame. But immediately following on this, there came a strange exhilaration. The letter was a diatribe, yet there was something not quite convincing about the outrage it purported to express, and it was from this falseness that his exhilaration sprang. The moral superiority which she claimed was bogus - she had slept with other men in Oxford, she could have infected him. Yet there was no sympathy in the letter, no magnanimity. It was pure attack. It was really overboard. She was protesting too much. And he knew in his bones that her falseness, her venom, came not from genuine hurt, but from her wish to foster guilt in him. Well, he would not accept it.

Some days later, his course of injections came to an end, but he noted with gnawing depression that the symptoms had not cleared up. The discharge was certainly less, but the irritation when he urinated was still there, and when he took a sample of urine in a small glass each morning and examined it, it usually contained a number of threads of pus. He decided to increase further his penicillin dose, to one million units a day for two days, to deliver what he hoped would be the knock-out blow.

The chemist's assistant showed no reaction when he ordered the huge dose, and they went into the cubicle talking of the weather and the cold at night. Dominic lowered his pants and underpants ready for the pain he knew the injections would bring. But if the quarter of a million units had been much more unpleasant than the earlier, weaker doses, the half a million units were now disproportionately worse. As the antibiotic was forced out of the syringe and into his flesh, it was like an acid searing his nerves. His whole body went rigid, and he felt his vision paling, retreating. He seemed to exist only where the invasion of flame scorched him. Yet he had to wait as the syringe was withdrawn, refilled, and the needle entered the other cheek with the same spreading stain of fire.

He stood up slowly, pulled up his trousers, and nodded with a small, twisted grimace at the assistant. He left without a word. He felt he had to get out into the street at once. He must move, move to ease the pain. He began to walk with brisk, rigid strides. Later he stopped, and the muscles of his legs and back began to tremble violently. He stood like a wounded animal, slightly stooped, on the dividing verge of the dual carriage-way that ran behind Sharia Merghani. Blocks of flats towered on each side, but on the cold February night, most people were indoors. The road was nearly empty, no-one seemed to be taking any notice of him.

Before setting off for the chemist's the following evening, Dominic heard a knock on his door. His first impulse was not to open it, but the knock was repeated more forcefully, and wondering if it was something important, he went to answer it.

'Hello, Dominic. So you are alive after all. Can I come in?'

'Annabel, what a surprise, please do.'

'I'm afraid I haven't got much time. I've got to go to a dinner with some agency people, but I had to come by to see if you were all right. Are you?'

Her slightly hooded, pale blue eyes looked into his. For a moment he thought of telling her his whole story - she filled him with such a strong sense of trust. But he did not, he fell back onto the reflex of dissimulation.

'Me? Why, of course.'

He broke from her gaze, and led the way into the salon.

'Come and sit down. Yes, I'm fine - more or less. I had a bit of tonsillitis but I think it's clearing up OK.'

'That's good. It's just that we haven't seen anything of you for weeks, since Emma went back. Rory says that he bumps into you occasionally at the Ministry, and that you looked depressed.'

This produced another reflex in Dominic, to deny that he was unhappy, that he was suffering.

'Nonsense. He was just imagining it. Probably suffering from blurred vision - hangovers. You know.'

Annabel would not follow this shift of focus onto Rory.

'Well, you don't look too bad, I suppose. A bit drawn maybe.'

He sought an escape.

'Would you like some wine?'

'A glass of red would be lovely.'

He left her to fetch the bottle. When he poured her a glass, she said:

'Aren't you going to join me?'

'No, I...', his brain worked quickly - 'I had far too much at lunch.'

'Well, cheers,' she responded vigorously, and drank half the glass. 'But you must come and see us more often in the evenings.'

'Us? You mean you're spending most of your time with Rory now? You two are solid - a going concern?'

She sat back on the sofa with a small bounce and pulled a hand through her golden hair.

'Well, I think so. We're living together now. But Rory has a way of taking things, of taking me, for granted. There's something very off-hand and at the same time very guarded about him. Don't you agree?'

'Yes, I do. I've never been sure where it all springs from.'

'I don't know either. But I try to get close to him. Maybe it'll just take time. I mean he accepts me all right, but it's as if I'm just tagging along, as we rush around from one place to another, visiting all his Egyptian friends.'

'The Egyptian social - what can one call it - treadmill? No, that's far too hash. It's really most enjoyable, but oh, so time-consuming.'

'Exactly. The only time we have any privacy together is when we go to bed.'

Dominic smiled.

'Now he's become interested in the Moslem Brotherhood. He wants to meet one of them, but it seems it's rather difficult to get an introduction. It's really a secret society. We've been on several wild goose chases already.'

'Why does he want to meet a Moslem brother? He hasn't talked to me about it.'

'You remember Ezzedine, the Palestinian we had dinner with once? Well, he's convinced that the only force for change in Egypt will come from them. Rory thinks he may be right and he wants to meet some of them.'

'I thought they died out with Suez and all that.'

'Evidently not. There's been a revival.'

'I wonder why.'

'Probably in response to Sadat's tilt to the West. That's the sort of thing Rory wants to find out. Anyway...' - she finished her wine - 'I'm afraid I must go now.'

She stood up and he did the same.

'But you will come round and see us one evening?'

'I will, I promise.'

He kissed her on both cheeks and closed the door behind her.

Later that evening he turned on the radio to listen to a simultaneous English translation of one of Sadat's long, rambling speeches to the People's Assembly. Most of it was an attempt to convince the deputies that the Israeli thrust across the canal in the Ramadan War had been just a lucky, fly-by-night affair. He would have crushed it, he said, had not the Americans forced a cease-fire on him and assured him that they would get the Israelis to withdraw in any case. But Sadat presented the story in such an extremely disorganised fashion, with so many non-sequiturs and dubious inside-story reservations, that Dominic wondered if there could be any truth in it.

The following day, another letter came from Emma. As Dominic picked it up, he feared with a sinking heart that she would announce that she too had developed his disease. He tore it open quickly and dropped into an armchair to read it. Again a page full of neat, spidery lines.

'Dear Dominic,

You may be surprised to be getting another letter from me so soon after the last one. The reason is that after I sent it, I realised that I had a lot more to say. I was so shocked at first that all I could express were my first reactions. Now I can see things more clearly. I can see, for instance, that your sanctimonious moral superiority to me over my so-called promiscuity is an utter sham. How dare you insult me for sleeping with other men in Oxford, when you are doing exactly the same with Egyptian women, and what kind, might I ask? I was stupid enough to feel guilty about what I did. I should have thrown your criticism straight back in your hypocritical face - talk about a double standard!'

He gave a raucous laugh. The mood of exhilaration in response to her attack was still with him. Now she was really getting into gear, she was letting fly. Oh, it was too good. And come to think of it, had he 'insulted' her for sleeping with whoever they were in Oxford? He was sure he hadn't. He remembered only the chill that hearing about them had caused him. This insult Emma referred to was a figment of her own imagination. He read on.

'Fortunately I have heard from my doctor that there is no sign of my having any infection whatever. That is just as well, because if you had infected me, if this horrible disease had got into me and spread in my body and damaged me - maybe for ever, they say that gonorrhoea causes sterility - then I would never have forgiven you. After all I suffered last year with the abortion, having my ovaries destroyed by your germs would have been insupportable. But as I said, I have escaped, no thanks to you.

I find it hard to end this letter on a friendly note. What is left of our relationship? I have no idea.

Emma.'

Now he understood the source of her attack. With just an oblique reference, she had revealed it: 'After all I suffered last year with the abortion...' This was where the real disgust came from. It was the disgust she had felt then, for what she had brought with her own will on herself. Now she was venting it on him. The embryo that had invaded her womb was also his - but she could not blame him for it, nor for her decision to scrape it out, to scratch it away in blood from her inner, living tissue. But these germs were different, they were all his fault. The tables had been turned. Now the guilt could be entirely his. At last she had her revenge.

As he lay in bed that night, waiting for sleep to come, his thoughts revolved endlessly round his disease. The huge dose of penicillin had not really worked. There was some improvement, there seemed to be less irritation, but he had been living with the symptoms so long now that he wondered whether he was simply ceasing to notice them. And all the while, he might be suffering irreparable damage, as Emma had so bluntly put it. He could not trust himself to the Egyptian doctor, of that he was sure. Was there any point in trying anyone else? He thought not. There had been that friend of Ronald's in Alexandria who had been under treatment for allergies for over a year, and who was diagnosed back in Holland as suffering from typhoid. He had very nearly died. No, Egyptian medicine did not inspire confidence.

He broke the vicious circle of his preoccupation by deciding that he would take leave and return to London. That was the only sensible thing to do. He had done all he could, but it was clear that he had to admit defeat. It would be folly to persist. He must put himself in the hands of some competent doctors.

His parents would be surprised to see him. Usually he announced his homecomings well in advance, and made sure he brought a friend with him. This time there would be no forewarning, and he would be alone. But fortunately one rule that was never broken in the Erbury household was the rule of discretion. His parents would ask him no searching questions about his sudden arrival, they would not pry.

That was it, he would go back to London as soon as possible. He would present a request for leave to the undersecretary at the Ministry the next day. With any luck, he would be away before the weekend.

His decision drained his worries of their power. He drifted into vaguer thoughts of London, and of his parents and their home in Horsham, and he was soon asleep.

He woke abruptly in the middle of the night, aware that a noise of some kind had broken into his consciousness. The moon had risen and was shining strongly through his bedroom window, which he had left slightly ajar. The night was calm and windless. Then, from so close outside that he started, a piercing cry flowed into his room. It was a karawan, he recognised at once. That was what had woken him, the strange, liquid call of the bird, as if from another world. He sat up in bed and tried to locate where it had come from. It was so loud, so unexpected, so preternatural, that it had ended before he could work out if it had come from the front or the back of the building. If he opened the shutters, he would make a noise and disturb it if it had settled nearby. He would have a better chance creeping out onto the front balcony. The door to that he could open silently.

He slipped from the bed and heard his breath coming in and out in the tense silence. He moved with speed and stealth to the balcony door. Easing down the handle, he opened it and then stepped out into the cold moonlight. Everything was a dim, silver grey. Steadily and very slowly he crept along the side wall to the edge of the balcony and looked down at the grassy square below. Bushes of oleander formed dark clumps with hugging shadows. He could see no birds.

After a minute, watching motionless, he was rewarded - three sharp notes away to his right, and immediately after, a whitish shape, about the size of a curlew, rose into the air from a nearby rooftop and flew off in the direction of the City of the Dead. He had seen it, but not clearly. He was just about to go back to bed when almost directly above him that call was answered by another - the full, descanting cry, trilling down in looping curves to the last note, which wavered and then suddenly stopped, leaving its echoes ringing in the night air.

The karawan must be on the roof above him. He crept back into the flat, and went out through his front door, and climbed the main staircase to the small door that led to the roof terrace. He pulled the bolt back carefully, opened the door and inched forward. The flat area of concrete was empty. Suddenly there was the sound of a flurry of wings behind him. He stepped quickly round the door gable and saw the chimney of the central heating system rising about six feet off the roof. The karawan was already ten feet higher, flying under the sharp, bright disc of the moon. He could see again the whitish plumage, there were no marks, no distinguishing bands on the wings or tail. The head was large, but unlike an owl, clearly separated from the body. The wing-beat was quick, vigorous.

That was all. In a second, the bird was no more than a dark

receding shape. But at least he had seen it up close. He had shared its palpable, living space. For a moment, as it had risen away from him in fright, he and the karawan had been one.

'Well, well, Dominic. Come in. You have been keeping to yourself. What's this about your taking leave?'

Before he could answer, Rory shouted over his shoulder: 'Annabel, it's Dominic.'

He heard her call from the bedroom: 'Oh, just coming.'

He was warmed by the obvious pleasure in her voice, but standing there in front of Rory, a part of him was disturbed - could one be just friends with a woman, especially when she was as desirable as Annabel? He felt it was impossible, friendship was a self-willed pretence. One would always want to go further. Now, of course, she was with Rory, and he would not go further. They sat down in the salon and waited for her arrival.

'I bumped into that British Council chap, Andrew, at the ministry, and he told me you were going off. What's up?'

'I'm just going back for a few weeks. You know I've been thinking of buying a flat in London. Well, one has come up that I think would suit. I'm going to have a look at it.'

He came out with this fiction with just the right amount of nonchalance. But if anything, he despised the efficiency of his lying. Why couldn't he just tell the truth? What did this subterfuge serve? It was another unnecessary pretence.

'I suppose I should be doing something similar,' Rory said. 'Inflation is ripping away. No point in keeping any money in the bank. Borrow, borrow, that's the way.'

'It certainly makes financial sense. And psychologically I feel I need a London base. This expatriate life is all very well, but it'll be good to have one's own place in the UK.'

Annabel appeared, wearing a buff-coloured galabiya. The

small embroidered cloth buttons down the front were undone. As she came towards him and leaned down to kiss him, a deep shadow drew his gaze down between her breasts.

'So you did come to see us,' she said. 'You weren't just being British.'

'Being British?'

'You know, saying -Yes, I'll drop round some time - and then never doing it.'

'No, no,' he smiled. 'I suppose Egypt must have worn away those hypocrisies.'

'Jolly good. It doesn't in everyone. I met a very nice couple at a dinner party last weekend, and a few days later, I passed the man in Maidan al Tahrir and he pretended he hadn't seen me. It was awful, and sad at the same time. There I was, just about to greet him, to be friendly, when I saw him clamp shut. I could feel him decide not to recognise me. Why on earth are people like that?'

'Insecure,' Rory said. 'In the dinner party context, he's re-laxed and open. In the crowded Cairo street, he's on guard, he's tense. Then you come along, and he just can't switch modes from reserve to openness.'

'But I felt quite hurt,' Annabel said.

'You needn't have. It was pure psychological mechanics on his part. He didn't mean it.'

'No, he probably regretted it as much as you did, Annabel.' Dominic agreed. 'He made an inappropriate response, We all do that all the time, don't we?'

'Do we?' she replied, and as he looked at her young, open face and the unclouded frankness in her eyes, he thought that yes, she probably was an exception.

'Well, most of us do.'

He thought of Emma's two letters, they were inappropriate, grotesquely so. For the first time, they had sown contempt in him for her. What would happen when they confronted each other in a few days' time in England?

Annabel insisted that Dominic stay for supper.

'Rory is preparing it,' she said with a laugh.

'He's not becoming domesticated, is he?' he asked, as Rory got up with an absent-minded embarrassment and went into the kitchen. A few moments later he reappeared with a tray on which were crowded bottles of beer, foole and taamiya sandwiches in brown pitta bread, and large green mangoes.

'Well, here you are,' he said somewhat apologetically.

The whole meal he had obviously bought in the street outside the apartment block. The sandwiches were the cheapest food available in Cairo, the staple of its poverty stricken millions. Yet they tasted very good, and were nutritious. Rory began to hand them round.

'What have your researches into the Muslim Brotherhood turned up?' Dominic asked.

'Not much, but what I have learned has filled me with such contradictory feelings. On the one hand I think - Good, Islam will provide them with the backbone to do something, to restore their honour. On the other hand, the idea that people are seriously considering the reintroduction of a theocracy, of holy law and all that, is infinitely depressing. Because, of course, it's antediluvian. It'll be a total failure.'

'The introduction of a theocracy in Israel, or at least of a religiously inspired state, hasn't been such a failure, has it? Dominic said.

'No, it hasn't,' Annabel agreed. 'Why should the Muslims fail, while the Jews succeed?'

'Firstly, I don't agree that Israel is a theocracy. They have their sabbath mania, but by and large, their society isn't much different from most secular democracies. It might become more theocratic in future, but right now it's liberal in the western tradition. These new Muslim brothers want to go the whole hog - if you'll excuse the metaphor. They want to make every aspect of life follow the strictest, purest, Islamic doctrine.'

'But even the early Islamic empire couldn't achieve that.'

'I know, but that's what they're after, and if they get the chance, they could go a long way down that road. But the other thing you forget when you compare Arab failure with Israeli success is that Israel has no autonomous success. Without the constant and massive support of America, Israel would sink in no time. So what Arab theocracy faces is not Israeli theocracy, which as I say I don't believe exists, but western technological secularism.'

'Islam and science can go together.'

'How far? Maybe I am too anti-religion, but I can't see how a society, a culture, which posits unique authority in one book, can contend with the scientific method and master technology. It'll give them fire in their hearts, yes, resolve, yes, but will it give them missiles?'

'They can buy them from the Russians or anyone else. I think you may be mistaken. You're looking at technologically backward countries, and saying that their religious beliefs are responsible. But there are just too many other variables in the equation. What about the crippling rule of the Ottomans, for example?'

'They probably succumbed to the same affliction. Do we know why the Turks were once great? Remember they were fighting pre-scientific Europe. One theocracy against another. It was only when Europe had overthrown the power of its churches that it surged to dominance. The irony of it is that the Jews with their archaic religious dream exploited that dominance to get into Palestine, and could not exist without it today.'

'So you don't hold out much hope for the new Islamic revival,' Dominic said. He regretted now that he had brought up the topic. Rory was unstoppable. He wondered how he could draw Annabel more into the conversation. It was from her that he wanted to get sustenance.

'No, I'm afraid not,' Rory went on. 'But as I said, I'm terribly sympathetic. Here are these people, defeated, colonised, and abused by us, and they are searching back into their mystic heart for the will and the strength to fight us. Islam is all they have. Faith is all they have. It reminds me so much of the Irish - the same hopeless odds, the same implacable defiance, and the same clinging to a religious faith as the only support. It's pathetic, and I'm afraid it won't work.'

'The Irish succeeded, Rory,' Annabel said with tenderness in her voice. 'Not completely, but they did succeed.'

'Yes, they did partly, but not in my part,' he said with a lopsided smile. 'Maybe the Arabs, too, will partly succeed. I hope they do.'

Twenty-five

The plane began its long descent towards London airport. Warning signs blinked on above the seats, and there was a relieving quietness in the rushing noise of the engines. The voice of the stewardess came over the PA system: 'Saeedati was seddati...Ladies and gentlemen...'

In breathy, guttural Arabic, she announced their imminent arrival at Heathrow. Dominic stared out of the window at the grey banks of cloud below, and imagined that they were the protective cover over the European world, where all was cool, well-organised, and secure - so different from the clear, blazing heat that flayed Egypt, in which human life could only be a remorseless struggle.

The plane fell through the air into the muffling blanket, and suddenly patches of cloud vapour were flashing past the windows, giving passengers the only true impression they got of the great speed of their aircraft. For a moment, Dominic imagined himself flung out into that rushing, damp world - falling, falling, his body turning over and over, his clothes torn away, his consciousness blasted numb.

A grinding noise and an unsettling vibration invaded the cabin. He looked out and saw the trailing flaps creep back and down from the wings, bending into the air stream. They trembled in its force, and trails of vapour condensed from their sharp edges. Then came the louder noise of the undercarriage going down and locking into position.

They broke through the cloud, and London lay, with its familiar mosaic of houses, roads, and gardens, beneath them. Dominic felt no particular emotion. He had made this trip home too many times from his various jobs abroad. But there was a certain pleasing contrast between this capital of his country, with the Thames winding through it, and Cairo, divided by the great double flow of the Nile.

The dreariness of the airport and the drizzling weather did not depress him. All this too was familiar and secure. It would obviously put off the foreign visitor, but it gave him comfort. He got through immigration and customs quickly and took a bus to Victoria. With any luck he would be home in time for dinner.

'Hello, son. Good to have you back. To see you again. Very glad indeed.'

His father shook his hand and welcomed him in his habitual, clumsy phrases. This is how it always was between them - any warmth, any tenderness, was felt to be incongruous. It could only be haltingly, imperfectly expressed.

'Good to see you, Father,' he replied in like manner. 'A bit unexpected. Jolly good to be home.'

He remarked again the strong clasp of his father's hand. This was not hesitant, it went with his military style - the clipped moustache, the flushed cheeks, the tweed jacket and cavalry twill trousers. Within these conventions and rituals, his father was sure and utterly reliable, and from them he drew a great personal strength, which Dominic always found impressive. It didn't equip him very well for the intimate realm of the family, that was all.

As they drove from the station to the house, a more casual and easy-going exchange developed.

'Your mother was delighted to hear that you were coming. But hadn't you told us that your leave was in May or June?'

'They changed the dates of this year's Alexandria conference, so I had to bring it forward. Hope it won't rain all the time I'm here.'

'Well, it may not. We've been having a mild spring so far. The daffodils are coming through at a cracking pace. I might be able to line up some gardening for you.'

His father and Dominic laughed together. This was one of the unfailing family jokes - his father always tried to get him out into the garden when he was home for a visit. Dominic would prevaricate, postpone, make excuses. But eventually he would have to submit. Over the years, it had become a good-humoured piece of family theatre.

They pulled into the short, cypress-lined avenue leading to the house.

'Your mother is out at one of her damned meetings,' his father said as they got out of the car. 'She's spending a great deal of her time at them these days. I prefer to work with plants, as you know. Much more predictable, much less wearing. I'm afraid she's overdoing it.'

This was the pattern of his parents' lives. His father, after retiring from the Ministry of Defence, had withdrawn to his garden, while his mother had moved in the opposite direction. Leaving her home, that had been her overriding concern for more than twenty years, she was now throwing herself into local politics. She hoped to turn the tide that had swamped the Heath government in 1974.

'Oh, I'm sure it's good for her,' Dominic said. 'Far better to be involved, doing something, than sitting at home complaining. Remember what she was like when Wilson got in first?'

'Indeed I do,' his father replied.

Next morning at breakfast, the family sat round the kitchen table. Everything was, Dominic noted, exactly as it had been throughout his childhood and adolescence - his father reading the morning's Times, propped against the teapot, his mother having her first cigarette of the day, the food they ate, the ritual silence, broken only by requests for marmalade or butter. He felt a small elation at this constancy, this immutable order at the beginning of each day. Yet he recalled how it had once filled him with a sense of claustrophobic panic. Years ago, before he had escaped for good, the mere presence of his parents and the awareness of their cast-iron ways and prejudices had exerted an insidious and awful pressure on him.

Now he looked across the table at them and felt only affection.

'You'd better hurry, Dominic,' his mother suggested. 'It's nearly ten past nine.'

He glanced at the clock. He knew his mother kept it some minutes fast on purpose.

'So it is. Well, I'll be back at about six, I should think. If I'm held up in town, I'll ring.'

He walked briskly to the station, and caught the nine-thirty to Victoria. On the train, he read the Guardian. There was a long article in it about the Sinai disengagement agreement, filed by the Jerusalem correspondent, who was obviously Jewish. That was clear from his name, but it was also clear from the pervasive assumption that underpinned the article - that what led to peace was good, and what perpetuated hostility was wrong. Of course the whole western world shared that assumption, for, as Dominic now understood, it was in their interests. He found it striking that in the article no credibility whatever was given to the line proclaimed by Syria and the Rejection Front. Yet in Britain's last great struggle, implacable hostility, the refusal of a dishonorable peace, had been the very cornerstone of Churchill's policy and the nation's will.

None-the-less, the Jewish correspondent's prose was subtly respectful of Sadat and the Egyptians. Things had changed a good deal since the '67 war, with its Israeli heroes and its crude abuse of the Arabs - not so much in substance, but in tone.

Dominic got a taxi from Victoria Station to Hammersmith Hospital. He knew that there was a V.D. clinic there. Victoria Street and the Embankment were grey and wet. They too were unchanged - the same old-fashioned London buses, the same ungainly black taxis with their noisy diesel engines. Why did the British cling so to the old?

In contrast, the hospital and clinic were modern and efficient. He was issued with a patient's card, and joined about half a dozen people in the waiting room. Four of them were black, and he felt a curious surprise that they too should be caught by afflictions similar to his. He felt, though he knew it at once to be a ridiculous sentimentality, that they came from a simpler, cleaner life.

Soon his name was called and he followed a male nurse into one of the surgeries. A doctor sat at the desk and Dominic began a long account of his infection and of all the antibiotics he had taken. As he came to the huge doses of penicillin, the doctor's eyebrows rose and the man muttered 'Good Lord'. He then began asking questions about Dominic's sexual life - who he thought he had caught the infection from, whether he had had relations after its onset, the number of partners he had. Dominic answered each question, and as he did so, a slow, disabling mood of guilt settled on him.

'Hmm, hmm' he doctor acknowledged his last answer mechanically. 'Do you practise oral sex?'

For a fraction of a second, Dominic was paralysed. In panic he asked himself: 'Do I or don't I?', but before he could decide what the answer was, he heard his voice saying 'no' into the tensed, empty silence that hung between himself and the doctor. He knew at once why he had been asked - gonorrhoea could infect the throat - and knew also that he had lied. A remorseless flush of shame crept up from his beating heart and spread over his face. Why, why, had he lied? What was to be gained from it? Why was he afflicted with this cowardice? Crippled by his embarrassment, he answered the remaining questions in a kind of daze. If the doctor had noticed, he was sparing him the torture of making it obvious, the torture of the piercing gaze.

'All right,' he said, 'let's have a look at you then.'

Dominic submitted to the examination with relief. Now he had no part to play, he had no further responsibility. He became a mere human object, passive and anonymous, as the doctor poked him, felt him, peered at him.

'Good,' the doctor concluded. 'Go for your tests now.'

Dominic followed the male nurse out of the surgery and into a small curtained booth. Here the nurse asked him to take out his penis and he milked it for a discharge sample. In doing so, he pushed the platinum wire a little way up the urethra and Dominic felt a sharp pain. Soon the wire was out and the nurse was applying it to a microscopic slide, and then wiping it deftly over the surface of a culture dish.

'Wait in the waiting room now, please.' the nurse said in his sing-song Indian voice.

Ten minutes later, Dominic was re-admitted to the doctor.

'Well, we have found no trace of gonorrhoea, whether you

had it in Egypt or not. In any case, we are going to treat the infection as non-specific until we have the culture results in a few days. Take these, four times a day. No alcohol and no sex. Come back on Thursday.'

He handed over the prescription and gave a brief smile.

Dominic walked out into the hospital forecourt, flooded with watery yellow sunlight, and glanced at the piece of paper the doctor had given him. The drug prescribed was tetracycline, one of those the Cairo laboratory had reported his infection was resistant to. Well, he would take it and see. He walked over Westminster Bridge, and the lofty towers of Barry and Pugin rose up before him, triumphant. His spirits lifted.

'Are you going to visit that girl you mentioned in your letters?'

Dominic knew that sooner or later his mother was bound to ask this question. He was ready with the answer.

'You mean Emma, Mother? Not for a week or so. She's very busy with her work at the moment.'

He was glad that his voice betrayed no emotion. His mother smiled at him with her usual, vague indulgence.

'In a week or so? That will be nice. Will you have some more apple tart?'

She stretched across and took his plate.

'Yes, that will be nice,' she repeated. 'It can't be much fun for you out here, so far from town, and all your old university friends.'

'Oh, it would be practically the same in London - most of my friends have moved far and wide. Except for John, he's still slogging away in Shell. May have moved up a few floors, that's all.'

'Well, it is a very good company, you know, Dominic.'

His mother was strongly in favour of established companies, established careers.

His own rather unpredictable progress in the world of international aid was worryingly unreal for her. Yet she was loyal when any acquaintance asked her how he was doing. Her reply was invariably: 'Oh, he's doing very well in ..." and she would name the country with a grave intonation which made it sound important and challenging.

'Yes, well, I'll drop in and see John when I'm up in town some day. Very strange, I heard from Hugh recently that he's gone religious.'

'That is surprising,' his father said. 'Wasn't he the chap who got a double first in maths and physics, something like that? Very bright?'

'He was. And he was also extraordinarily sceptical, and detached - probably because he didn't quite belong. His father was Austrian. He saw through most of our illusions and prejudices at university, I can tell you. Now he's fallen for the greatest illusion of them all.'

'Now dear, just because you don't believe, you mustn't dismiss other people's beliefs.'

His mother appealed thus to his politeness, and he was now free enough and fond enough of her to say:

'I suppose not, Mother. But it did surprise me.'

'Well, he's older now. He probably draws much comfort from the church.'

Dominic let this conclude the discussion. Once he would have argued on, relentlessly driving his mother back on the defensive. Her religious feelings were ill-defined and obscure, but she held to them with a doggedness which used to exasperate him. Their battles over religion had disturbed all his adolescence, and had usually ended with his father shouting: "I will not have you addressing your mother in such tones. That is enough!" Each of their clashes was thus frozen in unresolved tension by his father's authority. Now, it was different. He no longer felt the need to dispute. He could live, he had lived, and he could let live.

The tetracycline was working. With an immense feeling of relief, Dominic noticed on the third morning that his urine flowed freely and without irritation. The drug was curing him. So much for the Egyptian laboratory results. How utterly incompetent they had been. Had his cultures been contaminated with someone else's? He would never know, but it was the most likely explanation.

When he returned to the clinic on the Thursday, he was told that the culture tests confirmed the first diagnosis. The urethritis was non-specific.

'I shouldn't think there's any more to worry about,' the doctor reassured him. 'Continue with the course and come for a check-up in a week.'

Dominic felt intense gratitude. This doctor had taken such a great weight from him.

'Thank you very much. Thank you so much,' he said effusively.

'Not at all,' the man replied, dismissing him with a perfunctory wave of his hand.

Though he was now so close to Emma geographically, and cured of his disease, he could not bring himself to contact her. The idea of picking up the telephone and ringing her at her college seemed insuperably difficult. What could he say to her, how could he address her after those last two letters that she had sent him? The idea that they would be forced to exchange pleasantries on the telephone out of politeness was excruciating, impossible. Should he write to her, and propose a meeting? He shrank even from that, because he would have to explain and appeal to her. He would have to apologise, and this he would not do. If anything, he felt he deserved apologies from her.

The only solution to his dilemma was for him to visit her without warning, simply to confront her. He would hire a car and drive to Oxford. He would just walk in on her. Achieve a fait accompli - no apology, no falseness, just get to her again and see what there was between them. Yes, that was how he would do it, the third week, after his check-up visit to the clinic.

In the meantime, he travelled up to London frequently. He went to the cinema, catching up on a year's films that he had missed in Egypt. The one that made the most impression on him was Scorcese's 'Taxi Driver'. After it, he came out of the cinema pent up by the violence of the last scenes. They had had a strong physical effect on him, they had pumped adrenalin into his blood so that he floated in a kind of ecstasy. He wanted to go into the attack himself, to soar into a violent paroxysm with someone, with anyone. If a stranger jossled him, he would fly at him, and give vent to this palpable, thrilling violence. He felt his eyes ranging over the crowd that poured out of the cinema with him, as if seeking a victim.

Later, as he returned to Horsham in the train, a reaction set it. The film was horrible - a heartless, pornographic portrait of deranged individual aggression. It had a crucial moral ambivalence in it. It was pure Hollywood - crime, the criminal, presented with all the brilliance that the camera could achieve. Guns, prostitution, blood, the absolute horror as the anti-hero fires point blank at his rival at the top of the stairs and the great spray of red covers the wall behind - what was the point of it?

Why was it shown? Why did people troop in to watch it and be thrilled by it? It was simply evil, decadent, perverted. This was the state of Christendom, or rather the state of its art, that greeted him on his return from the world of Islam. He saw it with a new and shocking clearness - the cult of violence pouring out of Hollywood. Generation after generation in the West fed on Scarface, Al Capone, Bonnie and Clyde, and now this vicious killer in New York, all delivered in images whose beauty and slickness were completely false.

And the cult was not even confined to the cinema, it had infected literature. What was "In Cold Blood" but a literary "Taxi Driver", only even more brutal? This was the gladiatorial spectacle of our times, not public combat between profession-al fighters, but glamourised, vicarious regurgitation of private crime.

And had it always been the same? Wasn't "Macbeth" Shakespeare's Hollywood play? And the press with their mas-sive coverage of sex murders, particularly of children. Why did people want to read about them? Did they stir, like "Taxi Driver", evil impulses under the guise of moral indignation? Dominic felt intense revulsion against the culture of his own world that he had never felt before. Even if there were children raped and murdered in Egypt, the press did not pour it out on their front pages for the masses to feed on. As he sat in the train, watching the glistening bark of the birch trees that caught the light from the train windows, he brooded on the sickness of the West.

On his next visit to London, he could not bear to go to the cinema, but went instead to the National Gallery. He wandered through the familiar rooms to see his favourite paintings - the Gainsborough portrait of Mr. and Mrs. Andrews, Van Ruisdael's landscape with its pool of wintry light, Piero della Francesca's unfinished masterpiece, full of simplicity and rapture.

After these, it was the Rubens room that held him. He was overwhelmed as never before by the optimism and celebration of his wonderful nudes - the great puckered, creamy thighs of the women, their high, soft breasts, and the muscular power of the men. He sat down before each canvas and allowed his eye to feast on their glory of form and colour - the genial vision of a great human spirit, who had come to Britain and worked here. It was only right that his room in the gallery should be one of the richest.

Twenty-six

O nce he had decided on the method of his approach to Emma, he set about realising it without any misgivings or apprehension. He moved almost mechanically, borne along by his plan. He hired a pretty blue Renault 5 from a garage in Clapham and took the M4 west. He cut north to Henly and had afternoon tea there, looking out over the rippling grey water on which he had rowed with his school eight so many summers before. The flat river, almost level with the town, brimming against the green fields, always pleased him, and evoked now not just a nostalgia for his youth, but more diffusely a deep feeling for his country and its civilised traditions.

Then he drove on north, through small villages with their old, red-brick houses, and over the wide, rich farmland of Oxfordshire. He came into the university city as night was falling. Magdalen tower rose up a dark silhouette on his right. The streets were quiet, just a few cars, and students riding past on bicycles with scarves wrapped round their faces.

He went straight to Emma's college, and parked in front of the entrance. He walked past the lodge and crossed the grassy square to a row of Victorian houses on the far side. This was where she lived, where his letters from Egypt found her. Her house, number seven, was the second in the row. She had described her room to him, an attic overlooking the garden, so he climbed up the long staircase. His heart beat fast from exertion and agitation as he stood before her door and read her name tab on it. Impulsively he turned the handle. The door opened, it was unlocked. In the room a light was on, but almost at once, he knew that she was not there. He went in and closed the door behind him. He walked round the room looking at her books, her dressing table, her clothes strewn on the chair and on the bed. There were two photographs on a chest of drawers. He examined each of them. The first was one of Emma, caught in a bright, flecked light, looking up in surprise from a book, probably taken by her father in their garden in Alexandria. The second was pale and northern - greens and greys, Emma and a man standing by a river. The man had his arm round her, and she was smiling, carefree. She looked so happy that a needle of jealousy pierced him. He put the photograph down. He gazed round the room. There was nothing of him in it, no image, no keepsake. He felt suddenly drained, an intruder. Why had he come?

He slumped into a chair and gave way to a mood of resentment and withdrawal. Really, he was peripheral to Emma's life, someone she met in the holidays, who had no significance here. But he would not leave. No, he would stay and wait for her. He would vent his resentment on her. She would not be the only one to deliver blows.

He sat in the dim light, thoughts rolling over and over in his mind. He seemed to lose contact with time. He heard other girls in the house opening and closing their doors, talking, but they were very far outside this space, Emma's space.

A long time later, he could not tell how long, the door opened abruptly and she strode into the room. He did not move, but was instantly, sharply awake. She dropped a folder on a table and stooping to take off a shoe, she saw him. She straightened up slowly and her face showed fear. For a moment she was dumbstruck, only fear showed in her eyes. He saw it, and it gratified him. So, he had this purchase on her.

'Dominic, what? Why are you here?'

She had found her voice. It was hollow.

'Would you prefer me not to be?'

'What? But I... how did you get here?'

'I drove up from London and just walked in. You leave the door open.'

'No, but why are you in England? I didn't know you were coming.'

'Quite. It's something of a surprise.'

'Yes, it is. You gave me such a shock.'

She was recovering herself. She sat on the bed and pulled off her shoes.

'Ouf - I've been on my feet all evening. Rehearsals. Did I tell you? I'm doing the sets for the play.'

'You didn't.'

But he blocked her escape into small talk.

'For obvious reasons.'

'What reasons.'

'Your new boyfriend.'

He pointed dismissively at the photograph on her chest of drawers.

'I suppose he's the male lead.'

'Robert? That's Robert, the friend who stayed with me in your flat in Cairo last year. Don't you recognise him?'

Dominic thought quickly - Robert? Was that Robert? He hadn't recognised him at all.

'So, an old flame rather than a new one.'

'He's neither. It's just a nice photograph of me, that's all.'

'It is. You don't seem to have a care in the world.'

'I didn't then.'

'Before you met me.'

'Yes, it was.'

'Before I brought you pregnancy and disease.'

He noticed the flinch in her neck.

'Yes.'

'And now you've had enough.'

'Enough?'

'You don't want any more - your last two letters.'

'I was so angry when I wrote those.'

He waited. This was her first gesture to him. Did it mean that the rejection in the letters was past, done with?

'So?'

'So? I was just disgusted by the thought of catching it from you. Are you better now?'

'Yes, thank God.'

'I'm glad.'

'So am I. It was ghastly.'

'It must have been. Poor you.'

There was a clear sympathy in her voice.

'What would you know about it?' he said, and immediately regretted his perverse reply.

'Thank god you didn't get it,' he went on. 'It just rots your soul, a thing like that. Especially when you can't cure it. That's why I came back, to cure it.'

'That sounds awful.'

'The Egyptians are hopeless. First they diagnosed me wrongly. It wasn't gonorrhoea at all. Then they gave me drugs that didn't work.'

'Just like Christian in Alex - the doctors nearly killed him with drugs.'

'Fortunately I didn't put myself entirely in their hands. Then I came to London. It's been cleared up here in no time.'

'What a relief. You must feel so much better.'

'Yes, I do. And you? Any problem?'

'No, nothing.'

'El hamdulillah.'

She smiled at the echo of Egypt.

'So,' he looked around the room, 'this is your lair. It's very nice.'

'Isn't it? I was so lucky to get this room. Janet got it for me last vacation.'

'Janet?'

'She's next door. She's an old school friend.'

'And what about your men friends, do they like it?'

Again she was at a loss, he saw her mouth twitch slightly as she said:

'Which men friends?'

'The ones that stay overnight. Is it allowed?'

'Officially no. It's easy to get in at night, the problem is getting out in the morning.'

'So I shouldn't try it then?'

He would force himself on her, claim ownership of her, whether she wanted it or not.

'Well, I don't know... '

The fact that she was not refusing him outright gave him a cold pleasure. He wondered if she was actually prepared to sleep with him again. Could she change from hate to love, just as she had changed from love to hate? It might be so.

'No, I'll get a hotel room. It'll be easier.'

'If you like, Dominic,'

There was a delicate ambivalence in her tone as she said this that suddenly drew him to her. He got out of his chair and went to her. As she looked up at him, he wanted to put his hand on her hair, its shadow falling down her white cheek. But he could not.

'Shall we go out and eat something?' he asked instead.

'Yes, let's. I'm awfully hungry,' she said and stood up beside him. 'Let's go to Brown's. It's just down the road from here.'

A precarious normality was already established between them. She walked down the stairs in front of him buttoning up her coat. A girl passed them and smiled at her.

'Hello, Emma.'

'Hello, Janet,' she replied with a small swing of her hair.

The girl passed Dominic and gave him a full look in the face. A look of inspection - who was Emma with now? - and a look of unflinching hunger. He knew in that moment that she had no man, that she was one of the girls of Oxford who slept night after night, month after month, alone, in this university where men outnumbered women by so many.

It was raining outside, cold March rain. They ran to the car and jumped in, slamming the doors.

'She looked sad, that girl,' he said.

'Janet, you mean? She is.'

'Lonely, no boyfriend?'

'Well, she has a sort of one - Richard. But he's very strange. Janet says that he's never touched her. They've been together for a year now, but he says that he has no sexual feeling for her. He just likes her a lot.'

'And she puts up with him?'

'Yes. And what is strange is that before she came up to Oxford, she had an affair with a married man. She lived with him on and off for about six months. He broke off with her and went back to his wife. Now she's stuck with Richard.'

'Why doesn't she drop him and get somebody else?'

'Well, it's quite hard to meet men.'

'What, with the place teeming with students?'

'I mean it's hard to get to know them, to establish relationships.'

'The boarding school lives on.'

He imagined the extraordinary change it must be for Emma when she left this wet, cloistered world and arrived in Egypt, with its immediate intimacy and immediate sexual pursuit.

'Just down on the right. You can park here,' she said, pointing to a gap between the cars. He saw the yellow lighted windows of the restaurant hazed with condensation.

Over the meal they talked of Janet. Emma explained that she was the daughter of the headmaster of a school, and that she had gone to the school herself, and that her lover had been one of the teachers. For some reason his wife and children had not joined him at the school, and he lived during the week in a small cottage on the school grounds. At weekends he returned to Coventry to stay with his family. Janet had begun to visit him secretly on her free afternoons. Almost at once he had taken her to bed.

She had told Emma of the almost uncontainable excitement as she walked among her school-friends in his presence, knowing that whereas they were all virgins, she had already passed into womanhood, and that he, unknown to them, was her lover.

'And what about her parents? Didn't they sus her out?'

'It seems not. It was her last year. She went to Belgium to au pair the next year, and he fixed it so that they could spend the summer together in a friend's house in Brittany somewhere.

Her parents thought she was in Brussels.'

'How did it end?'

'He left the school and went back to Coventry. She never saw him again. She says that now she can hardly believe it all happened. She had this terribly intense love affair, and then she came to Oxford and well, now all she's got is Richard.'

'She's very attractive, in a rather gawky kind of way.'

'Oh, you fancy her?'

'I could fancy her,' he dissimulated. In fact her hungry gaze had excited him intensely, and he had felt a momentary intoxication that, possessing Emma, he could also, through her, enjoy these other Oxford girls in their starved, bookish world.

They went on to talk about Richard, and Emma speculated why he might be blocked sexually. The conversation loosened the tension between them, and Dominic lost his feeling that Emma was a moral prig whose blame he would not bear. It was strange, he reflected, how they could talk so freely of the sexual problems of others, and yet be unable to achieve a similar frankness about themselves. For they avoided their own problems as a topic of conversation completely.

As they drove back to the college, he reached across and took her hand.

'Will you come and stay with me tonight?'

There was only a short hesitation.

'If you like,' she said, and again her tentative way of consenting and exposing herself touched him.

'Do you want to get some things.'

'Yes, and I need to lock up.'

They returned to her room and she collected some clothes and toilet things and put them into a small carrier bag. He watched, and was filled with slow, quiet happiness. Her small possessions and acts of privacy were knitting themselves back into his life.

They drove out of Oxford onto the ring road and found a motel where he got a double room. The receptionist asked no questions - this was how easy it was now in England to spend the night with a young woman. Maybe in some years, Emma's college would be just as liberated, with men and women students living together in the same buildings, and if they wanted, sleeping together.

Once in the hotel bedroom, with its brightness and clinical style of decor, he felt a dragging inhibition and awkwardness afflict him. The unresolved sexual antagonism was reforming the barrier between them. They undressed quickly and got into bed. He would not turn out the light, but lay looking into her face, stroking her hair, as if searching for still more acceptance from her. He knew that he must break through the barrier, he must bring his lips to hers and kiss her, but some powerful paralysing force prevented him. The impulse, now that it was up to him to bring it to fulfillment, seemed to remain frozen for a long, long, time. He felt that there was no mechanism in him to carry it through.

Emma closed her eyes, and at each stroke of his hand, her head made a small movement. After many minutes her face suddenly became clouded, and though her eyes remained closed, their lids flickered and a frown cut down between them. This broke Dominic's stasis. He brought his head to hers quickly and began kissing her. She responded. The barrier gave way.

He turned off the light, but the room was filled with a white glow from a lamp outside in the parking place. In it he saw her body again, her thin flanks, her breasts with their pale aureoles, her long thighs. He kissed her and was assuaged. The antagonism of the past was behind them. He rolled way from her and got out a contraceptive from his toilet bag. Lying on his back he put it on carefully. She looked at him in silence, waiting, and when he was ready, pulled him over her and opened her legs to receive him.

Once in her, he remembered everything - the way she moved her body, the feel of her open mouth, the pressure of her ribs, her legs hooking themselves over his. She was exactly as she had always been. His orgasm came soon in spite of the rubber, and with him, she ceased to move. He almost fell into sleep, but forced himself awake and off her. He took the rubber off carefully and dropped it beside the bed. Then he lay against her, with his head on her breasts. Soon they were both asleep.

The next day he took her back to her college for a tutorial at eleven o'clock. He left the car outside the college and walked through the quad to St. Giles and then down to the Ashmolean Museum. Entering the forecourt he felt that the building, for all its classical character, lacked distinction. Was it because the street was too narrow, the site too cramped? But he went inside with a keen sense of anticipation - he had come to see the museum's small but very fine collection of Pre-Raphaelite paintings.

There was hardly anyone in the upstairs galleries. The atmosphere was so different from the National Gallery in London, with its hordes of visitors. He could stand right up against the canvases and examine their detail without getting in anyone's way. A large painting showing a monk hiding from a search party held his attention longest. The composition had such a modern immediacy about it, yet its subject came from the era of Anselm. He moved back and forth in front of the painting, noting its brilliant detail, and studying with astonishment how the painter had achieved it. The brushwork was so fine, so painstaking, for such a large work. Though the inspiration of Pre-Raphaelitism may have been sentimental, its execution was daunting labour. Perhaps that was why, as a movement, it had been still-born, a provincial flourish with no resonance abroad. The whole drift of modernism had been away from that kind of craftsmanship.

He met Emma for lunch in a pub near her college. The place had low ceilings and uneven wooden floors. They found a settle near a window, and drinking down the flat beer, he felt calm contentment - he was slipping back into England and its ways so effortlessly. The sun broke through running clouds outside and filled the street with gleaming light.

'What about the next few days, Emma? Do you have much on?'

'Not really. The next rehearsal is on Tuesday, and my next tutorial is a week away.'

'I was just thinking - why don't we go off and tour the Cotswolds villages?'

'That sounds super.'

'Have you been to many?'

'We went to Woodstock last summer, and I've been to Banbury once. That's all.'

'Let's do it then. Can you spare a few days? What about work?'

'Oh, I find work so boring these days. I'd love to go.'

'All right. There's one village I've always wanted to visit. It's called Shipton-under-Witchwood. No idea what it's like, but I saw it on a map once and the name just captivated me. Shipton-under-Witchwood - why is it so beautiful? I think it's the un-der-Witchwood part - witch-hazel, witch elm, Witchwood. We must see it.'

'It sounds lovely,' she said enthusiastically, but the adjective she used disappointed him. She could not feel the almost mystical aura of the name. It did not fill her with reverence, as it did him.

'Can we leave today, this afternoon?'

'Yes. I'll leave a note for Janet.'

In the wet, blowy weather of March, they explored the uplands of the Cotswolds, and their nesting valleys. They wandered through the villages made of ochre stone, staying in small country guest houses. One day, they looked down on the topiary and ancient roofs of Compton Wynyates. Often, they had afternoon tea of hot scones with jam and whipped cream.

Shipton-under-Witchwood was not the most beautiful of the villages. Dominic reconciled himself a little sadly to the fact that its ineffable mystery lay only in its name. The name was wonderful, limitless, and thrilling beyond the reach of his consciousness, but the reality of Shipton was not.

The village that pleased them most was Chipping Campden. Its curved main street and irregular houses were the most medieval in character -they drew the imagination back, back into England's past. The slow, unfolding vista of the street, with its darkened stone, moved them both. They decided to make this their last stopping place. They would spend their last night together here.

They had their evening meal in a pub. It was good country cooking, a vegetable pie with thick, dry pastry. Dominic drank beer, Emma cider. Afterwards, they walked up the street once again, buffeted by the wind, delighting in the glowing windows and dark ochre shadows.

As they got into bed, Dominic felt the gloom of impending departure. He cupped Emma's breasts in his hands and kissed them one after the other for a long, long time. Her nipples rose and fell with her waves of excitement. He thought of getting a contraceptive for himself but was reluctant to break off his slow, last exploration of her body. He would, this last time, give her pleasure, and forgo his own. He moved down the bed and lay with his face on her bush of hair. A sense of her passivity, of the vulnerability of this opening into her body, and of what she had suffered through it, filled him with a poignant love for her. He kissed her there, and lay between her legs, his tongue feeling into her, knowing the strange, soft flesh, its faintly bitter taste. Long, darkly, her explored her, with healing devotion.

She seemed inert. She lay quite still. He wondered if she liked these soft, intimate caresses. Eventually, he came away and moving up her body, he touched her shoulders and her mouth with his lips.

'Aren't you going to do it properly?' she said.

Clear irritation gave her question a cutting edge. He was shocked into a reflex of defence.

'But it's still your fertile period, isn't it?'

He could not explain that tonight he recoiled from the mechanics of putting on a contraceptive.

'You're too old, that's all. Tired out.'

She rolled away from him.

The remark wounded him with unexpected power. But a clamouring impulse to protest he stifled. She must understand the real reason, but she chose this barb instead. Lying beside her as she fell asleep, his affection for her reeled back into his heart in coldness and confusion.

The next morning he woke in a mood of frozen neutrality. She made small remarks, he answered them. They packed up their bags and had breakfast. They drove south, back to Oxford, with no celebration of their days spent together, and no talk of the coming separation.

When they got to her college, he said that he would press on to avoid crossing London in the rush hour. She accepted this excuse as if it covered no new breach between them.

'When are you flying back to Cairo?'

'On Tuesday or Wednesday.'

'I wish I was coming. Spring is so late this year.'

'Yes, well, I'll get your bag.'

He opened the car door and got out. The fact that she talked of Egypt and going there as if it might merely provide a climatic change and had nothing to do with him added new resentment against her.

'Here you are. Goodbye then.'

She was standing beside him.

'Goodbye, Dominic.'

He kissed her quickly on both cheeks in the French way. He waited in a moment's strained silence but she said nothing more. He turned from her abruptly and got back into the car. He started the engine and give her a small wave of the hand. He reversed out of the parking place, and when he looked round to drive forward, he saw that she had already gone through the college entrance.

'Right,' he said to himself.

He pushed the gear lever into first, and moved out into the flow of traffic.

He spent the last few days of his leave at Horsham. When the weather was fine, he went for walks over the Matling estate. The open fields and scattered copses had retained their somewhat unkempt appearance. He wondered if most of the land was rented out. It probably was - Lord Matling was a more or less perpetual absentee. He now lived in Rhodesia and had declared for Smith. There was an air of abandonment about the place. It gave Dominic the sense of freedom to wander where he liked.

The swelling buds of the beech trees, the flush of growth in the sodden fields, delighted him. The English seasons, that had been the rhythm of his childhood and youth, rolled round without ceasing. Abroad, now, he had lost contact with them, but reassuringly, they would always be.

He went up to town once more before leaving, to see de Sica's last film. "The Garden of the Fizti-Continis". He knew that de Sica would be free of the repellent violence of Hollywood.

Going up Regent Street on a bus, he was struck by how empty it was - dead and deserted compared to a Cairo thoroughfare at the same hour. Unlighted shops presented their black glass fronts to the night. It was wet and cold. He wondered whether the oil crisis had cleared the streets. Was it really biting now, and not just a figment of the newspaper headlines?

When he got to the cinema, he was a few minutes late for the start of the film, and had to find his seat in the dark. The images on the screen absorbed him at once, images of the lives of two Ferara families, one rich, both Jewish. The truthfulness and beauty of the film's vision transformed his mood, and as the story moved to its tragic ending, he felt overwhelmed by its moral power. The terrible quietness of the last scene, a daughter comforting her weeping grandmother as their lives were crushed, was perfect art. As the Jewish falsetto sang the hymn to the martyrs of the Nazi camps, rage and hatred consumed Dominic that such evil had been accomplished, and as de Sica showed, with such awful banality.

Twenty-seven

Dominic's flight back to Cairo left London at two o'clock in the afternoon. Soon the sun was reddening in the western sky, and for half an hour the aircraft flew between two thick layers of stratus cloud which enclosed all the sun's blazing light in a fluid, airy world. The metallic aircraft was the only reminder of the earth, hidden away below.

Later, the lower layer of cloud broke up, and the massed peaks of the Alps showed through, milky pink and black. Over this barrier of snow and rock, the Mediterranean waited, promising warmth. Dominic was happy to be returning. His holiday had rid him of his disease, but the bitterness of his parting with Emma and the rather empty ritual of living with his parents made Egypt seem his real home, where he would once again draw strength.

As the aircraft began its approach to Cairo, he looked out of the window for the lights of the city. There must have been cloud, for at first he could see nothing, then suddenly, out of the darkness, there appeared all at once a maze of roadways speckled with light. They were low over Cairo's heart. The plane banked steeply and with his body leaning with it, he looked sideways almost straight down onto the two great black bands of the Nile spreading round el Guizera island. The old, old river thrilled him - he felt now that he belonged to it, and to the enormous city that crowded its banks.

'Well, Dominic, how are you?'

Rory shook his hand and pulling him closer, kissed him as an Egyptian would.

'Ahlan, ahlan,' he said, repeating the Arabic formula of welcome.

'Fine - it's really nice to be back,' Dominic replied.

They sat down and ordered beers and lunch.

'You look better. A bit white, but better. You've missed a glorious spring here.'

'How have things been at the Ministry?'

'Pretty uneventful. Writing up reports mostly, on what hasn't been done.'

'The solar heating project - any progress?'

'None at all. They are going cold on it. Of course they hope to get the Sinai oil-fields back soon, so they think their energy problems are over. It's 'bukra, bukra' on solar power, I'm afraid.'

'Oh, well, what else has been happening?'

'A friend of Ali's has come back from Lebanon. It's getting so bad there, that he has decided to return to Cairo and settle. His family emigrated to Beirut after the revolution some time. Anyway, now they're back.'

'What's his view on the civil war?'

'What you'd expect - that it's all the Palestinians' fault. You know - blame the refugees, the victims, but don't blame the people who drove them there.'

'But it's not just Lebanese versus Palestinians, is it? It's Lebanese fighting Lebanese as well.'

'It's primarily that, and of course, it suits Israel down to the ground.'

'Good Lord, for a month I've been away from all this. You

know how all news on the box just becomes meaningless formulae - do you think it's because they read it off those damned idiot boards?'

'No, it's because it's somebody else's problems. Anyway, things are pretty depressing out here. There's civil war in the Lebanon, and inflation ripping away in Egypt. The economy is getting completely out of hand. They're going to renege on their repayments to the Russians. Now tension is mounting with Libya. Evidently the western desert is teeming with tanks on both sides of the border.'

'That's all we need, a war between Egypt and Libya.'

'Oh, it won't come to that. It's just muscle flexing.'

'As long as they don't close the desert road to Agami. Have you been down?'

'Once or twice, but I'm getting rather tired of all that scene, Lynda and Nefrititi. Everyone is in one camp or the other, bickering away. Oh, your Dutch friends were asking for you.'

'Ronald and Elizabeth?'

'Yes. I told them you were in England, with Emma.'

'Did you? Well, it's partly true, I suppose. I did see her for a few days.'

'Elizabeth asked me if I thought you two were going to get married,' he said and laughed.

'And what did you reply?'

'Told her there wasn't a hope in hell.'

'Oh really?'

Rory's blunt, dismissive certainty made his spirit contract. Who was he to pronounce thus? Why couldn't people mind their own business? But he was probably right, of course.

'Talking of marriage,' Rory went on, 'I've been invited by an Egyptian friend to a country wedding this weekend. Can you come? It should be fun. It's in a tiny village in the delta called Bish Bish.'

'I'd like to, but am I invited?'

'Of course, no problem. Besides, they'll be short of cars, so you'll be able to help out in the wedding cavalcade. You know the sort of thing, horns honking all the way. Have you finally got your car papers sorted out?'

'Yes, I'm legal at last.'

'Fine, I'll tell Ali you're coming.'

Dominic smiled. He was back. Horsham and England were like discarded husks. Where would one suddenly find oneself dragged along to a wedding there? They arranged to meet at Rory's flat on the coming Saturday morning.

On Friday evening, Dominic rang Ronald and Elizabeth. Elizabeth answered.

'Hello, Dominic. How was England? Did you see the Queen?' she asked in gentle mockery.

'No, she was at Windsor. Still, I enjoyed myself - went on a tour of some beautiful villages near Oxford.'

'With Emma? How is she?'

'Well, well.'

The artificiality of his reply was patent.

'When are you coming down to Alex next? Oh, here's Ronald. I'll give him the phone. Come soon, OK?'

'Hey, Dominic, I've been waiting for you to come back. Look, it's time to solve the mystery of the karawan. You agree? Good. Willem and I will come down to Cairo. The moon is growing now, it will be a good time soon.'

'Fine, Ronald. Not this weekend, Rory and I are going to a wedding somewhere in the delta. How about next weekend?'

He heard him consulting with Elizabeth in rapid Dutch.

'Ya, next weekend, that's fine.'

'Do you know how to get to my place?'

He described the ring route round the east side of the city, past Khan Khalili and the Mamluk tombs, to Heliopolis. As they said goodbye, he felt lifted by Ronald's eagerness. At last they would discover the hidden identity of the night bird.

Twenty-eight

The next morning Dominic's car followed Rory's red Fiat out of Cairo on the delta road. Ali was with Rory in front, and they seemed engrossed in conversation in spite of the dense, chaotic traffic. Dominic watched Ali's left hand describe eloquent, fluid movements as he talked.

Once out in the country, they raced along the flat roads. The front wheel of Dominic's car began to shudder. His old MG was, he realised, getting loose in the joints. Soon he would have to sell her, back in the UK. He would not get another MG - their hard suspension was no match for Cairo road surfaces. In any case, the whole design was completely out of date. There had been no progress since the fifties - same rear axle, same lever shock absorbers, same pushrod engine. Now MG were just living off their name.

The two cars passed through Mahalla Kubra, the Place of the Bridge. The town was large, sprawling, industrialised, but once out of it, they were again swallowed up in farmland that looked much as it must have looked in the time of the Pharaohs. This was the realm of the fellahin, the struggling, burgeoning, lowest stratum of society, from which Egypt drew its perennial strength.

Some minutes later Rory pulled off the tarmac road onto a dirt track, and Dominic followed in his dusty wake. Donkeys ruled this thoroughfare, trotting along with their riders bob-

bing up and down side-saddle. These were usually round-bel-
lied men, with fat legs dangling almost to the ground, which
they waggled rhythmically in time with the donkeys' gait, as if
to deceive the beasts that they were somehow assisting them in
their progress.

The cars left the track and took to what was more like a
path, running along the top of a dyke between cotton fields. An
irrigation canal ran alongside it. They drove slowly and carefully
- a clumsy movement of the steering wheel and one of the cars
might slip over the edge and into the brown water. Dominic assumed that it was teeming with bilharzia.

Soon a village spread out it front of them, and pulling off
the dyke, they crossed an area of cracked brown earth and drew
up outside a modern, one-storied house. Ali got out of the Fiat
and was immediately surrounded by a crowd of small boys in
striped galabiyas and bare feet who had come scampering at the
sight of the cars. Rory and Dominic joined him, and it seemed
every one of the boys wanted to shake them by the hand. Ali
pushed his friends clear and through the gate.

'No, no, you can't shake hands with the whole village,' he
said, closing the gate behind him and barking something to the
boys who clustered on the other side.

They crossed the small garden, and the family came out of
the house to greet them. There was Ali's cousin, Kemal, Kemal's
elder brother, his parents, grandparents, and young sister. All of
them were animated and talked excitedly in Arabic. Dominic
couldn't understand very much, but his and Rory's replies
seemed to please them greatly. They were welcomed into the
house for tea.

Kemal was a tall and thin young man. His manner was almost grave. He was obviously the star of the family. A student

at Cairo University, he would go out and conquer. His brother, Morsi, was more jovial and had achieved less. He owned a taxi which he plied round the villages.

But the member of the family that most impressed Dominic was Aicha, Kemal's sister. She was still a child, maybe twelve or thirteen years old, and though tall, her body showed no signs of womanhood. She spoke little, but he often looked at her pale face with its striking, unclouded beauty. Whenever she looked back at him, it was transformed by a brilliant smile. Her spontaneity, her innocence, filled him with wonder. Was she not aware of her extraordinary power? Had she never looked at herself in a mirror? Had she not learned to manipulate that smile for her own ends? It seemed not. No, it was utterly pure, utterly disinterested. As he received these silent, smiling glances from her, he felt an almost painful joy.

Later in the evening, the family began to get ready to leave for the wedding. More relatives arrived at the house to join them. Soon there were thirty or so people milling about, and the excitement of the women broke out again and again in gay ululations. Dominic noticed how they covered their mouths with their hands when making these strange sounds, but even so, he could sometimes see their bright pink tongues vibrating from side to side.

Finally they were all ready to leave, the men in suits, the women in western-style dresses cut far lower than their normal daily wear. Aicha had on a frock of deep purple, obviously her best. Her eyes flashed with excitement. They all trooped out of the house and into the cars. Dominic managed to fit eight into and on his, three beside him on the front seat, including an enormous aunt with arms like white marrows, three children crammed in the space behind the seats, and two older boys sitting astride the front wings, clinging to the wheel arches. The rest disappeared into Rory's Fiat and Morsi's huge old taxi.

Thus overloaded, they moved off. Everyone was so high-spirited that Dominic felt only reckless disregard as he heard his exhaust pipe bang again and again on the uneven road. All six inside his car seemed to be talking their heads off. This was the big night of the year - he must get them there, no matter what.

The three cars came to the centre of the village where many of the houses were made of unplastered red brick, and parked in an empty place. A short distance away was a street where chairs had been set in lines in front of a wooden stage, and lights strung across. The place was already full of people, and on the stage, the bride and groom sat with serious faces, surrounded by a band of musicians who were busy setting up their microphones and amplifiers. Kemal led Rory and Dominic up onto the balcony of a house on one side of the street, close to the stage. They had a privileged view of the whole scene.

The band started playing with the amplifiers turned up deafeningly loud. A wave of excitement passed over the crowd seated below. They began clapping in time to the music, many with their palms horizontal, one hand bouncing forward off the other. Ululations from time to time added to the din.

Dominic looked for Aicha in the crowd and at last found her. Her face was beaming as if in a trance. The huge aunt was on one side of her and some of the younger children on the other.

Ali joined Rory and Dominic on the balcony.

'Where have you been?' Rory asked.

'I brought the belly dancer. Look, there she is.'

He pointed and sat down with them.

'Wow,' Rory exclaimed, 'what a belly.'

Ali laughed and raised his right hand in the air. Rory put his out to receive the slap - the ritual reward in Egypt for a *bon mot* or witty remark. Dominic smiled to himself. Rory had really gone native, adopted so many of the small gestures and ways of the Egyptians.

The dancer had now come to the front of the stage, and when the band changed the tempo, she began to dance. She was in her thirties, Dominic guessed, and just as the Egyptians like their belly dancers to be, she was well covered. Flesh lay on her in rounded slabs, and shook in violent little shudders when she danced. Her dress, cut low over her ample breasts and clinging to her hips, shook with it. The clapping below gained force.

'Why are the bride and groom so serious?' Dominic asked Ali.

'That is the tradition, Dominic. It is a serious day - the start of married life. They are not allowed to joke and laugh.'

'Really? Well, the crowd are making up for it.'

By the end of the first dance, the belly dancer was dripping with sweat. The mounds of her breasts showing above her *decollete* glistened like lumps of creamy dough.

'She is, how do you say, she can't talk.'

'Dumb? Is she?'

'Yes, that is right. She is dumb.'

As the end of another dance approached, her movements became faster and more vigorous. Her flesh seemed to roll and shake of its own will. The crowd responded, clapping and whistles filled the air. Then on the last trill of the music, she spun herself round and round. Stopping suddenly, she bowed and accepted their applause with thrown kisses. Then she stepped back towards the bride and groom, and reaching behind her, took a hand of each. Dominic wondered if she was going to pull them up to dance with her, but no - leaning back between them, she planted their hands firmly on her breasts, one on each. She smiled broadly, and with her own hands pressed theirs into her soft, yielding flesh, and moved them in slow, circular caresses. Dominic could hardly believe it was happening. He looked at the crowd - young and old, children, grandparents, all were hugely pleased. They cheered and laughed. So, he concluded, that was the role of the belly dancer at a country wedding - to set the erotic fire alight, to excite the bride and groom and to celebrate the sexual pleasure that would soon be theirs.

When her first performance was over, Kemal invited Ali and his British friends to eat in one of the rooms of the house. There were no other guests in the room. A table laden with food took up most of the space. The dishes were traditional and plentiful. Dominic felt uncomfortable at this special treatment for foreign guests - why weren't the other relatives eating with them? But he knew that to betray his discomfort would be ill-mannered, so he joined the other two as they piled their plates high. After they had eaten, they passed compliments to Kemal, who received them with obvious pleasure. Opening a door leading to the kitchen, he shouted a request for drinks, and a few moments later, a plump woman appeared with a tray of Coca Colas. Kemal handed them round and introduced the woman as their host, the mother of the groom. She stood at the door and smiled warmly as Rory and Dominic congratulated and thanked her.

When they returned to their chairs on the balcony, they saw the crowd sending up contributions to the band. One of the musicians held a microphone, and as each banknote was handed up, he repeated a formula of praise for the home town or village of the donor. Rory and Dominic sent notes, and as the names of Londra and Irlanda - Rory assumed that Lisnaskea was too unfamiliar for the musician to get hold of - came over the loudspeakers, the crowd cheered and waved up at them. They waved back.

How astonishingly warm they were, Dominic thought. They had forgotten and forgiven so much. Ten years before, during the '67 war, they must have howled at the iniquity of the British and the Americans.

The belly dancer reappeared on the stage and the music began again. She received the last banknotes sent up and tucked them down the front of her dress. For this second performance, she called for a chair by gesturing to the people seated below. One was handed up to her. She placed in on the stage and began to dance round it, rolling her hips sensually at it. Closer and closer she came, and then, spreading her legs on each side, she stood over it. Now her movements became slow, twisting, overtly sexual. With each beat of the music, she lowered her body a fraction, and when she was finally sitting astride the chair, she gave herself up to a rippling, grinding motion. Her eroticism was completely unrestrained. Again Dominic was amazed, and this time the Egyptian guests below also seemed to think that the performance was exceptional. First the young children, then the older girls and women, and finally even some of the grandmothers rose up from their seats and began to shout and to throw and twist their bodies in imitation. A kind of erotic hysteria was taking possession of them. The dancer's movements became even more abandoned, and they cried out and ululated to her in unbridled response.

Then Dominic noticed a group of men in galabiyas advancing on each side of the chairs. They had long staves in their hands and they began beating down on the heads of the women and children who had been aroused by the dancer. At first the blows had little effect, but they beat on, and slowly they began to gain on the hysteria. Their victims subsided one by one, putting up arms to ward off the blows, and resuming their seats.

Rory and Dominic looked at each other in disbelief.

'My God, what a scene,' Rory shouted over the din.

It proved to be the climax of the night's festivities. When it was over, the band started dismantling their equipment and packing their instruments. The crowd began to disperse. Soon only close relatives and friends were left. The couple came down from their chairs of honour and were led up to the balcony where Ali, Rory, and Dominic had been sitting. Soon these three found themselves part of two lines which formed a human corridor across the balcony to a door. The door was opened and revealed a bedroom. Dominic realised that they were actually going to witness the entry of the couple into the bridal chamber.

The bride and groom passed along between the two lines of relatives, receiving blessings and good wishes. Rory and Dominic shook the groom's hand. Ali kissed him. On the other side, the women kissed the bride. There was not the slightest embarrassment, not the slightest prurience. Eventually bride and groom went into the bedroom and the door was closed.

Dominic assumed that the parents would wait outside all night, to see the display of the bloodied sheet, but he and the rest of them quickly dispersed.

Kemal led the party back to the cars. Dominic noticed at once that something was amiss with his, and getting closer, saw that his back light lenses had gone. He walked round inspecting the car. Every object that could be removed had been removed. The children of Bish Bish had stripped it for souvenirs - mirrors, wipers, lenses, hub caps, rubbing strips, fog-lights. All had been torn off. It was as if the car had been attacked by iron-jawed locusts. The shell had been left clean.

'What a night,' Dominic muttered to himself, as he got in and opened the other door for his numerous passengers.

But it was not over. At the house, he and Rory were shown into the main bedroom where they were to share a huge double bed. No doubt it normally slept half a dozen, but tonight it was theirs alone. Everyone else would pile into the other bedrooms and the sitting room.

Talking over the scenes of the wedding, they undressed and got into bed. Then they blew out the candle and settled for sleep. It did not come. No sooner were they in darkness than the bed came alive with the wriggling of innumerable fleas. They were everywhere, biting into the strange, foreign flesh for the first blood of the night.

'Christ, it's infested, infested!' Rory cried. 'And we've no matches. We've had it.'

They lay helpless victims, twisting, turning, slapping - all completely useless. The feast of the fleas went on.

'I can't stand it, I've got to get out,' Dominic said, and he leapt out of the bed. Rory heard him pacing round the room in the dark.

'They must put up with it every night. Can you imagine?'

'They probably don't notice it any more. Built up an immunity, I suppose. If only I could do the same,' Rory replied.

Dominic paced up and down. He could not get back into that seething mass. How could Rory stand it? As he paced, he heard Rory's breathing gradually getting deeper. Somehow he was able to accept the probing little jaws. After a while, the breathing roughened into snores. Rory was asleep.

Incredible, Dominic thought. He decided to trust himself to

the concrete floor rather than face the fleas again.

Stretched out with his bundled-up towel as a pillow, he passed a fitful night. Now and then he heard the pattering and scratching of mice round him, but to these he felt friendly - they were preferable by far to the ravenous fleas.

They woke next morning to the crowing of cocks and the braying of donkeys. Dominic was groggy from lack of sleep, but Rory did not seem any the worse for his loss of blood.

'I was amazed that you stuck it out,' Dominic told him.

'Oh, I was just too tired to resist,' he replied. 'Let them get me, I'm only a humble link in the food chain.'

The other people in the house were up and about before them. They could hear women's voices chattering in the kitchen.

They breakfasted with Kemal and Morsi outside on the small patio at the front of the house. Kemal's mother and Aicha brought them oil bread, cream, yogurt, jam, fruit, and mint tea. Again Dominic caught Aicha's eye whenever he could, and again she sent him her brilliant smiles. He realised that already he was tenderly, irrationally in love with her.

When the family gathered outside the gate to wave them goodbye, it was her gaze that he held last. He felt such sharp regret at leaving her. As he drove off, his head straining round to see the last of her, he narrowly missed a small child who had wandered in front of his car. The shock of this, the fear of adding death to his litany of country experiences, cut off his connection with her. Now she was left behind, lost.

Outside the village, he led the way along the dyke path. Soon Rory pulled right to go and pick up Ali from a nearby farm where he had spent the night. Dominic continued on to the main road and headed back to Cairo.

Twenty-nine

'**Y**ou're crackers, Dominic. It's an absurd idea.'

'But why? Let's say she's thirteen. All right, I'd only have three or four years to wait, then she'd be seventeen. It'd be worth it - she's the most beautiful, the most wonderful girl I've ever seen.'

'You're soft in the head. You're a gaga romantic. For God's sake, grow up.'

'You don't seem to understand the possibilities of love, Rory. I know it sounds ridiculous, but I also know it's profoundly right.'

The thought of marrying Aicha had formed itself in his mind as he drove back from Bish Bish. Why go on with Emma, with her manifest lack of commitment to him? Why struggle against her little darts of rejection? Here was this pure, generous girl. In her smile, he was sure he knew her. Knew all he needed to know. He would open negotiations with her family through Ali. By pronouncing the short formulae required, he would become a Muslim and overcome the religious difficulty. Emma would be at Oxford for a further two years in any case. After three, he could marry Aicha.

'Profoundly silly, more like it. Have you no sense?'

Rory sucked cigarette smoke deep into his lungs.

'What do you know of her? Is she still at school? She can't speak of word of English probably. Your Arabic is hopeless. How would you communicate in God's name - by sign language? Look, if you must drool and make an ass of yourself with young girls, stick to Emma. At least she's somehow on your level, she's in your culture.'

Dominic was surprised by the contempt in his attack. Did beauty have no power over him? He felt it was useless to answer back.

'For all you know, Aicha is completely ignorant. She's a peasant. This smile of hers that you're so hooked on - what can it tell you about her likes and dislikes? Look, I know something about country girls, they're as grasping and as materialistic as the rest. You've got this stupid Wordsworthian notion of the pure native and pure nature. It's all bullshit. After a couple of years, she'd be driving you mad because your furniture wasn't gilded and shiny enough.'

'You think so?'

'Of course. And where are you going to live? Here in Egypt? And when your contract is up? Could she survive in Britain? No way.'

Dominic regretted that he's come round to discuss his extraordinary dream with Rory. Obviously his friend could not see the point of it.

'Oh well, it was just an idea, a very attractive idea,' he said, getting to his feet.

'Right,' Rory shot back, 'now forget it.'

But Dominic did not forget it. He kept the dream at the back of his mind as a kind of refuge. The pure simplicity of it burned on - he had seen a young girl, he had fallen in love with her. When she was grown into a woman, he would marry her. It would be a surrender to the force of nature, an unknitting of his knots. It would humble him and it would transform him. Most of all, it would lift him to a new plane of moral certainty. He would become clear, integral.

In Egypt, such a marriage seemed conceivable. People here had a directness about sexuality. They were matter of fact. Life still ran in the traditional pattern, where marriage was the straightforward goal of everyone growing up. For Aicha, it would be a simple choice - would she want him for a husband or would she not? It would not be a question of whether she loved him enough, or whether she should pursue a career first. For Egyptians still, at least for the vast majority, marriage remained the categorical priority. A woman married young, and her first child came within a year. Certainly she could go to university, she could work, but all that was secondary. The family was the rock.

Thinking of Aicha, Dominic responded to this vision of life. It seemed a kind of absolution, stronger than the bankrupt romantic ethic, the constant quest for personal satisfaction that was destroying marriage in the west. It called for a humbling of the personal will, a surrender to the beauty man found in woman and woman found in man. It was simple, it was profound.

And it was not unreal or unrealistic. He had come across such a marriage. On one of his first jobs abroad, in Kenya, he had met just such a couple. The husband had seen his wife for the first time in a village up in the White Highlands. She had been a girl of eighteen, grinding corn like her mother, outside their two-roomed shamba home. She had waved to him as he passed in his Landrover. Later he had sought her out, taken her to a community centre dance. Within a year he paid the bride price for her and they were married. When Dominic met them, they had two light brown children, who were, like their mother, beautiful. They lived much like any other expatriate couple, if a little more privately.

Would he too make such a marriage, and follow this sweeping urge towards Aicha? Rory thought such an idea absurd. He wondered if Annabel would think likewise. Where was she these days? Rory had not mentioned her during the weekend in Bish Bish. Had they split up already?

Later in the week, he called at her apartment in Zamalek. There was no answer, and he was about to get back into the lift when the door of the apartment opposite hers opened and she appeared in it.

'Dominic, how nice to see you.'

She closed the door behind her and crossed the landing.

'You rang my bell? I thought so, I can hear it in Samira's flat. Lucky I came out.'

She raised her face to his to receive kisses.

'Why, were you thinking of ignoring it?'

'Well, I was helping Samira to prepare mehshi - you know how long that takes - and I thought it was Gamal. You don't know Gamal,' she said, opening her door and letting them in.

'No, I don't.'

'Well, he's a dreadful hanger-on. He comes here and moons about and expects me to give him my undivided attention.'

'That's the nature of Egyptian friendship, isn't it? It may not last, but while it does, it's all consuming.'

'Exactly, and it does get tiring. But how are you, how was your trip, how was Emma?'

'Oh, fine,' he said with as little enthusiasm as he could without sounding rude. 'And you and Rory? What gives? Have you two parted company?'

'I'm afraid so. What would you like to drink? Let's have some wine and I'll tell you about it. I've got over it now. I think I can...tell you about it, that is.'

She went into the kitchen and returned with a bottle and two glasses.

'Would you open it?'

He set about the task. For a moment she watched him.

'After it happened I was terribly upset. I didn't think he could be so hurtful.'

'Why? What happened?'

He pulled the cork.

'It was soon after you left. He was more or less living here by then, so that he could drop down to Cairo University whenever he wanted. He's met some radical students through Ali and Kemal who are mixed up with a new Islamic group, some sort of underground opposition. I don't know what they do exactly, but Rory spent more and more time with them. He seemed to find their company more stimulating than mine.'

'Well, politics is his main interest, you've always known that.'

'Quite, but it wasn't just politics. One of the group was a girl student - woman I should say. She's here doing a maters at the American University, something on American policy in the Middle East.'

'Ah.'

'She's from Kuwait, a rather exceptional woman.'

'Really? From Kuwait?'

'Yes. I came home from work one afternoon, and discovered that he had brought her here, to my flat. They had been in my bed. I was outraged. As soon as I could, I accused him of it. And do you know, he admitted it straight away as if it was nothing to be ashamed of. I was very, very hurt.'

She drained her glass. He refilled it.

'So, it's all over?'

'Yes, it is. I haven't seen him since. Now Gamal is trailing me. He knows I'm on my own again. He's the exact opposite of Rory, he clings, already. I really don't seem to have much luck with my men, do I?'

'It seems not, Annabel. I'm sorry you and Rory have broken up. I thought you might reform him, you know, get rid of that cold, rather egotistical machismo of his.'

'We were getting on quite well, but then he went and did that. Why?'

'He's a rather nervous character, Annabel,' Dominic said quickly - she was showing signs of distress, and he must pull her out of it.

'It's better it ended pretty soon. You see, he'd always told me that he never wanted to get involved with anyone. It's completely immature, don't you think? He just treats women as some sort of diversion. Or threat - he must feel threatened by them. That's why he's got to keep his distance.'

'But he doesn't keep it, that's the trouble. We were living together. He said he cared for me.'

'Did he? He can't have much, can he? They were just diplomatic lies. No, at bottom, he can't connect, he can't get close.'

'But why?'

'It's probably basic for him. He feels he must maintain some kind of inviolate individuality. It's neurotic, but it's part of his intellectual make-up. You know the way he dismisses all the usual opinions and beliefs, especially in politics. He thinks he knows better. Maybe he does, but he can only maintain his cynicism, his scepticism, rather, by keeping clear of everyone. And this is somehow caught up in his sexual nature too. He's got to be cut off, inviolate there as well.'

'I don't know,' Annabel said. 'I think it's more a matter of not respecting women. For some reason, he sees women as inferior. They don't merit his respect. No wonder he's happy here in Egypt. A harem is his ideal, no doubt. One woman one night, another the next.'

'You think it's as bad as that?'

'Yes, I do. He's been infected by this Arab male chauvinism. Woman is there to be bought and sold - treated like a chattel. Picked up and then dropped whenever the man feels like it.'

'Oh, I think he's been like this always, since long before coming to Egypt.'

After this, Dominic reflected, he could not possibly discuss his dream of Aicha with Annabel. She would dismiss his idea of marrying her as just another buying and selling of woman. And was it that, more or less? His confidence that it would be fundamentally good suddenly faltered.

'Well, living here certainly hasn't improved him. Just pandered to his worst instincts.'

'Maybe. But I think finally that Rory is rather sad - what can he get out of this constant chopping and changing?'

'Oh, I suppose it was stupid of me to get involved with him, I guessed what he was like right at the beginning.'

'It's funny that - how one commits oneself, willy-nilly. I suppose it's exactly the same for a woman. One commits oneself and then perseveres even though one knows that it isn't right.'

That is what he had done with Emma. And the reverse is also true, he thought. One pulls back from someone, and it then becomes less and less possible to change one's course and reapproach. He had felt drawn to Annabel when he first met her, but his impulse had been still-born because of Emma. Now they were stuck in the tracks of friendship. To break across them and to approach her sexually seemed enormously difficult. And now that she had become the victim of Rory's callousness, the idea was faintly repellent.

They talked on and finished the bottle of wine. He tried to console her as best he could, but, perversely, this inched him further and further back from her. When he got up to leave, he said that he would see her again soon, but he knew, with a sense of relief, that he would not make any special effort to do so.

Thirty

After his return from London, Dominic had felt little desire to write to Emma. But when ten days had passed, he forced himself to do so. On re-reading his letter, he found that it contained all the clumsiness of dutiful correspondence, lacking any inspiration. It ended with a query as to whether she had really enjoyed their tour together in the Cotswolds - she had expressed no appreciation of it to him on their journey back to Oxford. Nor had she written to him since. He was asking her in this way for some kind of affirmation, but he knew that it was also more to chide her for her ingratitude than to reach back into her heart.

The following Saturday as arranged, Ronald and Willem arrived at his flat just before lunch. They went to the club to eat and to discuss their bird-watching expedition.

'It's a very good time,' Ronald said in his usual vigorous English. 'We are very near a full moon, and it's the mating season! There should be plenty of them about tonight.'

'Yes, exactly,' Dominic agreed. 'They may come out this way during the night, but we should go to the river, don't you think?'

'Yes, the Nile is the only place where I have actually seen them. We saw four flying together at nightfall - it was too dark to see them clearly, but I'm sure they were karawan.'

'When was that?'

'Two weeks ago,' Willem answered. 'We came to Cairo for a party at a Dutchman's house.'

'We were sitting on his balcony overlooking the river,' Ronald continued. 'On Zamalek, and they flew past us.'

'How did you know they were karawan?'

'They called,' said Willem, 'that's why we looked for them. I saw them first.'

'Good chap. Well, tonight's the night. Have you brought your binoculars and your birdbooks?'

'Ya, ya,' Ronald said, 'we're fully equipped.'

'Listen,' Dominic went on with mounting enthusiasm, 'I think the best place is up-river, out of town a bit. Do you know Andre's, that chicken restaurant off the Guiza Road? A friend told me he heard them calling a lot round there.'

'But it's quite far from the Nile,' Ronald objected.

'Yes, but there's a big canal running alongside the road, and it's good open country. We'll try there first anyway.'

'OK, good idee,' Ronald agreed. It was one of his few mistakes in English - the final diphthong of the word became a single long vowel.

The sun was a shimmering orange disc, already sinking behind the palms, as they pulled off the Guiza road to follow the canal in amongst the farmland. They had left the strip of nightclubs behind, and soon the only buildings to be seen were low bungalows set well away from the dirt road. They were probably the country villas of wealthy Cairenes, who used them as refuges from the heat and noise of the city.

'Keep you eyes open, Willem,' Dominic said. 'We've got to see one before the light goes. Otherwise we haven't a chance of making a definite identification.'

'I don't think they're owls,' the boy said.

'Oh, why not?'

'When we saw them from Jan's balcony, they were flying quite close together, in a group. I don't think any owls fly like that. They are always alone, no?'

'I believe you're right. Surely owls always fly around alone?'

'So what night birds fly together?' Ronald asked.

'I really don't know. Maybe nightjars? I doubt it. The only thing I can think of is geese flying high at night, on migration. But obviously the karawan can't be any kind of duck or goose. For one thing, it's too small, and there's no long neck.'

'What about a coot or a moorhen?' Willem asked. 'A small water bird like that?'

'No, no, the cries of all those water birds are so different - nothing like the karawan,' Ronald said.

'But what about the corncrake, Ronald?' Dominic suggested. 'That has a unique call - quite unlike all the others.'

'Yes, that's true,' he conceded.

They drove on slowly, peering across the canal into the dusty yellow evening light.

'Damn,' Dominic said, 'We're looking into the sun. If we don't see one soon, we'll only be able to make out the shape.'

They passed the restaurant on their left. Half a mile further on, the eucalyptus and palm trees gave way to open country. Dark green clover rose lush in wide bands. In the distance, some women were walking back towards the road after the day's work. Soon the road parted company with the canal, and they were surrounded by the fields.

'We should stop, Ronald, We'll have a better chance of spotting them if we do,' Dominic said.

Ronald brought his Landrover to a halt by a clump of bushes and switched off the engine. They got their binoculars ready and waited. Across the fields from the city the high, wavering voices of the muezzin reached them, calling the evening prayer. Darkness was settling quickly, and colours were fading from the scene into muddy greys.

'What is that?'

Willem pointed. They trained their glasses on the bird, a black shadow, but the long forked tail marked it as a kite, flying to its roost after a day of endless soaring, endless gliding over the earth.

Ten minutes later in the thickening dark they realised that the karawan had eluded them again. They had seen only two, far off, obscure smudges giving their strident call, but soon lost from view, impossible to identify.

'Oh well, what a shame. Another time,' Dominic said to Willem, who was clearly crestfallen.

Ronald started the engine and they moved off.

'We'll go back to Andre's and have a good dinner anyway. Eh, Ronald?'

'Yes, good idee.'

Rejoining the canal, they heard more karawan calling, and saw some flying over the fields on the other side, but they were only dark silhouettes. Ronald parked near the restaurant and got out. Willem took up a pair of binoculars and scanned the night air. He would not give up. As if in encouragement, a sudden trilling call reached them from across the water. Its brilliance, its wailing descant made all their hearts beat faster.

'My God, that was close. Just over there on the other bank.' Dominic said in a strained whisper.

They peered into the darkening twilight. Where was it? On the canal bank perhaps?

'I see them! I see them!' Willem cried in a voice high with

excitement.

'Where?'

'On the ground. They are running. Look, look, near the dyke.'

Dominic tried to focus his glasses on the brown earth of the field on the other side, but at first he could see almost nothing. Slowly his pupils opened and a pale light began to pick out clumps of earth, small plants. Then he saw a round grey ball running across the field of view at high speed, almost like a rat running for its life.

'Yes, yes, I've got one,' he exclaimed.

'Give me the binoculars, Willem.'

Ronald grabbed them from his son.

'There's another. Oh, the place is full of them.'

Dominic caught sight of several more, making their dashes across the rough ground, stopping dead still, then dashing on. Two ran together and then suddenly lifted into flight. Their wild notes filled the air.

'How extraordinary. They're ground birds. They're runners. Do you see them, Ronald?'

'Ya, ya, I see them.'

Willem tugged impatiently at his father's arm.

A few minutes later, the last light of the day was gone. The stars shone through the dull glow that spread across the sky from the city. They went into the restaurant in high spirits and ordered mezza, oriental hors d'oeuvres, and chicken. Ronald and Dominic drank Stella beer. They had their bird-books open on the table.

'Do you think they could be plovers?' Dominic said. 'I remember in East Africa plovers running like that, not as fast though. Just a minute, I'll check Robert's for plovers. Maybe it's an African species.'

He opened Robert's "Birds of South Africa", one of the best bird-books he had ever used - the only good thing to come out of that racist culture, he used to think - and quickly scanned the illustrations of plovers. He turned to the text.

'Listen to this: "Typical plover habit of running in starts. Quite often feeds at night. Voice: an attractive whistle that carries far". No, that's not the karawan's call. Also it says that it is usually found in large flocks in tidal estuaries.'

He looked up at Ronald and Willem.

'No, and anyway, it's the same size as a golden plover. That's too small. We want something large - with a voice like a wader, like a curlew or an oystercatcher. Hey, oystercatchers flight at dusk and call very loudly. I've heard them in Scotland on late summer evenings.'

'Yes, and in Holland we hear curlews at night sometimes.' Willem said.

'The karawan is about the size of a curlew, but the beak is not long at all. And this is a real night bird, it must have big eyes, like an owl, or a nightjar. My God, the big eye - stone curlew!'

He smacked his hand down on the table in triumph. The dishes rattled.

'Hold on.'

He looked up the stone curlew illustrations in Robert's.

'There it is. Look at that great yellow eye!'

Ronald and Willem strained over the book.

'It's called "dikkop" in South Africa - that's Afrikaans. Dutch too?'

He found the text entry and went straight to voice and read out:

'A loud, but plaintive tcho-u, the end of the note drawn out and gradually tailing off. Very often heard on moonlight nights. That's it, oh we've got it. Listen: At night often comes about homesteads, where its melancholy whistling notes cause misgivings in the minds of the superstitious. That's the karawan, it must be. Check it in Collins, Ronald.'

In that book, there were two species listed for Egypt, the common stone curlew, found in open, dry, stony country, and the Senegal thicknee, confined to Egypt, with a more nasal, metallic voice, and frequenting orchards, gardens, and sandy river beds. They decided on the thicknee.

'Yes, I think we have identified it at last,' Ronald said.

Willem peered over the page.

'Burhinus senegalensis,' he read out slowly and deliberately.

'Burhinus senegalensis,' Dominic repeated, laughing.

They drank to their success.

Thirty-one

Some weeks later, Dominic was looking through the Egyptian Gazette, Cairo's English language daily, in his office at the Ministry. Sadat had decided to hold another referendum, and the paper was advocating the need for a " full participation" of the voters. Hardly necessary, Dominic thought, the last one had been a complete success, with 99.78% in favour. Yet here was the Gazette, not only discussing this new referendum as if it were something more than empty political theatre, but even trying to persuade people to make the effort to troop down to the voting booths.

Still, there was something to be said for referenda in Egypt - all government employees were given a holiday, to enable them to fulfill their democratic duty and go and vote. Foreigners like Dominic and Rory also had the day off.

He rang through to the Rural Development section.

'Have you seen this news, Rory, about the referendum?'

'Yes, I have. What a complete farce. If we voted against, do you think we'd make a dent in the figures?'

'Doubt it. But we might be sacked for ingratitude. We're getting the usual holiday.'

'We shouldn't take it. We should work in protest.'

'Well, this time it's on a Wednesday, next Wednesday. That means we can have a long weekend in Agami.'

'All right. I'm persuaded. I'll protest next time. We'll have to go in your car. Mine's being re-sprayed.'

'Oh, what happened?'

'Backed into by a bloody army lorry. I was buying bread at a stall, looked round, and there they were, grinding the whole of one side with their Volga monster, or whatever those old Russian trucks are called.'

'Bad luck, Rory, I am sorry.'

'Well, I suppose it was my turn. Yours was the onslaught of the Bish Bish metal scavengers.'

'So it was,' Dominic said and laughed.

They made arrangements for their departure to Agami at the weekend.

When they got out of Cairo onto the desert road on the Wednesday evening, conditions had turned stormy. There was a gale of wind sweeping across the western desert. The dunes smoked like volcanoes - sand whipping off their crests and billowing away in low turbulent plumes. And more sand, like beige smoke, rushed across the tarmac. In places the road was covered with drifts.

'I hope this doesn't get any worse,' Dominic said, 'If it does, it'll strip all the paint off the front of the car, and frost the headlights.'

'Just slow down,' Rory replied. 'We're in no hurry.'

Dominic eased back on the accelerator, and the low-slung car bored slowly into the streaming, gritty air. At times they seemed completely enclosed by the sand-storm, the daylight became obscure and ominous. A moment later, they would enter a clearer patch, with the sun hanging yellow, bathed in a limpid pool of sky ahead of them.

'What are you thinking of doing in June?' Rory asked. 'Will you renew?'

Their contracts ran from September to September, and June was the renewal month.

'I haven't given it much thought yet. In some ways I really enjoy living in Cairo, but I've been working abroad quite a long time now - longer than you - and maybe it's time I was getting back.'

'Shouldn't be too difficult for you, with your industrial experience.'

'I suppose not. What about you?'

'I'll stay on, definitely. You may be right, we probably are self-indulgent, hopping from one expatriate scene to another, but the Middle East is extraordinarily interesting. Something big is going to happen in Egypt soon. I 'm almost certain. I'd like to be here to see it.'

'What, another war, another revolution?'

'Either or both. It's like a morality play, the Middle East. A tragedy on classical lines. Sometimes I feel that the end of it all will begin here.'

'Better not be around then, surely?'

'Oh, being here or there will make not the slightest difference. We'll all be in it. Haven't I told you Ian's story?'

Dominic shook his head and kept his eyes on the road. Where was the white line? He had lost it again.

'Ian was a friend of my father's. Used to live in Derry before the war. Evidently the people of Derry used to promenade in the evening like they do in Spain. Anyway, one evening, Ian ran into a bloke he knew, a bit of a know-all. "How's it going?" he asked him. "Splendid," your man replied. "But it looks like war," Ian said. "Indeed it does." "You don't sound worried." "I'm not, I'm off out of it." "Really? But where?" The friend swung his cane in a stylish arc. "The other day I got out a map of the world and found the spot that's furthest away from everywhere - as safe as houses." "And where's that?" A dramatic pause. "Singapore!" replied the friend in triumph. The poor man spent the war in a Jap prison camp - damn near died,' Rory concluded with a chuckle.

'All right,' Dominic conceded, 'one might as well be atomised here as in London.'

'Exactly. And I would prefer to be an onlooker up close. You know, I was reading Thucydides last month - his history of the Peleponnesian war. It was absolutely brilliant. The war destroyed the classical world of Greece. It was cataclysmic. Thucydides charts the inexorable process by which it got under way. It was just like the Middle East.'

'How?'

'The same recipe, I tell you. Two big powers, Athens and Sparta, dragged into a war over a colony. Oh, it's described marvellously. The petty frictions at the beginning. The commitments of support. The threats to prestige. The impossibility of turning back. And most important, the desperate, suicidal ploys of the colony. They had nothing to lose, or rather they had everything to lose, and so they brought the whole Greek world crashing down on their heads.'

'That does sound a bit like the Middle East. The '73 war was pretty close - the Americans were on nuclear alert by the end of it.'

'They were, and remember, the Israelis were busting through in Suez at the time. Imagine what would have happened if it had been the other way round, the Egyptians or Syrians crashing into Israel. I mean the imminent collapse of the favourite colony. Without a shadow of a doubt, the Israelis would have used their nuclear bombs, and that, my friend, would have been it.'

'And we, the West, would have been on the wrong side.'

'Yes. That's nothing new, is it? Vietnam, Suez.'

'I suppose not.'

Dominic was suddenly struck by the haphazardness of history - the infinitismal acts of human will that set the awful tides in motion, that produced what seemed in retrospect to be inevitable. Rory's scenario was perfectly plausible, it could happen. It had already very nearly happened. He felt the hairs on the back of his neck rise.

'No doubt that's why the US is arming the Israelis to the teeth,' he said. 'Evidently they're much stronger now than ever before. To stop the Arabs from ever thinking of having another go.'

'Just a step in the inexorable morality play, towards doomsday - the putting so much into it that you can't go back. While the basic, underlying truth remains - your colony is rotten. It exists only by virtue - excuse the pun - of a completely indefensible principle, that some people have the God-given right to take, to rob, another people of their country. And that evil is eating away at the core. Soon it's gong to bring the world crashing down, and by God, we deserve it, we deserve it!'

'But what can we do about it?'

'Nothing, everything. But at least we must see it, recognise it, admit it. You remember the German excuse - "we never knew". We cannot allow ourselves to slip into that.'

'I've just had a disturbing thought, Rory. If one is completely powerless, mightn't it be better not to know?'

'Never. That is absolute moral cowardice. Anyway, one cannot completely not know. One always knows something, then one chooses to ignore it. Before the deed there is the thought - there is the world of thought in which everything is done. We are all part of that world of thought. We can't not be. That's the first step - the essential step, to take responsibility for your thoughts. To see if they are true or false, right or wrong, good or bad. Even if everyone else doesn't care, you must. And if they don't, you must make them. You know, I've been reading up about the start of Zionism. I told you I thought I was onto something. Well, I've no proof as yet, maybe it doesn't exist, but I know in my bones that I'm on the right track. I'm sure it's a fact, and it's a fact that, if it were widely known, would change people's perceptions, would affect the world of thought in which actions are possible.'

'What is it then, for God's sake?'

'That the whole thing was a cash transaction.'

'A what?'

'A purchase - cash for land. Their money for somebody else's territory.'

'Whose money? The Jews'?'

'Exactly. You know, it's always been an official mystery, why the British government played ball with the Zionists, why Balfour made his fateful declaration. There are all sorts of theories - he wanted to get rid of Jews from Britain and Europe, he wanted to get America into the war, he wanted to repay a Jewish scientist who had invented a new way of making explosives, he wanted a dependable colony in the Middle East to protect the life-line to India. After their centuries of experience in Ireland, the British knew that there was no more dependable colony than a religious minority. Well, those are some of the theories. And there's probably some truth in all of them. But even all of them together aren't completely convincing. They are just not a necessary condition. I believe there was a much more pressing motive - money. The government at that time, at one of the lowest ebbs in the war, was broke. They were desperate for money to support the war effort. Remember, this was the era of private capitalism - governments had to raise money in the capitalist market place and the Americans were being tight on loans.'

'So the Jews had the money.'

'And the British were about to go for Palestine. They got hard cash on a post-dated cheque. If it bounced, no matter, but they had to have the money. It was like Churchill's bombing feint in the next war, a calculated gamble, only this time, at someone else's expense. Who knows, like Churchill's gamble, it may have saved the day.'

'But what evidence is there?'

'Circumstantial. The financial crisis is well known - that's history. Then the declaration itself - who was it handed to? Not Weizmann. No, Lord Rothchild - the English end of the world's richest banking family. What could Rothchild and his other Jewish banking associates offer in return for a piece of conquered territory? Money, and lots of it. And Jewish bankers had been financing wars for centuries, all governments knew that. When the Russo-Japanese War was raging, a Japanese delegation came to London to ask for financial help under the terms of the Anglo-Japanese treaty. The British government refused, but put them in touch with Jewish bankers in London who took on the job. The Japs hammered the Russians and Japan has always supported Israel as a result.'

'So the whole thing, the start of it all, was a sordid money transaction. The Palestinians sold for a mess of pottage.'

'For vital national interests, money to stay in the war, to defeat Germany. Not for pie-in-the-sky colonial allies, or solutions to the Jewish refugee problem, or anything else. Money to make shells, to hold off the Germans in their final, desperate offensives. Palestine and the Palestinians were sold for that. They'd made the mistake of being on the wrong side.'

'And then the hypocrisy of the declaration itself,' Dominic said. 'You know the bit about - as long as the interests of the Arab population are not jeopardised - I forget the actual words.'

'That was the masterful stroke, eh? The absolute, blatant, two-faced humbug. The French are dead on with their "perfidious Albion".'

'But are there any records of the transfer of funds? Surely banks keep records? And the Treasury, what about the official papers?'

'There's nothing published on it at all. No mention in the history books. On my next leave I want to try to ferret something out. Oh, I'm certain it's there somewhere. You know, the Zionists tried exactly the same ploy with the Sultan of Turkey. Offered to pay him for a bite of Palestine when he was down and out at the end of the nineteenth century. But even the Sultan, for all his corruption, couldn't bring himself to do the deal. His sense of honour as a Muslim, as the Caliph , wouldn't let him. Anyway, that first attempt to buy Palestine is well known, though it was a failure. But they only had to wait about twenty years, and there they were, with the British government as the new brokers - the best in the business.'

'It is like a morality play, Rory. Maybe you can find something concrete on it in London. Prima facie, it's very convincing.'

'If I do, you'll hear about it. You know I worked a bit in the theatre in the sixties. I know the Redgraves. I've just heard that Vanessa is going to do a film on the Palestinians. She'd be able to use it. People would hear about it then, I can tell you.'

As they pulled off the road to cut across to Agami, it was

already dark. The headlights caught the sand still gusting across the road. They smelled the sea.

The following evening they drove into Alexandria and called on Lynda and Charles. Both were at home, and Lynda seemed glad to see them. Charles was also at ease. Dominic wondered whether Lynda's lesbian affair with Titi was all over. She certainly seemed back to her old self - surrounded now by three men and obviously enjoying it.

They joked about the referendum and Egyptian style democracy.

'If the vote ever fell to realistic levels, say 75%, that would be the end of the referenda,' Charles said.

'It's like Henry Ford and the colour of his cars,' Rory suggested. 'You know, you can vote as many times as you like, as long as it's always yes.'

Lynda turned the conversation into a more personal direction.

'Well, the referendum brought you both down here. We haven't seen you for ages.'

She smiled at Dominic.

'No, that's true. Well...' he searched for an excuse. Eventually it came. 'I was in England, you know.'

'But Rory, you haven't been down either.'

She was hinting at their disloyalty.

'Now you're here, are you free this evening? We're all going to the Solaris. You must come.'

'The Solaris?' Dominic said.

'A new nightclub. On the Corniche, just down from the Cecil. You must come - George will be there, and he's such fun, isn't he, Charles?'

'He's certainly unusual - a kind of Greek guru preaching

nudism and Platonic dialogue instead of Buddhist nirvana.'

'Where do you find these freaks?' Rory said, laughing.

Dominic thought this tactless, typical of Rory, but Lynda showed no reaction.

'Sounds amusing,' he said. 'We'll come along. We've nothing else planned.'

When they got to the nightclub at about ten-thirty, it was only half full. Dominic found it rather dingey. They went to a table, pulled other tables to it, and all sat down together. George sat next to Lynda and talked to her without interruption. He wore a highly original cotton pyjama suit. The sleeves were wide and billowing, the material thin. As they were sitting down, Dominic had noticed the clear outline of his genitals under the flimsy cloth.

Nefrititi and her husband were also in the group, as well as Adel and his brother, and another British couple, newly arrived in Alexandria. The wife, Christine, was sitting next to Rory, and he was directing most of his attention at her. Dominic strained over the music to try to hear what they were talking about. It seemed that Rory was giving her the lowdown on the Egyptian way of sex. Well, he probably knew something about it.

Nefrititi and her husband got up to dance, leaving the seat opposite Christine empty. Dominic went and sat in it.

'What's he on about?' he asked her, nodding at Rory.

'We've been talking about the Muslim attitude to sex. He's been telling me it's fundamentally different from ours, because for them, marriage is not a religious institution, but only a civil contract. Do you agree?'

'Yes, it must make for an important cultural difference - they're certainly incredibly open about marriage. Did he tell you about the wedding, in Bish Bish?'

'Yes,' she nodded vigorously and laughed.

'Christine can't stand the polygamy aspect,' Rory put in. 'That sticks in her feminist throat.'

'Yes, it does. Well, it's outrageous - young girls marrying dirty old men.'

'They're not forced to,' Dominic said.

'Often they are, by financial pressure, by family pressure. Even if they're not, the first wife is forced to accept the second.'

'Certainly, but maybe she's ready to.'

'Look, it's not so different in the west,' Rory said. 'Men, particularly rich men, have affairs all the time. The only difference is that with us, it's not institutionalised, so it breaks up the family.'

'Possibly, but at least we women can have affairs just like you men. If a Muslim woman wants another man, she's stoned in the marketplace,' Christine replied with vehemence.

'Well, she was stoned in the marketplace, but there had to be four adult male witnesses to the actual act of adultery,' Dominic said.

'It's still one rule for the men and another for the women - that's what is totally unacceptable.'

'Well, the issue is then, are men and women the same and should they therefore have the same rules? It's troubling - the older I get, the more I believe that men and women are different.'

But did that mean that they should have different rules? Dominic wondered where his conclusion left him. It had obviously antagonised Christine. She leaned away from him as she said:

'That's primitive. We'll never go back to that.'

'Of course not, Christine,' Rory agreed. 'Don't listen to him, he's just a romantic fool. He wanted to marry a thirteen-year-old the other day just because she smiled at him.'

Dominic was suddenly at a loss.

'That was different,' he countered lamely.

'No, the interesting thing, Christine,' Rory went on, 'is that though the Muslim woman is suppressed, she's so completely uninhibited. No shame.'

'Oh?' Christine said guardedly.

'I'm telling you. You expect them to be all shy, but not a bit of it. Take the famous Egyptian dirty joke. I've been with families - mothers, cousins, daughters - and out come the most outrageous jokes. Everybody rocks with laughter. Not a trace of embarrassment. None of this not-in-front-of-the-ladies nonsense, like we have.'

'That is surprising.'

'There seems to be no sense of guilt about sex - no internal moral repression. It's all external. If you can get round the rules, you know - girls must be home by six, they can never go out alone, that sort of thing - then you naturally let rip. With us, it's all internal, sex is sin, we stop ourselves.'

'Oh, that may have been true for our parents' generation, but not us,' Christine retorted.

'Are you sure? We've just changed the vocabulary, that's all. Now the religious puritanism has been replaced by the relationship puritanism. The internal repression is still there. We can't just be hedonistic about it. The Arabs are streets ahead of us there.'

'Hedonism is certainly not the answer,' Christine said.

Now Rory too had alienated her.

'There you are,' he mocked.

Nefretiti and her husband returned from the dance floor.

Dominic got up and gave back his seat. As he passed Lynda she caught his arm and pulled him down.

'What's the news from Emma? I wrote her a long, newsy letter and she never replied.'

'She's all right. Pretty busy with work. That's why she hasn't written.'

He wondered with irritation why he should make excuses for her.

'Anyway, she'll be out at Easter probably.'

'Are you still together? Rory said something about you wanting to marry an Egyptian girl.'

'No, no. That was just a...'

He sought a phrase that would release him from responsibility.

'An absurd fantasy.'

The music started up loudly, and a belly dancer came with short, running steps onto the stage, her hands high in the air, her head thrown back, and the black torrent of her hair falling behind to her waist. She began her dance.

'Emma and I are still in business,' he shouted to Lynda, but the music drowned his voice. He patted her on the shoulder as she looked up at him and then went back to his original seat.

They started to clap with the dancer, and Rory stood up, and just as an Egyptian would, began to roll his hips in reply to hers.

Dominic smiled to himself.

Later, when he thought back, it seemed to him that this smile had been endless, suspended without any conclusion. For in the middle of it, his senses were assaulted. There was a white, blinding flash and a vivid crack of noise that obliterated every sensation. His brain struggled to encompass it, to understand it, but it was so short and so intense that it left only an appalling scorched void in his head.

What was it? In dread and numbness he saw that blood was streaming from Rory's face. He watched his friend stagger and slump down into his chair, a hand going up to his eye, the fingers spread and trembling.

He realised that part of the stunning explosion had been a sharp, electric jolt in his own knee, and as he felt it with his hand, warm blood was already seeping through his trousers.

Smoke hid the people around him in the unreality of a dream. He saw Lynda screaming, her hands white, gripping the table in front of her. Other people were already stumbling, crashing their way out of the room. The dancer lay on the stage, a long wound across the front of her body. The flesh was sliced deep, showing shiny globular fat and tattered muscle. She was like a carcass thrown up on a butcher's counter, but her life was still pulsing in her. Spurts of blood came from the sides of her wound and spattered her whitish skin.

He sat transfixed. People were chaotic about him, rushing past, clawing the air, but he could not move. He saw Charles breaking Lynda's hold on the table, pulling her up. Beside him, Adel rose slowly from his chair, his white shirt-front covered with brilliant red stains, his face glistening carmine. But the colours, the horror, were becoming remote. They were apart from him, he did not care.

After a time, he too got to his feet and began to move vaguely. Someone caught his arm and he looked into the eyes of a young waiter who was steering him towards the door.

'Shukran, shukran,' he said with deliberation. He felt a flood of gratitude, almost a piercing love, for this man who was leading him as if out of hell.

He woke next morning feeling drugged, shock still clouding his mind with unreality. He saw that he was in a hospital ward. Raising himself from his bed, he grimaced at the jagged pain in the back of his right knee. Adel was in the bed next to him, asleep or unconscious. His round Egyptian face was greyed, the colour of earth and ash. His thick black moustache sprang out of bloodless skin. Bandages covered the top of his head.

Beyond Adel lay Rory. Dominic recognised his curly hair with its flecks of red. He too was inert. A great bandaged pad covered his right eye. He called 'Rory, Rory,' in a low voice, but the head did not move.

Slowly he lowered himself back onto his bed.

Some minutes later a doctor with two male nurses entered the ward and came towards him. They saw that he was awake. The doctor smiled at him.

'You are Englishman?'

Dominic nodded.

'How are you? Not bad? You are lucky one, just very small piece in your knee.'

He pronounced the 'k'.

'We take it out this morning. No problem, nothing damaged.'

A little piece, Dominic thought, why then is the pain white hot when I move?

'Your friends,' the doctor waved his hand towards Adel and Rory, 'they are worse. He has six, seven pieces in his chest. But not very deep, al hamdulilah. Your English friend has bad luck, two small pieces, but one in his eye. The eye finished now.'

The doctor raised his hands in resignation.

'Irish friend... poor chap,' Dominic whispered.

'Well, now we prepare you for removing the piece in your

knee.'

He gave instructions to the nurses in Arabic, and went to look at Adel.

One nurse took Dominic's pulse, the other began to unwrap the bandage round his small wound.

The fragment was removed an hour later. Though he was injected again with sedation, the operation was completed under local anaesthetic. He lay on his stomach and could hear the clinking of instruments in dishes and the occasional remarks of the surgeon to his assistants. There was no pain, but a strange gritty scratching that communicated itself up his leg to nerves that were not deadened.

When he was wheeled back into the ward, Adel and Rory were no longer there. A momentary panic seized him - they were dead. He tried to force the fear from his mind. Surely the doctor would not deceive him. They must be having their pieces pulled out too.

'What hospital is this?' he called over in Arabic to a patient in a bed opposite his.

'The Military Hospital in Smouhah.'

'Smouhah?'

'Yes, in Skandaria. We are near the race-course. Do you know it?'

'No, I'm from Cairo. Were you in the Solaris too?'

'Yes, I was there. Terrible, terrible. Are you all right?'

'Al hamdulilah, yes,' Dominic replied. 'And you?'

The Egyptian repeated the Muslim formula of gratitude and acceptance.

In the afternoon Charles came into the ward to visit him.

'What's the news of Rory?' he asked him at once.

'He's been taken to another hospital where they do eye surgery. It seems the shrapnel cut right through the eyeball and is lodged at the back. He's almost certain to lose the sight of the eye.'

'What rotten luck - if only he hadn't been standing up, larking about.'

'If only... if only we hadn't gone to that nightclub on that night. All day I've been tortured by the thought. Isn't time utterly remorseless? It goes forward, always forward. I want to go back, to those crucial points where we set ourselves on the course to the Solaris and take a different direction. One can take different directions in the future - why not in the past? It's maddening, maddening.'

'What was it, a bomb?'

'A grenade. A small explosion, but murderous bits of shrapnel, tearing into people'

'Was anyone killed?'

'The dancer, another chap in the band, one man at a table at the front. A piece went straight into his heart.'

'What about our table?'

'You three. Titi was hit in the arm, nothing serious. Adel's pretty cut up. He's gone to another hospital too - said he didn't trust the military. Your end of the table got most of it. Christine was unscratched, but she's in a terrible state.'

'What a rotten beginning to their time in Egypt. Who threw the grenade? Does anyone know?'

'Nobody knows. Nothing on the news or in the papers. It looks as if they're trying to keep it quiet.'

'They want to pretend it hasn't happened. You know, the strange thing is, I'm really not sure it happened either. If it wasn't for this dull ache in my knee, I'd say it was all unreal.'

'The doctor told me we can take you out tomorrow. Lynda

insists you stay with us in the flat. She's awfully upset because it was she who persuaded you to come with us to the Solaris.'

'Charles, you mustn't let her think that.'

'No, well, she'll be immensely relieved to see you back on your feet.'

As Dominic waited to be collected next day, he sat stiff-legged in a chair chatting to a male nurse who spoke English. He had worked in a London hospital.

'That was before the War of Ramadan. When the war started, I came back to help my country. Many of the wounded came to this hospital. We still have two wards full of the very badly wounded, the hopeless ones.'

'Poor fellows,' Dominic said.

'Yes, some with no legs, paralysed, burned all over, maybe they'll never go home.'

'Awful, isn't it, one just doesn't know about them. In any war. No sensational pictures of them in the press. When it works against you, you keep such horrors quiet.'

'Ah, here is your friend,' the nurse said, looking up.

'Well, goodbye then.'

Dominic shook his hand and hobbled, right leg stiff, towards Charles.

Two days later, Charles, Lynda, and Dominic went to see Rory. He had had his operation, but lay unseeing in his bed. Both of his eyes were heavily bandaged.

'Good God, what's the matter with your other eye?' Dominic asked him at once.

'Nothing, I hope,' he replied. His voice was thick, unused. 'The doctor told me something about optic nerve trauma. It appears if one nerve goes, the other can too. Bloody awful, eh? Got to rest the good eye completely or it might conk out. They say they'll take the bandage off in three days' time, and then I'll know. Could be blind as a bat.'

'No Rory, it can't be,' Lynda said. She sat on his bed and took his hand in hers.

'Well, it sometimes happens.'

His mouth made a strained smile under the swathe of white. In the silence that followed, Lynda's chin began to pucker, and large tears rolled out of her eyes and fell onto the sheet. Dominic struggled to find something to say.

'The whole thing sounds too much,' he eventually got out. 'Nerves can't be that concerned about each other.'

'You'd think not. But it's going to be bloody awful waiting to find out. I'm going to go absolutely batty. Mad as, not blind as.'

Again the mouth forced itself into a twisted smile.

'I'll stay with you, Rory,' Lynda said quickly, 'I won't leave you.'

He didn't answer her immediately.

'It'll be quite all right,' she insisted. 'The hospital won't mind. The Egyptians do it all the time.'

'Would you?' he said in a voice that Dominic, standing at the end of the bed, could hardly hear.

Over the next three days, Lynda stayed at the hospital. Charles came at lunch and in the evening with food which Ahmed had prepared. They ate together. Lynda left with Charles at about nine and returned next morning at seven o'clock by taxi with croissants and a thermos of tea for Rory's breakfast.

Rory wanted her to read to him, and when she asked him what, he replied:

'Something relevant - the battle of El Alamein, for instance.'

From a friend's library, she borrowed a book on the see-saw campaign in North Africa which ended with Britain's first taste of victory against the Germans. She read it to him in long stretches. It fascinated him and calmed him. He seemed to consider his own injury as obscurely part of that same old war.

Dominic went to see him once more before returning to Cairo. He was unable to wait until the following day, when the bandages would come off. He marvelled at the comfort and support that Rory drew from Lynda, and the way she had responded to him. He would not have thought her capable of such devotion. How strange that these two people, before casual and distant with each other, had now formed a strong, intimate bond. This was the astonishing unpredictability of human nature, the meshing of the unknowable urges and needs in men and women under the pressure and power of fate.

When Dominic rang Lynda from his flat in Heliopolis the next day, he learned at once that the news was good.

'Dominic, it's been a success. Thank God, thank God. They took off the bandages this morning as planned. I could hardly bear it. We couldn't even stay with him. But when we were allowed back in, there he was, sitting up in bed, looking at himself in a mirror. His other eye is perfect. It hasn't been affected at all. The doctor says the danger period is over. There's nothing to worry about. And the damaged eye is healing well. It looks so sad though. The pupil is dark and slightly milky. One can't believe that it's stopped working, but Rory says he can only just distinguish light from dark with it. The eyeball still moves all right, so the doctor says that one just won't notice anything. Isn't that marvellous.'

'Yes, it is Lynda. It would have been so unjust if he had been blinded completely. I don't know anyone who is more sympathetic to the Arab and Palestinian cause. I suppose you saw the report in the Gazette?'

'No, we only get the French language daily here.'

'Well, it said that they had "arrested a Libyan who was responsible for the recent attack in an Alexandrian nightclub." It might be true. Of course, there are thousands of Egyptian students and workers in Libya. It might have been one of them, trained by Gadaffi, and sent back. The Egyptians would probably just call him a Libyan for propaganda purposes.'

'But why should he throw a grenade in a nightclub? What is the point of that?'

'Why do civilians ever get bombed, Lynda? It's just that it happened to us this time. How is Adel?'

'He's all right too. He's covered in scars, but he's back home, eating all the time. His family are trying to rebuild his strength.'

'Splendid philosophy. When in doubt, eat.'

'Yes. Oh, Ronald and Elizabeth came round today and were sad to miss you. They send their best wishes.'

'Send mine back.'

'They want to know if you're fit for more birdwatching expeditions. I told them you were.'

'Good. Yes, I can walk fine now. The only permanent damage is that I can't flex my big toe like I used to. It curls half way down and then stops. Quite funny to look at. When is Rory coming out of hospital?'

'At the end of the week. We've insisted that he comes to us to convalesce. Can you imagine him returning to that messy flat of his on his own?'

'No, he'd be much better with you. You've really been very good to him, Lynda.'

'I still feel it was my fault.'

Her voice trembled. Guilt still haunted her.

'Nonsense,' he said quickly, and then in a more measured and almost academic voice pointed out that there was no causal connection between her decision to go to the club and what happened there. Guilt could only come from such a causal connection.

'So you simply can't feel guilty, Lynda. It's completely inappropriate. Remember,' he ended, 'post hoc, but not propter hoc.'

Thirty-two

The Easter holidays approached and Dominic received a letter from Emma. She apologised for not having written for so long. She explained that she had been having lots of fun with the theatre group, and that it had taken up most of her time. Work she had lost interest in completely. It now had little meaning after all she had been through the year before. Referring to his criticism in his last letter to her, she said she did appreciate what he did for her, the holiday in the Cotswolds and all that, and regretted that she didn't show it more.

As he read it, he saw that it was a positive letter, that she was trying to make amends. But though she might now be moving towards him, he, at a distance, could feel no urge on his side to move towards her.

Obviously she had not heard from her parents about the nightclub attack. She made no mention of it, simply ending her letter by giving him the date of her flight to Cairo and saying that she would stay with him for a few days before going on to Alexandria.

He waited for her arrival with a growing unease. The remark she had made to him in the hotel in Chipping Campden on the last night of their tour about his age crawled up out of his memory and surged back to the surface. He had pushed it down on his return to Cairo, but he had not forgotten it. The very tone of her voice, the gratuitousness of the cut, his shock, now he lived it over and over. It sent bitter waves through him, made him twist inside in rage and hunger for revenge. What was the source of her wish to humiliate him? He imagined cursing her for her viciousness, berating her. He imagined conversations between them in which he would give vent to his hurt, finally let go with her, tell her that he detested her. He would strike her, he would bring his arm up and crack it across her face. He imagined the look in her eyes after the blow. He savoured the long moment while she apprehended that he had struck her, while her sob of fright gathered in her face. He rehearsed her defeat with a hot, exacting gratification.

His hate rolled up in him again and again. It caught him in moments when he least expected it - as he did some minor chore in his flat, as he waited in a shop to be served, as he lay sunning himself beside the club pool.

Perhaps because it had brought him so many fantasies of release, his resentment seemed cauterised when he eventually picked her up from the airport and brought her to his flat. For two days he lived with her in an unreal, glassy pretence. They had meals together at the club or he cooked for them in the flat. They went to a film in the open-air cinema in Heliopolis. They talked about Oxford. They continued their sexual exchange in bed at night.

When he described the explosion at the Solaris, she reacted with a hinted incredulity which he found irritating and stupid. He described the injuries to himself, to Adel, to Rory. She expressed sympathy, but he was sure that he could detect a certain limit to her sincerity. It was as if she would not take completely seriously this dramatic event that had happened in her absence, without her. Noting this, he suddenly felt that he understood her, that he had got the measure of her egotism.

She wanted to see his uncurlable toe. When he showed her how its movement was impaired, she laughed. Looking down, he felt a sudden surge of rage against her, which evaporated in his brain almost before he could recognise what it was. It left only a tense black pulse.

'I suppose it is funny,' he said. 'It's just a scratch. I was lucky. Rory got the scratch in his eye, deep, deep in his eye. Right into the nerve, and it blinded him.'

'Well, that's what you'd expect,' she said.

In an instant, he was aroused, outraged. He sensed malignancy in her and now he would wrench it out into the open.

'What would you expect?'

His words were slow, cold, his limbs rigid.

'That he'd get the worst of it,' she said, as if not noticing the tension in him.

'And why would he get the worst of it?'

Now his voice was louder, threatening, relentless.

'Well, you know...' she faltered. She knew that she had transgressed and that he was going to break her open and expose it. She felt fear, but it was too late.

'I mean, he's always talking about politics, the Palestinians, all that, justifying the PLO, so now he's got a bit of his own medicine.'

Dominic stared in front of him. He could not bear to look at her, now that she had spoken this grotesque verdict. He reverberated in utter rejection of her. Space seemed to elongate round him, and she was far away, locked at a distance, shrunken.

'Are you implying in some way that he deserved it?'

'Well, didn't he? I remember him saying to me that if he were a Palestinian, he would join the PLO. So now he's on the receiving end of terrorism, and we'll see if he likes it.'

'I don't follow your logic,' he rasped out with open hatred.

'That's because you swallow everything he says.'

In an instant, he wanted to obliterate her, to kill her, to wipe her out. This immorality, this stupidity, were an intolerable affront. She must not be. He raged to eliminate her. Why should he argue, try to dissect her words, expose her fallacy? Easier by far just to end her, now.

He said nothing more to her that night. He washed and went to bed. He felt her get in later beside him, but he drifted into sleep with a sense of isolation that cut her off from him completely.

In the morning he had no further wish for her company. It was a Sunday and she was to take the train to Alexandria at noon. As he had always done, he went into the kitchen and made breakfast for them both.

But why, why should I serve her so? he thought. Why did I ever serve her, go on serving her, give her things, make my efforts for her as she lay around, taking everything, lifting not a finger, leaving her mess, her self-indulgent disorder behind her? Cocooned in the insouciance of her youth, or rather in my need for her. Now it is over. I will need nothing more from her, I will give nothing more to her. I will do nothing more for her.

Yet he prepared the breakfast tray and took it to the table. She had risen in the meantime and came to eat. He looked at her occasionally and noticed the pale colour of her cheeks after sleep, the slight puffiness of her eyes behind her glasses. He felt nothing but a cold objectivity about her, his will towards her was utterly annulled.

They drifted through the morning. He threw himself on the sofa and read. She prepared her case, collected her things from the bathroom. He heard her. The irreversible process of separation was under way. He had nothing more to do. It gave him a cold and remorseless fulfilment. He was freeing himself of her in space and time as he had freed himself of her in spirit.

He drove her to the station.

'When are you coming to Alex?' she asked him.

'I don't know,' he said, as if her question was immaterial.

He carried her case to the main door leading to the platform. He said goodbye to her without speaking her name. As he turned and walked away from her there was no waver in his will. Once outside in the bright sunshine of Ramses Square, the teeming crowds, the noise of the traffic, and the implacable statue of the great Pharaoh filled his attention.

Thirty-three

The following weekend he drove to Alexandria. He took the desert road as usual, and the sun swung lower in the clear April sky in front of him. About half an hour out of Cairo, he passed the turn-off of a track that led west and south to an ancient Coptic monastery. Looking across the endless sweep of desert he picked out the small cluster of green where the monastery stood, maybe twenty kilometres away. Around it on all sides was emptiness. He thought it a ghastly, torturing place, and yet celibate Christian monks had lived there for more than a millennium. It was true, sexual repression was at the heart of Christianity. As his eyes moved away from the monastery and over the searing aridity of the landscape, he felt prickling disgust. A religion might lock up old men out of reach of women and life, but one that forced this on young men, men like himself, was vicious. The thought of Islam sweeping Christianity aside, and replacing its repression with a love of women, of sexuality, and of children comforted him.

He drove to Agami. Lynda and Charles had taken a new bungalow for the coming summer, and Rory was staying with them. He found it at the end of a sandy track, right on the beach, with sand drifts piled up against a leaning fence that surrounded it.

There was no car outside, but lights were on. He walked in carrying his over-night bag and found Rory lying on a reclining beach chair in the front room. The air was loud with music. Dominic recognised Brahms' second piano concerto. He greeted his friend and examined him.

'You look very well, Rory. And the eye is hardly noticeable. Here, I've brought you a bottle of Jameson's Crested Ten from the duty-free in Cairo. Let's drink to your recovery.'

'Thanks,' Rory said, 'but better make mine a small one.'

Dominic poured the whiskey and they sat together through the rest of the concerto. When it was over, Rory said that he was still not allowed to read, so when he was alone, he listened to music.

'I'm almost living in music now. Or living on it. It's my mental food. This last week, it's been that concerto - the most moving thing Brahms ever wrote. And Shostokovitch's fifth. Those are my two constant companions.'

'What better. And Lynda and Charles, are they out?'

'Yes, they're out to dinner. They've been immensely kind. I have to force them out of the house, otherwise Lynda would never leave me alone.'

'And you'll stay on for a while longer with them?'

'Till the end of the month, yes. Then I'm going back home to get my lens. They don't have quite the shade of green out here.'

Dominic, smiling, looked into the good eye.

'Are they green? Yes, they are. And then, you'll be coming back? Your director was on the phone to me last week and told me to send you his best wishes. They're all looking forward to your return.'

'That was nice of him. But I don't think I will return somehow.'

'Really, not come back to Egypt?'

Dominic felt a sudden chill at the thought of losing his

friend.

'No. This eye business, everything, has set me thinking, I can tell you. More than ever, I am aware of the passage of time, of my time. I could have been killed by that grenade, we all could have. It has concentrated my mind wonderfully.'

'On what?'

'As I say, on my time, or what's left of it. I've only got this fixed span, like everyone else, in which to do anything. Up to now I've done practically nothing. This work, of course, it's fun, isn't it, but is it important? You know my concern for politics. Well, here I am, getting caught up in Middle Eastern politics, almost being wiped out by it, when my main concern is elsewhere.'

'You mean Ireland? Ulster?'

'Yes, I haven't taxed you with it much, Dominic. You're English, your father in the army, brought up in deepest Surrey, you probably think the British government is doing the best it can there. Don't you?'

'It's a terribly difficult task - reconciling the irreconcilable. Is there a solution?'

'That's just it, in those terms there is no solution. But in other terms, yes, there is.'

'What other terms, a civil war? Surely you can't want that?'

'It may have slipped your notice,' he said slowly, 'that a civil war is exactly what is in progress. Has been since sixty-nine. Look, I don't want to argue with you, Dominic. Let's just say that now I have decided to return home and see if I can't do something to change the terms. You know how I go on all the time about the received opinion, the official propaganda that people swallow without really thinking. Well, I want to get them thinking. I want to force them to think. I'm not sure exactly how I'm going to do it, but I must do it. I must stop wasting my time, and my life. That grenade took out my eye, just by chance, without any act of will on my part. Probably thrown by some young Egyptian who can't stomach Sadat's reneging. I can understand him perfectly. I sympathise with him. But why should I risk my life in his conflict without any act of my will, when I could have risked it in the conflict of my own people with my will? That's what had been torturing me these last weeks, the waste of this eye.'

'Thank God you still have the other, you can still see.'

'Quite. And now I must return home. I must fight in my own war.'

'But Rory, the I.R.A., surely you can't support them?'

His friend stared at him, one eye clear, the other blind. There was a silence.

'Remember Dresden, Dominic,' he said finally.

He looked away.

'But no, a one-eyed wreck like me wouldn't be much use to any army. I'll have to fight with the only weapons I have, my brain, my cunning, my will.'

'Isn't it hopeless?'

'It does seem so, doesn't it? We've been at it for eight hundred years.'

'I mean the odds are so heavily stacked against you.'

'Like against the Palestinians. Indeed. But you know how Terence McSweeney, dying on hunger strike, put it?'

Dominic shook his head.

'He said that victory would go not to the strongest, but to those who could suffer the most.'

'That's very bleak, Rory - turning the other cheek endlessly.'

'Yes, well anyway, I will go back home. I will start to suffer with the rest. Why suffer elsewhere, to no purpose?'

He pointed to his damaged eye. Its large, dark, unseeing pupil seemed to express outraged bewilderment.

'Time to do something. Probably all I can do is fight in the propaganda war. I will try to push the mountain of ideas.'

When Lynda and Charles came back from their dinner party, the talk of the four friends turned to Adel and the others who had shared the Solaris experience with them. The level of whiskey in the bottle fell steadily and they enjoyed the camaraderie of survivors. They had all been changed, and the sense of this change, they shared.

As they were gathering the glasses before going to bed, Lynda said:

'Oh, by the way, Dominic, Emma rang me this afternoon. She was surprised to hear that you were coming down. She's staying this weekend with the Fosters. Do you know their villa? It's over on the other side of the Gamaiya.'

'Yes, John and Sally's place, I know it.'

'She said she'd be there all tomorrow.'

'All right.'

She did not know, then, she had not realised that there was nothing left between them. He resolved that he would tell her.

But the next day, he felt that he could do it later, later. It was not immediate, it did not matter.

After yellow-green dusk had given way to darkness, he finally roused himself and drove to the Fosters' villa. He was welcomed in by Sally. Emma sat, her bare legs drawn up under her, on a flat couch. She had been reading. He sat down beside her and because of Sally and John, for some moments carried on a normal, social conversation. He told them that he had come down by the desert road, that he was staying with Lynda and Charles in Agami, that he had to return to Cairo for Monday morning.

'I didn't know you were coming. Lynda told me,' Emma said, and as she did so, she put her hand across and laid it on his arm. It seemed to him such a decisive gesture - a claim, an appeal. Had she never touched him like that before? Was it so strange, her making this declaration to him, in front of the others?

It was too late.

'Could we have a talk somewhere?' he said and held her eyes with a cold stare.

She withdrew her hand slowly. It had been incongruous, useless. Tension made her face a mask.

'Yes,' she said, and gave a small shrug of acceptance.

'Let's go out for a walk.'

They excused themselves and went out into the dark road-way. There were no lights. He could hardly see her face. She was just a presence beside him. It would make it easier. They walked towards the sea. A cool wind blew against them.

'I only wanted to tell you Emma, that it's finished between us.'

'Finished? Why...why?'

He was surprised by the shock in her voice. Was it anger, was it hurt?

'It's pointless. It was never any good. It's best to end it.'

'And you decide, just like that. Why didn't you tell me before I came all the way out here from Oxford.'

'You would have come to see your parents anyway.'

'I came to see you.'

'Did you? I never felt it. I never felt anything particular from you.'

'That was your fault.'

'How? There was precious little to feel.'

'That's not true. I ...' she hesitated.

He waited, tense, for her denial. Could she utter it? Would he accept it - slide back into intimacy with her?

Eventually it came.

'I always had a crush on you.'

The last thread broke in his mind. It was final.

'There you are, your choice of words betrays you. You use an empty, juvenile formula.'

He threw up his arm towards her in contempt and turned back. She followed a few paces behind in silence.

They reached the car. He said goodbye in a toneless voice and got in.

As he drove away, his lights swung across her. She had turned and was walking back to the villa. He saw her in the dark space, but he did not feel anything for her.

Thirty-four

Long, long after, years and years later, he held her letter in his hand.

ISBN 141207265-4